Circle of Lies
Alien Prophecies
Book One

A novel by
Fiona Riplee

Print ISBN: 978-0-9974756-0-9
eBook ISBN:978-0-9974756-1-6

This novel is dedicated to my husband. His loving support and encouragement kept me going from the very first mention of being an author. He put up with a lot through the writing process, probably more than he expected, but he wouldn't let me give up. I love you so much! This novel wouldn't be written if not for you.

I'd also like to thank my family and friends for their understanding and support. This novel took a lot of time and energy and they cheered me on even when I was feeling down and sad. You all inspired me to reach for my dream. I am so very grateful for having you in my life!

Circle of Lies

CHAPTER ONE

RAZ DONOVAN STARED at the slender curve of Sandra Robins's backside, jealous of the diamond-studded pockets. Tight denim hugged all the right places as Sandra combed through the junk mail scattered on the kitchen counter.

Her efforts were useless. The contact information she searched for wouldn't change his mind. Paris was Sandra's best friend, but Paris had been a part of his circle first. He'd leave with Paris and their son, Sean. They'd forget this cozy house and this family-oriented town like every other one they'd lived in before.

Raz feasted his eyes on Sandra. *Damn. Her sexy body will be the death of me.*

Like a beacon, the gems on her rear pockets winked at him in the afternoon light streaming from the breakfast nook's windows. The glittering jewels laughed at his weakness for her the past six months. Funny, he'd always thought of himself as a boob man, until recently. *Snap out of it!* He had responsibilities that didn't include ogling women. Raz snorted. Not a single human would classify a Sixxer as a man, only alien, but the knowledge didn't stop his lustful musings about the human woman standing before him.

Raz's torture was impossible to end until he left Sandra. She wasn't his. "I haven't agreed to call Cameron. It's added complexity."

Cameron Mason, probably a good colleague to Sandra, was about as useless as a gnat at this point. Raz trusted the fewest amount of people possible. Zero. Besides, the university where Sandra and Cameron worked wouldn't have squat to help Sixxers. The type of technology needed to hide a Sixxer's Nexus, or energy signature, didn't exist in the human world, unless Sandra had contacts with a Sixxer military unit.

"I don't remember asking your permission to call my friend." Sandra slapped a handful of envelopes on the granite countertop. "Last time I checked, we live in a free country, and you aren't my boss."

Raz bit his lip against a smile and choked back his laughter. There were days, like today, he could do without the sass. Yet, he provoked her at every opportunity The words kept physical distance between them and helped him stay in control. A tingle of power ran along his arm. He looked at the currents flowing over his skin and tamped them down.

Shaking his head cleared his mind. *I lie to myself because of her.* His control was on a hair trigger.

Sandra organized the items in her hands, effectively ignoring him, which was good since she didn't notice the show of alien power seconds ago. Despite her pissed-off mood, at least she was talking to him. Finding out just a few hours ago her best friend was moving away for good probably chafed her always-know-the-facts and be-prepared scientific mind. He'd taken the easy way out and avoided Sandra, too. He hadn't spoken to her in weeks in preparation for this moment. Finding out her lover was leaving, too, probably didn't help her disposition. Raz would be in a sour state as well.

There was a time when he believed he'd have the white picket fence, a dog and kids. Father's stories of a time when Sixxers didn't run and weren't afraid to live on this planet filled his childhood and made Raz long for the same. Yet, his vision of a future like that with Sandra was impossible. He had to leave her behind.

"What I'd like to know …"

Sandra's hesitant words brought him out of his musings, and he focused on her profile.

She flipped her bangs out of her eyes with a toss of her head and sighed. "Why tell me now?" She cast a quick glance his way then focused again on her task. "You should've kept to yourself. Told Paris to stay away from me then I wouldn't have gotten close to her or Sean."

"Did you hear the words coming out of your mouth?" Raz

laughed. Sandra didn't know Paris at all. "Paris does what she likes. She's more obstinate than you are."

Sandra rolled her eyes and turned back to her search. She snorted. "If you're the fearsome leader of the group, why doesn't she listen?"

Controlling Paris was like ordering a bee to fly south for the winter. Although, Sandra did have a point. His objective had always been to stay away from humans. Raz ignored his self-imposed rule, but now it had to be followed. He focused on his circle, which included a sick mother and her six-year-old child. He was all Paris and Sean had. There were no other Sixxers he trusted with their lives.

Since Sean's birth, Raz picked the next town and kept them moving, hiding them from the Chasers, keeping them safe. They traveled their way north twelve months ago. The three of them wanted Angelville, Pennsylvania to be their permanent settlement after years of suitcase living. Paris begged him to stay. The illusion of safety allowed friendship and hope to blossom within their small group. Angelville became a false reality where they were just like the humans living around them. Raz accepted this town as their home. He hadn't expected, or wanted, to move his circle to a new location.

Another lie. Raz knew better than to dream. He straightened to his full height and crossed his arms in a move against Sandra's bullheadedness. "Why don't you listen?"

"Being overbearing and bossy isn't defending anyone." Sandra leaned against the countertop. She tossed a handful of papers into the recycle bin. "And you've said nothing to convince me leaving is absolutely necessary."

"Paris and Sean will do what I say. I keep them safe."

Silence permeated the room. Sandra shrugged. "You're the boss. Am I included in your macho heroics?"

"You can't come with me."

She shook her head. "What's so horrible you can't tell me? You're a good man."

"You know nothing about me."

Her brown eyes met his. "I do know you." She turned back and continued rummaging.

The infuriating stack of papers didn't have answers. She was a bulldog tugging on a rope, and the embodiment of the local university's mascot where she worked.

Raz wasn't surprised. Hamilton University of Pennsylvania, aka HUP, was full of tenacious types. She, along with Cameron, thought the place had all the answers. Raz couldn't let her unravel the truth about his people. Sandra allowed him to forget the harsh reality of his life during their time together. He paid the price and exposed his circle to Chasers. "When Paris wakes up, we'll be leaving."

"I'll follow you."

Of course, Sandra would argue. As the last living Sixxer Transor, Raz would easily lose her if she trailed his circle. The amount of Sixxer power and Nexus energy a Transor held was no match for humans. If he left right now, he'd be out of the city before she could think of how to track him. Doing so would keep her safe, yet he wanted to say goodbye. Years of running from Chasers engraved the ability to hide into his soul, but he didn't want to hide from her.

His gaze traced the line of Sandra's back and stopped in the middle where her hair fell. The dark, fitted jacket hugged her curves. Sunlight glared in the window and created red highlights in her mass of brown waves. He wanted to twist the strands around his wrist, kiss the tender spot below her ear and hear her soft moan. He breathed in her lilac perfume floating around the room and clenched his hands into fists. A ball of energy leapt out from between his fingers and fell to the floor. The sphere dissipated until the glow faded into the sunlight. Would he ever stop wanting her? Wanting what he couldn't have?

Sandra stepped toward Raz and broke his fantasy.

Then he recognized the desire in her eyes and caught his breath. Her cheeks flushed a becoming pink. Brown irises rimmed in pure gold searched his. Could she see the carnal thoughts floating at the surface of his mind? Did she know the extent of his hunger for her?

"How will you stop me from chasing you?" Sandra whispered.

He cringed at her word choice. He didn't want to associate Sandra, in any form, to the human bastards who were ready and capable of hurting his people. "I know you don't want to be responsible for putting us in danger."

Sandra gasped. Her eyes narrowed, and her lips pinched together. "That's low."

"I do what I have to." Keeping them alive meant keeping them apart. Sixxers apart from humans.

She leaned back onto the counter and crossed one foot over the other. Her hair covered her face, and she brushed it behind her ear. Irritation dripped from her lips. "You're so melodramatic. Suddenly, we're in mortal danger. It's a bad B-movie. If you'd tell me what's really going on, you'd realize the best choice is to stay here. Cam and I can help Paris."

Raz clenched his jaw. A tic pulsed under his eye. Why was she so damned aggravating and sexy at the same time? "We help ourselves. It's the only way."

Sandra will never understand. Sixxers and humans didn't mix. The Nexus bonds between a circle healed Sixxers but harmed humans.

Killed humans.

Sandra's nostrils flared. "You're so damn ornery. Paris said you'd be like this. I told her you'd be reasonable."

Paris had manipulated Sandra as effectively as she had Raz. She wanted nothing more than to stay here in this house he rented for her and Sean. She used her empathic abilities against him every chance she got. Roots grew from her feet and burrowed into the ground.

Raz had his bag packed at all times, and it was already nestled in the backseat of the van.

The automatic coffeemaker light turned blue. Fresh coffee dripped into the pot near Sandra's elbow. Paris re-filled and programmed the pot to brew every two hours. She wanted java continuously, no matter the time: morning, afternoon, right before sleep. Any amount of caffeine provided her with enough energy to make it through the day. Bitter house blend wafted through the house. The hated smell increased the tension in Raz's shoulders.

"Please, don't follow us." Raz rubbed his forehead. Damn it. Sandra forced him to beg. Again, the tic fluttered under his eye. "The three of us must go alone. Paris knows this."

"I won't let Paris leave while she's sick. She should be in the hospital."

The accusatory expression and low tone cut him to the core. "Paris has a cold."

"It could be pneumonia."

"She's fine," he said with an emphatic nod of the head.

With wide eyes, Sandra pleaded, "You're in witness protection. Why can't they protect you at the hospital? It's the most logical and safest place to be right now. Also, if you have guards there, your fear of these bad people finding you would be alleviated."

Raz raked his hand through his hair and swore under his breath. He regretted using the witness protection program as a cover. Sandra would easily figure out the lie the longer they were around her. He inhaled a deep, soothing breath and relaxed against the wall. The solidness grounded him. Life with Paris taught him love didn't exist, only survival. His unnatural attachment to Sandra placed each of them in danger. "Nowhere is safe. We'll travel for two days, maximum. I promise I'll take Paris to the nearest Urgent Treatment for evaluation. I won't let her die, which she's far from."

A harsh cough echoed from the bedroom.

They both froze, heads tilted. Paris still moved, with what little strength she had. For how much longer, Raz couldn't guess. Her power, along with her physical strength, weakened every damned day.

"The university lab has medication." Sandra's voice wobbled. She cleared her throat. "Cam has access to it."

Raz preferred Sandra's anger to her hesitant words. He focused on her lips. She worried the bottom one with her teeth. He wanted to kiss those full lips, taste them one last time and soothe her. What harm would come from a goodbye kiss?

For one, arouse me to a point where I'd do anything to keep her.

He scratched his chin. A day's growth of stubble abraded his fingers. "We can't go to HUP. Not only for our safety, but helping us in such a way will ruin your career. Paris will be fine until we can call the marshal and find a safe house. You're worrying too much."

Would Cameron's medication help Paris? Sixxers didn't respond well to human drugs, but with her so fragile he might have to rely on something man made. Raz hadn't engaged Nexus energy through a render for over a year. He intended to keep a low profile by conserving circle renders for emergencies. Chasers had technological means of detecting Nexus energy shifts generated by the process. They had to be out of range before he attempted such an act.

Sandra tittered. "Worrying too much? You're running for your lives —"

Raz slammed his arm into the wall behind him.

Sandra jumped.

He peeled his body from the paint. A small indentation marred the plasterboard. He lowered his voice and calmed his power. "I know this situation is new to you, but we've been here many times. I know what I'm doing and how to keep us safe, including you."

"Don't be a jackass." Sandra's lips thinned, and she turned her back to him. "In any of those previous times, was Paris sick?"

"No," he whispered.

She didn't hear him or pretended not to.

Raz suspected General Taft would discover their location within days. Paris's illness had to have resulted from General Taft's targeted biological weapons. The general and Dr. Nazier used Paris as a guinea pig for years before she came upon Raz's circle. What would've happened to Paris if he hadn't been an M83 agent? She was his responsibility.

Raz wouldn't sacrifice Sandra to General Taft's evil by taking her with them. "Stop." He straightened.

Sandra pulled open drawers and cabinets. "Cam is trustworthy." Her anger took on an edge of desperation. "I've known him for seven years. I'll find his number. It has to be here. I wrote it down when he changed it. If my crappy phone worked, I'd have the number in my contacts."

Raz walked up behind her. The tension in her back increased in proportion to her chattering. His hands grasped her shoulders and pulled her against his chest. Instant heat flared at the contact. She melted into his arms in such an erotic way, sparks of Nexus energy tingled along Raz's fingers. Her panting was replaced with slow inhalations, full of … arousal. Her hair tickled his face, but he loved the sensation. The lilac fragrance from her shampoo filled his nose. He branded the sensations into his mind. If he could only touch her skin.

Sandra wiggled out of his arms and brought him back to his senses. She clutched a mini-market receipt in her hand. A phone number had been scrawled over the print.

"Angelville isn't safe for us anymore." Raz grabbed at the paper.

She evaded him, stuffed it into her coat pocket and strode out of the kitchen.

"We're being watched," Raz called out.

Sandra stomped down the hallway. "How do you know?"

"Listen to me." Raz trotted over to her. He didn't need proof. If he had any, it'd be too late. They'd be dead or captured. The Nexus provided enough warning and was all the evidence he needed to tell him danger was close. "Stop being so goddamned bullheaded and think."

Sandra turned a one-eighty. Her white-knuckled fists shook by her sides. "I think all the time. I won't let Paris leave here in pain." Her chocolate brown eyes locked onto his. A crinkle formed between her brows.

Sandra's anguish hit him, and he jerked back as though she'd slapped him.

She pointed a finger at him. "You listen, for a change. Cam knows stuff. It's scary how much he knows. If the last thing I do on this earth is risk my life, I'll do it for y—" Sandra blushed but didn't look away. She whispered, "For Paris."

Raz hadn't missed her slip.

Why would she risk everything for them, for him, without even knowing what they were? His heart ached. The seconds ticked by as they stared at each other. Desire pulsed low in Raz's stomach. He wanted to kiss her but couldn't afford any emotional entanglements. The warm aura of her body and the silk of her skin tempted him. He moved closer without his conscious permission.

Raz's hands cupped her jaw. His nerves sang in ecstasy at the skin-to-skin contact. Her pulse jumped against his fingers. His lips found her ear. "Why can't I resist you?"

Sandra sucked in a breath.

He skimmed his hands along her throat to the curve between her neck and shoulders. The hard, knotted muscles tightened under his fingers. They hadn't touched in weeks. Her soft skin against his hands made thinking difficult. He massaged the muscles, and they relaxed. For a moment, her eyes flickered to gold. Her shampoo scent surrounded him in lilac essence. He soaked in the touches so he'd have sweet memories of her for any dark days ahead.

Raz loved her hair. He threaded his fingers into the heavy mass and rested his forehead against hers. "I won't allow my past to hurt you." His fingertips memorized the curves of her face. "How can I make you understand? Being with us … with me, will hurt you."

Her hands snaked around his wrists and held tight. "I *can't* lose you. I can't lose Paris. She's like my sister."

He caught the tears from the corners of her eyes before they fell. "Sandra." They weren't worth this amount of pain.

"How will I say goodbye to Sean? I need more time."

Her voice had a scratchy hitch. Raz wrapped his arms around her and kissed the top of her head. *I hunger for more time, too. Unfortunately, fate doesn't give me what I want.*

Sean burst into the kitchen. The screen door banged against the wall.

Sandra jerked and brushed more tears from her face with the heel of her hand.

The light played tricks with Raz's mind. Her eyes glistened like the rarest of yellow sapphires.

"Sandra, come see my new bike." Sean jumped from foot to foot. His six-year-old body vibrated with unconfined enthusiasm.

"What've you been doing outside?" Sandra sniffed.

Sean grabbed her hand and pulled. His dusty jeans complemented his inside out T-shirt.

Raz was suspicious of Sean's happy attitude. Each move made Sean crabbier than a hornet. A six-year-old shouldn't have developed empathic power. Sixxers didn't go through their change, or elevation, until they were much older. His little boy couldn't be going through Sixxer elevation, but Raz saw the subtle signs of Sean's transformation every day, growing uncontrolled and stronger. He was gaining his Nexus energy.

"Paris bought him a bike a few days ago. I taught him how to ride." Raz let go of Sandra. Coldness seeped into his core.

Sean pulled harder on Sandra's wrist.

She moved closer to the back door. "Wow. That was fast. I'm impressed."

Sean stood straighter, and a prideful grin appeared.

Sandra hugged him. "You're a bike-riding prodigy."

"What's a pro diggy?" Sean mumbled and bounded out the door.

Sandra continued praising his newfound bike riding skills.

Irritation gnawed inside Raz's gut. They'd have to go to HUP now, but not for drugs. Sean and Paris were absorbing Sandra's heartbreak. Sandra's love for Sean was apparent, and her love would bring out his circle's empathic instincts of protection. With two out of three Sixxers being empaths, Raz was outnumbered. An energy transfer at HUP would generate enough circular energy for them to break away from Sandra and still mask their trail from the Chasers.

What a fucking mess. Raz needed time. If he pulled away from Sandra too soon, he'd have a Sixxer fight on his hands. Not a good situation to have when hiding.

Chapter Two

MUFFLED FOOTSTEPS ECHOED behind Raz, and he looked back.

Paris stood in the kitchen entryway like a lost child. "So, we're staying?"

The transformation in her weight shocked Raz every time he saw her. She leaned her sunken and bony frame against the doorjamb. A blue hoodie engulfed her body from shoulders to knees. Her gaze seared through him. Gold and green flecks flashed among the brown irises. The dim light of her Nexus energy was still present within her. It might buy them a few days before her health declined again, but would it be enough?

Raz feared a render couldn't wait. If Raz threw his circle back on the grid by increasing their energy signatures, he had to keep them moving. He kept his suspicions of General Taft's soldiers being in Angelville to himself.

Paris hated the bastard's guts more than he did. Inciting her anger would further drain her Nexus energy. She shuffled her feet. "I thought Sandra would persuade you to stay."

"What's that supposed to mean?"

Paris pushed off the door and hobbled toward the kitchen counter. "The coffee smells heavenly."

"Don't change the subject." Paris's actions all screamed her desire to stay in Angelville. Unfortunately, she had no other choice but to leave with him. He grabbed a travel mug from the cabinet, filled it to the brim with black liquid and handed it to her. Raz couldn't comprehend how she drank the swill.

Paris inhaled, sighed in pleasure and blew over the mug before cautiously sipping the steaming liquid. She shrugged with a knowing look in her eyes. "Sandra is the red in your rose these days. Why is it, exactly, my best friend is chummier with you than with me?" She eased into the kitchen chair and unsuccessfully covered a grimace. Her dark blonde ponytail swayed along her neck.

Raz shook his head, and his lips twitched. "Sandra is my what?"

"Stop pretending." Paris gulped at the mug and winced. A swirl of steam hovered under her nose.

Raz's tentative smile disappeared. A Sixxer empath read nothing or everything about the mental states of those within a circle. Raz thought he'd figured out how to hide his emotions from her better than a human, but he'd been wrong about Paris's ability before.

She sipped her coffee. "Why can't we stay?"

"I encouraged the friendship between the two of you, but your relationship must end. Sandra and I … We leave nothing behind, like every other time we've moved."

She dropped her hand, and the mug clanked on the table surface. The contents sloshed over her fingers. "We'd be better off staying where we can defend ourselves. Home turf advantage. You know this. I shouldn't have to spell it out to an M83 agent."

Ex-agent. They didn't have a home turf. Every location was temporary.

At his silence, she gripped the mug tight to her chest and shivered. "At least I have my cup-o-Joe to keep me warm."

"Don't start."

"You don't even block me anymore. Do you do it to hurt me or make me angry?"

Raz leaned a hip against the countertop. Maybe both. "You knew we'd eventually have to leave. If Chasers find Sean, you know what they'll do to him." Raz pulled a porcelain cup from the cabinet. He needed clarity and focus. The brewed coffee offered both. He poured liberal amounts of milk and sugar into the cup. The dark contents of the mug turned fair and sweet.

Paris gulped her beverage and gained fighting power. She jumped from the chair and stepped toward him. "We'd be better off if we stayed right here. If we combine our energy, and you create a shield —"

"Are you hallucinating? A shield would advertise our location to every Chaser in the state! The circle's safety is our number one priority. Don't fight me on this." Disgusted with her proposal, he dumped the mocha liquid down the drain. Raz no longer needed the java buzz.

Paris's gaze followed the stream of coffee. "Tsk-tsk. Such a waste," she whispered. The longing and greed in her voice chilled him.

He leaned over the sink. "Your proposal is the last thing we should do."

"It'll protect Sandra, too." Paris refilled her mug, tucked the pot close and shuffled back to the table. Her burst of life fizzled out with a flip of a switch.

Raz wouldn't have been surprised if she drank straight from the carafe. "A shield will kill Sandra. Like it did to the last human who tried to enter a render with us."

The chair held Paris in place as though she were a rag doll, the mug and pot her table anchors. Raz ignored how tired she looked and the wild set to her eyes. Staying here wouldn't improve her condition. "The Nexus doesn't want humans. There's no point in wishing differently, no matter how much we both want it."

Paris reached for his arm.

Raz shrugged her off. He wouldn't be swayed by her need for human connections. Their goal was to keep the Chasers away.

The effectiveness of the coffee was a human crutch. Her illness took charge. Shudders vibrated Paris's small frame. Twenty layers of clothes covered her, despite the unseasonably warm October weather.

Raz rubbed his hand over his face. The sicker she became, the harder he struggled to appear calm and unaffected. Fearless. The detour to HUP held the potential of a render and a possible delay in Paris's next attack. If they were on the move, it might be worth the risk.

"Have you said anything to Sandra?" Paris asked.

Tell Sandra they were alien? *Hell, no.*

Raz squatted, pulled her hoodie together and zipped it to her chin. He removed the gloves from her pockets and helped place them on her trembling fingers. He wasn't sure they'd be warm enough to thaw her ice-like skin. "Worry about yourself. Worry about Sean. Our son's safety comes before any human."

After rising, he marched down the hallway. *Don't I have the right, as Sandra's lover, to keep her safe, as well?* His desire for Sandra made him possessive, irrational. The sigh reverberated through his body. The energy bond Raz had with Paris prevented him from fitting anyone else into his life.

Raz entered the dark bedroom. He tossed an empty suitcase on the bed and loaded it with Paris's clothes. She should've packed days ago. Paris wanted to slow him down. He didn't like being an ass around her, but it was the only way to get the hell out of this town. "Sandra will never find out what we are," he said. The words echoed around the empty room. He wouldn't think about Sandra's reaction to the truth–to the lies, especially after their last night together. The hours they'd spent with each other caused him to forget his obligations. When he was with Sandra, the circle didn't exist. He pretended for a moment he had happiness, and that everything was perfect. Pretended Sandra wouldn't hate him for what he was.

Paris shuffled into the room. She sat on the edge of the bed.

The walk to the kitchen and back had cost her a lot of strength. An apology teetered on his lips, but he wanted her anger. She didn't want to leave Sandra behind, either. How could he blame her? Their friendship held strength. There was something about Sandra, a quality about her, an acceptance she gave, which all three of them craved.

"You can't keep ..." Paris brought her hand to her mouth and coughed. "Sandra away from us. We need her."

"Lie down while I finish this. You're overexerting yourself."

"Don't treat me like a child." The next cough shook her body. She caught her breath and placed a hand on the bed to keep her balance. Her eyes dimmed to a dark brown. "I decide what's best for me and my son. We're happy here. The happiest we've ever been." Another coughing spell curled her into a ball. She recovered with choppy words. "Small towns are better for Sean. This is his home."

"Happy doesn't mean safe." Raz tossed several hoodies in her luggage case.

"You act like you're running from her."

Raz paused and looked at Paris closely. His decisions weren't based off whether or not Sandra was near. His bond was with his circle. "We've been running for seven years. I don't care about humans, only us."

Paris arched an eyebrow. "Sandra can come with us."

Damn, to some degree, she senses my feelings about Sandra. "No."

"Then why take me to someone you don't trust because Sandra suggested it?"

Raz hesitated over loading her shoes into the suitcase.

"Don't look so worried. I heard parts of your conversation." Paris grabbed the Nikes and shoved them into the side pocket of the carry-on bag.

"HUP is a delay. It's an opportunity to boost your energy, instead of relying on caffeine. We'll initiate a render before leaving."

Paris leaned back until she lay flat on the bedspread. "You're definitely in emergency mode. A render will create a call-out within a mile of us. A mile around HUP! Here we are, Chasers. Come get us." Laughter rasped from her throat and make her cough. "And you're worried about a shield which would, at least, protect us when they found us."

"Sandra's emotions are encouraging your empathic power inside you and Sean to protect her. A refocus of that energy will strengthen you and get us moving. Away. The damn Chasers won't have time to find us after they realize a render occurred. We'll be gone."

"You don't want to leave, either."

Raz shook his head. "I want to get the hell out of here."

Paris eased up on an elbow. She snorted. "Like I said. I *heard* you. You don't even know you're doing it."

Raz ignored her empathic analysis. If Paris read his longing for Sandra, did she also feel it? A longing he'd never admit to himself, now they were forced out of Angelville. "The ride to HUP will give you time to detach. Once polite hellos are exchanged, we'll engage the render and deal with the consequences." He ducked into the small bathroom and came out with Paris's toothbrush and hairbrush. He tossed them onto the bed. The small carry-on was now stuffed to the gills. It should be enough until they found somewhere new.

Paris fondled the suitcase's leather strap. "Everyone's emotions come at me like a hurricane. They hurt as much as my illness. How can you trust Cameron's medical analysis when a rendering and a shield can heal me? Right here! We can make our stand—"

"I protect you. I don't trust you … or anyone." Raz wanted Paris safe. She was the mother of his child, and their initial relationship, before the death of his parents, had filled him with hopes and dreams of a family. Yet, her foolish mistake of trusting a human always had him on edge. He carefully examined her friendship with Sandra when they met. The promise of a normal life had him, also, believing a human could be trusted.

Paris's face drained of all color. She sat up. Green specks of light flared and dimmed several times in her eyes. Her lips thinned, and she tugged the hoodie higher on her neck. "Without Sean, you would've left me years ago." She rambled. "Why would you stay? The young girl I was … She's gone." Paris re-folded and rearranged the clothes in the bag. "I never expected you to forgive me. I still don't, but I'd suggest nothing that'd expose Sean to danger. HUP is a red flag."

Raz sat in the corner chair. He didn't want to bring up the past. It wouldn't help them and would push Paris away when he needed her on his side. "Because of your illness, my Transor power won't be enough to keep the circle safe if we're attacked." He held out his palm to stop her interruption. "If we stayed here, I'd have to render the circle first before using that energy to form a shield. Most of it would heal you. A shield won't last a day under those conditions. We can't risk draining the circle until we've left Angelville."

"But, you *are* a *Transor*. Your power and Nexus bond is immense."

Raz leaned forward. His elbows rested on his knees. A Transor wasn't a miracle-worker in such a weak circle. He didn't look at Paris, because he didn't want to see her disappointment. "We stayed too long. Got too comfortable. HUP will provide an opportunity to boost your strength. At least, give you some strength. Once we're on the road, we can dart enough so our Nexus energy can keep you strong. We'll have time for goodbyes, especially for Sean."

"We should tell Sandra the truth—"

"Tell her what?" Raz wanted to tell Sandra everything but never would.

Paris clenched her teeth. Nexus light flared in her eyes, again. The mix of yellow and green sparks danced along her irises. Small bursts of Nexus energy triggered Paris's empathic ability. "They're in Angelville." Her eyes brightened with knowledge. "How long have the Chasers been out there?"

Raz couldn't hide from her anymore. "Possibly a few days, maybe as much as a week. They haven't marked us."

Paris leaned forward and put her elbows on her knees. "You haven't attempted a render since we've lived here. It's kept us hidden. Why do you think they haven't marked us?"

"I have no clue. The no-render idea was worth a shot." He gathered Sean's toys from the dresser. "We lasted over a year before I sensed the Chasers."

Green light flashed then dimmed from her hands, and gold flecks sparkled from her irises. The power faded. Her eyes appeared human, normal brownish-hazel with yellow and green highlights. Soon, Paris would have no Nexus connection left. HUP now became a necessity for Raz's Nexus healing.

"What if Cameron is one of them?" Paris asked.

"You trust Sandra, don't you?"

Paris nodded.

"She trusts Cameron. That's enough, for now." Raz sensed Chaser eyes watching, waiting. One wrong move sentenced them to experimentation as Sixxer lab rats.

Sandra's trust of Cameron ran deep. He'd keep Sandra safe after they left. General Taft wouldn't think twice about using Sandra to get to Raz, to get to Sean. Cameron wouldn't endanger Sandra any more than Raz already had. "Sandra will be safer if I leave her at HUP."

Paris blubbered, raw and awful.

She blinked her tears away. "Sandra is a part of us. Our circle. You're tearing our family into pieces."

Raz hated hurting her. "Sandra can't be a part of our circle." He tossed the toys on the bed and went over to sit beside her. He hugged her shoulders. "I remember the render with the human. You almost died. Your coma lasted three days. None of us saved my parents. I knew then we had to keep hiding, maybe forever."

Paris shook her head. "A render with Sandra won't be the same."

"I can't. Not with Sandra." Raz couldn't hide from Paris any longer. Her empathic power easily read him, and he didn't block her. His choice wasn't to punish her but to make her understand. The struggle was too much for the circle and weakened their Sixxer life-force.

"Sean would keep Sandra safe," Paris said. "I've sensed his power growing. Raz, he's capable."

"He's not that powerful."

"You were younger and unsure of your abilities back then. Sandra's strong, too."

Raz squeezed her tight. "Too much energy is exchanged. The surge would be like blowing a circuit in Sandra's brain." He pulled away and zipped the luggage.

Paris picked up Sean's teddy bear and hugged it tight. "Sandra's different."

"She's human. Don't speculate on what might happen. I'm a Transor. If I couldn't do it before, there isn't anyone who can."

Paris squished the teddy bear into the front pocket of the bag. "I sense something … Sandra's not like—"

"She's nothing like you."

The blood drained from Paris's face. "Comparison shopping doesn't become you, Raz." Sarcasm dripped from her lips.

The jealousy flares quick, no matter what I do or say. My interest in you, dear Paris, has long faded.

The floor creaked. Raz flicked his gaze to the doorway.

Sandra stood in the entrance. One foot crossed the threshold, but she hesitated on moving her other foot inside. "Are we leaving soon?"

Raz stood and grabbed the suitcase. "Time is the enemy now." He wouldn't answer the questions in Sandra's eyes. "We have to go."

CHAPTER THREE

SANDRA STEPPED BACK as Raz exited the room. His bicep lightly swept over her breasts as he squeezed past her. Her jacket and shirt weren't enough to prevent the flush of heat tingling along her skin. Her face flamed. Hopefully, Paris wouldn't notice her reaction. Sandra composed herself. She'd overheard a few words from their conversation, but they had made no sense. She called from the door. "Is everything okay?"

The room was a dungeon, dark and lifeless. Paris sat in a sea of white on the bed. Her jacket was a splotch of navy and contrasted with her pale face. Paris focused on her. She licked her cracked lips and smiled. "Are you ..." Paris scratched her brow. Her smile faded. "Your eyes are ... glittery."

They were probably bloodshot from lack of sleep, and the crying jags Sandra couldn't stop since she'd found out they were leaving town.

Paris grabbed at her chest. "Oh." She moaned and inhaled a raspy breath. Her body shuddered from the effort to breathe.

Sandra rushed into the room but hesitated. Paris wanted no one to touch her when the body pain intensified. Sandra stopped a foot from where Paris sat on the bed. Her illness was more than a cold. Sandra reached for the paper in her pocket. The receipt's smooth surface, and the phone number it contained, calmed her. Cameron would know what pain medicine to give her. "Let me take you to a doctor."

Paris's cheeks were red from the exertion of coughing. Clearing her throat, her spell passed, and she breathed without incident. "I'm fine now." Her complexion returned to normal. "Where is Sean?"

Sandra smirked. She was proud of the kid. "Riding like he's training fro the *Tour de France*."

Paris grinned. "He's always been a quick study." She studied Sandra's face. "The light in here ... for a moment, your eyes brightened."

Indigo walls framed the single window. Beams of late afternoon light entered through the slivers between the blinds and fought the shadows. Sandra hoped the semidarkness masked any redness from her earlier tears. Her eyes were now irritated and scratchy. She blinked the dryness away. "They're the same muddy brown as usual."

Paris snorted. "Your eyes are beautiful."

"Flattery is appreciated." Sandra leaned closer. "Do my eyes say I'm pissed, too?"

Paris smirked. "Shouting surprise doesn't help? You hadn't planned your day to include running from bad guys?"

Her friend's weird sense of humor eased Sandra's anger. She bit her bottom lip. "We all have secrets, but really? Witness protection?"

Paris scooted to the edge of the white comforter. She bumped Sandra's knees and held out her hand. "At least we aren't spies." She giggled and grasped Sandra's fingers before winking. "Then we'd have to kill you."

Sandra allowed Paris to pull her down toward the edge of the bed. Sandra sat beside her, and her smirk was automatic. *Maybe they are spies, and the witness protection is the cover. What a wild thought.*

Paris coughed and loosened the phlegm hindering her breathing. "Ug. That one sounded bad." Paris squeezed Sandra's fingers. "It sounds worse than it is."

Her voice scratched from her throat like a seasoned smoker. Sandra squeezed her hand tight. "Let me take you to the hospital."

"I wanted to tell you for a long time. I thought we'd be in Angelville for years."

"You don't have to explain—"

"My father, Dr. Nazier, he's the one we're running from." Paris's next cough was rough and wet, but over quickly.

Sandra reached for the box of tissues on the bedside dresser. "Don't tell me." *Yes, tell me. Please. I want to know what drives you so desperately.*

"My father wants us, dead or alive," Paris whispered.

Dead. Sandra's worst fear. "I want you safe." Once the words were said aloud, a vibration filled the area around Sandra as though someone had hit a tuning fork. Strange currents of air swirled around her body.

Paris brought the tissue to her face as another coughing attack shuddered through her body. She regained control but gawked at Sandra with large saucer eyes. "Did you feel that?" Paris ran her hand along Sandra's arm.

Distress oozed from Paris's grip. Her fingers searched and poked Sandra's arms and stomach. Sandra couldn't stop her or speak. The pulsation ended. Sandra shook her head. *What the eff just happened?*

"For a second, I was scared you'd pass out." Paris forced out a chuckle. She patted Sandra's bicep. "I don't have the strength to catch you. So, please don't, okay?"

Spots in Sandra's peripheral vision floated in front of her, and she blinked them away. Paris came back into focus. The weird sensations were just vertigo. What else could have happened?

Paris drew in two quick inhales followed by an exhale. She arched her neck side-to-side. Pop. Snap. "I'll ride with you to HUP. I'd rather not be with the Mayor of Crab Town anymore today."

Paris's humor brought Sandra back to reality, and she smiled at the description of Raz. She flexed her fingers and rolled her shoulders. "An appropriate title." They giggled.

Sandra guessed, if she carried the weight of protecting Paris and Sean on her shoulders, she'd have little time for relaxation. Although, Raz's mood most likely resulted from his displeasure with her for screwing up his exit plan.

"All we do is argue." Paris examined Sandra's face.

What had Raz said to her? Was Paris searching for ... what? Friendship? Betrayal? Sandra studied the carpet pattern at her feet. Paris had done everything possible to get closer to Raz. Guilt bubbled to the surface. Sandra hadn't wished for the same. Sandra wanted Raz for herself, and her desire twisted her gut into knots. She wanted the life Paris had with him.

"The conversation I walked in on was none of my business." A hundred questions formed, but Sandra couldn't bring herself to ask one. *Did Raz tell you we're lovers? Do you hate me?* She sat on the edge of the bed and waited. *Tell me Raz isn't mine. State your claim on him, Paris.* Time slowed. Sandra pulled at the edges of her sleeve.

"Don't worry." Pairs bumped shoulders with Sandra and grinned. "Raz gets irritable when we move. I'm rusty dealing with him."

Wait. Raz hadn't told Paris about their relationship?

Paris pushed off the bed, swayed and bounced back onto the mattress.

"Can you walk?" Sandra held on to Paris's arm.

Paris laughed. "I'm fainting. You're fainting. We're not a good couple right now." Tears sprang to her eyes. "I don't want to leave."

"You have to—"

Paris hunched and tilted her head. "You don't want us to go, either."

Guilty as charged.

"Raz can save … Keep us … Right here," Paris said.

Sandra shook her head. *Dead or Alive.* The danger they were in was too great. "You're hiding for a reason. This house isn't safe anymore."

Paris squeezed Sandra's arm. "If anything happens to me, you'll take care of Sean."

The burning behind Sandra's eyes returned. *My God! How can she ask me this?* No. Didn't ask. Paris demanded it. Sandra's heart skipped a beat. She loved Sean like her own, but the request was too overwhelming. After a few slow breaths, Sandra eased her arm around Paris's waist and helped her stand.

Sandra blinked against the flow of tears, but they escaped and moistened her lashes. Now, *she* needed an escape plan. "Raz agreed to take you to my lab. I can't promise Cam can help, but he's gotten me out of a few scrapes with my ex. He doesn't blab, and he's practically a doctor. I'm not sure why he's working for HUP's biology department."

"What can he do to keep us here?"

Sandra ignored the question because her answer included one hundred ways to keep them here. "The lab has painkillers."

Paris latched on to Sandra's hand and stepped carefully toward the door. "Promise me you'll keep my father away from Sean."

Sandra urged Paris to keep moving.

She ground her feet into the floor. "Promise me."

Sandra couldn't tear her gaze away. The green flecks in Paris's eyes mesmerized her. Sandra couldn't deny her and nodded. "I promise." She positioned Paris toward the hallway.

Paris shuffled out of the room. "You remind me of a childhood friend."

"How so?"

Paris leaned on the wall outside the door and looked Sandra in the eye. "You're stronger than you believe."

They reached the kitchen table. Paris grabbed her coffee mug.

Sandra helped Paris walk down the porch steps to the rundown 1969 Camaro SS parked in the drive.

Paris snickered. "Aw, you have Thom's baby with you."

Sandra cringed. The car was the only baby she'd ever have from her ex-husband, or anyone else. *I have* … The air sailed out of her lungs. *Sean doesn't count!* She reached the last step. "It runs."

Paris shuffled her feet, and small clouds of dust hid their legs. "I can't believe you wanted this piece of shit. You should've asked for the Mercedes."

Sandra grinned. "Yeah, I should've, but Thom wanted the Camaro."

Paris eased into the passenger seat of the muscle car and closed the squeaky door.

The car needed a good scrub. Dirt and grime coated the black paint. Thom would throw a little-girl fit if he saw it at HUP. A rush of satisfaction went through Sandra at imagining Thom's suffering. Cell phone in hand, she retrieved the receipt and punched in Cameron's digits. The phone flashed 'No Service'. She cursed and tucked it into her pocket.

Raz opened the hatch of the minivan. The muscles in his back flexed under his T-shirt. A slight breeze tossed his dark hair over his forehead.

Sandra leaned against the van. Dust fell from the metal and settled on her blazer. She didn't care.

Raz finished his task of loading Paris's bag into the cargo area.

Sandra didn't stare him in the eye because she couldn't take her gaze off his delicious physique. Her fingers tingled. They ached to touch him. The rush of desire gave her courage. After today, she'd never see him again, so why not clear the air? "You and Paris were arguing about me."

He stacked additional boxes and bags in the back.

She called his organization skills a mix of catty-wampus and I-don't-give-a-shit. Paris would have fun finding stuff.

"We have the same argument every time we leave. It wasn't personal."

Sandra raised her gaze to his. "How much does she know?"

Raz glanced in the back window of the Camaro. The partial outline of Paris's head was silhouetted in the front passenger seat. He looked back to Sandra.

The directness of his blue gaze sent a ripple of hard, hot lust into the pit of her gut. He had to feel it, too. Dark stubble covered his chiseled jaw drawing her attention to his full lips.

"Coming to your house that day was a mistake. I'm sorry." Raz tapped his hand onto his jeans. Dust fluttered from his palms to the ground.

Sandra's gaze snapped to his as her jaw dropped. She pushed away from the van. The heat that had flooded her body turned into ice. The pounding in her head increased. *An apology?* Sandra didn't believe him. She stepped closer and hissed. "We aren't a mistake." Her fingers itched to slap him. *Why did he say their relationship didn't matter, today of all days?*

Raz rubbed his hand over his mouth. He sat on the leftover inch of space in the van's cargo area like nothing was amiss. The vehicle sank from his muscular weight. His black T-shirt hugged his chest and flat stomach.

She remembered all the hard planes underneath and hated pretending she didn't. He was the sexiest thing alive.

"We haven't had to move in a year. Paris is being difficult. You'll be fine."

One step forward. "How can you say it was a mis—"

"The Chasers are worried about us, not you."

She wanted to punch the forced smile from his face.

He snickered and arched a brow. "Sean calls them Chasers. They are evil men who have a grudge against me. I dragged Paris and Sean into this mess, and I can't get them out."

She stepped closer and reached out. "Talk to me—"

"The university will be our goodbye."

The small distance between them stretched into a chasm.

He moved his hand out to touch her but brought it back to the bumper. He opened his mouth then pinched his lips together.

Did he want to tell her how much he'd miss her? This really wasn't happening. She'd gotten her life back. Dreams of a family were right around the corner. So much for clearing the air. He wouldn't let her speak. She hadn't wanted their last bit of closeness to be in Paris's kitchen, but that's all she got.

Sandra glanced back toward the house and caught Sean in her peripheral vision. He zipped around the end of the dirt driveway and onto the country road on his bike. "Does Sean realize you're never coming back?"

Raz's gaze lingered on Sean, mastering his new skill.

The uneasiness in his face made her heart ache.

"Let's get going," Raz whispered.

She almost didn't hear him.

He cleared his throat. "I don't want to stay at HUP for longer than a half hour." Raz called Sean and loaded the bike into the back of the van.

The little boy hopped in the passenger seat.

Sandra couldn't catch her breath. Her chest ached. Dust blew in her face as the van accelerated down the drive.

Sean held his teddy and waved the bear's arm at her.

She waved back, grateful this hadn't been her goodbye. Short and sweet would've taken longer. Sandra had been pissed moments before, but those emotions were nothing compared to the present. How dare Raz treat her like this!

A fine layer of grime coated everything as the van disappeared. She squinted to keep it out of her eyes. The drought this summer lasted longer than predicted. Hot, humid air clung to her body. Sandra longed for a fresh breeze, like on the day she met Raz. That day had marked a new start for her life. Her carnival excursion had, also, been the beginning of her current mess.

Her memory came with the scent of blooms and crisp air. Mechanical thrill rides clattered as happy families enjoyed the afternoon in the heart of Angelville. A sweet and salty mix of fried dough and sizzling Italian sandwiches teased her nostrils and made her mouth water.

The man barely glanced Sandra's way, but his blue eyes could've pierced the blackest night. Her entire body still experienced aftershocks several minutes after he turned away. She sat at the picnic table. He lounged against the metal carousel gate. Her gaze gobbled him up like a chocoholic starring down a triple ganache cake.

Six months ago Sandra finalized her divorce. She needed to start living again. She occupied herself by observing her newly-found dessert, standing there, tempting her. Who was she hurting? Thom had done much more than admire other women when Sandra still had a ring on her finger.

The stranger's slender and wiry body curved, giving her an excellent view of his backside. He leaned against the railing, and his gaze darted between people as they rode. The muscles in his shoulders and arms rippled underneath his T-shirt as he shifted into a more comfortable stance. Danger came off him in waves, despite his casual demeanor.

Sandra itched to touch his shaggy dark brown hair.

Paris walked up the boardwalk.

Sandra waved before her gaze again flickered to the man at the railing. Paris would get a chuckle out of her fascination. An image of the man's naked chest flashed in her mind. Did he have a six-pack? This stranger didn't know she devoured him from a distance.

Then, the blue fire of his eyes met and held hers.

Her face heated, and her breath hitched. Mortification paralyzed her for a second. She ducked her head, yet she couldn't resist another peek at those baby blues and fine body.

The man was turned back to the ride. Had Sandra imagined his interest?

Paris stopped beside him and snaked an arm around his waist.

Sandra's chest tightened, and she stopped breathing.

He placed his arm around Paris's shoulders and laughed.

Sandra's gut rolled, and her mouth fell open. Paris obviously knew him well.

Unfortunately, Sandra had never stopped wanting Raz for herself. Guilt punched Sandra in the stomach, and she snapped back to the present. The trail of dust behind the van settled to the ground. Knowing Paris loved Raz hadn't stopped Sandra from getting involved with the man. She eased into the bucket seat of the Camaro and started the engine. Her heart galloped as she dreaded every word she needed to say in order to wash the dirt off her soul.

Sandra focused on the windshield. "I have to tell you something."

Paris patted Sandra's hand on the gearshift. "You're my sister." She placed her other hand over her heart. "Here, where it counts. You can tell me anything." She coughed into a wadded tissue.

I've just been sucker-punched by Paris. A coating of dust settled on the window. Sandra sighed. She released the parking brake, lifted her foot off the clutch and they coasted backward to the turnaround and stopped.

"What did you want to say?" Paris asked.

"Me and Raz ..." Sandra peeked at Paris. Was it her tone, or the breathy way she said Raz's name, causing Paris's extra-pale face and shimmering eyes? Sandra's throat tightened. She blinked back tears. She'd stay strong and admit her betrayal. Several tense moments passed. Sandra tried to speak, but the words wouldn't form. She cleared her throat.

"My history with Raz is ugly. He took care of us when we couldn't take care of ourselves," Paris whispered.

"You love him." Sandra's voice turned raw and painful.

"My love was never enough." The shimmer in Paris's eyes flared and then faded to light brown.

Is the afternoon light reflecting in her tears?

Sandra's gaze fell to her lap. "I'm sorry." Teardrops welled, and one sneaked out from the corner of her eye. She brought up her hand to staunch the flow and clear her vision. She put the car in gear and drove down the drive. A good friend wouldn't rip another's love out from under her.

"He needs you."

"Do you understand what I'm confessing? Get angry at me. Yell. Do something!"

"I'm dying, Sandra."

Sandra braked hard. They both shot forward. The seat belts jerked them back. "What are you talking about? You have the flu, or pneumonia, or something. When you get out of the state, Raz can call the marshal—"

"There isn't a marshal. We aren't in witness protection."

Sandra squeezed the steering wheel. "What? But Sean made up the phrase Chasers because criminals are after you?"

"Sean didn't make up the word, Chasers have been after us before he was born." Paris tossed her tissue onto the floor by her feet.

Sandra's head hurt so badly she had a hard time comprehending Paris's words. She set the parking brake and pushed the seatbelt latch then opened the door. Her feet landed on gravel, and a wave of nausea hit her. Gasping for fresh air, she got humid thickness instead. Had she wished for this? It was her fault. She should've taken better care of Paris, taken her to the doctor. Stopped wishing for her life. Ignored Raz.

"I don't think I'll make it much farther," Paris said. "Maybe to the next state. I have only days left." She coughed.

"I'll take you to the hospital right now." Beads of sweat broke out on Sandra's upper lip. Bile rose in the back of her throat. *Focus. Swallow. Breathe.* She refused to throw up. Paris was wrong.

"No hospital."

"Paris!" *Why won't she go?*

"You want them both. I want Sean to have a mother."

Sandra raised her head and eased back against the seat. A cool current filtered through the heavy air, which relaxed her turbulent gut. She couldn't stop shaking her head. *No. No. No.*

Paris stared out the window and pulled another wadded tissue from her face. "It's too late for me. I need you to take care of Sean."

"I don't want your life." *Liar.*

"Other than Raz, I only trust you. Raz can't do this alone."

Sandra knocked her head against the steering wheel. Moisture ran along her upper lip.

"Oh, shit." Paris thrust a clean tissue in her face. "Your nose is bleeding."

Sandra pulled wet fingers from her face. She grabbed the tissue and blotted. Red blossomed onto the white material.

"Are you okay?" Paris asked.

Sandra scoffed. "You're worried about me? I haven't had a nose bleed since I was a kid. It's nothing." She leaned her head against the wheel, blotting a few more times. Peering into the visor mirror, she made sure everything was okay. The light reflected from the hood of the car, and her eyes became a honey color. *Definitely the afternoon light.*

"It's over," Paris said.

What part? Sandra glanced up.

Paris frowned.

Their warm camaraderie was gone. Sandra had nothing now. No lover. No friend. All ties had been cut.

Chapter Four

A BROWN THREE-by-five card flapped from Sandra's empty name plate. Someday, she'd have her name on this door and really belong here.

The horrible handwriting scrawled on the paper said, "Professor Bombshell's New Time: 8 pm. Be there or be scared. We know where you live. ~ The Six." The students she tutored loved to make jokes at her expense. There weren't many women in the biology department at HUP, but at least the students wanted to learn from her and not Thom.

She removed her arm from around Paris's waist and helped her lean against the wall. Raz hadn't been discussed on the drive. Sandra's confession had been one-upped by her friend's death prediction, leaving their relationship teetering on the edge of a cliff. Sandra searched her bag, the key to her office hidden in the depths.

"A love note from Thom?" Paris grimaced.

"Not this time." Sandra had told Paris about Thom's harassment a month ago.

Paris's lecture started with new job searches and ended with figuring out a way to get Thom fired. Unfortunately, a new job was out of the question. HUP contained the one lab in the country able to test Sandra's research. She shouldn't be the one to sacrifice her work because Thom was an asshole.

Paris closed her eyes and coughed into her hand. No longer able to stand without help, she slid down the wall a few inches then caught herself.

Sandra gasped and leaped forward.

Paris waved her off. "I'm all right."

"Yeah." Sandra helped Paris sit on the floor instead of falling on her face. "And I have a fairy godmother. Are you having more pain?" She found the office key in the bottomless pit she called a handbag.

"The same."

Sandra didn't believe Paris after noticing the squinting in her pale, sunken eyes. In Sandra's urgency, she fumbled the key. It pinged onto the floor. She bent over and scooped it off the tile. *Relax. Paris won't die in front of your office.* "My badge is inside. Somewhere. If I can find it, I can get us into the lab, but I'll also call Cam and see where he is. He'll open the security lock." Sandra tore the paper from the door and kept at least one eye on Paris. Without a doubt, Cameron would be on campus somewhere.

Paris braced herself with her back against the wall, and she stretched out her legs in front of her. Under half-closed eyes, a green sparkle flashed. "You get notes on your door often?"

"My students sometimes leave messages this way." Sandra inserted the key. "The Six is a campus group that thinks they're hilarious." A line of static shot from her finger to the doorknob. Lightheadedness crawled over her. Her ears rang. "Damn it," she mumbled under her breath. *What's wrong with me?*

"Don't tell me you have the wrong key?" Paris pushed off the floor and stood. She swayed. Her weary eyes held more pain than she let on.

Sandra unlocked the entrance. "It's okay. I have the right key. The door knob zapped me."

Paris slumped, and her lips twisted. Pulling off her glove, she reached out to touch the doorframe. "Why'd you get shocked?"

"Static electricity, I assume."

Paris furrowed her brow. "Does this happen often?" She removed her other glove and gently touched the door with both hands. A gold luster popped into her eyes from the light filtering into the hallway. Paris stood on wobbly legs.

Sandra got the willies. Her overactive imagination was on the high-alert today. Nothing happened. She shook off the bad vibe. "It's just me. I'm electric." She laughed.

Paris tilted her head. The intensity of her eyes increased. A puzzled expression wrinkled her face, and she moved her hands to Sandra's arms.

Her fingers burned Sandra through her clothing. Paris's brownish-green gaze trapped Sandra's.

She couldn't look away. Her skin crawled. Sandra turned the doorknob behind her. "Come on. Let's get inside."

"Are you getting headaches, too?" Paris squeezed Sandra's biceps.

The vibration Sandra experienced at the house returned. "Static won't hurt us." *The hum is nothing real. It's my imagination.*

"What if I'm contagious? Sometimes I have hallucinations and headaches."

Sandra pulled back and held Paris's icy hands. She rubbed heat back into them. Sandra typically formed wild theories in her head, and she knew to ignore them. The light and noise she thought she heard and saw wasn't real. She'd been around Paris long enough to know the illness wasn't going to affect her. "You're the one we need to worry about today." A deep breath calmed her nerves. She pushed open the door.

Sandra prepared to battle another of her quirks in the small space of her office. Sandra counted. *One. Two. Three. I thought I had a handle on this fear of tight places, especially at HUP.*

As Paris entered the room, she tripped and fell onto the bookcase before righting herself.

Sandra didn't rush inside. Any guests who entered Sandra's office were on their own in the corn maze of junk until she could work around her phobia. She scooted the door stopper under the edge of the door with her foot. Now she could enter.

Sandra set the note, along with her computer bag and purse, on the desk and moved aside a few papers and books. "I'll clear a chair for you." Her keycard wasn't there. A curse of her profession, or personality, she'd get so wrapped up in her research she never left the badge in the same place. "I hope Cam is here this weekend. Thom could get us into the lab, but I'd rather avoid him right now. He'd ask too many questions."

"He'd want to protect you," Paris mumbled and sat down.

Paris is delirious. Sandra rolled her eyes and dug her phone out of her jeans pocket. "Bug the shit out of me is more like it." The blank screen stared back at her. She leaned over her desk and plugged the cell into the charger.

The hair on the back of her neck stood up. Sandra spun.

Raz stepped into the tiny office, and he filled the entire space with his body.

Sean was suctioned to his side. He'd found an old bandana and tied each end to his teddy's arms. The bear's arms looped around his neck piggy-back style.

Instead of holding her breath, she inhaled Raz's scent, spicy and sweet, like Red Hots candy. Her attraction to him was magnetic.

"I parked the car as close as possible," Raz said. "I circled forever. I didn't think the lot would be full on a Saturday."

"Classes six days a week," Sandra said. "My space is reserved."

Raz was so … immense. A light buzz of euphoria filled her like a stone massage she'd gotten for her birthday a few years ago—pleasantly heavy and warm, soothing. Sandra intended to step away from Raz. She needed a clear head but instead took a step toward him. She created a distance of approximately three inches between them and swore another spark of static electricity snapped.

Paris cleared her throat. The jealousy on her face twisted her lips.

Tingles of embarrassment squirmed along Sandra's neck. She snapped out of her daze.

Sean crawled around Raz and hopped over to his mother. He climbed into her lap.

Sandra held her breath, afraid all the oxygen would get sucked out of the room.

Sean turned toward Paris. "Are we going to see a Chase now?"

"We're going to go see my friend Cam," Sandra said on an outward breath she immediately regretted. *It's okay.* The open door allowed plenty of air circulation. She piled the papers in her hands onto the desk. A few fluttered haphazardly to the floor.

"Sandra, why's The Six written here?" Sean pointed to the script on the brown notecard.

Raz grabbed the paper out of Sean's hand, scanning the message. His gaze flew up to Paris's face then Sandra's. "What's this?"

Sandra placed her hand on her hip. His tone irritated her. She repeated her inner mantra to ease her panic at the tight enclosure.

Keep responses short. Retain as much air as possible. No deep breaths. "A joke."

"A joke?" Raz's incredulous tone raised the pitch of his voice. "Looks like a threat."

"Is it because I'm six?" Sean wiggled in excitement at his advanced age, swung his bear around and hugged it close. "I just had my birthday."

Sandra ruffled his hair. "The Six is a campus group. They're biology students I tutor two days a week. I have a pretty good idea who the author is." She removed her laptop from her bag and placed it with a click on the docking station.

"Did you read it?" Raz's voice deepened.

Sandra raised her eyes from her laptop. Raz's direct gaze captured hers. His eyes, while still blue, appeared crystalline, as though small specks of light flooded the iris.

Hallucinations. She yanked the paper from his hands, crumpled it up and threw it in the recycling bin. "Of course, I read it. Like other nonsensical messages I get from my students, it's nothing to worry about. It's not why we're here."

"We can't be too careful, Sandra."

She pulled out the receipt with Cameron's handwritten number and pushed the power button on both her computer and the phone. The faster she contacted Cameron, the quicker they could leave this room. "Raz, these are kids. Your paranoia is showing." Both power indicators of the electronic devices lit up.

"The Chasers are soldiers," Paris whispered. "We've never encountered them in an environment like this." She rubbed her neck, and trickles of perspiration beaded on her skin.

"HUP doesn't have a military presence on campus." Sandra rubbed her forehead. *Who in the hell are they really running from?*

Raz crouched between the chairs and held Paris's hands in his own. "We can't make a stand here. This is too much of a coincidence."

Paris hugged Sean closer. "Let's find out what Sandra has in the lab." She gripped Raz's forearm as Sean scooted off her lap.

Sean perched on the edge of the second chair. He didn't take his gaze off Paris. An energy surge, like someone would experience before a lightning strike, filled the room.

Sandra's heart galloped. She had to get out. Sandra picked her cell phone off the desk. "I'll call Cam so he can get us into the lab."

"Where's the restroom?" Paris tugged on Raz's arm and stood.

He straightened and accepted her weight against his side.

Paris turned green. "I'm going to be sick." She clutched the edge of the desk and leaned forward. Deep, even breaths bowed her back.

Sandra tossed her phone on the desk, grabbed the empty trashcan, and pushed it between them. Raz's body crowded against her. She stumbled and all recognition of her surroundings left her awareness. He filled her senses. His hands came up to steady her, and his nearness muddled Sandra's brain. Had he always been this tall? His massive body, all muscles and heat, was pure sex. She wanted his hands on her flesh, his lips on her neck, his tongue on her breasts. Her face grew warm from her inappropriate thoughts.

"I saw the restroom when we came in, Mommy." Sean grabbed the trashcan from Sandra's hands and held it in front of his mother.

Sean's words jarred her back to reality. She allowed Raz to ease her out the door. Breathing the fresh air into her lungs, like the lifeline it was, reminded her to focus on the here and now. Allowing her hormones to drive her current actions put her friends at risk.

Raz looked toward the restroom sign. "I saw it too, buddy. I'll take your mother down the hall."

His voice rumbled beside Sandra's head, sexy and deep. Their only connection the touch of his lips on her ear. The moist air of his breath flowed over her cheek in pleasant waves. *Stop this. Focus.* Sandra brought up her hands and pushed him away.

He grasped her shoulders. "Keep aware around these students. If you were hurt because of me ..."

Again, Raz's eyes appeared lit from within. Sandra became entranced, but she looked away, breaking her obsession. Raz assisted Paris through the door who clung to his chest, weak as a newborn. Sean trailed behind them with a worried expression on his face. He gripped the wastebasket as tight as he did his precious stuffed animal. The trio walked down the hallway and away from her, always away from her.

Anything and everything proved to be dangerous to the three of them. A note from students had Raz alert and on guard. They needed Sandra's help, whether Raz wanted it or not. Especially now, after she witnessed the severity of Paris's illness. She partially closed her office door. With no one else inside, the irrational compulsion to escape was gone, but Sandra had to make sure the room had air circulation.

Sandra raced back to her desk. The phone had a one-hundred percent charge. She removed it from the charger so she could have movement while talking. Her fingers shook as she dialed Cameron's number.

He picked up on the first ring.

Sandra pounced. "Are you in the lab?"

"I'm here. You're missing. Where in the hell have you been today? I tried to call twice."

She stepped over to the whiteboard calendar on the wall. The day was circled in red marker. "Oh no! I'm so sorry, I was going to help you with the Brighton study today. I completely forgot about it. My cell died."

"Jesus, Sandra, get a new one for crying out loud. Why do you sound so strange?"

Her scratchy voice didn't sound bad. Did it? "I'm in my office. I need the biggest favor." She made sure the doorstop kept a two-inch gap between her door and the hallway. Once in front of her monitor, she entered her password into the logon screen.

"You sound breathless. Don't tell me—" Cameron interrupted before she could say anything. "Thom is harassing you."

"I've been avoiding him. He's getting really creepy around me." On autopilot, Sandra brought up her email and scanned the new messages. She switched her mobile to speaker and held it close to her mouth.

"He needs the testing results you promised." Cameron's voice boomed in the tiny office.

She adjusted the volume. "Too bad for Thom. I don't give a rat's ass what I promised him."

The line crackled over Cameron's voice. "He'll get the dean involved and make your life miserable."

She shook her head. "I'm not sure it could get any more miserable than it already is." Her divorce had seriously impacted her career, but she trudged on.

"I don't want to hear any negativity," Cameron barked. "Get your ass down to the lab, and let's get this Brighton shit started."

She sighed.

"What's the problem?"

Cameron immediately picked up on her anxiety. He was freaky like that. A nervous laugh escaped her lips. "I'm in a bit of a pickle."

He half-sighed and half-moaned on the phone. "I know that tone. What're you trying to get me into?"

She leaned back in her chair and ran her fingers through her hair. "I'll take any heat."

"Damn it. I can already tell what you're going to say next will ruin my day." His voice had softened.

"I'm sorry, Cam. I need help." Her gaze darted around the room. The bland contractor's white on the walls glared back. One landscape painting in cool blues and greens broke the monotony. Cameron had given it to her years ago, to cheer her up during the darker days of her marriage. Cameron was a good friend. Was this too much to ask?

"This isn't about Thom, is it?" Cameron asked.

"No. Besides, you've reached your quota for the month on making Thom's life miserable. I'll be forever grateful. I have a different problem right now. My friend is in trouble. She's in a lot of pain. I have to get her out of town, the faster the better. We can't go to the hospital." She sucked in the deepest breath she dared in the enclosed room. "Do you have access to the lab meds?"

The silence on the other end of the phone deafened her. She pulled her long hair back into a ponytail. Would he answer her? He wouldn't report her to campus police, would he? Asking for medication like this was illegal. She was going to jail. Sandra leaned forward and turned her mouth closer to the phone mic. "Cam, are you still there?" she whispered.

"It's not a student, is it?"

The beeps of the security keypad pulsed in Sandra's ears. The ker-chuck of the locks released and she knew Cameron had entered the laboratory. "I'd never get involved with a student." She chastised.

"I never expected you to ask for something illegal."

His deep baritone cut her. What was she doing for a man who

didn't want her? Repeating the past? She sighed. "Your name will never be associated with the inventory. I take full responsibility. They're running from very bad people and ... I can't go into the details. Please, trust me."

"You're willing to risk your job for this person? What the fuck is going on, Sandra?"

She chewed on her lower lip. The whole story was on the tip of her tongue. "I can't tell you."

"Did you say *they*?"

"I need pain meds Paris. She's a mother and needs to keep her son safe."

"She's the neighbor you hang out with?"

"Yes." Sandra nodded even though Cameron couldn't see her. Who's the other one?"

"Raz takes care of them."

Cameron snorted. "Sounds like it." Glass tinkled. A chair scraped across the floor. "Wait. Who's the guy? You mean the same dude you've been dating?"

Sandra squeezed her head between her hands. "Dating is a little strong of a description. He's no one, really. I do this, and they're gone. Out of my life."

"Damn. He's messing around on you?"

Sandra stood and paced in front of the desk. "It's not like that, Cam."

"If you want my help, you better tell me something. Not only have I had to deal with your dipshit husband—"

"Ex."

"—and his crazy psychic experiments. Now I'm your dealer. How will you fix the logs? The supply numbers will be off."

She set the phone down and leaned over the desk. Placing her hands on either side of her phone, she spoke into the mic. "I'll get Thom to sign for anything we take. He'll never find out until the whole mess is over." Cameron had no clue how often she'd signed Thom's name. Her forgery was almost a perfect match to his own signature. "You know you want Thom to suffer over something like this. He'll be tied up in HR for weeks and out of our hair."

"Damn. That does sound fun." A short laugh came across the

wire. "I'll never get on your bad side. Get down here before I change my mind."

Sandra let out a sigh of relief. She'd owe Cameron for the rest of her life. "Will you let me in? I'll have to search for my badge for an hour—"

"I said, get down here."

"I'll repay you for this. If there is anything you need. Anything. I'll be there to help you." Sandra hurried back to the chair to shut down her computer system. She skimmed her computer screen, and an email from Thom jumped out at her. She clicked on the message.

To: Sandra Robins
From: Dr. Thomas Robins
Subject: Second Chance

Sandra,

We had our problems, but we called it quits too soon. Our divorce happened so fast. I didn't try to figure out what went wrong, and how we screwed up. I made poor choices, and I'm not asking you to forgive me, but to listen. Families are important. I think we have many options. I was selfish when I told you adoption was out of the question. Please give us a chance. I still love you.
Love Always,

Thom

In disbelief, Sandra stared at the email. She read it several times. Yet, she still couldn't comprehend Thom's message. After all the heartache and horrible moments that'd occurred in the months prior to their official divorce, he wanted to try again?

"You there?" Cameron asked. "Earth to Sandra. Hello?"

Sandra obviously missed what he'd said to her. She blinked out of her memories. "Don't worry about the logs. I'll be down in ten seconds."

Disconnecting the call, Sandra deleted the message from Thom. She wanted to ignore him and erase all evidence of her past. She jumped at the rapid knocking on her door. A small scream burst from her lips. She grabbed her chest and nearly tipped her chair over in surprise. Under the door was a large shadow. Raz, and no Paris? What happened? She ran over and swung the door wide.

CHAPTER FIVE

"DID YOU GET my email?"

Sandra flinched at Thom's familiar voice. How dare he send her such an infuriating email? Avoiding him at all costs wasn't easy on her current research projects, but this was the first time since the divorce he'd intruded into her office space.

The mahogany door creaked. Thom slid the doorstop in place with his foot.

At least he was considerate of her phobia, but more likely he used the action to manipulate her into thinking he cared. Her hands tightened into fists. Punching him on her day off would still get her fired.

Thom towered over her. He spread his arms wide and placed a hand on either side of the door frame, trapping her. The expensive cologne he always wore slithered under her nose. On any other man, the woodsy marine notes would please, but the scent sickened her.

Every one of his female students worshiped him and called him Dr. GQ. Why not? Each strand of his bleach-tipped hair was perfectly styled in the messy just-got-out-of-bed look. Ice gray eyes, the irises surrounded by a dark blue ring, pinned her like a captured butterfly. The twin orbs examined her for flaws and waited for her to squirm so he could pin a twitching wing again.

An unpleasant heat flushed Sandra's skin. She pulled her shirt collar away from her neck. "What're you doing here?"

"You owe me your virus research and the four units you promised." Thom bullied his way inside the tiny office and pressed against her.

Sandra stepped back. He'd never lost those tight abs or hard biceps from their high school days. She learned the hard way to stop judging him by surface appearances and remembered the most beautiful flowers on earth killed people. After another step away, the backs of her knees hit her swivel chair. The wheels rumbled over the scarred floor.

"I didn't want to beg you in an email, but I didn't think you'd be in the office today. Lucky me," Thom said.

"Unlucky me—"

"I want a second chance," he whispered.

The heat of his body overwhelmed Sandra. The room shrank, and her breathing became labored. *Months ago, I gave you plenty of chances.* "I provided my notes to your team last week. Cam needs the rest for the Brighton project. So, you'll have to wait."

"Of course, Cameron needs it." His dry lips came closer to hers. "You didn't send the files."

Sandra ducked her head in panic, but his kiss grazed her cheek. He fanned his breath along her throat, and goose bumps spread over her skin. Her hands blocked his face from further invasion. The static between them crackled.

"Ow!" Thom pulled back. His nose wrinkled. "You shocked me."

"Maybe you shouldn't get so close."

Thom wound his arms tight around her waist. "But I love kissing you. It's what I miss, Sands. I miss you. Why won't you come back?"

Irritated at the hated nickname, Sandra leaned back as far as possible in the confines of his arms. "If I give you my notes again, then will you leave?"

Thom hunched his shoulders, and his muscles rippled from the movement. He brushed his lips across hers.

All the moisture drained from her mouth, and she found swallowing difficult. Thom stole her air. The door was still open. She could leave at any time. Yet, being trapped in his arms sent nothing but fear into her soul. She didn't move. Her paralysis didn't discourage him.

His boa constrictor arms crushed her tighter.

Sandra couldn't push him away, and his closeness fueled her panic. She had to get out. Now. Her chest heaved, and she struggled to loosen Thom's grip.

He chuckled. "Why are you being so pissy? I'm a nice guy." The coffee and chocolate smell on his breath mixed with the cloying heat of his mouth. "I gave you the Camaro, didn't I?"

I remember the giving differently than you. "Let me go."

Grande cafe mocha with soy milk was his typical breakfast at Starbucks. Over a year apart, and Sandra still knew all of his habits. *I want to forget everything about him.* They used to get breakfast every morning before work in his precious Camaro. Thom was always behind the wheel. Now Sandra skipped breakfast. It left a bitter taste in her mouth. He always expected her to concede to his ideas and plans. Not anymore.

Thom stroked her cheek.

Troubling pinpricks woke every nerve. Sandra clenched her teeth so hard her jaw ached. "We're over. There's no going back after what you did." A rush of surprising strength filled her. She pushed against his chest and broke free.

He jerked back. Rubbing the spot of contact, he snickered in amusement.

The modest space wasn't enough for Sandra's liking.

Undeterred, Thom clamped his hands onto Sandra's hips and squeezed. "Are you working out? It's sexy when you push me." Thom winked and didn't budge. "I have to say, I'm enjoying this new you. Feisty."

"All I wanted was a simple life. I wanted to grow old with you and my children. That was it." Sandra pushed again, hard.

Thom stumbled backwards into the small bookcase full of biology references.

A knowing smirk spread across his face as he righted himself. The charming smile made Sandra itch to slap him. "Now everything has changed. I don't want anyone, anymore."

"Really?" He picked up a fallen book from the floor and placed it on the shelf.

She sat in her office chair, and her fingers flew over the keyboard. Damn him. She'd take all the meds in the lab and place the blame on him. He deserved it. He knew nothing about her and had no right to make judgments.

Thom lounged on the edge of the desk. "I saw the troupe come into your office. You banging the big guy, or planning to kidnap the kid? He's pretty cute."

Sandra paused her typing. Cold tingling trickled along her lower back, curled around her midsection and flipped her stomach. He'd been watching them? She gazed directly into his eyes. "That's a low blow, even for an asshole such as yourself." She'd never admit anything, but his guess was too close to the truth. Clicking print, her old-but-trusty printer churned out the form.

"Why are you with them?" Thom's eyes narrowed.

Instead of making him appear mean, the expression enhanced his physical perfection. Her stomach churned and bile rose in her throat. Why hadn't she recognized his true nature before making the mistake of marrying him? "We no longer share the most intimate details of our lives anymore. What I do—"

"You're totally boning the guy."

Heat flooded Sandra's face.

Thom leaned closer. "How could you do that, Sandra?"

He accused *her* of betraying *him*? After all the women he'd paraded in front of her on a monthly, then weekly, basis?

"Paris is my neighbor. We're friends. It's a foreign concept to you I have friends and don't sit at home all night awaiting longingly for your reconciliation. Will you please move?"

He didn't budge.

Sandra swiveled in her chair and pointed to the printer.

He grabbed the paper in a rush of well-remembered irritation. Greed overcame his curiosity about her visitors. He wanted Xnix-624 and her virus test cases badly, which should've made her nervous. Sandra had too many worries to wonder what he intended to do with her research. "This lab report record tracks where the samples are being used. I've added your project to release them to you. Sign it now, and I'll send it to Cam. You'll get the last of the Xnix-624 virus."

"Your precious Cameron." Thom's face twisted into an ugly mask. "I'm surprised you didn't bang him after you left me."

He still had selective memory on who had actually left. "You know I wouldn't. Cam's physical features remind me too much of you," she stated quietly.

Thom laughed without humor. "He wishes he looked like me. He'd certainly never screw like me." His gaze darted along the form.

You got that right, Tommy. Sandra pursed her lips. "I'm sure no one does." Thom had screwed her over, and all the other women he brought between them.

He grabbed a pen out of her cup, and the rattle echoed between the walls. He read and reread.

Sign it, for crying out loud. His OCD was obvious to anyone but himself. Third scan, fourth, how many times would he read the the form before committing pen to paper? At the rasp of the ballpoint across the document, the rising pressure inside her head abated. She'd print out the meds list in the lab and trace his signature. A copy was always better than a forgery.

"This would be so much easier if I had access to a T6," he mumbled.

Sandra had difficulty keeping her frustrations to herself. She didn't care what a T6 was. Thom suspicions of someone stealing his work forced him in his OCD way to create his own short hand coding system for his projects. He tossed terms around like candy waiting for some naïve young co-ed to ask what they meant. She didn't take the bate.

Thom pulled back his arm, playing a devious game of keep-away. "I know the girl." He cocked his head to the side. "Paris. Your neighbor. She comes into the lab once a week because she thinks she's psychic. She's crazy."

He was a master of lies. Sandra crossed her arms over her chest. "You're unbelievable."

"Promise me you'll stay away from her, or you won't get this. I can tell how much you want it." He held the form over his head.

His coffee-scented breath surrounded her. Always suspicious of his motives, Sandra narrowed her eyes. Thom wanted her to get up and touch him. She wouldn't physically wrestle him for the paper.

A smile spread across his lips, but it didn't reach his eyes. He stroked her cheek. "What's wrong with the virus?"

"There's nothing wrong with it." Sandra slouched in the chair and nonchalantly pushed away the keyboard.

"You've been dodging me on your notes for four weeks now."

What would he accept as the truth? He knew Paris and was now doubtful of Sandra's generosity in giving him the last of the virus. She walked on eggshells. The reaction bothered her because it was so familiar. "I might have new experiments for the Brighton project that won't work with Xnix-624 as well as I'd like. If I don't have any more of it left, I'll have an excuse to create something better."

Thom stared at Sandra for a few seconds in his maddening way that made her squirm. Perspiration formed under her arms.

He passed her the signed document.

An internal sigh of relief went through her. Outwardly, she calmly placed the page in her bag.

He grabbed her hand and wound his fingers between hers. "Your offering works out for both of us. See what a great team we make? This never would've been possible if I hadn't shown up today. Let me look at the new stuff you're working on and give you another set of eyes."

Never in this lifetime, bucko. "Relax. I would've given the last batch of Xnix-624 to you anyway, so I wouldn't have to see you anymore." Yanking away her hand, she shut down her computer and grabbed her charged phone and purse. She slipped past him into the hallway and headed for the elevator. After a split-second decision, she turned to the stairs, instead. Getting trapped inside a box with Thom was her worst nightmare.

"You forgot to promise me you'll stay away from Paris." The shout echoed through the bare hallway. Thom's footsteps closed the distance between them.

He was wrong. Paris would've told her if she'd seen him. "You have her mixed up with someone else—"

"The likelihood of two women named Paris living in Angelville is low. You shouldn't be associating with someone like her."

"Guess what? You don't get to boss me anymore or make my decisions." Sandra's footsteps clipped on the tile floor. She looked right and then left, but no Raz, no Paris, no skipping from Sean. Where were they? She grabbed the railing, and her foot settled onto the first step down to the basement lab.

"I'm sorry, Sands."

Thom's sincerity stopped her cold. *Don't turn around. He doesn't mean it.*

"We ... *I* shouldn't have thrown away five years of our lives. Honestly, I'm jealous. You're not really with that guy, are you?"

Was she with Raz? He had his family and had no room for her in his life. Their relationship couldn't be successful, not when other hearts were involved, namely Paris. Sandra had no claim on him. "I only have myself, Thom."

He walked up behind her as she tried to decipher her emotions. Strong hands stroked the back of her arms. He'd caressed her like this hundreds of times and used a tender touch to persuade her to his way of thinking. After all the months of arguing, and trying to get on with her life without him, he wanted back in.

"You think my research is ridiculous," Thom whispered. "Several people we study aren't right in the head."

Black spots formed in her eyes. She struggled to come out of the vertigo as he squeezed her biceps.

"You need to be careful." Thom held her left hand and tugged her backward.

Sandra was forced back up the single step she had taken on the stairs. She refused to turn around. The tenderness in his touch almost had her believing in him again. From behind her, his right hand encircled the back of her neck and moved down to caress her collar bone.

Raz had touched her earlier in a similar fashion, but a greasy ball of anxiety hadn't settled in her stomach. She was powerless to stop Thom and couldn't figure out why.

"What I did a year ago was unforgivable." Thom stroked her neck and her hair.

If she had heard those words eight or nine months ago, she might've given him a second chance, but his poor attempt at an apology was too late. Sandra had more important concerns now. People who were counting on her.

"I don't expect your forgiveness." Thom's voice cracked. "I had my reasons. These months without you have been awful. I need you. I love you." He kissed her temple and her cheek.

Sandra's eyes burned. She brought a hand to her trembling lips. A different Sandra would've welcomed the affection. Her skin crawled.

He offered no good reason for the agony he put her through. An inner strength she didn't realize she had allowed her to pull away. No. It pushed her away. She'd never feel anything for him again.

The three people whose lives were in danger were her only concern now. They were her family.

Sandra spun on her toe.

Thom towered over her.

The sincerity on his face let her know he'd meant every word.

<CENTER>CHAPTER SIX</CENTER>

ONE. SANDRA WAITED for the inevitable shouting match. Panting from her sprint down the stairs, she bent at the waist and caught her breath in front of the laboratory entrance.

Cameron peered out the door's window and entered the security code. He swiped his badge, opened the lab door and snatched the form from her hands.

Two.

His brows shot up to the top of his forehead.

Three.

Cameron's head popped up from the signed request form. "This is bull."

"I can make more." Sandra breezed into the room and headed straight for her work table. Their project would benefit from Xnix-624, but the virus was her creation, to be used in projects at her discretion.

Cameron rubbed his forehead. "You're giving all of it to *him*? We need Xnix-624 for the Brighton project."

The commanding tone in his voice gave her a slight chill. Sandra focused her attention on his military haircut. She'd never noticed the style before today. The short strands were naturally blond in contrast to Thom's artificial color, but an odd choice for a university research scientist.

She sighed. "The project will have to wait. I won't be able to work on it, anyway."

Cameron followed her to her workstation. "Yes, you will. We agreed to move Brighton to the top of the schedule."

Cameron's unblemished lab coat flared open and closed,

exposing a tan shirt and green cargos. Six-feet-four-inches of muscle, broad shoulders and quiet demeanor oddly comforted her, despite his obvious annoyance at the change in plans.

"Where are the medical forms? I'll transfer Thom's signature—"

"It's all done electronically." Cameron picked up a bottle of aspirin Sandra kept on her desk.

In seven years, he'd never taken any medication in front of her. In fact, he always refused any if she suggested a dose to ease a headache. "Are you ill?" She touched his elbow.

Cameron shrugged her off and sauntered to his desk.

Okay. He didn't want to comment on the aspirin intake. I'll take a hint. Sandra hunted for the stack of blank forms stored on the countertop. Paranoia had rubbed off on Sandra after Paris's earlier Jeopardy quiz on headaches and visions. She'd have to print a new document. Cameron's reaction was male pride, nothing more. His macho shit drove her crazy. In fact, she'd probably given him the headache.

Cameron snagged a bottled water from the cooler. "Where are your junkie peeps?"

Sandra put a hand on her hip. "Not a funny joke, Cameron."

He snickered.

"Does Thom still have lab access?" She hurried over to a computer, searched the file share, and clicked on the supply template document.

"Not this lab. I removed his badge access weeks ago." He narrowed his eyes. "Is Thom stalking you again?" Cameron popped the top off the bottle and shook three pills into his hand.

Sandra printed a blank form and hooked a pen from the supply tray with a finger. She overlaid the new sheet and traced Thom's John Hancock in the signature box. "I'll scan and save this so it looks like Thom signed the med lab supply form. You can fill it out with what we need for Paris, or anything else you might want."

"Anything?"

The smirk on Cameron's face caused a similar smile on her own. She shook her head. She couldn't help it. He always appreciated actions which resulted in Thom's downfall.

Cameron sighed. "The pain you let me hand out to Thom is one reason I'm in love with you."

"Can it."

"Ouch." He clutched both hands over his heart. "Don't you love me back? I'm hurt." He made a pathetic, lovelorn face and choked out fake sobs until she laughed.

Without Cameron as her research partner, she might've fallen into a deep depression after her divorce. He was a good friend, and his good-natured ribbing always brought her back into the right perspective. She didn't take his declaration of love as anything more than teasing.

"So, what's the drama with Thom?" Cameron asked.

He always assumed the worst, but considering the constant shit her ex dealt her, he was spot on.

He shook the pills in his hands as though ready to throw dice. "You usually let me ruin Thom's day." Cameron tossed the pills into his mouth and gulped the water. "I hate to admit it, but it's very satisfying."

"Hate is an awful strong word, isn't it?"

"Okay, fine. I love fucking up the guy's life. Most pleasurable part of my job." He grinned. His dark eyes sparkled with amusement.

Sandra sucked in a huge breath and then let her frustrations tumble out. Cameron made it easy to let go. "Thom says he wants me back. You won't believe it, Cam, but he sent me an email declaring his undying love."

He choked on his second swig of water.

Sandra let him regain his composure before telling him the kicker of her story. "And then … he told me he loved me to my face on my way down here."

Clunk. The bottle slammed onto the desk, and a small spurt of water flew into the air. "You're shitting me. He's the most conceited person alive. You told him what to do and where to shove it, right?"

Sandra scanned the forged document. "Giving him the virus will get him out of my life. The only satisfaction I'll have is that he won't get it today. The committee will have to approve it."

Thom would come out of the chaos she created unscathed.

Unfortunately, Cameron had to clean up the mess Sandra left behind. A tight knot settled under her ribcage. Cameron blocked

Thom's progress on tests and facility access. The university political system was at his disposal. None of those actions ever traced back to Cameron or her, but continuing to use him would ultimately strain their friendship or get one of them fired. Sandra hoped Cameron wouldn't end up hating her. This was the last favor she'd ask him.

"You shouldn't have to sacrifice your research in order for Dr. Thomas Robins to leave you alone." Cameron leaned back against the work table, arms crossed.

Creating viruses to combat existing genetic plant defects and diseases was important, but she'd rather start from scratch than have the constant attentions of her ex. "I'm sending this to your email because I'm not going back to my office. Thom is there." Sandra shuddered. She dialed Paris's number and walked back toward the row of lab coolers for privacy. All of her progress was nestled inside cooler thirty-nine. Sandra didn't like keeping secrets from Cameron. She paced as the line rang. Yet, the less information she gave Cameron, the safer he'd be.

Paris picked up on the fourth ring.

"Where are you?" Sandra asked.

"I'm still in the restroom." Water gushed in the background.

"Thom came to my office. He saw you leave." Sandra observed Cameron check is email inbox for the scanned attachment.

"What do you want me to do?" Paris rasped.

Sandra examined the emergency exit map on the wall above the fire extinguisher. She traced her finger over the highlighted path. "Take a right after the entrance we came in. Then go down the hall. You'll see the stairs, but the easiest way is for you to take the elevator just a few more steps along the hallway. Once in the basement, the lab is the first door on the left."

"On my way."

"Paris?" Sandra chewed her lip. "Thom says he knows you. Is that true?"

The line crackled and seconds passed. Had the call dropped?

Paris coughed. "I volunteered for his research testing last month. After you told me what he did when you couldn't get pregnant ... I messed with him a little and pretended I was psychic."

"Does Raz know?" Sandra rubbed her forehead. Did it really

matter if Thom knew Paris?

"It was a psychic study." Paris shifted the phone and feedback broke on the line. Sean chattered in the background, and Paris dropped her voice to a whisper. "Raz wouldn't find my participation funny, but the examination was harmless. Besides, he doesn't know about Thom, so I kept that to myself."

Relief washed away Sandra's tension. The right moment for the big ex-husband discussion hadn't presented itself. "Thom warned me to stay away from you. He thinks you're insane."

Paris laughed a genuine belly laugh.

Sandra wondered if she'd be able to stop.

"Me? Crazy?" Paris mumbled through her chuckles.

Paris's infectious giggling brought a smile to Sandra's lips.

"Devious, maybe," Paris said between laughs.

"He might be onto something. Be careful he doesn't see you again." Sandra disconnected the call and walked back to her station.

Cameron pulled up the queue. He had placed the request form under processing. "Approval will take a few days." He winced and clutched the side of his head. He bent over and rested his forehead to the table surface.

Sandra hurried over. "What's wrong?"

"A stupid headache."

Paris's comments outside her office popped into her mind. Headaches were the start of Paris's illness, and any symptom, real or imagined, had Sandra on edge. "How long have you been having headaches?" Was she a carrier and had inadvertently brought it to the lab to infect Cameron?

"Off and on for the past few months. I didn't think you were such a 'chrondriac. My guess is it's from working on the Brighton tests this morning and waiting for you to make our appointment."

"I'm so sorry I forgot." Pin prickles crept along the back of Sandra's neck, and the same aura of strength and power filled her body as when she'd pushed Thom upstairs. She waited for them to pass. The tingles worsened, and black spots appeared in her peripheral vision. Her hands curled around the edge of the table, but they slipped past the solid surface as though the bench had melted in her hands. She whimpered, "Cam?" Her legs gave out.

His warm arms slid around her waist. "I've got you."

"I'm dizzy."

"Thanks for stating the obvious." He pulled her over to a stool to sit and pushed her head between her knees. "Take deep breaths. What have you had to eat today?" He rubbed her back.

"Nothing. I had to get Paris here. You don't think I'm getting what she has?"

Cameron twisted is lips. "I don't know what she has. You probably fainted from low blood sugar. You don't eat when you're stressed out. Take a deep breath. I'll find a cookie or something."

Sandra drew in a slow breath, and the fog cleared from her vision.

He came back and handed her a package.

She examined the white-and-red wrapper and arched her brow. "A fruit roll-up?"

"Don't judge me. Eat it."

Sandra peeled back the paper and untwisted the fruit rope. The fluorescent lights flickered, and before the artificial strawberry flavoring touched her lips, the dizziness went away. She blinked against the harsh flare of the overhead lamps and bit into the snack. Tingles feathered up her limbs. The hairs on her arms stood straight.

Puhhh … The room fell silent and dark. Sandra's heart kicked into turbo speed.

"The generator should compensate," Cameron said, low and steady, a few inches from her face. "Keep taking deep breaths. Count it out like we discussed."

Warm hands rubbed Sandra's back as she counted down from ten. Her instincts had her face the row of refrigerated storage coolers, even though she couldn't see them. She might lose months' worth of effort from an outage. Then she remembered the contents didn't matter because she wasn't coming back.

Thom would get what was inside, ruined or not.

She sucked in large gulps of air and came back to her center. *Cam's here. Raz, Paris and Sean are coming. All is good.* Her racing heart slowed to normal.

"You're leaving, aren't you?"

Cameron's question reinstated the jackhammer in her chest.

The darkness of the basement lab increased her panic. Her eyes convinced her brain the air didn't exist. "I ... no ...." For the first time in her life, Cameron scared her. How had he guessed her intentions? "I'm helping them. They're in danger."

Glass clinked, and something fell over. Cameron snapped on the flashlight and illuminated the room.

The tightness in Sandra's chest eased. It wouldn't completely abate until the overhead fluorescents came back on. Cameron stood in front of her like an ominous presence, but he was her friend. She had nothing to fear from him. He was supposed to help her fight the dark. She arched her neck back and looked him in the eye.

The flashlight cast shadows along his face. "You haven't any idea what kind of mixed-up shit they're running from."

Sandra wanted to tell him the truth, but at what cost to Raz, or Paris? "It's okay." She reached out toward Cameron.

He shrugged her off and stomped toward the back of the lab.

A shout for him to stay lodged in her throat.

Halfway, he stopped and shined the light directly in her face.

She closed her eyes against the glare.

"Are you going to risk your life for these people? I need you here."

"Cam, please lower the flashlight." She covered her eye with a hand, but she still couldn't see his dark figure through the blinding light.

"Our research is too important to abandon." Cameron didn't lower his arm.

The light was too harsh, the darkness too black. Why was Cameron so upset? Yes, their research had the potential to change the world, but she had enough knowledge so they couldn't start again. Cameron had always understood her, supported her. Helping Paris had been too much to ask. "You're a good friend. Please understand I have to do this."

"You don't know what you're talking about. Nothing good would come from you leaving Angelville."

Rapid-fire knocking on the door spun her around. Cameron's light followed. The glow fanned around her. Sandra didn't move.

"Time's run out." Cameron strode toward the entrance. The light bobbed and weaved in front of him before he opened the door. Cameron guided Paris to a seat near his workstation.

Sean stayed close to her and patted his bear's back. He typically raced over to Sandra, talking one hundred miles a minute. Maybe the darkness of the basement scared him.

The blank interior of the room terrified her. Sandra focused on Raz, and his eyes reflected the light of the flashlight. No. His eyes brightened from within, like they had in her office. Ripples of muscle flexed under his T-shirt. *God. He's so sexy.*

Cameron was right. Sandra didn't know what she was getting herself into. Her decisions and thoughts weren't rational around Raz.

Raz's eyes narrowed at her position on the stool.

Her elbows rested on her knees. She hunched over as though she'd fall off the chair any second. She eased back into a sitting position.

"Are you okay?" Raz asked.

"She was lightheaded." Cameron touched Sandra's shoulder. "I'll be right back. I'll check the generator. There's another flashlight in the drawer cabinet."

Sandra pointed to the drawer. "Sean, will you get the extra one?"

Sean found the flashlight, switched it on, and set it beside his mother. The impromptu lantern bathed the front of the room in a semi-glow but left her and Raz in the outer fringes of darkness.

Cameron retreated for now, but Sandra sensed he'd confront Raz. About what, she couldn't be sure.

Raz stared. "What happened?"

"Nothing sugar won't fix." She held up the last of the fruit roll-up.

Raz leaned closer to her face, as if to kiss her, and his spicy scent created a laser beam of heat straight between her legs. Her face flushed, and she broke eye contact. She glanced to the right.

Paris and Sean weren't paying attention to them.

Raz reached out and caught her hand as she eased off the stool. He pulled her back to the seat with a gentle tug.

She didn't resist. Her body wanted to be closer. She stared at their joined hands, not sure what was happening. Heat oozed from his skin.

"Why didn't you tell me you didn't eat today?" Raz whispered.

His lips almost touched her ear. Warm breath fluttered along her neck. The promise of heat and the softness of his lips teased her body.

He moved closer, and her every nerve ending came alive. "We had other, more important matters to worry about."

"Stop making me worry about *you*." Raz cradled her hand, and his fingertips caressed her palm. Feathered. Stroked. His soft lips brushed her neck.

Her eyes fluttered closed from the sweet and erotic kiss. Tingles ran down her skin, and a small moan escaped her. She swiveled in the high stool, her mouth centimeters from his. Cinnamon aroma enveloped her as their breaths entwined. She wanted this kiss more than anything. She didn't care who witnessed it.

"Sandra," Cameron quietly said behind her. "I need you."

Sandra froze. Her lips were millimeters away from Raz's. She looked over her shoulder.

Cameron stood four feet away. His low voice drew the attention of Paris and Sean. All gazes fell on Sandra.

She refused to blush, but the heat crept along her neck. Jumping off the stool, she took a tentative step toward Cameron's outstretched hand. Raz's grip on her arm stopped her.

Cameron no longer wore his lab coat. His khaki shirt and moss green pants were more intimidating than his words. His steely gaze made her uncomfortable and unsure. Sandra always teased Cameron that he was more at home at HUP than she was. Thom had alienated her from the majority of the staff. Yet, at this moment, Cameron didn't belong here, either.

Cameron oozed danger. He continued, in that disturbing tone, "I can't get the generator started." He'd nixed the friendly aura they'd shared a few minutes ago. The words contained a hardness she'd never heard before. His expression suggested he wasn't as concerned with the generator as he was with what in the hell had been going on in the dark corner. Between her and Raz.

She wanted to know, too, before she lost her mind.

Chapter Seven

SHARDS OF FIRE transformed Raz's nerves into a hypersensitive network. Kissing Sandra's neck had been foolish, but Raz couldn't deny the urge to mark her as his. The Nexus warning in the room was too strong to ignore. Raz controlled his oncoming Transor blitz. His Sixxer power and Nexus energy bond recognized the Nexus life force emitting from Cameron. The internal energy warning sent every protective instinct Raz had into overdrive.

Sandra's mine. I must keep my circle safe. Constantly aware at Paris's and Sean's location, he focused on keeping Sandra close. "We're not staying." Raz tightened his fingers around Sandra's arm and pulled her back against his chest. He had to get her out of here.

No matter who Cameron was, he had fooled Sandra for years. Cameron couldn't hide from a Transor's Nexus. The longer they stayed, the more Raz wanted to rip apart Cameron with his bare hands.

"Hey, man." Cameron held his arms low. His fists were clenched and ready to fight. His tone didn't match his stance. "You just got here." His predatory gaze followed Raz's movements and growing physique.

The pain of Raz's tissue growth bunched the muscles in his legs and back. He was ready to pounce at the slightest provocation. The show of dominance fed the Nexus energy between them. A surge flooded Raz's body. His biceps flexed as they grew. His chest tightened as heat rushed into his pecs and abs. Would the little amount of light allow Sandra to see his alien transformation?

Every ounce of rage in Raz's body burned in anticipation of a

Nexus release. Then he'd easily snap Cameron's neck. Yet, Cameron gave no signs he recognized an impending Transor blitz.

Raz encircled Sandra's other arm. Flashes of light glittered under his fingertips. Desire, hot and fierce, zinged along his skin, and traveled to his solar plexus. The battle between lust and fury sent out energy waves from his body as the Nexus attempted to connect the circle with a shield and claim Sandra as his. Her wanting enveloped him with her lilac scent. He must guard his woman.

Mine.

Raz had to stop the process or he'd kill Sandra. She wasn't a Sixxer and couldn't accept the energy of a shield. Raz forced himself to ease his grip and ran his fingers down her arms.

Sandra shivered at the caress.

He entwined his fingers with hers. Another low growl escaped as shards of Nexus fire pricked his flesh. His control was held together by a thread. Sandra's life depended on him.

Another buzz of power coated his joints and energized him. The Nexus wanted to break free. It commanded Raz to protect the circle. Yet, his circle excluded Sandra. The threat against her shouldn't agitate the Nexus. Had she been involved with Cameron? Was a past relationship with this human causing this baffling puzzle of Nexus energy?

Paris stood on wobbly legs. "Let's leave."

Sandra reached in her direction. "You need the pain medicine."

Raz stepped in front of Sandra and blocked her attempt at touching anyone else in the circle. He was unsure what the Nexus might do. Cameron was a constant in his sights. All Raz wanted to do was fight, which would throw him into a blitz. Sandra's death would then be a guarantee.

Cameron motioned for Sandra to move toward him. "What's Thom's access code? I'll get the drugs."

She struggled to maneuver around Raz as she shouted the code to Cameron, but the Nexus wouldn't let her go to the enemy, and neither would Raz.

The Nexus brought the circle together and invigorated Paris. The air crackled around her and Sean. For every move Raz made, her body tensed. He attempted to stay calm, but biological instincts flooded his mind. His clenched jaw ached. Energy emitted from him in waves, and Paris braced herself against the chair.

Raz couldn't believe his eyes when Sandra wrenched her arm free. She gazed at Raz as though he were a hideous bug. He watched in disbelief as she stepped away. How had the Nexus failed him? *How can she leave me right now?*

She narrowed her eyes. "Cam needs me."

I don't care about Cameron. I need you! "Coming here was a mistake," Raz whispered under his breath.

Sandra placed her hands on her hips. "We're already here. Let's do what we came for and leave."

In his current energized state, Raz lost the ability to reason. Sandra made sense, but the Nexus sent waves of strength toward Paris and Sean to join the fight. "We can't trust him." His voice lowered, so only Sandra could hear.

"You're acting like a jealous fool, and so is Cam." She shook her head, and her ponytail swayed. The studs in her ears sparkled in the dim light. "Cam is my very good friend," she hissed. "Let him help us. Then we can get the hell out of here. What was with the whole kissing my neck thing? You brushed me off back at Paris's house."

She wanted the kiss as much as I did. Raz had wanted to mark her as his own in front of everyone as soon as he'd entered the room.

Cameron walked over to Paris and Sean. He spoke in low murmurs.

Raz should've sensed Cameron's movement toward the others, but Sandra's tirade had distracted him. If Chasers were here and he couldn't focus, all was lost. Raz tamed the impulses inside him as best he could with Cameron ten feet away.

The kiss claimed Sandra as his and only his. Cameron should've gotten the message loud and clear.

Raz turned Sandra to face him.

She stomped her foot and let out a guttural cry. Everyone in the room turned toward her. She ducked around him and trotted down the hallway.

"Sandra!" Cameron called.

"Hurry up." Sandra's long strides got her as far as the end of the lab table when her knees buckled underneath her.

Cameron got there before her head hit the floor. "You little dumbass. You passed out two seconds ago, and you thought you'd sprint to the medical cabinet?"

Raz arrived seconds after Cameron caught her.

The circular connection affected Sean. He ran halfway between Raz and Paris, reaching for Sandra, but looking back toward his mother.

Raz held out his hand for Sean to stay put, but protective Nexus vibrations shook his body.

Paris touched his shoulders and neck, but Sean's eyes radiated a brownish-green glow.

"Raz, take her." Cameron eased Sandra into Raz's arms and reached for a small zippered bag.

How does Cameron know my name?

"I don't know what's wrong with me," Sandra whispered.

Cameron checked her pulse.

Sandra raised her head. "Do you think I'm sick?"

The fear in her eyes sent Raz into fix-it mode. "You're not sick." He eased her onto the floor. Grabbing Cameron's discarded lab jacket from the end of the table, he placed it under her head. Stroking her hair, he did everything he could to push his power back so he wouldn't accidentally hurt her.

Cameron's hands shook as he unpacked a small device. "I'll check your blood sugar. The results should convince you of the real problem."

"Why do you have a meter?" Sandra whispered.

"Because you're bullheaded and don't listen."

Sandra attempted to sit up, but Raz and Cameron pushed her gently back to the floor.

"What does this device do?" Raz asked.

"Sandra doesn't like to eat when she's under pressure. She's had symptoms of low blood sugar before, after not eating for days. I've asked her to go to a doctor, but she refuses."

Sandra shook her head. "He's such a worry wart, after one bad result."

The Nexus eased back as it recognized the caring radiating from Cameron. Raz couldn't wrap his mind around the relationship between Cameron and Sandra. The jealousy within him burned dark and selfish. He wanted to punch Cameron in the face, but the Nexus told him the threat was gone. The lingering emotions made no sense. Was it because Cameron loved her, or because she was human and the Nexus was reaching out for her?

Cameron squatted beside Sandra, glucose monitor in his hand, and poked her finger for a pinprick of blood.

Sean slipped behind Cameron. Unwavering curiosity spread over his face as Cameron handled the small lancet then inserted a test strip into the device. Sean observed everything Cameron did. The flickers of the Nexus slowed, and then dissipated in Sean's small body. The entire circle had come down from Raz's near blitz high. *How?*

Cameron ducked his head. The device flashed a number. He sighed and held the unit to Sandra's face. Cameron glared at Raz. "You aren't leaving until Sandra rests a few minutes, and I find something substantial for her to eat." He rummaged in his desk, pulled out a package of peanut M&Ms and a juice box, and handed them to Sandra. This closeness between the two of them ... Raz never had it.

She's mine. Cameron has no claim to her. Jealousy was a mean and spoiled bitch. "We get the meds, we're gone," Raz said.

Cameron trotted to the corner of the room. He entered the code into the locked cabinet and pulled open the glass door.

Raz didn't want to linger here any longer. Sandra needed more than junk food, but candy was better than nothing.

Sandra touched his arm. "I'm coming with you."

"Damn straight, you are. I'm not leaving you here. You're weak—"

"I needed food." She held up the bag of candy. Sandra worked her legs under her as though to stand.

Raz pushed her back against the desk. "Don't get up. We'll get real food as soon as we can. We all need to eat." His stomach growled. The attempted energy transfer in the restroom had left him, Paris and Sean starving. They'd also be drained and weak from the Nexus energy just released.

"I won't slow you down." Sandra cleared her throat. "Paris needs help, and so do you."

"I'll talk to Cameron for a few minutes." Raz held up a finger as she opened her mouth to protest. "I'll have a friendly chat."

Raz trotted back to the cabinet and was aware of everything in the room. Was it possible Cameron was M83? He hadn't recognized the Transor blitz, but Chasers weren't storming down the lab door either.

Cameron examined each container of pills in the cabinet. He acknowledged Raz with a nod. "I know what you are."

Snaps of electricity danced along Raz's arms and pulsed along his spine.

Over his shoulder, Sean and Paris hunched over the glucose meter. Sean pricked his bear with the lancet and inserted a strip into the monitor. At least the Nexus only raged inside Raz. This time.

Sandra sat on the floor, eyes closed. Her chest rose with each breath. She crumpled the empty wrapper in her hand.

Was the Nexus affecting her, as well? He wouldn't leave her here not knowing what Cameron's ultimate goal was. He, also, couldn't leave her in a weakened condition. He never thought she fall ill, too.

"You better ease up before you nuke the electrical grid on this campus." Cameron held several medicine bottles in his hand. "That's how I figured it out." He placed the vials on the desk. The flashlight moved from container to container as he read the labels. "The generator never fails during an outage."

"Who are you?" Raz squinted and his nostrils flared. Deep, slow breaths brought the pressure building inside back down to a manageable level.

"I can help you, but I won't let you destroy Sandra's life. She has to continue her research here. She can't be running off happily ever after with you and your ..." Cameron gestured to Paris and Sean. He raised his eyebrow. "Family?"

Raz moved to the farthest cooler. The engraved numeral thirty-nine marked the door in front of him. He turned to find Cameron had followed. At six-two, Raz wasn't small and refused to be intimidated by this ... what? "Are you M83?"

Cameron backed him against the cooler and shoved his face centimeters from Raz's. "What the fuck are you thinking? Humans aren't supposed to know about us. What have you told her?"

The Transor in Raz ached to get out. It hurt to keep his power tamed, but he had to find out who Cameron really was. The knowledge that Cameron was a Sixxer and not a Chaser helped tamp down the fire. Barely. "She knows nothing, and it will stay that way." He shoved Cameron. A small burst of energy from Raz's palms moved Cameron back two feet.

Cameron's shocked face froze for a second before he arched his neck with several pops. "We've claimed HUP as our territory. Report back to your commander and stay away."

The *stay away from Sandra* Raz heard loud and clear. He hadn't encountered another Sixxer or M83 agent in seven years, and Cameron had been in Angelville the entire time his circle hid here. Raz had left the Corp the moment Paris went into a coma from their failed rendering. He'd allowed an infiltrator into the circle, a traitor within M83. Including the false Sixxer in the render had killed his parents. The shame had been too great to remain an agent, and too risky, considering Paris had been pregnant with Sean.

"Sandra's vital to our fight." Cameron raked his hand over his buzz cut.

"Sandra isn't yours."

Cameron laughed. The darkness transformed his face into something menacing. "She certainly isn't yours. Sixxers don't own or claim humans. At least, the good ones don't. You starting to mark humans like Chasers mark us?"

Sandra didn't belong to Cameron, either, no matter what relationship they had.

"I know you're running from General Taft," Cameron said. "You have something to hide. Sandra?" He touched his head with his index finger. "It's Paris."

"She's been intentionally infected with a Sixxer illness."

Cameron didn't blink. "I'm not surprised. My unit, Omega, can get you somewhere safe."

"I'm not with the Corp anymore. We'll leave the state and keep low. My circle won't get involved."

"Determining what sickens Paris has could help us." Cameron scrawled something on a notepad stuck to the cooler door. He handed the scrap to Raz and walked back to Sandra. The paper contained contact information and coordinates to a location approximately thirty miles outside the town of Center, in the heart of the Appalachian Mountains.

The one place Raz thought they were the safest crawled with M83 soldiers, which also meant it crawled with Chasers. He didn't know if Cameron worked for their allies or enemies. The suggestion of studying Paris's illness didn't sit well with Raz. It's what Dr. Nazier would have wanted done. Some rogue Sixxers have been known to work for themselves. The promise of money and control over humans was too tempting to pass up. The emphasis Cameron placed on Sandra's research also made his gut churn. Omega had been watching all of them.

Raz folded the paper and tucked it in his pocket. No need to get Cameron suspicious, but he had no intention of contacting Omega Unit after they left. Even being an ex-M83, Raz thought Cameron had been too quick to give Raz information or accept on faith Paris's illness without further questions. Sandra didn't even realize Cameron had used her to get to them.

CHAPTER EIGHT

SANDRA LED THEM out of the lab. At every sound, Raz and Paris twitched and jerked like the boogieman would to jump out at any second. Maybe they were right. Still woozy from fainting, Sandra concentrated on putting one foot in front of the other. She hadn't heard Cameron and Raz's conversation, but whatever they'd discussed had Raz on edge.

Is he suspicious of Cam? He was her research partner, not a threat. Needle-like sensations bounced along her spine, and the hairs on her arms rose. The hallway transformed into a shrinking tunnel. One option remained. Escape.

Paris shuffled beside Raz, but she was so weak he held her upright. Her feet dragged under her every few steps.

Sandra didn't like the ashen cast to her face and held out the water bottle. Paris batted it away in an ungrateful punch. Sandra almost dropped the container, but she didn't let Paris's action stop her from trying again. She pressed the bottle to Paris's stomach. "You need the water so you can take the pills."

Paris grimaced and shook her head. "Keep moving."

The desperation in her voice petrified Sandra. HUP was safe. *No one will snatch us in the open.* She tried to make sense of what happened in the lab, but her brain wasn't cooperating.

Sean tucked the water bottle to his chest. Grabbing Paris's hand with his free one, he swung her arm around his neck. His small legs did little to help her.

Sandra pushed open the main hall entrance, and they tumbled out into the dark evening. All they had to do was get to her car and they could continue with the original plan: leave PA, get away from the Chasers, take Paris to a medical facility. This list became Sandra's priorities. Concentrating on anything else was just a distraction.

"What were you thinking back there?" Paris asked.

Sandra lost hold of the door and scrambled to keep it open. *The kiss.* The door banged shut. When she turned to face Paris, she realized that the question hadn't been directed at her, but at Raz. She stared at him waiting an answer, but he wouldn't look toward her. *Thinking about our kiss, too?*

Raz jogged down the steps his arm around Paris's waist.

Paris stumbled and latched onto the railing. Raz pulled her forward, but she jerked away. "Get the van and pick me up."

Paris's legs gave out. She fell onto one of the stone steps.

Sandra crouched beside her. "Cam won't tell anyone about the medicine."

"We won't split up again," Raz released Paris and jogged down the stairs. He kicked up the fallen leaves pooled at the bottom.

Paris stared at Raz, eyes wide. "He'll tell them all. Did you see what happened?" Her fingers clamped onto the handrail, and her knuckles went white from strain.

"I felt what happened." Raz turned. His eyes glowed with the reflection of the evening parking lamps.

Paris sighed. "If he's a Chaser, we're all dead."

Sandra didn't understand why they would conclude Cameron was out to harm them. "Cam tried to help us," she hissed.

Raz jumped two steps back up to where Paris sat. He grabbed her shoulders. "Get up. Now."

Paris ground her feet into the step and Raz couldn't budge her. "Take Sandra and Sean to the van."

"Get a move on, soldier!" Raz's yell boomed around them.

Sandra stifled a scream.

Raz shook Paris like a rag doll. "I'm not leaving anyone here!"

Paris flinched and wrenched away. Her face twisted into a grimace, and she pulled her body off the step, leaning on the rail for support. Blood drained from her face, and she lurched to the side.

Sandra caught her.

Raz held out his hand to Sandra. "Give me your keys."

Paris inched along the railing and down two more steps. "He's M83?"

Raz nodded. "He's M83 Omega, but he could be working with an infiltrator. I'm not going to stick around and find out."

Paris's face blanched.

They act like Cam is a soldier. Sandra helped Paris down another step. How far would she be able to go? "He's a scientist." Raz arched a brow and snorted in disbelief at Sandra's proclamation. Cameron wasn't a scary infiltrator, whatever that was.

"Mommy, I need to get my things." Sean ran over and tugged on Sandra's sleeve.

Paris took two more steps. "There's no time, sweetie." She stopped and caught her breath.

Sandra didn't understand why Raz wasn't helping Paris. She grew weaker by the minute. Sandra removed the bottle of pills from her purse.

Paris grabbed the vial and thrust it into her pocket.

Sandra grabbed her arm. "Take them."

Paris ignored her. Her focus was on Raz. "If Cameron is associated with General Taft, let alone an actual infiltrator, he wouldn't let us leave like this."

Sean stomped and huffed. "We can't leave my bike."

Paris grabbed Sean's hand, but nothing calmed his tantrum. Her pitiful soothing attempts agitated him more.

Sandra placed a hand on his head, and he stopped moving. "We'll come back for it later," motherly instincts made her croon.

Sean clutched at her jacket sleeve and whined. "We neeeed to get it. Please. Please. Please."

Raz pulled Sean with him. "We've left before with the clothes on our backs. We have to go."

Sean continued to pester both of them.

Sandra had too many unanswered questions to fully concentrate on him. "Who's Taft? Aren't you running from Paris's father? Cam isn't in the military." Yet, the combat boots, demeanor and elusive answers Cameron had given today created doubt in her mind. Cameron had been hiding a secret life from her for seven years. *No. Impossible. Cam wouldn't lie to me.*

Sean jumped up and down and cried. Big fat tears rolled over his cheeks. "You promised I could take my bike."

Sandra leaned over and looked in his eyes. "I'll take care of it for you while you're gone."

"Can't," Raz said. "You're coming with us."

What? He really *had* told her earlier she was coming with them. She hadn't imagined it. "To where?" Sandra was now unsure she wanted to leave Angelville.

Paris arched her brow at Raz. "This is interesting."

Sandra swiveled her head from Paris to Raz. "Two hours ago, you couldn't get rid of me fast enough. I begged you to come here."

"Keys. Now. I'll explain on the road."

Sandra hesitated for a few seconds. Her hand gripped the keys in her purse tight enough they dug into her flesh. "Cam isn't the one chasing you. He tells me everything."

Raz's lips pulled back from his teeth in a sneer. "Does he, really?"

Offended by the question, Sandra reared back. "Yes." Why did her answer sound so tentative?

"Wrong. He's lied from the first moment he met you. Why do you think he didn't want you to leave with us?"

Sandra snorted. "He cares?"

"He wants your research."

Just like Thom? His comment cut her to the core. "You're going too far. Cam has never stolen my research."

Paris leaned against Sandra as she moved forward again. "They're called Chasers, Sandra. They're the cats, and we're the mice. And like cats, they like to play."

Sean scurried up the steps, putting him face-to-face with his mother.

Paris cupped his cheeks. "I'm one weak little mouse right now."

Sean handed her the water.

She drank. "Although, I haven't sensed Chasers, Raz."

Raz placed his hand on his hips and tapped his right foot. "It's the illness. You aren't reading anything right. Failing to use your gifts right now isn't your fault."

His tone suggested Paris was to blame for everything.

"You have five seconds to decide, Sandra," He said.

Eyeing his outstretched hand, Sandra wanted to leave but also wanted to stay. Cameron always had her trust and support. Turning her back on him after he'd done so much for her made her sick. Yet, her friends were running from someone out to possibly kill them, and she couldn't turn her back on the three of them and live with herself. Sandra placed the keys into Raz's hand.

Raz's smile stopped her heart.

"You get shotgun because you drive like a grandma," He teased.

Sandra gasped. "I do not."

Raz scooped Paris into his arms, cradling her like a child, and continued into the parking lot.

Sandra had to trot to keep up with him as Sean raced ahead.

Raz helped Paris and Sean into the back seat of the Camaro and jumped in the driver's seat. The engine roared, and he backed out of the parking spot before Sandra opened the passenger door.

Once she hopped inside, she clicked her seat belt.

He shifted into first and headed toward Center.

Sandra couldn't get over the personality change in Cameron. She refused to believe he was any threat to Raz, or Paris, and certainly no threat to a little boy. After several miles of road buzz, Sandra broke the uncomfortable silence. "What did you say to Cam to piss him off?"

Raz glared. "You told me Cameron was trustworthy."

"He is. What's going on? First you don't want me around, then you won't let me go. Cam wouldn't hurt me or any of you."

Sandra glanced in the backseat. Paris closed her eyes and a serene expression came over her face. She had to be exhausted. Sean attempted to keep his eyelids open, but they drooped in the sweet way they do on kids and sleep overcame him.

She turned back and settled into the passenger seat. The dials on the speedometer glowed bright orange. Raz cruised at ninety. The passing scenery changed from gray to black. Lights from the distant houses were sprinkled over the hills and twinkled in the night.

"Cameron would do whatever was necessary." Raz turned on the heater. He concentrated on the road. Headlights beamed into the darkness and covered his face in shadows.

Sandra hadn't registered the chill in the air. "Ridiculous. He had the perfect opportunity in the lab to alert the authorities, but he let all of us leave."

"Cameron knows who's after us."

Sandra couldn't fit the puzzle together. "He knows Paris's father?"

"No."

She hit the dash. "I'm here. In this car with you. I made my choice. Tell me what the hell is going on."

Raz squeezed the wheel. His knuckles turned white. He pushed the pedal to the floor. The needle hovered over one hundred on the speedometer. "I know what Cameron would do, because I used to be him. He's deep undercover, Sandra, and he would never tell you about it."

"Undercover as in—"

"Military ops." His gaze flickered from the mirror then to her face before he continued to watch the road.

"How—?"

He shook his head. "I can't tell you more."

"Or won't." This revelation suggested Raz was undercover ops, as well. For who, and why? Sandra searched her memory for any clues Cameron had given her about this secret life and came up with … nothing.

"You broke the law for us today," Raz said.

Sandra's head popped up.

"You can't dispense medicine from the lab."

She adjusted the seatbelt. "Cam won't tell anyone. He's done worse favors than stealing medication from the labs. He acts like it's against his moral code—"

"How come you never mentioned Cameron before today? You've been working with him for years."

For the same reason Sandra never mentioned Thom. She observed Raz's tense shoulders and the angry curl to his mouth. "Are you jealous?" Why did Raz's possessiveness give her a perverse burst of pleasure?

Raz clenched his teeth, and the muscle in his jaw twitched.

"Of Cameron?" Sandra laughed and shook her head. Spreading out her cold fingers, she rubbed her hands together in front of the vent. The warm air thawed her fingers. What reaction would Raz have when he found out she had an ex-husband? Cameron had never crossed her mind as a romantic partner. Even after the divorce. She hadn't been ready to share any personal details of her life with Raz. Hadn't been ready to answer questions. Cameron was the only one who knew her past.

"He's not an old boyfriend, if that's what you're worried about." Beyond the passenger window, an endless number of trees whizzed by the car. House lights in the distance broke through sections of forest. Cameron had been there through the wedding, the marriage, the loss and the end. How could she describe the gory details to Raz?

"I don't like him." Raz adjusted the rear-view mirror.

She snorted. "Cam is a softy and a good friend. He wouldn't hurt a fly."

"He's lied to you."

Sandra tried to control her anger but exploded. "Have you? Lied? I trust him. Jesus, Raz! What's your problem? You're just like Thom, constantly questioning the people I'm with. Maybe Cam has a valid concern, too. I know nothing about you. Who or what you're running from. Paris tells me it's Nazier, then I hear General Taft. Has anything either of you told me been the truth? You aren't even in the witness protection program, and now you're some type of secret military fucking soldier."

A hand squeezed her shoulder. Glancing back, she saw Paris had leaned forward in her seat. A worried frown pulled down her face. Sandra had blasted Thom's name to everyone in the car, and the secret Paris had entrusted to her. The sudden buzzing in her ears muffled whatever Paris said next.

Raz's attention diverted off the highway for a split second to gaze into the rear-view mirror.

"You need to tell her," Paris pleaded.

"Our conversation is none of your business."

"This circle is my business, Raz. We must tell her all the truth, not half. She's changing. We're all changing. What happened back at the lab wasn't normal. Her neurons called out to the Nexus. The connection would keep her safe during a render. Her eyes–"

"No." Raz snapped back to Sandra.

Terror etched his features, which made Sandra's blood run arctic.

Yet, she couldn't respond. The motion of the car didn't sit well, her stomach churned and a rash broke out on her hands. It crawled along her arms, and their conversation became an underwater chorus, muffled and slow.

"If the Nexus protected her, it would've energized her back at HUP. Instead, she collapsed," Raz said.

"You need to trust me." Paris griped his shoulder.

"Something happened at home," Sean whispered.

The hum of the engine and the road noise buffeted the car. The vibrations in Sandra's head subsided. Her scalp tingled, and she turned sideways in her seat to see everyone. Didn't they notice something was wrong with her? The conversation jumbled and jumped in her mind. She couldn't focus. The illness attacking Paris was also attacking her.

"I'm sick." Sandra held her stomach, and the cramping heightened. Her voice was so tiny, barely a whisper. She hoped the confusion and floating sensations would pass soon. Piecing together what they said was impossible. "Something's not right." Had she spoken aloud, or had the words only echoed in her mind?

"I didn't want Sandy to be scared," Sean said.

"I'm not." Of course, she was. They kept secrets. She didn't know what they were running from. Cameron could be a bad guy. Her stomach muscles contracted. She moaned. Now her health was in question. "I don't feel good." Paris had nothing like this.

"Are you doing this?" Raz demanded.

Is who doing what? Help me.

Sean snuggled closer to Paris. His small little boy voice was barely audible. "I'm not sure."

"I didn't realize he could reach her. He must've done the same at HUP." Paris held Sean close. "I can't sense anything anymore."

"What happened at the house?"

Sandra tried to follow the conversation, but none of it made any sense. She watched Raz and Paris get more and more anxious. She looked from Raz to Sean and back again.

"I didn't do anything." Sean sat up straighter. "I wanted us to be safe." Small hands held the back of Raz's seat.

Paris pulled Sean back. "Sandra had a nosebleed and nausea right after you left."

"I used to get those as a kid," Sandra offered as an explanation. She needed more air and rolled down the window. The wind cooled her clammy neck.

"Can you calm yourself, Sean? She's reacting to you," Paris whispered.

"The charge in the restroom must've affected her," Raz said. "Cameron insisted she fainted. It must've happened while we tried the energy transfer. She's either connected to you or Sean."

Paris stroked Sean's hair. "Focus on the sound of my voice, buddy. Sandra will be safe with us. No one will hurt her."

Sean bounced from Paris to the console between the bucket seats. "They *will* hurt us."

Raz half-hugged him with his right arm while still maintaining a steady hand on the wheel with his left. "Of course not. I won't let them."

Sandra's head ached, and her mind refused to focus. "Pull over." What in the hell were they talking about? All Sandra heard was a secret language they'd perfected over the years, and not knowing what the words meant aggravated her. Something dripped on her. A small, dark circle formed on her denim-clad leg. She reached up and wiped at her nose. Warm liquid covered her fingers.

"Stop the car," Paris said. "Sandra has a nosebleed. Sean, relax and take deep breaths. Everything will be fine."

Sandra pulled out tissues and old napkins from the glove compartment. She needed to prevent further damage to her clothes or the seat. Then she remembered she wouldn't get in trouble for ruining the car. It belonged to her now.

"It will be okay," Raz said.

Sandra pinched her nose, leaned forward, and pressed to staunch the flow of blood.

Raz parked at a mini-market gas station. "We'll get a bite to eat, fill up the tank and then get back on the road."

Sean and Paris tumbled out of the car and walked to the store entrance.

Raz pulled Sandra closer. He examined her face, and the back of his hand settled on her forehead. Satisfied with the results, he relaxed. His hands lingered on her skin.

"I'm better," Sandra said.

Raz brushed his thumb across her lower lip. "Tell me again the moment you feel anything strange. Anything."

"What's wrong?" she whispered.

A light flashed in his eyes. He closed them, and his forehead touched hers. "There's so much you won't understand, but Paris is right. You need to know."

Sandra waited for the truth, but the touch of his lips on hers destroyed any need for explanations. This kiss was innocent, loving but had the faintest sweep of heat. The touch woke a dark hunger in her body.

He opened his eyes.

The raw need there scared the bejesus out of her.

Raz jerked back into the driver's seat, back into the shadows. "Go clean up. This stop will be short." He got out of the car and shrugged into his jacket. Inserting a credit card into the kiosk, he pulled the gas cap off the tank.

Sandra opened her door, and the cold night shocked her. Her uneven breaths puffed like smoke before her. She wished she had something warmer to wear, hot days and cold nights left her unprepared. She pulled the collar of her blazer around her neck and followed Paris and Sean inside the building.

The ladies' room spanned three stalls, and Sandra entered without the walls trapping her. She grabbed paper towels and ran hot water over her hands. They shook. Sandra examined herself in the cracked mirror.

Stress, anxiety, and lack of proper food for the entire day all added up to what she saw reflected back. A tired thirty-one-year-old woman who decided on a whim to run off into the sunset with her lover and a questionably contagious friend. She ran the moist paper towel across her face. Raz knew more about Paris's illness then he let on. *I'm infected.* It's the only reason they hadn't left her behind at HUP.

CHAPTER NINE

SANDRA WALKED OUT of the restroom and scoured the shelves for convenience store food. Paris and Sean browsed the aisles probably as hungry as her. Sandra paid for the snacks and walked to the gas pumps. Raz wanted to be out of Pennsylvania by nightfall. Yet, they were still on the outskirts of Center. The last delay had been her fault. The one before that, too. Raz finished washing the windshield and placed the squeegee back in the solution of cleaner. She stood as close to Raz as she dared, not sure if she'd be welcomed.

Opening the passenger door, she tossed her bounty on the dashboard. "Paris and Sean are still shopping."

Raz turned to face her and trapped her between the car and *him*.

Her heart thundered at the contact. She wanted to know his secrets, no matter how frightening. So, she propped herself against the door, and it clicked shut behind her. The cool metal penetrated the cloth of her jacket and shirt. She trembled. Yet, more than her body was chilled.

Sandra waited for Raz to confide in her after all they'd been through. With the toe of her shoe, she kicked the loose gravel at her feet. It scattered across the pavement. She lifted her gaze and studied his eyes. If Raz spilled his secrets, then she'd have to do the same.

Am I ready to tell him? "Cam won't mention the pain meds."

Raz narrowed his eyes. "That's the least of my worries." He tucked a loose strand of hair behind her ear, and his fingers lingered at her neck.

She smelled a faint hint of gasoline, and the exotic scent of leather from his jacket. "Cam isn't a part of your secret military." *Is*

Raz crazy? Did he escape from a loony bin before moving to Angelville? Raz being insane would certainly tidy up all the crazy talk. Yet, Sandra believed they really were being chased.

One touch from Raz, and Sandra wanted to follow him to the ends of the earth. If he'd stop touching her, then she could think straight, but the pleasure she found with him couldn't be resisted. She couldn't take her eyes off him. His crystalline gaze mesmerized her.

"Are you afraid?" he asked.

Sandra swallowed, but didn't answer his question. Fear was becoming the constant companion of the day. "You told Paris Cam might be working with an infiltrator, which implies he'd have wanted to get on your good side, not piss you off."

His thumb grazed her bottom lip as he edged closer. "He tried getting on my good side. He gave me intel for Omega's location, but I'm not taking us there."

Another touch seared her flesh and made her mouth go dry. She parted her lips and leaned back onto the car door. "He's not after my research."

Raz scrunched his face. He smoothed the fly-aways from her cheek and rubbed his nose against hers. "Maybe not, but my experience suggests he wouldn't have such a close relationship with you if there wasn't a benefit for him. You have something he wants. Maybe he just wants you."

She shook her head. Raz's warm breath tickled the side of her face and neck, sending delicious shivers along her body. "We work together. We're friends. I'm confused. If Cam is the enemy, he'd want to get to you, not me. He's M83, and so are you, right?"

Raz shrugged. "Technically, not anymore."

Sandra rubbed her brow. "But you were. Doesn't that put you both on the same side?"

"Something is going on in Angelville. Omega is a small unit. Cameron implied dozens of Chasers are in the area. The ratio isn't normal protocol."

She pushed against his chest. Cameron wasn't a liar. "He's at the lab every day. He wouldn't have time for what you're suggesting."

Raz wrapped his arms around her in a comforting embrace. His warmth thawed the cold deep within her. He brushed soft kisses on her hairline which made her tremble.

He misinterpreted her shiver. "Don't be afraid. Nothing in the universe would make me hurt you."

Does that include my heart?

Raz lifted her chin. His gaze penetrated deep within her soul. "I never thought an infiltrator would be an M83 spy before one killed my parents. I wasn't leaving you at HUP. Not with so many uncertainties."

He stroked her hair in a soothing motion that tugged at her heart. Was he admitting they weren't a mistake? Sandra reached for his waist and wrapped her arms around him. She couldn't help herself. She needed to be closer. Her body craved his.

"Sandra." He breathed her name in her ear. "We shouldn't temp ourselves."

Goose bumps erupted along her neck, and a pleasant shudder pulsated down her back. He nuzzled her at the spot above her earlobe, sending shards of desire through her body. A flush of heat sensitized her, and her breasts tingled. She tightened her arms and pulled Raz closer. She wanted his kiss she hoped as much as he did.

Raz lifted her a few inches off the ground and then covered her mouth with his. Wet and deep, his tongue swept inside.

His five o'clock shadow abraded her face. Her feet came back to the pavement.

Bracing one arm on the roof of the car, he plunged the other into her hair. He angled her chin so her mouth was in the exact position for him to plunge his tongue even deeper.

A quick burst of desire heated her lower body.

Raz seized what he'd been denying them both since this morning. The cool metal of the vehicle contrasted with the intense fire of his body and the hard length of his erection against her thigh. She pressed back against him.

The gas attendant squawked on the loud speaker, but the sound was background noise to Sandra. She didn't care. Her hips undulated in small motions, and she reached for the front of his jeans. Her hands, hidden by his leather jacket, popped the button.

Raz groaned. "I can't get enough of your touch. One time was supposed to be enough." He grabbed her face in both of his hands.

"You belong to me. Only me." He pulled back his head, and they locked gazes. He pressed himself against her, exactly where she needed him.

Sandra sucked her bottom lip between her teeth. His physical reaction told her how much he wanted her. Raz owned her, body and soul. Yet, doubt sent a slight twinge into her chest, and her breath hitched. Did he mean their one time together had been a mistake, or had everything between them been a mistake? *He hates that he can't control his urges around me. He doesn't want to love me.*

The lights of the gas station radiated around him. His eyes were the brightest blue she'd ever seen. His strong jaw and dark hair filled her vision. Stubble shaded his face. His breath puffed out a cloud of steam in the cool air. *Am I a slave to this lust between us?*

Raz dragged a finger down the shirt opening at her throat and stopped at the barrier of the first button.

Anticipating his hands on her sensitive breasts caused her nipples to tighten, and with every inhale, the fabric of her shirt abraded them.

He manipulated the fastening between his fingers but didn't undo it. He opened the buttons on her jacket. Both hands snaked beneath the coat and covered her breasts over her shirt.

She moaned and arched against his hands. "Don't stop."

"Damn it. We have to stop." Raz growled. He jerked her away from the car but grabbed her ass to keep her against him and delivered another molten kiss.

Her hands traveled under his jacket. She first touched his back, and then, when that wasn't satisfying enough, she dipped down below his waistband. Her breasts crushed against his chest.

He swore again, opened the car door, and gently pushed her inside.

She panted inside the car and the window fogged. Reality set in. Her blazer was now stifling hot. The blurred glass framed the crowded gas station. Customers walked to and from each vehicle parked around them. Loud, gasping breaths filled the quiet of the car. *I'm panting like a marathon runner. Or a nympho.*

A few patrons stared at the car. A combination of tingles and flame built in her cheeks.

Raz replaced the gas pump and grabbed the receipt.

The mixture of arousal and embarrassment created an excitement she wanted more of and brought her attention to the slight dampness between her legs. *What am I becoming?*

Raz eased into the driver's side of the car and sat for a few minutes.

Sandra was glad he had a difficult time coming down from their flight of passion. She wasn't the only one.

"I didn't bring you with us for this. It was a—"

"Mistake." Sandra stared.

He lifted his head and leaned toward her. The close space sucked them toward each other like a black hole drinking in light.

"You brought me because I'm sick," Sandra added.

He snapped back his head. "No. I meant what I said about Cameron. I don't trust him, and I don't trust him around you."

"You don't trust anyone, from my perspective. I've delayed you twice. You can leave me here, and your mistake will be over and done with."

He bounced his head back against the headrest. The steering wheel creaked under the pressure of his clenched fists and white knuckles. "Does Cameron tutor The Six like you do?"

The Six were unrelated to Raz's situation. Sandra rubbed her aching brow. "We help each other. What does that have to do with us?"

"How many times have you helped each other?"

"How many times have you lied about being in the witness protection program?"

Raz held her hand and brought it to his lips. The kiss he placed on the back was both erotic and protective. "Do you want to know what Chasers do? Who they really are?"

"Absolutely." *Finally, I'll know what's going on in this messed-up relationship.*

He turned her hand over and placed a kiss on her wrist. He licked her pulse point and lightly sucked her skin.

"Raz," she said on a throaty moan. His mixed signals were sending her body into a state of hypersensitive turmoil.

"They take, Sandra. They take everything from us. M83 was a way for me to give back to my people, but my service didn't work. I had to leave. Paris and Sean have special skills which Chasers want. They are done taking from my family, *anyone* in my family. If Cameron or The Six have taken from you, then I'll stop them."

A sting of tears made her blink a few times. What was he saying? No one had made such a promise.

Ever.

She had taken care of herself this past year using her inner strength as her guide. Maybe even before then, after her marriage fell apart and divorce was the only solution. She had no one to help her fight, help her win. The thought of Raz fighting for her, and with her, was the sexiest damn thing she'd ever encountered. "They haven't taken anything."

Raz cupped her jaw and kissed her again. Neither fought the magnetic attraction. His mouth was gentle, yet savage at the same time. He nipped at her lips. His tongue swooped in to taste and tease. The air was too hot. Her body too hot. Yet, craving his skin against her own pushed her over a precipice, an indescribable free fall. She pushed his jacket down his arms.

He ripped the coat from his shoulders and tossed it in the backseat. "I want you," he said, between mouthfuls of liquid fever. "Right here."

Under Sandra's half-closed eyelids, customers walked from their cars to the store. How many of them watched in voyeuristic pleasure? Or perhaps disgust? Raz kissed a line of blazing embers on her neck, onto her collar bone and into her cleavage. Sandra's embarrassment left her. She didn't care who spotted them. Moisture pooled between her legs. She wished the fabric would disappear. Despite her heightened state, reason argued with her desires. This display of passion wasn't keeping a low profile. They were still on the run. "We should talk … about this," she gasped.

And they should. She needed to stop before they were naked.

He pulled back but thumbed her beaded nipples through her shirt.

The sensations coursed through her in a high-speed race to the center of her body. She reached over the middle console for the zipper of his jeans, glad she'd already popped the button. One less obstacle to meet her goal.

He grabbed her hands, but not before she stroked him. He moaned. "People can see us. I don't care, but bringing attention to ourselves in a public place would create memories for those around us. An easy way for Chasers to track us."

She agreed. "I can't stop touching you." She clutched at his shirt. "The thought of never touching you again is making me crazy."

"I don't want you to stop, but if Cameron is to be trusted, Center is crawling with Chasers."

Sandra caught headlights out of the corner of her eye, and the shock of it splashed cold water over her burning skin. She gasped. If Sean or Paris came out and saw them, she couldn't repair the damage. The tension between the four of them was complicated enough. She withdrew and sat back against her leather seat. Her erratic heart skittered against her chest as she brought her heavy breathing back to a normal level. The euphoria faded. She blinked out of her haze.

Focus came into Raz's eyes, and his gaze darted around the parking lot. He cursed under his breath. His breathing slowed to a normal pace, and he narrowed in on the mini-market like a hunter sensing prey.

Sandra's fight-or-flight senses went on high alert. "What is it?"

The light in his eyes shimmered.

A tickle along her arms made her glance down, and the fine hairs on her forearms stood upright.

"They've been gone too long." Raz concentrated on the market entrance. His large frame blocked her entire view of the store. Swearing under his breath, he braced himself against the steering wheel as he searched their surroundings.

The muscles in his forearms bulged and flexed. How could a man look like that without spending hours in the gym?

He reached for the ignition and zap, a faint light of static shot forward.

She jumped. Her heart pounded out of her chest.

Raz didn't take his eye off the store. "I'll pull closer to pick them up at the door."

Someone shouted from the store entrance, and Sandra noticed a group of people standing around the ice cooler. Several people pointed inside the building. A blare of sirens wailed in the distance, and she twisted to identify which direction it came from. Swiveling back, Sandra couldn't speak through her fear. Cameron had betrayed her.

One of the store patrons dialed furiously on his cell phone. The hairs on Raz's arms and the back of his neck stood up. His fingers remained on the key, poised as if waiting for a signal. The sirens increased in intensity. His gaze darted around the entrance.

Sandra leaned forward to gain a better view, and more people ran from their vehicles to get closer to the front of the store. *Where are they?* The lights under the weather roofs flickered and blinked out for a second.

Paris exited the building and collapsed onto the pavement.

"Shit." Raz bolted from the Camaro.

Chapter Ten

THE SIRENS GREW to deafening levels and echoed under the gas station roof. Raz scanned the mob for the best extraction point to remove Paris from the fray. Running around two parked cars, he focused his senses on Paris and Sean. He could feel the circle's connection to Sean, but had yet to spot him.

His muscles burned. Zaps of electrical heat bolted from his nerves and increased his strength. Bringing Sandra with them had been a mistake. He cared too much about her. She was a huge distraction from his circle. Raz jumped the curb between the gas pumps.

The humans surrounding Paris cut off Raz, and they offered no aid. People inside the market jogged toward the glass doors. Others milled around the sidewalk. His Transor power sparked along his arms. He pushed and shoved people aside until he reached her.

Pale and gaunt, Paris lay on the concrete. A thin sheen of sweat covered her face and neck. Instincts drove him. Past M83 training came back. Raz found every ounce of his control. Chasers' Nexus Emissions Unit (NEU) detectors probably littered the area. Once the NEUs registered the tiniest hint of Nexus energy, the Chasers' descent on the mini-market would be quicker than the ambulance's arrival.

Where was Sean? He couldn't see him over the building numbers within the crowd. Exposure of the circle guaranteed Sean would live a life of captivity instead of a life on the run.

Raz struggled to calm the desire still raging through his body. He'd lost control with Sandra in public. Their connection was unbreakable, and more than sexual frustration and lust. The pending blitz, edgy and rough, clued him in to just how attached he was to his human.

His senses warred with having all three of his circle members in different locations. A shield would try to connect them all if he didn't hurry.

Yet, his human wasn't a part of his circle. *My human? Yes, she's mine!*

Cameron's assertion that Raz's possessiveness wasn't politically correct mattered little. She was an addiction.

Raz reacted at a gut level and located Sean running from the entrance of the mini-mart. A burst of Transor power filled every muscle. He had minutes before he'd be on the nightly news and his family lost to him forever.

"Daddy, I didn't do it." Sean sobbed. His legs pumped like pistons, and he ran straight for Raz.

"I know—"

"Mommy couldn't hear me. I told her we needed to leave. She couldn't hear me."

Raz dropped to one knee and clutched Sean in a bear hug. Sean's tears soaked through Raz's T-shirt. Wisps of azure energy cocooned them. If Raz touched Paris, he couldn't stop the resulting shield from forming. The physical connection with Sandra moments before, combined with Sean's fear, made Raz's fight against the surging Nexus energy hopeless. *My M83 training is worthless.*

If he distanced himself from the crowd and sent Sean to Sandra for safety, he might stop the blitz and the shield from forming. Raz stood.

Sean wrapped his arms and legs around Raz like a baby monkey holding on tight in high trees.

He stepped away from the crowd and scanned the mass of people for Sandra. Where were these people coming from? The small distance from Paris already decreased his urges.

"Hey, bud. Listen," Raz whispered in Sean's ear. He tugged small arms from around his neck, but Sean squeezed. His anxiety was a tangible force keeping them together.

Sean's sobs increased and his hold tightened. Raz pulled back, Sean's brown eyes filled with Nexus light and unshed tears. The aura cocooning them swirled around their heads. Sean hiccuped. "I didn't hurt Mommy."

What was Sean talking about? "This isn't your fault."

"We need Sandra's friend. He can help us."

Raz cursed his luck. Sean felt that Cameron was an ally. "We can't go back."

Sean nodded. "We must. He's good. I'm like Mommy. I can tell."

Empaths. Their uncanny ability always shocked Raz. Before he met Paris, he'd never encountered an empath. Trusting a developing Sixxer power in a child tested Raz. He rubbed Sean's back. Cameron could very well be the reason they were in this situation. Someone tugged on the back of his shirt. He swiveled.

Sandra stood there like an angel of mercy.

A sigh of relief escaped his lips. "Will you take him to the car? I need to—"

"Go to Paris." Sandra tugged on Sean's arm. "Hurry. The ambulance is coming." Sean reached out for her. She pulled him tight into her embrace.

Yet, the urge to protect Sandra was almost too much to resist. The swirling mass of force within Raz eased. His reactions in her presence bobbed up and down. He suspected she created the ticking time bomb inside of him, but then, in the next instant, she tamed the Nexus energy he struggled to control.

Raz noticed a deep red line running from her nose to her upper lip. "Your nose is bleeding again."

Sandra reached up, but he'd already wiped the small streak of blood from her face. The slight brush of his fingers against Sandra's mouth sent his Transor powers through the roof. Light oozed from his fingers, and he quickly lowered his hand. His body ached from the massive amount of strength infusing his arms, legs and back. He couldn't hide the change from her.

Sean lifted his head. One look at the smeared blood on Sandra's upper lip, and another meltdown swept over his face. Sobs shook his shoulders.

Raz cupped Sean's cheeks and placed a kiss on his forehead. "Remember to focus. Everything will be all right."

Sandra blotted her nose with her sleeve and stared at the blood on the fabric. "This shouldn't be happening." She pressed against her nose a few times to staunch any more fluid.

"It's over. Get Sean to the car. We don't know who'll be in the ambulance when it arrives."

Sean clung to Sandra and blubbered into her neck.

Sean somehow linked all of them through the Nexus. The consequences of Sean having such power over a human meant death if Chasers focused their hunt specifically on him. Raz's mind raced with all the possibilities of what scientists, the military or any other crazy person would do to Sean if his abilities were discovered.

"I didn't do it. Mommy said," Sean whispered.

"I know, sweetheart. You didn't do anything." Sandra rubbed his back. She nodded at Raz. "We shouldn't be separated, but what do we do?"

"Chasers aren't aware of us, yet. They would've already isolated the gas station. Keep Sean away from us. I'll do what I have to get us through this."

Rage blurred his vision. He'd fight every last one of them to protect his son. To protect Sandra. His need to defend overshadowed his need for control. His body expanded and gained mass. The seams of his black T-shirt stretched to the limit as stitches popped. He backed away.

"Don't leave me," Sean cried. His arms extended toward Raz, but Sandra held onto him, and for that Raz was grateful. The blitz was a touch away.

"I've got you." Sandra stroked Sean's hair to soothe him. "Raz, help Paris." Sandra ducked her head and murmured to Sean. Her lips moved against his blond hair. She wiped away Sean's tears with her jacket and glanced up when Raz didn't move.

He prayed his eyes weren't glowing.

She backed away. Fear, confusion and need battled on her face. If she witnessed his full power, would she back away forever?

He whipped around and pushed people aside again. Paris needed him. A few of the humans cast mean looks his way and protested his intrusion. "She's with me," he barked. "Make room." His knees hit the pavement beside her head. The people baked away and made a ring around them. Someone said help was on the way. Others told the crowd to give them breathing room. The gawkers thinned a little but not enough for Raz's liking.

"Raz," Paris sputtered.

"I'll get you the hell out of here." He reached under her back and lifted, but she cried out in pain.

Paris's hands clamped onto his forearms. "Someone called 911." She dug her nails into his skin.

He leaned down to her ear. "I know. They're getting here fast."

Paris tried pushing him away. "You need to go. You'll blitz. People are taking pictures, possibly video."

"I'm not leaving you." His other circle members were safe. He concentrated on Paris. He'd transfer the swirling energy bubbling from him to her for a few seconds and keep his blitz under control and give her a boost so she could get up.

"Keep Sandra and Sean safe. You need to."

Heat and electricity built in his hands. He hugged her. His fingers burned from the effort of passing the energy without the very willing audience seeing. "Cameron set us up."

She panted and gasped as his power entered her body. "Has he followed us?"

"The pain pills were something else. They made you collapse." He eased back to see if his transfer did any good.

Her face contorted. "I didn't take the medicine. Your hands are like ice on my skin, and the pain gets worse. The transfer isn't working." A gloved hand pulled the bottle of medicine from her hoodie.

Raz helped her sit. "Why didn't you take them?"

"I didn't read Cameron wrong. I'm weak physically, but my power is true. The drugs would've dulled my senses. I can't … Not when Sandra is with us. I can't go on. You'll need M83's help."

"I'm not getting us involved with Omega. Can you stand?" He crouched and held out a hand to her

She pulled on his arm, but she had no strength. "You might have to, for Sean's sake. He'll need the training we all receive at elevation so he can hide his Sixxer power and Nexus energy from humans."

"Is Sean hurting Sandra?" Raz transferred a small pulse of vitality to her again, and she grimaced. A transfer wouldn't work. Only a render or a Sixxer healer would help her.

Her gaze darted back and forth. Tears streaked her face. "He's changing. It's more than we imagined."

"Not possible. You're feeding off his emotions."

"His control is so bad. He's terrified. His fear is like a monster eating at my soul." She stroked his cheek. "He hasn't learned how to use the circle. He can't fight the instinct to protect us. Nexus energy comes from him. To protect Sandra. He loves her. You must perform a render with Sandra before he loses control."

"She can't be included." *Sean is too young. Sandra is too human.*

"You have to see the possibility—"

"I have it under control." He wouldn't dare tell her how close to blitzing he actually was.

"Are you sure? Your muscles have popped … not because of me," Paris murmured.

Raz's face heated. In their seven years of running, he'd never lost control. Paris knew how unlikely his muscle mass change was from her fall. Wanting Sandra had incited the change, and the potential threat to the object of his desire as well as his entire circle. "Try to stand up, again."

She shook her head. "You're already getting bigger." She squeezed his growing biceps.

The panic in her voice was a force, urging a deeper Nexus connection.

"Your shirt is tearing at the seams. The Nexus will break free, soon."

Raz monitored the remaining humans. So far, no one had made a threatening move toward them. "I'm not leaving you for the Chasers like some kind of Sixxer sacrifice."

Whirling red lights entered his vision as the sirens careened between the station columns. The EMTs raced from the vehicle.

Sandra stood a few feet from the car. Sean clung to her. The lights of the ambulance cast a reddish-gold halo around her body. The tornado-like wind picked up and blew her hair in front of her face. Sandra took a single step toward him.

"Stay there!"

The EMTs recorded Paris's vitals and placed an oxygen mask onto her face.

Paris fidgeted during the examination.

If she had the strength, Raz knew she was two seconds away from bolting. He answered the medical team's questions and kept Sandra and Sean in his line of sight. He promised he'd sacrifice his life to ensure they all got out of this safely.

Paris motioned for Raz to come closer, and the EMTs let him get in the back of the vehicle with her.

So far, no Chasers had arrived. *Where are they? Is Cameron lying to us?*

Paris tapped his arm. "Keep them safe, Raz. You have to."

"I'll keep all of us safe, don't worry." He held her hand.

The tension left Paris's body. "Good. He'll need you. They'll all need you."

Paris's relief and the distance from Sean and Sandra helped suppress his instincts.

"Wait!"

Raz turned at Sandra's shout.

Sean broke free of her arms and ran to the back of the ambulance. "Is Mommy okay?" Tears cleaned a path down his dirty cheeks.

"The doctors will have her feeling better in no time." With a hand on Sean's chest, Raz pushed him back, preventing his climb inside the ambulance. A burst of power zapped them both, but Raz absorbed most of it so Sean's aura wouldn't embrace them.

Sean stomped his foot. "We aren't supposed to go to the doctors."

"No. We aren't supposed to. I'll stay with Mommy to keep her safe, and your job now is to keep Sandra safe."

Sandra stopped behind Sean and crouched down to his height. "You and I will be right behind them, okay?"

"I didn't do it, Sandra. I promise." Sean shuffled his feet.

Raz knew Sean was responsible for more than he realized.

"Of course, you didn't do anything," Sandra said.

"I hurt you."

"No, baby. What're you talking about? You can't hurt me."

Sean touched Sandra's upper lip. "Your bloody nose."

"It's not your fault." Sandra's lashes were wet, but her eyes were clear and a little wild.

She was Raz's brave and beautiful human. He had to leave them behind, but they would follow the ambulance to the hospital. He trusted Sandra would protect Sean, but could he trust Sean not to hurt Sandra? Raz went against his gut instinct and made the decision to ask Cameron for help. The area was unstable, even though no Chasers had found them. Yet. Cameron knew where the Chaser garrisons were located, and Omega could protect Raz's unstable circle. The situation forced Raz to consider using the Corp. "I'll get her out."

Sandra nodded.

"We'll all leave together," Raz promised.

"Okay."

"Be careful." Raz almost told her to beware of the Chasers but couldn't risk it around the EMTs.

"Will the Chasers get us now?"

Goose bumps rose on Raz's arm. Sean had read his mind.

Chapter Eleven

THE AIR CONDITIONER kicked on. A cold blast of air hit the back of Sandra's neck. She shivered. Low music whispered from the speakers, but the soothing tones did nothing to calm her nerves. She bounced her foot against the end table. Other than she and Sean, no one occupied the small hospital lounge.

Sean flipped through a stack of magazines, and his blond head moved to his own tune. His head bobs certainly didn't match the hospital's poor music selection. He had wedged his trusty teddy inside his shirt, and the bear's head poked out of his collar.

Sandra hugged herself. They'd been here for hours and hadn't heard a word about Paris's condition. The longer they stayed, the wilder her thoughts became. *What if Chasers find us? What if they already have? Should I take Sean and run?* The cords at the base of her neck ached. Her heartbeat blared in her ears. Four cream-colored walls and the ugly furniture surrounding her provided no comfort. The interior decorators were clueless at this hospital. Disjointed colors and patterns destroyed any focal point, and the lack of warmth maximized her discomfort.

Sandra snapped out of her obsessive focus on the room. No one cared about the hospital furnishing committee. Criticizing the room and wall color made an appealing distraction, but Sandra had to sort through the events at the mini-market. She wanted to forget what happened at the gas station.

Her brain balked at the images still darting through her head. A force field had surrounded Raz and Sean before she'd reached them. Sean vibrated with … something she couldn't explain. Holding him had been both painful and tender. She must've imagined it. A spike of pain shot through her brow, and she rubbed her forehead. Everything had happened so fast. Sandra closed her eyes.

A growl emerged from her stomach. She covered it with her hand. She hadn't eaten since HUP, hadn't been hungry. The chaos and adrenaline in her body squashed any remnant of an appetite, until now. Again, her stomach growled. The fruit chew and M&Ms from Cameron had been digested hours ago. The snacks from the gas station sat on the car dash, untouched and were too far away to be of any use. Despite the rumbling in her belly, a sour ball settled in her midsection.

The events prior to the ambulance's arrival had to have been a hallucination. Energy shifts, or whatever the perceived phenomenon she observed, made little sense. As a scientist, she examined everything from a rational and scientific perspective. Yet, logical answers eluded her.

Sandra remembered the variations in the air. Like tendrils of transparent corn silk, blue in color and very real, they'd swirled around Raz. When she came up behind him, she'd choked back a scream and wrenched back her upper body as the coils rushed at her face. She'd blinked. Then nothing. Only Raz. The smoky air hadn't been real. Hallucinations? The smoke had to have been a trick of the lights, and her overactive imagination gone wild.

I'll find a doctor to examine me. Although, my symptoms are similar to Paris's. If they can't help her, they can't help me, either. Sandra opened her eyes.

Sean sat in a mauve chair beside her and browsed a women's magazine. He waited patiently. Well, as patiently as was possible for a six-year-old. He wiggled and bounced and flicked the pages with a snap. The faded flowers on the upholstery behind him danced with his movements.

Sean clenched Sandra's coat sleeve. "Why can't we go see her?"

She expected to see more tears from him, but they'd dried up upon arrival and hadn't returned. "They have to do tests—"

"The doctors will think I hurt her!" Sean's face drained of color. His upper lip trembled. "I have to fix her."

"Sean." She grabbed his chin and eased up his face until she caught his gaze. "Mommy is okay. The tests will help the doctors treat her. You didn't cause her to get sick."

"She might die," he whispered.

Paris's ragged whisper entered her mind. *I'm dying, Sandra.* Sandra feared for Paris, but no way in hell would she repeat her thoughts to a six-year-old. She pulled him onto her lap. "Raz will be back soon. He'll tell us what the doctors are doing for Mommy, okay? Then we'll be able to see her."

Raz's leather jacket was on the chair beside her. She'd grabbed the jacket only to have something of him with her. She'd wait for ten more minutes, and if Raz didn't come get them, she'd leave. Although, she didn't want to. A warm pulse of remembered desire flushed her skin. Sandra rubbed her face and pushed back her hair. Her out-of-control hormones were a different issue to contemplate, and she brushed aside those thoughts. The wait gave her too much time to think.

Something black flickered through the large glass panel of the waiting room door. Sandra peered out of the etched geometric pattern. Raz stood at the nurses' station. A sigh of relief and a tingle of unease surged through her. The stamped glass blurred his image. He spoke to a large man behind the desk. Sandra eased Sean off her lap and walked over to the entrance. *Run to him!* A glimpse of Sean held her back. She wouldn't let anyone hurt this child. *He's mine.* She had to protect him.

The man behind the counter shouted wrestler, not high school wrestling but Wrestle Mania. He was taller than Raz. She'd bet he was taller than Cameron or close to his height. His massive shoulders and biceps swelled with power as he moved. His large body, intimidating and hard, was most likely used to fighting and winning.

Sandra rubbed her arms. Raz had her suspicious of everyone.

The man's long dark hair was pulled back into a low ponytail. The color contrasted with the white skin of his neck. A gem glittered from his ear. Her gaze followed their discussion.

Raz shook his head.

His new companion gestured wildly with his arms.

She wished she could read lips. A head appeared at the windowsill beside her.

Sean moved to the edge of the pane. A magazine dangled from his hand. He stared as intently out the window as she did. "Will Daddy come get us?"

Sandra sensed a bad vibe from the other man. Was Raz avoiding them because of the same danger? If she didn't divert Sean's attention, then he'd seek answers, too. They both needed a distraction, pronto. "Why don't you grab one of the kid books over by the small table? I'll read it to you while we wait for your daddy to finish talking."

Sean walked backward to the children's area. He never removed his gaze from the window.

Sandra looked away. No point in torturing herself. She wouldn't leave Sean. "We up and left your stuff in the van. How silly of us. It's a good thing they have a stack of books here."

"Why didn't we bring the van?" Sean kneeled and sorted through the stack of brightly-colored readers.

"Raz was in a hurry."

Sean studied two readers, one orange and one green.

She touched his arm. "We'll have time to read both." Sandra moved back to their designated chair.

Sean nodded his head. He climbed next to Sandra in the oversized chair. "Do you think Daddy knew Mommy would fall, and we'd need to get here faster?"

"I don't think so, sweetie." Her arm went around Sean.

He settled in beside her. "Because your car is the fastest."

Sandra laughed, and Sean grinned up at her. The teddy bear's eyes twinkled in the light.

"Only when Raz drives." She tweaked his nose.

Sean leaned into the snuggle of her arm, and she welcomed the contact. How she'd longed to do this with her own six-year-old. A day that'd never come. She glanced at his reading choices, and her hands wobbled. She almost dropped it on the floor before Sean caught it. The title read, *Two Moms Love You: Surrogate Mothers*.

"Why did you pick this book?" she asked.

"I picked one for you and one for me." He pointed at the second book. The title read, *When Mommies Must Leave*.

Sandra gasped. "Honey, why did you pick these books?" *Why in*

God's name did the hospital have such books in the waiting room? Even her panic wanted to run away like a scared kitty.

Sean shrugged in a quick upward movement. "Mommy might leave us." Pointing to the first book, he grinned. "And you're my second mom."

The words should've warmed her soul. Instead, they created a chill. Sean placed Paris at death's door without her having said anything. "You have one mother. She's not leaving us." Sandra couldn't face him. "She's down the hall."

Lunging out of her seat, she squatted in the children's area and hunted for more appropriate reading material. She sat cross-legged on the floor. Books fell over in her search for a better topic—puppies or ducks.

Sandra couldn't escape the past. Bitter memories of her marriage intruded. Images of the child she'd never have. Thom's numbers had been off the chart in terms of fertility. He could've been a stud for hire and had hundreds of children. Sandra wanted one, just one.

She remembered Thom's plan as if he'd told it to her yesterday. A light sweat broke out on her arms and chest. Thom hadn't asked or discussed his idea with her. The toys before her swirled and blurred into the unpleasant memories of her marriage.

"We'll hire a surrogate," Thom informed her. Late afternoon sun streamed in the windows of his study.

"Hire who?" Sandra's head popped up from her hunched-over position. Tending to her bonsai tree had become unimportant.

Thom sat at the massive oak desk, reading a scientific journal. His laptop and research notes created a ring of paper around his body.

His physical beauty almost overwhelmed her.

"I've been interviewing candidates." The dark and light liquid in his glass swirled together. Ice tea sweetened with two sugars and flavored with a squeeze of Arizona lemon. Thom had the fruit shipped in special.

The house had smelled like lemons for three days.

"I found students who are interested."

Her heart still pumped. Her breath still flowed in and out of her lungs. "Students interested in being surrogates?" She sounded so calm, which went against the electrifying streams of rage inside her body wanting to pummel him.

Thom smiled over the top of the report he was reviewing. He was a Cheshire cat licking feathered lips. "Yes." He chuckled. "They're very eager to find out the details, especially when they considered the cash aspect. I don't know why I didn't think of it sooner. You could be a mother by December."

Sandra didn't respond.

Thom stood and approached her with slow and deliberate footsteps. He reached under her chin and pushed her gaping mouth closed.

Her teeth clinked together. He'd spoken to his students about her inability to become pregnant. Sandra placed her favorite pruning shears on the table. The action had saved Thom's life. "You talked about buying a baby from one of your research students?" Inside she was calm, but her words flew like daggers. She sat on the matching leather chair. The furniture filled the room with a masculine aura. Sandra had picked out the set for him as a birthday gift. "You said you wouldn't consider adoption."

"I'm not. The child would be mine, of course."

Her lungs deflated, and she wheezed. "Of course." A sob caught in her windpipe. She cleared her throat and stiffened her back. Her body went numb. Any remaining love she had for Thom disappeared.

Thom rubbed her shoulder. "Making a baby isn't going to work with you."

Sandra shivered as the heat exited her body. "Because I'm broken? Is that what you're saying?"

"Sands, you're infertile. We shouldn't keep pretending you're not. We've been on fertility treatments for years with no results."

Hot tears fell onto her chest. "Why are you doing this?"

"Sands, it's not personal. I need an heir. Your family doesn't give a shit if their grandchild isn't theirs. I won't do that to my parents."

A hand tapped her shoulder, and the harsh antiseptic odors of the hospital registered in her confused brain. Queasiness flopped in the back of her throat. The past faded, and the day's events came back in a rush.

"You're not mad at me, are you?" Sean asked. A shiver ran along his arms and goose bumps appeared.

"Heavens, no." Sandra rubbed her hands rapidly against his bare skin. The thin T-shirt he wore was useless against the cranked air conditioning.

"Are you mad at Jamie?"

"Who are you talking about?" She squeezed his arms and shifted her crossed legs behind her so she leaned on one hip.

"Your little boy."

The air left her lungs as though someone punched her in the gut. "Not funny, Sean. Why would you say that?"

"He makes you sad." Sean pushed out his lower lip.

"Sean. Enough. Jamie isn't real. Why are you lying?"

Tears sprang to his eyes, and Sandra wanted to hide in a dark hole from shame. She had to get both of their minds somewhere else.

"Hospitals are famous for making people cranky." Sandra continued to rub Sean's arms, hoping to generate heat. He sniffed back the tears. She wiped his cheek. "I'm not mad. We should read something fun. Don't you think?"

He scrunched up his cute face. His words came out choppy and hoarse. "Since you're my surge rogit mom, I thought you'd like to read that book with me."

Each time she heard the word surrogate a sharp needle entered the back of her skull. "I'm your friend."

He hopped up and down. "You'll be my mom soon."

"Listen," Sandra said.

Sean bit his bottom lip.

She wiped away more tears. "Are you listening?"

He nodded.

"Paris is your Mom. She'll always be your Mom. What you saw today was confusing, but Mommy will be okay."

"She told me you'd be my mom, too. I'd like that. I want two moms!" He cried and stomped his feet.

Paris would've never said those words to Sean. Not after Sandra had confided to her about Thom. Sandra pulled off her blazer and placed it around Sean's small shoulders. "When did Mommy tell you you'd have two moms?"

Sean inserted his arms into the jacket.

Sandra rolled up the sleeves and buttoned it closed.

"She didn't tell me."

"You imagined it?" Sandra raised her eyebrows.

"No." His eyes were sad. "But she'll be able to tell me again soon."

"What do you mean soon?"

His brows came together. "We won't have to say anything to each other, but we'll know what the other says in our heads. I'll be able to do that. Both me and Jamie."

"Miss?"

Blue scrubs covered muscled legs and blocked Sandra's line of sight. She glanced up and up. The same large man who'd been talking with Raz stood before her. *Why him? Why isn't Raz coming for us? I need help.* She arched her head back in order for her gaze to reach the man's face. Her heart rate accelerated to the bursting point. She needed to escape. Right now.

"Are you Sandra?" he asked with an arched brow.

Sean tensed beside her then shrank back under her arm.

Sandra must've nodded, because the man broke into a huge smile full of white wolf-like teeth. She wanted to run even more.

"I was there when they brought Paris into the ER." He held out his hand. "Leon."

She squeezed it in a firm handshake.

His fingers wrapped around hers and became an iron handcuff. "She's stable. The doc is on his way."

Sandra consciously relaxed her neck then her arms. "Thank you for telling me." She pulled her hand free.

Sean crouched closer to her ear. "I don't like him," he whispered.

"Sit, sweetie. I want to hear what he tells us. It's about Mommy." She pulled Sean back and down to urge him to sit beside her.

"He'll hurt her," Sean insisted, louder.

Leon reached out toward him. "Hey, buddy—"

"Go away!" Sean lurched backward.

"This man is here to help us." Sandra made Sean face her, and she pushed the hair from his forehead.

Sean jerked his head and pulled away. He stomped over to the toys in the corner and narrowed his eyes.

"I'm so sorry." Sandra's cheeks heated. She fluttered her arms.

"Kids."

"Is he yours?"

"Paris's." *Shit. I shouldn't have said that.*

The man offered his hand to help her.

Sandra refused. She stood by herself. Leon towered over her, but standing was better than being on the ground. She'd do anything to stop the dread swirling in her gut at his presence and sprint out the door, if needed.

"No wonder the reaction."

Sandra's gaze darted to him in shock, but she realized Leon referred to Sean's behavior and not hers.

"He needs reassurance she'll be okay. Scary thing for kids to go through."

She crossed her arms over her chest. "What's happened to her? We haven't heard anything since we arrived."

Leon guided her by the elbow to the opposite side of the room.

As soon as he touched her, a pleasurable tingle ran up her arm, full of comfort and peace. Her fear never evaporated, but her muscles relaxed and her pounding heart slowed.

"Her state when she arrived was very strange. Were you there when she collapsed?"

Leon never let go of her arm, and Sandra wanted to unburden herself of the stress the last few hours had brought her. "I was still in the car, but Paris has been sick for a while."

"How long?"

A sharp jab poked the skin above her left eye. "Perhaps a few months. The past few weeks she's gotten worse."

"What was going on?" Leon gestured for her to continue.

"No one could tell us." She rubbed her eyebrow with cool fingers. Why did thinking hurt?

"You took her to a clinic?"

Don't tell him the truth. "I took her to a doctor. Raz didn't want me to, but I wasn't going to let her sit in pain every day. We have her med—"

"Whoa." He reached into his pocket, pulled out a tissue, and thrust in under her nose. His hand on the back of her head pushed her forward.

She licked the blood from her lip, and the metallic flavor burst on her tongue.

"Ease forward. Apply pressure."

Pain lashed at her forehead. "I'm gonna pass out," she whispered.

Leon quickly moved her to one of the chairs and positioned her head between her knees. "If you have to pass out, don't worry. I've got you."

As the room enclosed and folded in on itself, a tunnel formed around her eyes. Feelers of air searched for her. Similar to what came after her when Paris fell, the wisps were different in color, not quite blue or silver, but a combination of the two. They came toward her faster and grew in size. The fingers reached around Leon's head, swirling and prodding. They touched her.

CHAPTER TWELVE

THE RADIANCE OF the silver-blue threads obliterated the hospital waiting room. The ephemeral ribbons stretched around Leon. They shifted and grew and blocked her vision, grazing her face. Her heart pounded. A scream lodged in her throat, and her limbs froze. She squeezed her eyes tight, but the darkness didn't erase the flashbulb imprint of the strands branded on her retinas.

What were they? Claws of panic scratched her chest. *They're not real. They can't be real.*

One. Sandra floated in a black abyss. The unwelcome images of the encroaching smoke-like fingers faded, and her heart rate slowed.

Two. A warmth immersed her into a languid dreamlike state. A kaleidoscope of colors burst in her mind.

Three. Hot and humid air spread butterfly kisses over her face. A layer of moisture beaded the surface of her skin. Tiny droplets of sweat ran down her neck. She wanted to ease the tickling sensation, but movement failed her. Heat caressed her everywhere and burned her from the inside out.

Yet, the sultry air comforted her and reminded her of summer. She dreamed of being home, of being safe. The shower of light on dark gradually focused into a recollection. She visualized the picturesque landscape of her backyard and the small trailer she called home. The property was the farthest, both physically and mentally, from the house Sandra had shared with Thom.

Despite the humidity, the sky refused to surrender a welcome rain for days. Sandra's clothes stuck to her skin, even inside with the air conditioner working overtime. A fine layer of salt coated her face and neck. She propped her feet on the coffee table and fanned herself with a handful of loose papers.

A burst of ideas bubbled to the surface, and Sandra scribbled them in the margins of her research notebook. Her pen flew across the page, and her hand cramped. She'd have to create a new round of testing, but if successful, these new ideas would be the breakthrough she needed. The engineered Xnix-624 virus infected her diseased plant specimens and acted as she predicted.

Sometimes.

Instead of the plant dying, the virus enhanced the health of the plant. *I can combat fire with fire and use the virus to kill the plant's disease.* Unfortunately, the experiments couldn't be repeated every time. Sandra had more dead plants than surviving ones. She hadn't discovered the missing link.

A soft boom echoed in the room and disrupted her concentration. An eerie stillness surrounded her. She glanced toward the open kitchen. The stove console was dark and the AC silent. In a matter of minutes, the power outage would heat the living area to sauna-like conditions. Her laptop had fifty percent battery remaining. Sandra saved and shut down her computer. She grabbed her notebook and pen. Perhaps she could get a few more minutes of work time before the storm hit full blast. She walked out onto her small porch.

The deck was more comfortable, but only by a tiny measure. Pages under her hands ruffled in the breeze. She feared she'd have to start from scratch. *All my years of sacrifice will be dead, like my plants.* She crinkled a page into a ball. The heavy air made her as restless as the thin sheets of parchment under her hand. On the flip side, if she trashed her findings, she admitted Thom was right. He doubted her research from the beginning. *Stop thinking about Thom's opinions.* She tossed the pen on top of the journal and gazed out into the yard.

This heat is sautéing my brain. A quick call to Paris would determine if she had functioning electricity and blessed air conditioning. She could drive over and hang out with her and Sean for a few hours, and take her mind off the past.

Will Raz be there?

A different heat consumed Sandra. In stolen moments, the simmer between her and Raz had sparked erotic caresses. Kisses labeled chaste by an observer fueled her hunger for something more. She experienced lust at the first stroke of his lips against hers. Forcing herself to ignore it was impossible.

Another breeze disturbed the calm, this one cooler. Raz's touch created an inferno on her skin only his mouth cooled. Sandra fantasized about him standing in front of her without a shirt. His muscles were slick with sweat. She couldn't stop the images of glistening pectorals and a tight abdomen that rippled with each movement. The thin cotton of her T-shirt clung to her chest and stomach. A trickle of perspiration raced between her breasts, and she wanted Raz's mouth there.

She tortured herself with these daydreams. The wind tore through the clearing. Leaves and dust chased each other in wild pursuit around the yard. The vortex thrilled her. Nature's building turmoil mirrored her internal war. The breeze lifted her hair off her neck, and she wished Raz's hands had done it. Wished the currents flowing over her body were his breath. Cool drops of rain splashed her face. Thunder purred in the distance. Without leaving her chair, she reached over and slipped her precious notes inside the sliding glass door before they blew away.

Cold and hot air surrounded her. The pressing whirlwind created by Mother Nature titillated her body. The approaching danger provided an anticipated release of her repressed desire. Rain drops cooled her overheated flesh. She stepped into the yard, arms spread. Her head fell back. She opened her mouth and caught a few droplets on her tongue. Lightning might strike her. An updraft could sweep her off the ground. At this moment, she welcomed the threats. Strength infused her body. Rainfall drove into the ground.

Sandra looked out into the yard. The deluge played tricks on her. No. She shook her head, and the rain wetted her hair. Strands clung to her face.

Raz stood beside the willow tree.

Her heart skipped several beats then quickened. *Is he an apparition? Wishes don't come true, but he's here. He's real.*

Branches enfolded him. Their spindly forms groped his body as the air picked up with a vengeance. Rivers of rain hastened over his bare chest. She gasped and blinked in rapid succession. *What magic have I created with my fantasies?* His heavy breathing denoted how alive and substantial he was. *He's solid flesh. Not my imagination.* Lightning flashed and illuminated his sculpted muscles. *He's magnificent.* His body never faded. She became drunk on the sight of him.

As a woman of science, her hypothesis must be tested. Compelled forward by her need to verify his presence, she took one step and another, releasing the anticipation.

They both ran, but an unnamed force stopped them before they embraced.

"What are you doing here?" Sandra shouted the words, but the wind snatched them from her mouth in an instant. The rain saturated her clothes.

Raz opened his lips, but no words came out. His gaze devoured her feverish body then came back up to her face.

Her every nerve ending was on fire. "Am I dreaming?"

Raz smiled, brilliant and dazzling.

She was in a fabrication created from her overactive hormones. *How can he be real?*

The rising temper of the storm blared.

Raz leaned close. His breath hit her neck, just as she'd imagined him doing a few minutes ago. She trembled.

"I couldn't stay away any longer." He stepped closer and ran the back of his fingers along her cheek then her mouth.

Her greedy body bowed toward him.

His voice was a flat growl in her ear. "You needed me. Didn't you?"

Raz's whispered words echoed the desire inside her soul. *Oh, God. Yes. I need you. I want you.* The wind thrashed her hair and stung her face. She didn't register the pain, only the heat of his touch, which she craved again and again. "I'm scared about what I feel for you. Paris—"

Raz shut her up with a quick press of his mouth on hers.

Sandra fell apart.

"I'm not here for Paris. I'm here for you." He cupped her face, his hands marked her as his. "I want you." His fingers tangled in her hair.

Sandra wrapped her arms around him. Her hands were everywhere—his chest, his back, his ass, all of him. She couldn't get enough. "You feel so good," she whispered.

Raz pulled off her shirt and spread his fingers over her breasts. The rain plastered the material of her bra over her nipples. He nipped a tender peak through the fabric. Shots of electricity glanced off the tips, and hot lava flowed into her lower body. The flashes of light, the rumbling and crashes coincided with each caress and staccato heartbeat. They fell onto the grass and gave in to the desire that chased them for weeks. The rain peppered their bodies as they shed their remaining clothing.

Then Raz was inside her, and she fractured in half at the intense pleasure. He stopped and starred into her eyes. He moved his hips. She wrapped her arms and legs around him afraid he would stop and leave her at any moment. The momentum built, and she relished every sensation. Flashes of lightning flared in the sky, and thunder crashed as they both reached climax.

"Sandra?" a masculine voice asked.

The dream was torn away, but her body shimmered and pulsed with the memory like their past interlude had occurred seconds ago. The relaxing aftermath rippled like waves through her mind, but the blackness of consciousness returned along with panic. Her eyelids were weighted bricks. Sandra labored to open them. A child's sobs pulled her to the surface, and she struggled through the chasm to wakefulness.

"Sa-an-dra," Sean blubbered. "I d-didn't mean it. I w-wa-wanted him to leave."

"Don't worry, buddy." The voice was distinctly male but didn't belong to Raz. "I have something for her to eat."

Sandra blinked and brought the emptiness of the waiting room into focus.

Sean petted her hand, and fat tears rolled down his cheeks.

Leon's face came into view. The diamond stud in his ear twinkled. His massive grin stretched from ear-to-ear. "There she comes." He rubbed a cool cloth on her face and neck. "Welcome back."

"Sandra, you fainted." A hiccup popped out of Sean's mouth. He bit his bottom lip and sniffled.

Sandra lay on her back, legs bent at a ninety-degree angle, and her feet were propped on the chair. Raz's jacket covered her. She lifted her head.

"Easy."

Leon's hand weighed her shoulder and prevented her from sitting up.

"I put you on the floor for a reason."

She pulled her legs one by one from the chair and sat up with his help. Her uneasiness around Leon came back with a vengeance. "I've had little to eat today. I'm so embarrassed. There's been too much … the ambulance … Paris."

Leon scoffed. "People faint on me all the time." He laughed at his own joke. "Good thing I was here. If you hit your head, you'd be in a hospital bed." He rubbed her back.

Sandra's fear faded but never disappeared.

He'd picked the right profession with his uncanny ability to put people at ease. "Sean is good at taking care of you." Leon smiled again. "He told me you were hungry. He was brave enough to stay here with you while I grabbed a sandwich."

Sean mirrored Leon's grin, proud of his courage. Although, it didn't mask his swollen eyes.

Sandra wound her fingers with his and squeezed. "I'm sorry I scared you." She'd find Raz and Paris and get the hell out of here.

Leon plopped a deli sandwich in her lap.

Her stomach flipped at the same time it growled. Loudly.

Sean giggled.

Leon held a paper cup in front of her. Steam floated above the rim. "It's from the dispenser. Sean assured me you'd like it."

She sipped the hot liquid and stifled a grimace at the taste of vanilla-flavored coffee. She hated it. Flavored coffee reminded her too much of Thom. She preferred plain cream and sugar, but she sipped again. At least the semisweet flavor and caffeine brought her clarity.

"It's stressful when a loved one is in the hospital, but you shouldn't neglect yourself. You need to take care of this little guy." Leon tousled Sean's hair.

Sean tensed his shoulders.

Sandra couldn't shake her distrust of Leon, either. *How do I get rid of him?* "Thanks for the meal."

"Don't mention it. We had an extra box from our lunch run. I can find an empty room so you can sleep."

Shaking her head, she pointed at the beverage and sandwich. "This will change my perspective. I don't want to go far in case Paris needs me."

Leon rubbed his forehead and squeezed his eyes shut.

She frowned. "Are you okay?"

"A minor headache. Nothing to worry about."

"Headaches are going around."

Leon shook his head. "Nah. They're typical for me. When I grabbed the sandwich, I looked in on Paris. She's doing good. The doc will stop by her room soon." He consulted the wall clock. "Duty calls, but I'll keep you updated. I'll check on you in a few."

Sandra flipped her bangs out of her eyes and shook her head. She smiled. "I'm fine." Why hadn't he told her Paris's room number?

Leon squeezed her shoulder. He walked to the exit.

Sandra spotted an intricate tattoo peeking from under Leon's scrub shirt. She bit into the triangle of turkey on rye. The swirling design surrounded his bicep and reminded her of the grasping arms that'd reached toward her before she passed out.

Sandra had to get out of here, but her need for answers was even stronger. Will the doctor help Paris? Will the doctor help Sandra? Why did she experience such conflicting emotions around Leon, who was a stranger? She kicked herself for telling him details about Paris's illness. *Why wouldn't I tell him? He's a nurse. He's here to help us.*

Sandra swallowed another bite of her sandwich. It tasted like dry paste. The nourishment was a necessary evil. Energy filled her cells and cleared her foggy brain. A spurt of cold air hit her neck, and a shudder ran through her upper body. She pulled on Raz's jacket. His scent enfolded her in a cocoon of remembered passion. *Focus on the here and now. The past is over.*

Sean never left her side. She wiped his nose with a napkin and handed him the second sandwich triangle. They both ate in silence. Although, something in the back of her mind bugged her. "Sean, you know you didn't hurt me, don't you? People can faint when they don't eat enough."

He stopped chewing. A pair of brown eyes, identical to Paris's, stared at her with such maturity and fear, she knew they couldn't stay here.

"I wanted the man to leave us alone."

"Leon?"

Sean nodded and picked at what remained of his sandwich.

"He's here to help us," Sandra said.

"He's … different. I wanted him to go away."

Sandra wrapped the paper around the food and placed it on the chair in front of her. She pulled him tight into her arms. A burst of static jolted her arm, and she jerked back. She reached for Sean a second time. The static didn't zap her. "We need Leon close so we know when to go see Mommy."

His brown eyes held a faint glow and narrowed into slits.

The heat and vibration Sandra experienced at the gas station came back.

Sean crawled up on his knees and cupped her face in his hands.

His freaky eyes hypnotized her.

"He's gonna hurt us."

The same conclusion had crossed Sandra's mind, as well. What Sandra didn't understand was why Sean's declaration of the same scared the crap out of her.

Chapter Thirteen

ABOVE RAZ'S HEAD, the *No Cellular Use Permitted* neon sign flashed off and on in fits. From this vantage point, all entrances and exits into the medical wing were visible. He lounged against the wall and again dialed the Omega contact number. The absence of Chaser activity had him on edge. With a shrewd eye, he observed the nurses as they performed their nightly tasks. The phone rang in his ear. No answer. Raz hung up. The smell of cleaner and sickness mingled together. Two nurses entered a room at the end of the hall.

What was Sandra's involvement in M83? Cameron had to be after her research. Although, such reasoning made little sense. M83 never cared about human studies or drugs. They had different biochemistry. An orderly rolled a laundry cart past him. Raz knew jack squat about Sandra's research. Guessing about a connection between Sixxers and humans wasted precious energy. Had Cameron been behind this current predicament, or were they here because of the obvious 911 calls from the gas station? Chasers didn't appear to be at Center Medical, which was too weird. A M83 unit wouldn't be stationed here unless the threat against Sixxers was large.

Omega must have deployed observers on them. Hell, Raz wouldn't have let his group leave HUP if he were in charge. M83 wouldn't risk Sixxer exposure to humans. Unless Cameron wasn't to be trusted. Raz sighed. Unlikely, considering both empaths in his circle identified Cameron as safe. Raz faced the truth. HUP or Omega Headquarters guaranteed their safety. His earlier argument with the nurse had Paris staying in the hospital for a few days. Raz agreed only to get the guy off his back. Raz refused to wait any longer. Paris was stable. Any sign of Chaser activity was absent. Time to leave.

His footsteps clipped on the tile floor as he made his way to the lounge. White walls stretched before him. Darkness nipped at his heels. The cell phone tucked into his back pocket accentuated his separation from the Corp. Every decision was done in complete blindness. For years, he avoided places like this for that very reason. Combing his fingers through his hair, he walked closer to the waiting room. Inside the interior window, Raz spotted Sean kneeling beside Sandra.

A violent Nexus energy wave smacked into Raz. His body shuddered in pain, and the Nexus expanded his muscles for a fight.

A nurse gasped to his right.

After a moment, Raz regained his bearings. The wave came from Sean. He emitted enough energy to be detected on a NEU device. Sean's Sixxer power was the same as Raz's, Transor. Raz didn't dare enter the lounge, or Sandra was dead. They were all dead. He ducked into an empty patient room and pounded his hands on the edge of a newly-made bed.

If Sean generated this small burst of Nexus energy without harming Sandra, he could receive a Nexus communication from Raz. He sent a tentative mental link to Sean. They weren't always possible, but it was worth a shot. If Raz could control Sean's Nexus flare, he could get into the waiting room. A Transor stopping another Transor. The possibility blew his mind.

A voice in the hall stopped Raz's connection attempt.

"The Sixxer is now stable."

Raz tensed. His senses went into overdrive. Finally, Chaser contact. He'd rather fight the enemy he could see instead of hiding from the enemy he couldn't. He flexed his biceps as the Nexus nourished the blood in his veins. Years of training kicked in. He controlled his energy with precision.

"What's going on?" a second man asked.

Raz moved to the shadow behind the open doorway and peered out the small gap between the wall and door. One Transor and two Chasers. Good odds.

The two men faced away from Raz. One wore scrubs, and the other a lab coat. Despite not seeing their faces, familiarity prickled

Raz's neck. He stared at the man in scrubs. He'd never seen the man before, but the sense of knowing him wouldn't leave Raz.

The man consulted a patient chart. "Preliminary results suggested a Zenith build is unlikely. Our subject *is* Sixxer. Therefore, she has natural immunity to the virus."

Raz's suspicion of deliberate infection was now confirmed. They'd been trying to guess if Paris was a natural Sixxer or a Chaser-made Sixxer. A Zenith's false Nexus bonds made their energy highly unstable, but the humans were desperate to gain Nexus energy for themselves without understanding the deep biological dependencies required.

"You haven't determined what made the Sixxer stabilize. The drugs reacted abnormally, especially Z-211," the man with the chart continued. "

"Her symptoms *are* from the Xnix-624 virus," the man in the lab coat said.

The scrubs man shook his head. "Xnix-624 only will infect a Zenith. Something else is wrong with her."

Was that true? Maybe the virus affected both Sixxers and Zeniths? He and Sean could be ticking time bombs, as well. Cameron had neglected to tell Raz a team of Sixxer specialists used Center Medical for an infection facility. Danger had been their neighbor for a year. Never again would Raz pretend his circle was safe.

Scrubs pulled a phone out of his pocket and glided his finger across the screen. After several swipes, he tapped the device. "You reported in April that Xnix-624 was bogus. Test trials were negative. All Sixxers had no symptoms or illness." He held up the phone to the other man's face. "It makes sense. The original intent of the virus was to fight plant diseases. I told you not to waste your time."

Plant diseases? That's what Sandra studies. Chasers wanted to eradicate them through infection. Raz glued the pieces together. Omega's mission was to find out how this virus worked on Sixxers. To Raz's knowledge, Paris had been the only Sixxer who had succumbed to human disease. Plant viruses were their weakness. The idea was insane.

"Then it has to be the Z-211 drug causing her symptoms. She's weakening like a Sixxer should," Lab coat said.

"You injected her with Z-211 two months ago. The treatment wouldn't have taken so long to affect her. The drug lasts for a small window, days, if not hours."

"Something is off." Lab coat rubbed the back of his neck.

Raz ached to grab it and squeeze the life out of him.

"I injected her with the treatment, not the drug alone," Lab coat continued.

Cameron hadn't come forth with this Chaser activity. He wouldn't have let them leave HUP if there had been a threat of infection. Sixxers cared for their own. Omega must have suspicions on what these two men were doing. Raz couldn't leave this intel behind. The man in front of him had access to Paris two months ago, and that realization sent a shot of pure hatred through Raz. He could prevent more Sixxers from getting sick.

Lab coat shook his head. "Her reactions must be from the drug and virus combination I created in the ADZ virus treatment. The two administered together might've delayed the symptoms." Lab coat pushed away the other man's phone. "The virus and drug are enhancing one another."

Scrubs shook his head. "She's getting weaker."

"Exactly. The Xnix-624 virus is supposed to disrupt Nexus bonding," Lab coat continued. "The Z-211 drug enhances a Zenith's Nexus energy, and she's not Zenith, that's why she's declining. Z-211 must have awakened Xnix-624 in her Sixxer body. They are both working beautifully. Turn on the NEU. We can discover the other circle members. If we give up, then General Taft will come here. We won't get any credit. I've worked too hard for this, and so have you."

The staccato beat of the scrub man's phone alert broke through the conversation. "Her lab work came through. I have to go. Don't do anything stupid."

Lab coat didn't speak. Which one led the experiments, and where had they experimented on unwilling Sixxers? He'd kill the human responsible for hurting his people. Hell. He'd kill them both and do the world a favor.

The two men walked down the hall and rounded the corner.

Raz raced back to Paris's room. The urge to turn around and go after the men was unbearable, but he pushed forward. Above anything else, he had to protect Paris and Sean. The men hadn't activated the NEU, yet. They'd have registered the recent signature Raz witnessed from Sean. With all the residual Nexus flux floating around the hospital, Sean and Raz were sitting ducks. How much time did he have? Raz entered the room and closed the door behind him.

Paris opened her eyes and waved him closer. "Come here."

"We're going back to HUP. The university is the safest place for the circle and Sandra." Raz clasped her hand. A glint of light surged between them. Then the visible animation of the Nexus fizzled and died. Her bonds were breaking. The virus did infect Sixxers.

Paris pulled away as best she could in her weakened state.

What twisted, messed-up experiments were they facing? Raz urged her to sit up. "Sean and Sandra are in the waiting room. We have to hurry."

Paris shook her head. Glassy eyes and feverish roses brightened her face. "You have pure energy flowing from your skin. I need it." She clawed his hands. "Render with me."

Five seconds ago Raz wouldn't have hesitated, but after overhearing the conversation in the hallway, the option had been taken from them. "We can't do it here. It's too risky," he whispered in her ear. "I won't put all of us in danger. Chasers know who you are. They have a NEU here, and they'll use it."

Paris sunk back into the bleached pillow. Her skin faded into the sheets, and they swallowed her alive. "There isn't much time, Raz." The freckles across her nose were prominent against her sallow flesh. Her voice was quiet and determined. "You have to render with me."

"The transfer at HUP failed. The hospital can't experience a black out. Chasers are using a NEU as a bull's-eye on all of us." He'd have to help Paris some other way.

"I've been open." Paris stared.

Her eyes burned into his flesh.

She caught his gaze and held it. "Whatever has infected me is destroying the bonds between us. I have no control."

They might be outnumbered, but once a NEU discovered three Nexus signatures— two containing the strength of a Transor—all exits would be closed. A render would make that happen all the sooner.

"Sean's elevation has arrived."

Paris gasped.

Raz helped her into a sitting position.

Paris gritted her teeth. She swung her legs over the side of the bed. "Whatever's happening won't make it easy for him. Render with me now. It'll increase your own power and help Sean. He's too young. He can't control excess energy." She cleared her throat. "The poison they've given me is shaking my hold of the Nexus. I can't focus." Paris clasped his shirt. Her forehead fell onto his chest.

The two of them weren't getting out of here alive.

Raz lifted her head. He wouldn't keep lies between them. "I was going to tell you about Sandra."

"I already know." Paris glanced at him under her lashes.

Torment clouded her eyes. "I jeopardized our lives. She got too close." Raz gently pushed her back against the pillows then paced in front of the window. He rubbed the back of his neck. Shame heated and cooled his skin simultaneously.

"I used to kid myself you might fall in love with me after all these years. Once you met Sandra ..."

Raz understood the bonds between them couldn't be broken, but they couldn't force love or forgiveness. Outside the window, the night sky was fuzzy from the city lights. A faint hint of light grew along the horizon. Dawn was approaching fast. They'd been here long enough. He grasped the sill.

"I'm green with jealousy you can love a human and not me," Paris hissed.

"I don't love her—"

"You can't lie to me."

Raz punched the glass. His knuckles bled, and his hand went numb. A small crack spread in the pane from where his hand hit to the top of the frame. "Loving her isn't in the cards for me." He had to get out of there before his entire life fractured. "Our circle and Sean are the most important things to me. It's ingrained into my DNA. There aren't any choices. Especially ones dealing with humans. Now the threat of Chasers is staring us in the face. Sandra will remain in her own world. We move forward in ours." *I can't leave her behind.*

Paris rubbed her temples.

Her illness called to his protective instincts. Yet, the distrust he always had around her threw up his guard.

"We don't have time to discuss the past," Paris said. "There's more to Sandra than either of us can imagine. You've told me it is impossible to render a circle with a human, but something is different with her."

Raz grunted.

"Let me finish. Her energy is wrong. You and Sean have sensed it. She's already bonding to you. Maybe to Sean, too. I saw the Nexus light in her eyes several times."

"The Nexus won't take her."

"She can catch the same illness I have if it does."

No. Sandra isn't getting sick. Yet, the evidence stacked up—the headaches, nosebleeds and dizziness. She worked with the viruses the men were talking about. She would've shown symptoms long before Paris had. "You know the rules. Humans—"

"To hell with the rules, Raz! The rules have been broken. A render will save her."

"Save her from what?"

"Someone infected me on purpose. The drugs they give me are supposed to keep me weak." Paris's bottom lip trembled. "I've been participating at the university as a test subject for psychic research. Before you lecture me or get upset, my powers were already weakening. I went to help Sandra, but they must've figured out I was a Sixxer."

"Help her do what? God damn it! Un-fucking-believable." His power touched the window again. Several fissures spread from the center. "Why am I worried about getting you to safety? You go looking for trouble in our backyard! They more than suspected. They had you pegged and targeted immediately. What have you done?" He smacked her water bottle off the tray table.

"I'm sorry! Sandra is my friend, and I'd never risk her life. One of her colleagues was bothering her and I just wanted to get him off her back. I never thought the study would be real or headed-up by a Chaser."

"You've risked everything, and we're losing. Your psychic game gave *a Chaser* ample opportunity to dose you with a virus."

Paris nodded. She swallowed back what could've been a sob. "Everyone is changing, Raz. You don't believe me, but I have no proof to back them up. My evidence consists of gut feelings. My empathic power is weak, and I can't filter the emotions. We can't stop what's coming. We have to take this chance to protect both of them. If Sean is emanating power and energy in Sandra's presence, then the Nexus has already accepted her."

"It's not possible." Raz pushed aside the hospital tray, ready to shake sense into her ever-loving mind. He crouched beside the bed. Her eyes had sunk into her face, and the hollows of her cheeks were a light shade of purple. The virus sucked the life out of her.

Paris raised her hand off the bed. She hissed in a breath and tensed in pain. The small amount of Nexus light remaining in her body flared in her eyes. "Help me." She doubled over. Her face twisted in agony.

If she suffered an attack, the hospital staff would invade her room and they'd be trapped. He found his center, the place where his Transor powers rested. Like always, Paris gave him no choices. He'd render with Paris by herself and give Sandra and Sean a chance to run.

Heat built between their hands, signaling their circle would swirl and connect them in a matter of seconds. The longer it took, the more nervous Raz became. Circular energy ceased increasing. The Chasers were winning.

"It's not working." Paris rolled onto her left side, and the heat between their hands dissipated. Her shallow breathing quickened. "I'm dying." She squeezed his fingers in a pathetic display of weakness.

"No." Chasers had found a way to destroy them from the inside.

"You must close our circle. Leave me behind. If you don't, the NEU will find you."

"I'm not leaving anyone here."

"You have to. Our son is your key to freedom and I'm dead weight," Paris whispered.

CHAPTER FOURTEEN

RAZ'S BICEPS FLEXED. A muscle jumped under his eye. No one was getting left behind. He eased open the door and stepped into the hall. A few nurses ambled in and out of the other rooms on their night shift rounds. Paris needed enough energy to get the hell out of here. Raz would render with her and Sean. He'd keep out Sandra.

Sandra hadn't become a Sixxer within a day, and Paris was delirious to think the Nexus had accepted a human. Raz approached the waiting room with careful steps. He stopped outside the door. The Nexus flare wasn't present anymore.

Thankful Sean had released his energy, Raz turned the doorknob, and the latch clicked.

Sandra's head snapped up. She jumped to her feet and flung her arms around his neck.

His forearm encircled her waist, and he planted a possessive kiss on her mouth. He tasted the vanilla coffee on her lips. Her body pressed against his. A flush warmed him, and arousal pulsed low in his body. This brief contact soothed his raw nerves, even though it sensitized him. Her lips lingered on his mouth. The heat of her encouraged the animal instinct inside him. A flare of pure Nexus energy crackled between them.

Sean tugged his arm. "Your lips are lighted."

Raz broke away from Sandra.

She gazed into his eyes, and her brows drew together.

Every muscle in his body tensed, and his aura quickened in preparation for a render. He wanted it to be impossible, despite his body's response. Sandra had bonded with the Nexus. Paris had been right.

"How bad is Paris? Can we see her?"

Sandra brought him back to reality. Raz closed the door. He motioned Sean closer. "We're leaving, ASAP. They've given Paris drugs, which means they know we're S—" *I'm mindless.* Running his hand over his mouth, he let out a ragged breath. He almost blurted their identity.

Sean's eyes rounded and his mouth dropped.

Raz shook his head. "The medication is making Paris weak."

Sandra tapped her foot. "Then we stay until she's well. Have you heard from her doctor?"

"Chasers are here." Raz caught her shoulders. "We're going back to HUP."

The blood drained from her face. Sandra stroked her fingers along his jaw, and her eyes followed her movements.

Raz didn't think she realized her actions. The warmth of her fingers penetrated his skin. They'd touched each other more in the past twenty-four hours than they had in weeks. After all that had happened in the last few hours, Raz couldn't stop her. He didn't want to stop her. Her gaze darted over his face. Was she searching for the truth? Every caress brought him back to that day in the rain. The day they stopped denying the passion between them. Desire painted her face and left ribbons of reddish-pink across her cheeks.

"What do we do?" She asked.

Raz forced himself to focus on their situation, and not the woman in his arms. "Has anyone talked to you?"

"A nurse came in earlier. Leon."

The same nurse Raz had spoken to fifteen minutes earlier. Raz didn't trust Leon. Until Cameron, or an M83 official, cleared the guy, he was the enemy. "Don't talk to him again."

Sandra bristled and her brows scrunched. "He said Paris was stable." Her eyes widened. "Is he a Chaser?"

"I don't like him." Sean tugged on Raz's arm. When he made little progress, he walked over to the glass door and peered out. "Let's get Mommy."

"Leon took care of us. He fed me." Sandra continued.

Fed her? An energy transfer? Raz tightened his grip on her waist.

His blood surged in his veins as his adrenaline spiked.

Sandra pushed him away. "It was a turkey on rye sandwich."

Raz let out a sigh of relief. She was talking about food and not Nexus energy. He'd overreacted and the stress he was under made him irrational. The spikes of jealousy were becoming difficult to curb. He feared his edginess would tumble him over a precipice. *Focus on getting out of here.* "I'll be the only one taking care of you and Sean."

Raz picked up Sean. His son was growing so big, soon Raz wouldn't be able to carry him anymore. Sean would have to learn how to run, how to live on his own, in case they were ever separated. *Not today.*

Sean's fingers touched Raz's mouth. "I saw the light. It was the Nexus. When you kissed Sandra," he whispered.

Raz ruffled Sean's hair. How could he explain the bonding to Sean when he didn't' understand it himself? "I need both of you in Paris's room ASAP. I'll follow close behind. I might have to redirect anyone who questions us."

Sean bobbed his head up and down.

Sandra narrowed her eyes and turned her lips inward.

Raz suspected she wanted to pummel him with questions. At least she trusted him. Raz cupped her nape and pulled her close for another quick kiss. "Stay alert to anyone who stops you or comes into the room before I get there."

Sean leaned close. "I'm scared, Daddy."

"Don't worry. I'll be there lickety-split." Raz placed a raspberry on Sean's neck, and the boy giggled. The laughter covered Sean's fear, as was Raz's intent. He brushed Sean's hair out of his eyes.

Sandra rushed around the room, gathered their belongings and Sean's teddy bear. The worn stuffed animal had seen better days.

He leaned down and stared into Sean's eyes. "Once I'm in the room, we'll be complete."

Sean's eyes widened. His head moved from Sandra then back to Raz. "The spark?"

"Mommy needs us. We have to keep out Sandra. I'm counting on you, buddy."

Sean swallowed.

Raz hated putting so much responsibility on a six-year-old.

"I don't want to hurt her," Sean whispered. Tears welled in his eyes.

"You won't. Just focus on Mommy." Raz shifted Sean to his other hip and held open the door.

Sandra fidgeted with her purse. Her gaze darted back and forth between him and Sean. "You're not thinking of taking Paris out of here, are you?"

"We don't have a choice. If someone comes in, make sure they don't linger. I'll be right behind you." He stood Sean on his feet. From the way Sean clung to Sandra, he wouldn't be able to separate them in the future.

Sandra cleared her throat. "There has to be another way."

"Maybe before we stopped at HUP."

Sandra straightened her shoulders. "This isn't my fault—"

"This is just how the situation is." Raz kissed her again. "We move forward now. Time is our enemy. She's in room 344."

Sandra swallowed.

Either her tears or words, Raz guessed. Her worried eyes drilled into him.

Sandra pulled back her shoulders and marched out the door. She walked down the hall, holding Sean's hand in hers.

Raz waited a few seconds for them to get past the nurses' desk. He followed then slowed when a man in scrubs marched up the opposite hall and stood behind the counter. He searched a computer system. It wasn't Leon, but the itch of recognition tingled everywhere. Raz had the same sensation while eavesdropping on the Chasers earlier.

The man raised his head. "May I help you?"

Why couldn't he have let me go by? "Do you know where I can find Leon?"

"He should be around here somewhere."

Raz recognized the man's voice from the overheard conversation. Chaser! What bothered him was the familiar face. Raz didn't remember meeting him, but the sensation was a nagging tug in his mind. "Are you a doctor?"

"Yes."

Raz pointed a thumb over his shoulder. "The people in the

waiting room are expecting news, I think. Are you the messenger?"

The man leaned over the countertop to get an unobstructed view of the closed lounge door. He went back to the computer monitor and nodded. "I was actually on my way there now." He cocked his head.

The air of anticipation made it clear this new information was intriguing to him. He knew Paris was a Sixxer. Therefore, anyone associated with Paris, or concerned about her welfare, had the potential of being a part of her circle. He'd want to immediately find out who was in the waiting room.

His gaze surveyed Raz. "Why did you need Leon?"

Raz suppressed the urge to squirm. "We're old friends. I'll check back later." He tapped the countertop and left. Was he successful in misleading the man? He passed room 344 so the Chaser wouldn't see him enter. He could've screwed his plan all to hell if Leon and the doctor were acquainted.

The prickly crawlers along Raz's neck was the Chaser's gaze. Suspicion now surrounded Raz, and time ticked by faster each second Raz was separated from his circle. He entered a family restroom and locked the door behind him. A large mirror encompassed the entire wall above the single sink basin. How in the hell was he going to get back to Paris's room? Were the Chaser and Leon working together? The potential of three Chaser eyes on them threatened. After hours of silence, they kept accumulating.

Having had no communication with M83 for years, Raz accepted certain facts, such as not knowing hot zones, or key Chasers that had moved up in rank. Yet, the actions and lack of activity between the two Chasers at the hospital confused him. They'd identified Paris as a Sixxer. Why weren't they looking for her circle? Why drag out the capture?

Raz placed his arms on the edge of the basin and leaned toward the mirror. He focused on his eyes and brought his Nexus energy to the surface of his mind for the first time in six years. After fighting it for the past few hours, he gathered his concentration and created the communication link. His blue eyes appeared normal in the mirror, but then the Nexus energy illuminated the outer ring of his pupil. It filled with white light. The Nexus pulsed in his veins and made them more prominent against his forearms and neck.

There. Raz sensed Sean's presence. In less than a minute, Sean connected to their Nexus ring. The outer circle of Raz's iris became encased in the white light. His heart pounded, and the bottom of his stomach dropped. Sean bridged the Nexus artery without hesitation. His power was true, and definitely that of a Transor.

"*Daddy?*" Sean asked through the Nexus connection. His voice rang in Raz's mind.

"*I'm here, kiddo. Are you and Sandra okay? How's Mommy?*"

"*Yeah, we're all right. Sandra is scared. Mommy is sleeping. The light keeps popping into her eyes. Will Mommy wake up soon?*"

Paris was tapped out of power.

"*Don't let your energy form a shield. It'd hurt Sandra.*"

"*Oooookaay. I used to talk to Mommy like this, and now I can't.*"

Fear gripped Raz at the extent of Sean's power. Sean could communicate through the Nexus without a render. He needed Sixxer elevational training. An individual had to have the mental maturity to understand the Nexus. Adults had trouble. The Sixxer power which emerged, signifying elevation, typically occurred in their twenties. How would Sean survive it?

"*I'll be there soon. Then we'll complete a circle. You won't have to talk at all. We'll send our thoughts to each other.*"

"*Sandra, too?*"

"*No, bud. You must pay attention. If you think we're hurting her, you must break free, okay?*"

"*I can do it.*"

"*I'll be there soon.*" Raz pulled out of his trance and stared in the mirror. The light from his eyes faded. He unlocked the door. The hall was quiet, too quiet. Where was Leon? More importantly, where was Raz's identified Chaser? Hell would break open after General Taft was notified of a circle. Raz padded down the hall to the third door, room 344. He entered Paris's room.

An aura near the bed reached out and struck him. A glow flashed under Paris's lids, a Sixxer pain reflex, then it faded. She hadn't the strength for any aura emissions. The temperature of the room suggested the Nexus united the circle, but Paris didn't have the strength for that, either. Sean didn't have the knowledge.

The glow graduated around Sandra in soft waves of gold light. The aura came from her. Raz didn't understand how it was possible for the Nexus to want her or accept her energy without harm. Raz had to trust Paris.

The render must include all of us.

Chapter Fifteen

SANDRA GRAVITATED TOWARD the blue glow of the bedside computer. The light of the monitor broke up the hidden shadows of the sterile room.

Paris lay motionless on the small hospital bed. She wouldn't survive a move.

The alternative … fear clawed at Sandra's skin. Was Paris doomed to death no matter what decision they made? Another flare of light shimmered under Paris's lashes. Sandra directed her attention from the monitor to Paris's face. Sandra stared and waited for the next flash of light. Nothing happened. Weariness filled her, and she rubbed her tired eyelids.

This vision, like the one in the lounge, destroyed any sense of reality Sandra had. Her impaired judgment left her lost and confused. She patted her cheek, bringing alertness to her mind. When they got back to HUP, she'd have to sleep for a few hours. She only needed to concentrate long enough to find Paris's treatment. The codes on the electronic chart flashed on the computer screen. Sandra scrolled though the list of prescribed medications—so many unfamiliar names.

Cam will have them at HUP. Her finger paused on the mouse.

Sandra never questioned Cameron. Her trust in him was absolute. She'd ignored his access to drugs, supplies and the other projects he couldn't talk about. No one at HUP had the same level of autonomy and freedom in the labs. Sandra had rationalized Cameron's every action with a lie of her own choosing. Until now, she'd never thought Cameron's actions strange.

Cameron's resources would help Paris. She trusted him. She had to.

Raz stood beside the bed.

Paris moaned.

Sean ran over and tugged on Raz's shirt.

He squatted beside Sean, their heads bowed together. Another vision appeared. An aura of mist cocooned them.

She was tired and hungry. Focus on something else. Sandra zeroed in on Raz's flat abs and lean torso. A distraction her mind readily accepted. His kiss in the waiting room had electrified her. She ached for his touch. Her desire couldn't be ignored, but it must be. The form-fitting T-shirt hugged his muscular chest and arms. His disheveled hair made her fingers yearn to tame it. A fire burned inside her, despite the low temperature of the room. Sandra's fingers twitched, longing to touch him.

Paris's hand grazed Sandra's side. "It's good he brought you."

She snapped Sandra out of her haze of lust. "How are you?" Sandra clicked through the chart. She crossed her fingers. She'd find the dosages. "I'll text your meds to Cam."

"Cameron isn't answering his phone," Raz said.

Paris tugged on the edge of Sandra's shirt, but her hand flopped on the bed after one pull. "Don't want the medicine. Poison."

Paris was talking nonsense. If she didn't get treatment, then she'd be worse off than she already was. How could Raz think of moving her in this condition?

Sandra placed her hand on Paris's forehead. Her fingers burned from the contact. "No offense, but you look like dog crap, and that's putting a positive spin on your condition."

Paris laughed then winced as she shifted on the bed.

Sandra squeezed her hand. "You need the medicine."

Paris gasped for breath. Her skin turned a grayish-blue.

Anxiety pumped through Sandra like a shot of espresso. Not another attack.

Sean clutched Sandra's hand.

Her jitters subsided. She pulled Sean close, thankful for the comfort he provided. They needed human contact, not charts. She tightened her fingers around Paris's hand and squeezed. A buzz vibrated along her arm, and Sean jerked back.

Paris opened her eyes. Another flare of light flickered in her brown irises.

The light is real!

Paris whimpered and thrashed on the bed sheets.

"What's wrong?" Raz rushed to Paris's side and seized her shoulders.

"You know what to do." Paris cleared her throat. "She's ready to connect."

"You said not to," Sean cried.

Paris waved her fingers. "Come closer to the bed, buddy. Let's get ready."

Sean's body trembled. "Mommy, I'm scared."

The room was freezing. Sandra plucked the extra blanket off the end of the bed and wrapped up Sean like a burrito. When would they leave this awful place?

"It'll be okay," Sandra said the lie automatically. She had misgivings about them getting out of here without incident. Then raw desperation to get closer, as close as possible, to Paris overwhelmed her. Her feet moved without her permission. An invisible hand snapped out and held her back. Were Paris's eyes *glowing*? The hallucinations were out of Sandra's control now. A green mist hovered above Paris's head. Terror pummeled Sandra's heart.

"Raz, do you see?" Paris asked.

Sandra panicked. Fanning her face did nothing to cool her embarrassment. Her head teetered from Paris to Raz. Did he see the crazy mist? She focused on everything except Paris—the tile floor, the crack in the window, the leather jacket tossed on the guest chair. Avoidance didn't change what was in front of her eyes.

Paris tugged at Raz's hands. Her weak attempts didn't move him. Worry lines creased his forehead. He moved closer to Paris's face. "What're you saying?"

Sandra released the breath she held. None of it was real.

"I saw, Mommy." Sean jumped up and down in his excitement. He pushed between Sandra and the bed, tripped on a cord and knocked the hospital tray askew. "It happened in the waiting room."

Sandra brushed her bangs out of her eyes. *Is he referring to the kiss, or the smoke when Leon helped me?*

"I saw it when Leon was there."

Sean perceived the mist, too? Her breaths heaved. *Did Sean just answer the question I asked in my head?*

"We should wait." Raz examined the call buttons and turned on the TV.

The blaring commercial made Sandra jump.

Raz lowered the volume but left it at a high level. "Sean's agitated. He's lost control several times today."

"Mommy, I did see it. We can be complete now. Can't we?" Sean smiled at Sandra. "It'll make Mommy better. You, too."

Sandra batted for the remote. "Does this have to be on?"

Raz held it away.

The loud volume irritated her and muddled her thoughts.

Raz wove the cord through the bed rail opposite her. His hard gaze flickered with silver flashes of light. "The sound will hide our conversation and movements." He rubbed the stubble on his chin and backed away from the bed.

"We have to hurry," Paris growled.

"We can't do it here. Sean, get her stuff from the closet. We'll help her get dressed."

Sandra didn't understand. "Can't do what? Nothing is more important than leaving, even though I don't want to take her out of here." The decision to leave had been made. They needed to follow through.

Sean raced over to the closet and pulled out a plastic bag of Paris's personal items. He gathered the edges of his blanket tight around his body.

Sandra helped him empty everything onto the bed.

Paris yanked the bed sheets to her chin. "Her eyes have changed, Raz. I've seen them hold the Nexus. There's no time to wait. It's now or never for me. I can't leave like this."

The loud ticking of the wall clock coincided with Sandra's heartbeat. Paris's declaration made the room too small, too cramped. The mist encased Paris in a cocoon of light. She fell onto the chair. The jacket in the seat slid onto the floor. She wished Raz's arms held her, but that couldn't happen. She had to ease this panic on her own.

Sandra focused on her breathing. *One. Two.*

"My father—"

"Paris, this isn't the place." Raz unlaced the shoes Sean tossed onto the bed and found a clean pair of socks from the hospital stash. "Wait until we're clear."

Paris waved her hand for Sandra to come closer.

She couldn't move. The stupid television wasn't helping her focus, either. Noise from the speakers crowded out Paris's words.

The newscast intro music paused. "My father was … is a scientist, Dr. Nazier," Paris said. "He did very bad things to me, experiments when I was a child. If he catches us, he'll experiment on Sean next."

The room swayed. Sandra held onto the arms of the recliner. The white-hot rage transformed her into someone she didn't know. What kind of sicko experimented on children? On his daughter? "He's not getting either of you."

Raz grasped Paris and shook her. "Stop talking. You've no idea who's listening."

"Doesn't matter anymore."

The surrounding walls closed in on Sandra, but she swallowed her panic. "We are wasting too much time. Let's get out of here."

Paris tried to sit up but fell back on the bed. "If he takes Sean—"

"If he takes you then finding Sean won't be difficult for him." Raz pulled the blankets back and helped a reluctant Paris sit on the edge of the bed. "You can't tell Sandra anything else. The more she knows, the worse it will be if she's caught. Sean, hand me your mother's clothes."

Sean hurried over with a shirt and pants. He plopped them on Paris's lap. "Here, Mommy. You need to wear these."

Sandra stood on wobbly legs. "I'll call Cam. He'll get us out."

"Sandra's instincts are right. Cameron and M83 can help us." Paris eased her pants up her legs under the hospital gown. Her movements were methodical, but she couldn't hide her moans of pain. "Dr. Nazier is here. I can feel him in my bones."

"Cameron's silent," Raz said. "But I've decided that we go back to HUP. It's the best choice."

Sean hesitated at the bedside. "Mommy," he whispered. "Let's go."

"Your senses are warped by the drugs," Raz continued. "You can't be sure Nazier is here. You're detecting Chasers. I know at least two, possibly three, are here." Raz put the socks and shoes on her feet then tied the laces.

Sandra grabbed her purse and the fallen jacket on the floor. She turned around. Sean's dark eyes glowed with silver and violet accents. Wisps of silvery-blue light reached out. She gasped. Everything in her hand landed with a dull thud on the tile. The hair on her arms stood.

Weird convulsions undulated through Sean's body with each move. He ran by the air conditioner.

Sandra noticed the large crack threading along the window pane. Every shake of Sean's body spread the crack into an intricate web. Sandra sank back into the chair. She focused on the smooth vinyl and cool circulating air. This wasn't happening. Her stomach muscles contracted, and her insides churned. Regaining her composure was a necessity. She pushed away her fear.

"The NEU will detect Sean. We don't have time to wait," Paris said.

"Sandra," Raz whispered.

Her head snapped up. Paris motioned her closer to the bed. Sandra pushed against the chair, but her legs were glued to the surface. The thump of Sean's feet on the tile competed with the jagged line on the heart monitor beside the bed.

"You know what we can do to give me strength. Then I won't be deadweight. Raz, help her." Paris's eyes fluttered closed, and a glimmer appeared under the lids.

Sandra stared at Raz. His blue eyes became a swirling mass of light. She sucked in a sharp breath. They reminded her of the waves of blue mist at the gas station. Her feet stuck to the floor.

Raz stepped toward her.

She shook her head and blinked several times. Sean's eyes returned to normal. Raz's did not.

Paris wouldn't walk out of here, she was too weak. If Raz carried her, then Chasers would stop them for sure. *What am I thinking? Ordinary hospital staff will stop them from taking a patient as sick as Paris.* Sandra's head hurt. Her eyes hurt.

"You have to do it," Paris murmured. Her gaze darted from Sean to Raz. "Can't you feel the connection?" She whispered, "The Nexus responded to them both in minutes after Sean walked into the room. If Chasers have turned on the NEU, we're vulnerable without a render."

"How? I never sensed Sandra."

"You don't listen."

"You didn't hear me, neither." Sean pulled the curtains closed. "Mommy says we have to. No one can take Sandra. No one." He clasped her hand. He tilted his head up and flashed a huge grin. "This will make you my second mom."

Sandra couldn't follow the conversation. Her neck prickled in mortification. "No, Sean. Paris, he's confused."

Sweat beaded on Paris's forehead. She continued her argument with Raz. "If you'd listened we'd still be at the house and not in this shit-hole."

"We'd be in a capturing facility if we stayed at your house," Raz grated out between clenched teeth. "The time isn't right."

A news anchor's voice interrupted. "This is a Late Night News, five-minute update. A young woman collapsed at a local gas station at around 8:00 pm local time. Authorities say she's in stable condition, but the local patrons are telling a different story. Be on the lookout for any suspicious activity."

They stared at the screen. Every beep and pulse from the monitors rebounded in the room. The camera narrowed in on a young man in his early twenties with an upper lip piercing and backwards hat covering short brown hair.

"So, what did you see tonight?" a feminine voice asked off-camera.

"It was creepy. I felt bad for the woman. I hope she's okay, but this guy came out of nowhere. He was yelling and screaming for everyone to get back. All the lights in the place started whacking out. I mean really going nuts."

The microphone went back the reporter. "You mean a power outage?"

The microphone switched back to the young man. "No. Like flicking on and off and shit. When I looked at this guy again, I saw this weird gas coming from him, and people started choking and stuff."

"Were you the only one who observed this gas?"

"Oh, no. There were a few others who saw it, too. I know because they were pointing. I would've called the police, but someone had already called 911 for the lady who passed out."

Sandra froze. The news report was a dream turned nightmare. She hadn't imagined the vapor floating around them at the mini-market, but no one else had noticed. This kid was lying.

The camera panned to the woman presenting the field report. Both she and the kid were in the frame. "Local patrons who frequent this establishment say nothing out of the ordinary happened. The woman collapsed, the man came over and the ambulance took them both to the hospital."

"The gas-stuff was real, man … er … I mean, lady." The young man wouldn't be silenced. "The police should've looked into it further."

The news reporter turned back toward him. "Do you think the gas caused the woman to collapse?"

"Something like that. They're pod people. Trying to take over our bodies. We need to track the people who inhaled the gas. There're gonna turn—"

The camera swung to the reporter. Her lips twitched as she tried to cover her amusement, but her eyes laughed. "There you have it, folks. Strange acts in the night outside the city of Center. If anyone else has reports of gaseous substances coming from strangers, call 911 immediately. Sounds like this woman narrowly missed a predator or turning into a pod person. Back to you, Chuck."

"The smoke. The light. They happened in front of me." Sandra couldn't stop her head from shaking back and forth in denial.

"There's not enough time to explain. We have to leave now. We've no choice," Raz said.

Paris sat up. "How can I make you understand?" They spoke over themselves

Sean grabbed her hand. "It'll be all right."

The news report had been about them. Not everyone had seen the same thing, and the interviewee didn't appear as the most reliable of witnesses. The news reporter didn't believe him. Yet, Sandra had witnessed the same.

Sandra's number-one priority was Sean. She'd made a promise she wouldn't break. "I'll leave with Sean. Get him out of here. Raz can focus on you," Sandra spoke to Paris without turning away from the television.

"Separation weakens us," Paris said.

Sandra faced her.

"Please. Come closer. We won't hurt you." Paris held out her hand to Raz.

Sean climbed onto the bed, sat beside Paris and placed his head on her shoulder.

Sandra perched a hip on the opposite side of him. "What do we do? The news report exposes you."

"You'll know everything soon." Paris's chest moved up and down in exaggerated effort.

Raz hadn't moved and looked hesitant to do so.

"Mommy." Sean's scared cry competed with the ongoing newscast.

"It's okay, sweet boy." Paris kissed Sean's forehead. "Raz will fix everything." She flopped back on her pillow and stared at Raz. "Please."

Beads of sweat marked Raz's forehead. He pulled Sean to the edge of the bed. Paris held Sandra's hand. Raz entwined his fingers with Sandra's free hand and kissed the back. The mix of emotions running through Sandra paralyzed her. Raz's tender lips soothed her so much. The three adults encircled Sean with their arms.

"What happens next will frighten you, but it's the only way." Raz caressed Sandra's face with their knitted fingers. "I don't know what you'll see."

Sean hugged his mother, squishing his teddy between them.

Paris caught her gaze and held it. "Trust us."

The hum began as more vibration than sound, resonating from deep within. Internal tremors baked her insides. She focused on Raz's touch. The same frightening gas formed in front of her, and she couldn't escape. Panic increased and threatened to burst from every pore in her body.

The annoying beep of the heart rate monitor competed with the TV.

Raz's eyes turned to white light, as did Paris's. A warm aura appeared on Paris's skin and her breath normalized. Sean sat up, and the blanket around his shoulders floated to the floor. He touched his mother's face and splayed his other hand across Raz's chest. A blinding, incandescent shimmer exploded from Sean.

Sandra hovered over the floor. Trapped in the circle of their clasped fingers, she couldn't pull her hands from Raz or Paris. Brain synapses flashed, creating a starburst of colors behind her eyes. Tears fell as information bombarded her too fast. She gasped and moaned. Struggling to break free from their hands, Sandra watched the visual fireworks fade. Blackness weighed her down. The panic won. Not being able to escape, combined with the raw energy racing her heart, threw Sandra into a full-fledged panic attack. Tunnel vision enfolded her, and she couldn't breathe. She heard someone tell her to hold on for a few more minutes.

Sandra wouldn't last longer than a few seconds.

Chapter Sixteen

RAZ INHALED THE smell of sweet cookie dough coming from Sean's aura. Raz didn't recognize the pungent scent of lemons. The Nexus warned him to finish the render. A Chaser approached. Raz bristled. His skin crawled at their circle's vulnerability. Wild fluctuations in energy came from Sean, and they were difficult for Raz to control. He scattered more heat and fire into the void of the circle.

Sean broke his connection, and their circular glow blinked in the middle like an eye.

When the eye closed again, Raz watched in disbelief as Sean scampered off the bed, raced to the door and peeked out. How could Sean leave an active render without harm? "Come back," Raz shouted, but the force of the Nexus energy swirling among them ripped his words from his throat.

"Why is no one there?" Sean slammed the door and hurried back to the circle. He stepped under their arms and touched the Nexus beam encasing them in the render. The Nexus threw Sean back, and his small body bounced against the hospital tray. It bucked at the impact. The Nexus allowed Sean to leave, but he didn't understand how to return.

Without the brilliance of a circle ring blurring their surroundings, they had an open circle, and no way to complete it with Sean outside the perimeter.

Sandra tried tugging her hand free of Raz's hold. He gripped her tighter. The panic in her eyes was clear. She struggled to free herself from Paris's grip, and their hands slipped from one another. A stand of Nexus light arced between their fingers.

Raz dug deep inside to finish the process. They only needed a few more seconds to boost Paris's energy so they could escape. A break on his right made him turn. Paris had slipped from his hold as well.

Yet, Sandra pulled on Raz's hand and shuffled her feet back from the center.

Raz held onto her, but the circle slipped. They no longer held hands. The Nexus light grasped their fingers to keep them connected. How long would seam last? Raz reached for Paris's hand, but another force prevented physical touch. Raz couldn't maintain the connection, and the added strain broke the circle. He staggered backward and pulled the bed curtain off the rails in his disorientation. He fell to his knees beside the bed. The luminous sparks from the render blinked out and plunged the room into darkness.

How would they survive? An open circle was a highlighted trail for Chasers to follow wherever they went. NEU devices weren't required for tracking the residual energy broken from the Nexus. It'd be visible to the human naked eye.

Openness was a common problem with newborn Transors. Raz had made a rookie mistake. He blinked away the blurry shapes and attempted to stand. Grasping the bed sheets, he pulled himself up. His knees wobbled.

Sean cried. He pushed on the backs of Raz's legs in an offer of assistance and clung to him.

Raz squeezed his head and laughed at the irony of a six-year-old holding him up as he fell forward against Paris's legs.

Sporadic energy rumblings created a mental fog. Sandra's brown eyes flashed with golden light as the Nexus accepted her, but the render hadn't completed. The excess energy in an uncompleted or open circle would bombard her with Nexus energy.

How's this possible?

The addition of the strange Nexus energy Sandra emitted disrupted Raz's ability to control his own and depleted him. A wave of mist swirled in front of his eyes and down to his fingertips, where oscillations of white heat flickered. The room was a mix of motion and glare. Nausea and fatigue overcame him.

"Daddy, what's wrong with her?" Sean climbed onto the bed and sat beside Sandra.

Her chest caved and then filled with each frantic breath. Her gaze darted back and forth as Sean patted her face and rubbed her arm.

The render, despite being incomplete, had pulled Paris from the grip of death. Her face held a healthy pink glow. Her breaths were full and clear. She helped Raz to his feet. "The circle is open, Sean. We have to close it."

Sean wrapped his arms around Sandra's neck.

She pulled and tugged at his grip. "Let go. I can't breathe." Nothing stopped her sobs and trembling.

Fear entered Raz's stomach like a white-hot knife. He shouldn't have experimented with her life.

"Why's she so scared?" Sean tightened his hold. Sparks of flickering violet energy cascaded from Sean's hands down her back.

Sandra pried his arms away.

Sean dropped back to the bed.

"I have to get out of here." Sandra stood.

Sean jumped up and threw himself against her. His arms and legs hung onto her for dear life.

Despite his weakened state, Raz stepped in front of her. "You can't leave. We didn't have time to explain—"

"Bring her closer, baby. I can help." Paris waved her arms encouraging Sean to guide Sandra to her.

"Mommy, she won't listen."

Paris yanked Sandra back to the bed. Sandra's gaze darted around the room, and she bucked against Paris's hold.

"Sean, you have to talk to her." Paris wrapped her arms around Sandra's shoulders.

Sean held Sandra's hand. "I am. She can't hear me."

Raz grabbed the back of Sean's jacket. "Don't telelink with her in an open connection. We're too vulnerable." Raz hesitated. He couldn't dare touch Sandra until his energy charge dissipated. Assuming the render had incorporated her into the circle was too risky. "The Nexus might be hurting her. Stop touching her."

Paris stood. She whipped the hospital gown over her head and pulled on her shirt. "Let's close it."

"But, Mommy, we need Sandra to close it. I can't do it without her."

Paris reached for Sandra's hand.

Raz stopped her. "We can't touch her. The pulses are hurting her human body."

The door squeaked open. A doctor entered, followed by a sharp and vaguely familiar citrus note. Raz reared his head back at the odor that'd been similar to the Nexus warning moments before the circle broke.

The blond man narrowed his eyes, and the corner of his mouth tilted up.

Cold rooted in Raz's bones as recognition slapped him in the face. The man was the one from the overheard conversation in the hallway. This doctor was also General Taft's right hand. Raz had identified him on his last mission before the infiltrator had breached their circle seven years ago. The man must've somehow recognized Paris, identified her as a Sixxer and administered her weakening drugs when they'd arrived.

Sandra tugged several wisps of hair from her ponytail, and the untamed curls sprang out at odd angles.

With Raz's energy at such a low, any display of Sixxer strength would only bring retaliation from any Chasers. This man of General Taft's would figure out they were Sixxers. Before long, every exit at Center Medical would be barred.

The doctor frowned at Sandra and rushed to her side.

Sandra froze. "Stay away."

Good girl. If Raz couldn't touch her, no one else could, either.

"What're you doing here?" The doctor snuck closer. For each step he took toward her, Sandra backed away by two. "Sands, you can stop it."

Unease fluttered up Raz's spine. This Chaser knew her.

"Stay back." Sandra paced back and forth beside the bed, roped into a corner. Every few seconds she bent at the waist, flung out a hand and moaned.

Raz watched for signs she'd collapse like his parents had. Fear and distrust coursed along his spine.

"Breathe," the doctor said. "Fall back on your coping mechanism."

What the ...? This Chaser ass-munch had no right to tell Sandra what to do.

"What's wrong with her?" Paris whispered. She wasn't asking the doctor.

A low buzz hummed in Raz's ear, but nothing spanned the circle. Was Paris or Sean forcing a telelink? Nothing was as it should be.

The doctor stepped back. "It's a panic attack caused by a severe claustrophobic event. She needs space now. If she'd focus on me, she'd come out of it."

Raz cleared his throat. "Are you her doctor?"

The man straightened to his full height. "She'll fight it, but we need to get her into a larger space without so many people."

No! Raz towered over him, but a physical confrontation wouldn't end in Raz's favor.

Ownership came off the doctor in waves. He lifted his head and stuck out his peacock chest. "I'll take her to the lobby. Dr. Nazier asked me to check on his patient." His eyes traveled over Paris, head to toe. "I'll tell him you're looking much better."

Paris paled.

The telelink shouted in his ear. Her communication was loud and clear. *Fuck.* Her father had found Paris, and this Chaser knew him.

Raz narrowed his eyes. Did this Chaser realize who Dr. Nazier was, or was this a coincidence he was at the same hospital? Sandra had to come out of her panic attack. Raz couldn't let any of them be captured. He rounded on Sandra.

She fell to her knees.

He risked touching her, even though the energy hadn't dissipated from his hands. He helped her back up, but her shoulders remained hunched over. A zap of electrical fire traveled from his hands to Sandra.

She cried out.

He immediately let her go.

The doctor intervened and forced up her chin. He cupped her cheeks. "Sands, focus. Look at me. That's a girl. Look into my eyes." He grabbed her shoulder. "Remember, five two five. Ready?" The doctor gazed over to where Raz stood.

Was there a smirk on this fart knocker's face?

The doctor steered her away. "She needs common and

recognizable things to come out of this attack."

The intimate way the doctor touched Sandra incensed Raz. *I'll rip off his arms.* Raz's muscles strained the fabric of his shirt. The familiarity this man had with Sandra boiled his blood worse than Cameron had. He connected to the Nexus for a telelink, but nothing happened.

Paris touched his shoulder. "Let the doctor help her."

Paris's wide eyes warned Raz confronting their visitor exposed him and Sean.

The doctor watched in rapt attention where they touched.

Too late. Visible Nexus light communicated between them.

Sandra jerked her head back and forth. "I need to leave. Not enough air in here. I don't need your help. I can do it on my own." She backed away until she bumped against the air conditioner.

Paris grabbed her jacket and Sandra's purse. "Is there anything we can do?" She nodded toward Sean.

Raz agreed. *Take Sean and run.*

"No. She has to focus." The doctor's voice echoed in the room. "There's plenty of air, Sandra. Your office is smaller than this room. If you can breathe there, you can breathe here."

"No." Her gaze darted from Raz to Paris. "I … can't." Her breathing increased.

Do something now! We can't wait any longer, or he'll mark Sean. The shouted telelink across the Nexus came from Paris. She grabbed Raz's hand and added her energy to the circle. The extra surge was pointless with the open connection. They were helpless to ease Sandra's distress.

"She has severe claustrophobia," the doctor said. "Sands, five two five. Take a deep breath. Five. Four. You're so stubborn. A fight every time."

"No," Sandra gasped. "I can't." Her voice became high and thin.

"Grab my hand. I'll take you home."

Sandra shook her head.

"Remember how big and open our house is? You'll feel better." The doctor's voice dropped low. "I'll be there to keep you safe."

The screech of metal on pavement reverberated in Raz's head. *Our house?* Sandra lived alone. Raz reviewed what had happened in the last twenty-four hours. Paris squeezed his fingers. Sandra knew they were trying to get out of town. Yet, she'd deliberately prevented them with delay after delay. His gut tightened, and the contents churned. Sandra had been the one who'd persuaded him to go to the university. Was Cameron Mason an M83 spy? Was Sandra an infiltrator?

Raz masked his emotions and clenched both fists until the veins on his arms almost burst. He wouldn't lose it. He was the only weapon they had left to save the circle.

Sean ran past.

Raz threw out his arm and barred him from touching a traitor.

Sandra refused direct eye contact. Their entire relationship had been a set-up to gain his trust. Sandra had deceived Raz from the moment they met. Her pretended attraction had made Raz loosen his guard. His past came back to haunt him.

"Thom?" Sandra called.

Raz stepped toward her before comprehending she wasn't calling for him. That was the name she shouted in the car before the gas station incident.

Thom escorted Sandra toward the door. "Paris, I'll come check on you tomorrow. Okay?"

"You mean Dr. Nazier will check on me."

He paused. "Yes, he'll be in soon."

Raz had the edge now because General Taft wasn't here. The Chaser standing before him was working with Nazier on his own, or they would've been surrounded by a capture team and not allowed to wait on Paris's *doctor, aka father,* to arrive. They had a chance at escape.

Thom led Sandra out the door.

Raz tasted a small bite of the panic he observed in Sandra. How much time did he have before all hell broke loose? Calculating how many soldiers Thom and Nazier had was impossible. He gathered Sean and Paris close. He whispered in Paris's ear, "Is that the man you went to see for the psychic study?"

"I didn't know he was a Chaser."

Her eyes were wide and innocent, but Raz had a hard time believing her, or anyone, right now. "You didn't recognize him? He's one step down from General Taft. He was there the night my parents died."

Paris gasped. "It can't be."

"It's him. Sandra knows him."

Paris's gaze darted around the room. A few mumbles came out of her mouth.

Nothing satisfactory to Raz. "Why didn't you tell me?"

"Sandra's not a Chaser, Raz. It was her personal choice to tell you about her history. I couldn't betray her privacy."

Raz was ready to leave Paris behind. He thought this would be an easy relocation, but nothing regarding Paris was ever easy. "She's betrayed us all. Now we're weak and in the hornet's nest. She personally knows a Chaser. You kept information from me." He nodded at Sean. "From us."

"The Nexus never sent off a warning for either of them—"

He snatched the purse and coat from her hands. "We can't worry about Sandra anymore. Let's get out of here before Dr. Nazier arrives."

Paris nodded.

As much as Raz wanted to, leaving Paris behind wasn't an option. Sean needed her.

"What about the circle?" Sean tugged on Raz's hand.

The circle was still open. Possibly why Sandra had her panic attack. More likely, she wanted to get out as fast as possible after gaining proof they were Sixxers. In any case, he'd close the circle without her. "We won't wait long."

Paris barreled into Raz. "No. I won't allow you to do this to Sandra. You saw her eyes. The Nexus wants her, and we need her. We can't close the circle without her. The Nexus wouldn't take a Chaser."

"You've taken the choice out of my hands. I'm not sure our circle can survive, now."

CHAPTER SEVENTEEN

THE WISPY ENTITY acted as a living thing. It encased Sandra before she broke free of Raz and Paris's grip and wouldn't let her go. The fingers of air squeezed the breath out of her.

Thom hurried Sandra through the narrow tunnel that used to be the hospital hall. He guided her away from the thing hurting her.

She couldn't take her gaze off the sight behind her. Dark feelers of air hunted for her. Their hot embers had tattooed her body through her clothes. An invisible barrier stopped the ash-covered limbs. The grid that had flared on her hands faded the farther they traveled. Sandra squeezed her eyes shut and allowed Thom to lead her away.

What I'm seeing isn't real. No mist or no imaginary organism is stalking me in this hallway. After the gas station and news report, the denial rang false. She couldn't shake the panic after years without such an attack. The last one had occurred when she began fertility treatments after weeks of Thom's badgering. Fuzziness clouded her mind. Images flashed and vibrated behind her eyes like a slideshow, and none of them made sense.

Sweet aftershave lingered in the air, and her stomach flipped.

Thom's hand tightened on her bicep. "Such a foolish move. I warned you to stay away from Paris."

"What're you doing here?" Sandra clenched her jaw, yanked back her arm and stopped Thom in his tracks.

His vise-like grip cut off her circulation. Shaking her so hard he made her teeth clink together, his saccharine-sweet grin rang as false as his words. "You've no idea what you're involved in. Do you?"

"How did you find me here?" The walls of the narrow hallway

squeezed in around her. Before another wave of panic struck, Sandra breathed deep. Her lungs expanded. Air in through the nose. Out through the mouth. Again. Antiseptic fumes abraded her nostrils and cleared her lungs. The attack was over. *Why can't I focus?* Spots floated in front of her eyes. Each fluorescent light they passed sent a shooting pain into her brain.

Thom yanked her closer. "You put yourself in such a high-stress situation. No wonder you had a panic attack."

"You're not my keeper—"

"In five years of marriage, I've never seen you like this. Those people are messing with your head. Paris will only bring you suffering."

Sandra almost believed him. She expected blistered palms from where Paris and Raz had ensnared her. Yet, her flesh was unblemished. A migraine throbbed in her temple, but the tightness in her chest eased into a manageable ache.

"Paris isn't the cause of my panic attack." *Of course not, but what in the hell had caused it?* She remembered the grip of fingers and a flare of heat, light followed by shadows, then the burning embers surrounding her.

Thom sneered. "You think my research is foolish, but people exist who can control you. Do you ever wonder why you sacrifice so much for them?"

Sacrifice. Thom didn't comprehend her sacrifices. Her legs weakened and almost gave out. Her stomach pitched. If she vomited, maybe it'd land on him. "Anyone can manipulate. Our marriage taught me that lesson."

Thom twisted her arm behind her for a few agonizing seconds. He released her in disgust. "The last thing you need right now is to be alone. I'm the only one who can help you after an attack."

Always the master of deceit, he replaced his ugly mask with one of concern.

His hands massaged her shoulders. "The email … I meant every word." His thumb went under her chin and gently forced up her head.

She met his ice-cold gaze.

"I worry about you. You're not taking care of yourself."

"One panic attack doesn't mean I can't take care of myself."

He caressed her cheek. "You're already recovering faster because I'm here. You need me, Sands. I need you."

His tenderness was a lie. Another glance behind her, and the world tipped. The hospital hallway had turned into a vortex. She couldn't go back. When she faced Thom, the spinning stopped.

The closeness they used to have came back in a rush. Thom comforted her. He became her Thom, the one she loved.

No! I don't love him anymore.

"I know all about your friend. I'm sure by now she told you she participated in my research."

Hours ago, Sandra laughed at Thom's accusations. She believed Paris manifested about as much psychic power as she did. *But now? What is she?* What had happened in Paris's hospital bed couldn't be explained. *Psychics don't spurt energy from their fingers and ooze gaseous substances. Just like that kid witnessed at the mini-market.*

Thom guided her toward the elevators. He placed his warm hand on the small of her back.

Sandra allowed him to guide her away from the crazy unknown. Yet, her scrambled brain screamed at her to turn back, to help her friends, her family. Thom's familiar presence cut away the terror, but why did it have to be *him* offering her sanctuary? Their marriage was finished. Why was he so concerned that Paris tricked him into thinking—

Sandra stopped walking. "You know why Paris is sick."

A sneer appeared on Thom's face. "Poor Sandra. So naïve."

An icy sensation broke out on her neck and arms. "What have you done to her?" Her knees gave way. She grazed her hand along the cool wall and used its support to prevent her collapse. She couldn't afford to pass out again and end up trapped in the hospital, unable to fight for her people.

My people? The three she left behind. She claimed them.

No matter what happened, they belonged to her. Thom wasn't getting them. Yet, she couldn't force herself to turn back. Thom held a power over her more frightening than the dark smoke which chased her out of the room. How was he doing it? She pried herself away from the wall, but he still had a hand wrapped around her arm. He had some sort of invisible control over her body. She couldn't escape, even though she desperately wanted to.

Sandra understood, now. Thom was the Chaser they'd been running from.

A chime rang from Thom's lab coat pocket. He released her arm and pulled out his cell. The device flashed several notifications, but he didn't respond.

Someone is waiting on him. Who?

He shoved the phone back into his pocket. "Paris's illness is caused by an unstable psychic connection. There's no help for her," he said in a reasonable tone.

"Can you hear yourself?" Whatever he'd done to Paris, she had to find out. "Psychic connection? Paris is very ill. She needs a real doctor to help her." As soon as the words flew out of her mouth, she realized her mistake.

Thom's head snapped up. After two quick steps towards her, he smacked a cart from the wall.

Sandra jumped as some of the contents bounced onto the floor and startled two nurses exiting a room.

Thom smiled his charming smile, the one which never reached his eyes, and waved them on.

Icy pools of gray swirled in his eyes. The display of aggression failed to bring anyone to her aid. This wasn't the man she knew.

Thom's hot breath blasted her ear. "I'm the only one who can heal Paris. Remember that," he whispered.

"I didn't mean … let the hospital do the approved medical tests and treatment on her. Treating people without consent is unethical." *Your research is also experimental and not proven to work.*

"They aren't people." Thom tugged her hair from the ponytail holder. A few strands caught in the band, and he pulled them out by the root.

She tensed the right side of her face but kept the wince inside. He threaded his fingers through the waves of her hair, and his aftershave invaded her nostrils. The faint citrus spikes curled her stomach.

Thom's dry lips grazed her cheek. "You never supported me, did you? Our relationship was all jokes and laughs. You've no clue." He pulled her hair taut. "After everything I did to help you."

"Help me?" A black cloud settled over her. Focusing on the fear would bring back her panic. So she allowed her past anger to consume her. "You never helped me. You wanted to replace me with other women." Instead of the static electricity that'd pushed him away at HUP, she experienced a revolting attraction to him. Her knees gave way in shock.

Relax. You'll get away from him.

"Everything I did was for us," Thom said.

His familiar smell, both pleasant and offensive, increased Sandra's unwelcome arousal. An arm crowded around her waist, and another at the back of her neck. He inhaled along her collarbone, which created a stifling heat and a flare of desire low in her body. Her mind shoved back, despite her body's response.

How is he controlling me?

Thom's phone chirped again, and he scrambled for it in his coat pocket.

"All I wanted was a family," she mumbled.

"You won't get one from *them*."

The break in contact rolled Sandra out of the hazy drought of need. What was happening to her? Her reactions repulsed her. She didn't trust herself. Thom proved repeatedly he only looked out for himself. Had he drugged her, or was she going mad? Paris's room had held darkness, but the all-consuming fear she experienced in Thom's arms terrified her.

He responded to the text message. His thumbs flew across the small keypad. "Dr. Nazier and I determined Paris was an unlikely candidate for my treatment. The indicators for psychic bonding were missing."

Paris's father is really here. Her heart skipped a beat. "Because she isn't psychic." *Oh my God, is she?* "Psychics aren't real."

Thom snickered. "If you had the slightest bit of interest in my work, the truth is written there. Her skills are impressive, just not enough to raise any alarms on her true nature. Unstable during times of stress. Like now. She was our control for the experiments, but it looks like she's responding, now."

Instinct cried for Sandra to warn Paris. She stepped back. Thom's fingers ran down her arm and took possession of her hand before she could get far enough away to sprint back to Paris's room. Once he gripped her hand, her feet moved towards him without her permission. Tremors of hunger fluttered along her fingers.

These sensations aren't right! She followed Thom like a puppy no matter how much she tried to force her legs to run.

They neared the elevator enclave, and a discordant number of tones echoed throughout the floor. Behind them, chaos erupted. The elevator doors opened, and her panic returned. In both directions, a tunnel formed. Behind her, the black tentacles of smoke swirled like a sideways tornado. In front of her, the elevator shrank to the size of a shoebox.

A man in scrubs trotted from the adjacent hallway. "They attempted a render. The NEU detected the energy signature."

Sandra gripped Thom's coat. "There's too much noise. I can't get into the elevator."

Thom smiled. "See? You need me, baby. Take deep breaths. I'll help you in two seconds." He kept a hand on her arm and bowed heads with the newcomer. "Where did you go? I thought you were checking on Paris."

"I had an emergency call to the ER. Besides, they aren't going anywhere. The leader won't have the strength to leave her after a failed render."

Sandra attempted to control her fear with deep breaths. The comfort Thom's hand provided lasted a few seconds before a visceral ache throbbed low in her gut. She ignored the pain. These men had answers, and she wanted them, but she also wanted to get away. Her body ignored her internal commands.

"If they sense danger, he'll do anything. Why didn't you keep Sandra away from them?" Thom asked.

The man's gaze drilled into Sandra. "Make sure you test her. To be sure."

Thom narrowed his eyes. "She's not infected."

"Think again after what you did to her."

The nausea kicked up again, and sweat broke out along Sandra's neck. A thousand memories flashed in her mind of Thom convincing her to take drugs she didn't want. She stared at the other man. *Do I know him?* She remembered Paris telling her about the experiments her father performed on her as a child. The resemblance between him and Paris became clear. This man was Dr. Nazier.

Thom brushed past his colleague. He stepped into the elevator and dragged Sandra behind him. "We've got to go. Close your eyes, sweetheart."

A hand wrapped around her neck, and the hated desire flooded back into her veins.

Thom massaged her neck muscles. "Imagine an open field. Use my hand as a guide to keep you grounded."

His visualization technique would've worked if Sandra still trusted him. Closing her eyes on the enemy was impossible. His hypnotic scent filled the enclosure, and his mouth behind her ear sent chills careening down her spine.

Nazier stood in the hallway and grinned. He nodded with a slight tilt of his head. "Well done, sir."

The doors shut, trapping Sandra with Thom in a private hell. How could she warn Paris her father was coming for her?

CHAPTER EIGHTEEN

RAZ PROPELLED HIMSELF forward, despite his weakened state. They reached the opposite wing without being spotted by a Chaser or hospital employee. The Nexus connected them in fits of energy, but in doing so also drained their Sixxer power to almost nothing.

"Let's take the stairs." Paris pushed open the exit door.

Raz jerked her back. Running down two flights of stairs wouldn't give them any additional strength.

Sean pumped his small legs and rushed to the door. He'd wrapped his teddy bear around his neck, and the stuffed animal flapped behind him like a cape.

With his arms around Sean's waist, Raz scooped him up. "It's the first place they'll ambush. Surgical or delivery elevators conceal better and are a faster exit."

Paris flew down five steps. "You want to hunt for elevators with Chasers on our tail? You're crazy. I haven't been this strong in months." She stopped and tapped her foot. "We're already here. Move your feet, soldier."

Raz's heavy breathing echoed in the stairwell. His earlier demand from HUP chafed. Why did she have so much strength during an open circle?

Sean flung Sandra's purse over his shoulder. The bag covered his entire torso.

Paris tied her coat around her hips. She raced back toward them, pulled Sean from Raz's arms and carried him on her back.

Raz had no choice but to follow them. A surge of strength entered his muscles, and he scaled the first flight of stairs. Fatigue returned on the second.

"Where's the car?" Paris jogged another few steps.

Sean clutched Paris's shirt. His hair bounced wildly with each hop Paris took. "I know where it is."

"Raz?"

Paris's quizzical expression was out of place. "I was with you, remember? We arrived in the ambulance," Raz said.

Paris blinked. Her hand rested on the bar of the first floor exit.

He caught up to them, panting from the sprint. They shouldn't have used so much circular power after Sandra left. Paris's gaze drilled in to him as he hopped off the last step.

She scrunched her face. "We were in the car when we left the university. Didn't you drive it here?"

"Then we stopped after Sandra had her nosebleed."

Paris shook her head. "That was before we left the house."

Raz cupped her face and examined her eyes. "Are you okay?" She'd lost time after this render, which had never happened. He feared her burst of strength wouldn't last for long.

From his piggyback position, Sean climbed up her shoulders and kissed her cheek. "Mommy? What's wrong?"

"Nothing, sweetie." She patted Sean's cheek. "Sandra had another nosebleed?" She rubbed her forehead. Beads of sweat broke along her upper lip. "I must be dazed from the render. Sean, tell me. Where's the car?"

"Row B. No, row D."

Raz placed his hand over Paris's. "We'll find it." He opened the bag on Sean's shoulder and pulled out the keys to the Camaro. Guilt pecked at him for stealing Sandra's car, but they only needed it to get out of this town. He'd ditch it then and find another to steal.

Raz poked his head out the door and looked left then right inside the garage. No one was in the immediate vicinity of the exit. He lifted his hand and waved for them to follow. They were underground. Raz couldn't determine what direction to take. He edged along a wall, searching for an exit sign for the parking garage. A chilled breeze, tinged with gasoline odor, flew in between the cars. The main exit was close. Raz moved to the left searching for the rows Sean had mentioned.

"Mommy, go this way." Sean pointed behind him.

Paris followed Raz.

Sean wiggled off her back and sprinted up a ramp.

"Wait for us!" Paris ran after him, but his quick feet disappeared around the corner. Gasping for air, she held her ribs. "Why's he going outside?"

Raz caught up to her. He threw an arm around her back and urged her to keep going. "We can't lose him. Not with the circle open."

They struggled up the ramp. Shouts rebounded along the cement pillars. Their head start was quickly disappearing.

"Guys, hurry." Sean stood at the payment booth, eyes bright. His hands threw violet sparks along the ground.

Paris moaned, and her legs gave out. The open circle took back the energy it had given them earlier.

Raz hoisted her in his arms and battled the last few feet. The ping of a dart hit his shoulder, and the drugs inside spread scalding bites along his flesh.

Chasers shouted behind them.

Sean rushed forward and a flicker of his Nexus energy ricocheted off the ground and smacked Raz in the chest.

Raz yanked Paris to his side. "Run, Sean. Don't look back."

Sean froze. His sobs broke out in a burst.

Paris touched Raz's face. "Let me go." A dart protruded from her chest, and her light dimmed in her eyes.

Each step weighed down Raz. "We're leaving together. Sean will meet us at the emergency site." His knees slammed into the concrete, and sharp agony zinged behind his kneecaps.

"I only hope God forgives me when I see him." Paris's fingertips trembled, and the Nexus energy built in her hand. "This is all I have left to give you." Rivers of Sixxer power coursed along her fingers. She forced a circular connection.

Raz couldn't stop her. "Don't do this."

"I loved you the moment I saw you. After that, nothing else mattered."

Another thump slammed into Raz's neck. He dropped Paris. He waited for the scorching discomfort, but the pulses of energy from

Paris counteracted the spasm caused by the dart. His muscles bulged, and strength filled his bones.

Sean screamed and ran straight for them.

Raz stood and lifted him before he touched Paris. He dragged the two of them up the ramp.

"Mommy! Moooommmy!"

Raz fought Sean's moving jumble of arms and legs. He struggled to ignore Sean's screams. Each one cut him in half.

"Noooooo!" Sean's pain echoed through the garage.

Raz pulled Sean backward and glanced at Paris's still body. The glow missing in her open eyes socked Raz in the gut. A numbing sensation melted over the side of his face. Her body held no life, no essence. He whipped his head around as another shot flew past his ear, missing him by what must've been millimeters.

Sean scratched and clawed.

Raz refused to loosen his bear hug. The shots contained tranquilizers, a tactic for capture. There was no stopping until Raz found safety. Adrenaline saturated his body. He blew past the guard station and into the open parking lot. Sean's body swung away from Raz as they rounded the corner. He hooked his fingers into Sean's shirt to keep a hold on him. The energy from Paris zipped along his muscles and bones. Darkness and cars hid them. Raz crouched behind tailgates and bumpers.

Sean hunched behind Raz, protected from additional darts. *My body is the only shield I can create right now.*

Raz put his faith in Sean's instincts. "Which way do we go?"

Sean pointed.

Raz hooked him on the shoulder, and half dragged him as they ran. The phone vibrated in Raz's pocket. He guided Sean into the outside parking area and searched the rows for the Camaro. Sandra's keys jingled in his hand and fell.

Sean scooped them up. His teddy bear fell to the ground, and Sean scrambled back to grab him.

They were rats in a maze with no exit. His and Sean's aura became a bonfire in the night. The electrical fire spit and sputtered around them. Raz used all of his Sixxer power to bring the light back to them so the wouldn't be spotted by the Chasers. Cameron's name popped up on the phone's screen that he'd programmed into his contacts. Tapping answer, he lifted the phone to his ear.

"Is Sandra all right—"

"Where in the hell have you been?" They ducked behind an F-150. *Will M83 provide us protection, or is Cameron another avenue for capture?*

"What's going on?" Cameron asked.

Sean panted and clutched his stomach. His wide eyes searched for any movement around them.

"Paris is dead," Raz said, without feeling. "Our circle is open." He had no time to process her death—only time to move.

Cameron stuttered on the line for a moment then caught himself. "Shit."

Sean spotted the car and ran ahead to unlock the doors.

Raz threw Sandra's purse in the back. He'd search it later. "Can you get us out?"

"I need to talk to Sandra. Put her on the line."

"Cameron, can you get us out? This place is crawling with Chasers. A warning would've been polite."

Sean climbed into the backseat and buckled himself in. The remnants of the render still pulsated in his eyes and fingertips. "We need to get my bike, Daddy."

"It was our emergency plan, buddy. We have to do something else."

"Sandra should be with us."

Raz knew Sean wouldn't understand Sandra's betrayal. The line crackled.

"Raz, put Sandra on the line. Now," Cameron commanded.

"Were both of you working against us the entire time? The medication you gave Paris was intended to slow us down." Raz scanned the surrounding cars. Where were the Chasers? Would Cameron take the bait? Paris had denied taking what Cameron had given her.

"What in the hell are you talking about? I gave Paris aspirin."

"Bullshit—"

"You're still in Center? Where the fuck is Sandra?"

"She's with a goddamned Chaser, Cameron. If you knew this … If

I learn you put me and my family at risk, I'll kill you." Raz didn't threaten. He promised.

"What happened with the render?"

"You detected the render?" Raz ducked as low as possible in the driver's seat.

"We've had reports of a Nexus flare," Cameron said.

"You can detect a Nexus flare from HUP to Center Medical?"

"I placed a sensor on Sean before you left."

Shit! I've been out of M83 for too long. Movement raced two rows away from them. Raz tensed and ducked behind the steering wheel. There wasn't time for this. "We need safe haven. Can you give it to us?"

Cameron spoke to someone in the background. "You've been approved for clearance. I have more to debrief you on. Damn it. I didn't want it to come to this."

Raz enabled the speaker phone and tossed the device into the passenger seat. The roar of the engine gathered attention. Chasers fired on them. Pops blasted the side of the car. Raz pushed the pedal to the floor and tires squealed. They careened around a van. Raz's number one rule: if it looked too easy to get out, then it probably wasn't.

"Sandra left with a Chaser. She's out of the picture." Raz exited the hospital drive and headed east. At the main intersection, for a split-second he hesitated on which way to go. He turned right onto the main fairway, heading south. The Camaro rumbled over the road, but if Cameron pulled through they'd be safe in a matter of minutes, and the Chasers would be none the wiser.

Cameron's voice echoed through the car. "You're not joking. Sandra isn't there."

Sean sobbed. "Sandra isn't with Chasers, Daddy."

"They took her," Cameron said. "She wouldn't go willingly."

"Kidnapped? I'm not buying it. Her own two feet walked her out with that fucker." The speedometer reached one hundred.

"What exactly happened? I had an inside man. He didn't make contact?"

"No inside man contacted us!" Raz shook his head. "Why in the hell should I trust you?" He didn't expect Cameron to answer. There wasn't anyone else to trust at this point, and they needed help.

"It's M83 protocol, Raz. Get your head out of your ass and think. You've had trauma. Find the rational after what's happened. Granted, I've given you no reason to trust me, but one thing our team doesn't do is let Chasers gain intel, or capture our people. That's what you're accusing me of, isn't it?"

"You didn't do a very good job, did you? The Chasers knew the moment Paris entered the hospital. They toyed with us."

"I stationed Leon at the hospital in case we had any suspicious ER visitors. His reports stated Paris had been transported by ambulance to Center Medical. He was supposed to get you out. Once you get to HUP, I'll get you supplies and a debrief," Cameron said.

Leon hadn't done squat to help them. "I'm retreating for Sean, but I can't leave Paris behind. He stays at HUP. I'll go back for her. You don't realize—"

"No, Daddy. I wanna be with you." Sean cried.

The rearview mirror showed the Nexus glow lit up Sean like a live wire.

Cameron said with conviction, "There's no way you'll get her body out of the hospital."

Raz didn't respond. The rest of her was fated to the butchers for dissection.

"Come on, man." Cameron broke the silence. "We're the good guys, whether you believe it or not. We'll find Sandra."

Raz didn't have enough time to explain Sandra's role in the render and about recognizing the Chaser as General Taft's go-to guy.

"I'm heading your way, Cameron. I hope you have my back."

"There's classified info on Sandra. It's not what you think. I tried to protect her. I can't tell you more until you get here. You'll need a safe place to close the circle."

"I know what I have to do."

"You need to finish the render if it failed at the hospital."

"There hasn't been time." *I've got Chasers on my ass, dimwit.* With Sean this unstable, Raz had to close the circle without Sandra. Everything about living in Angelville had been a mistake. *Never again will I give into my fantasies of a normal life.*

"Son of a … you need to make time," Cameron said. "That's a

direct order. Any Chaser will track you until you get it closed. HUP has a small anti-NEU, but it won't cover the lost energy."

"I have a child to protect. He's my only priority." Raz crested the hill. The university lights popped out like fireflies. The university shield, in the form of an anti-NEU, wouldn't be as good as his own, but it'd give him time to figure out their next move.

"Everyone has their own cause, but we're Sixxers." Cameron paused. The line cracked. "Reconsider coming back as an M83 operative."

The line disconnected.

Cameron had no way of knowing his career history in M83. The knowledge was too high up in security clearance for a field unit to have access to.

Sean cried in low, wailing sobs.

The rearview mirror caught the reflection of his tears. They glistened like icicles. Sean's face was far too aged.

"Sandra didn't understand, did she?"

"What're you talking about, buddy?"

"She didn't understand about Mommy. He'll take her away. He'll take Jamie away."

"Explain."

"I'm not a little boy anymore," Sean whispered. A ball of electricity formed at the edge of his fingertips. "Sandra needs our help." The ball floated closer and grazed Raz's cheek like Sean's own hand. "We need her."

Déjà vu slithered over Raz's neck. Had he traded one betrayal for another?

CHAPTER NINETEEN

SANDRA'S HEAD THROBBED. The world floated and spun around her. She felt as though she'd drunk too much champagne but didn't remember the celebration. The sway of the car bounced her against soft leather, and a new car smell hovered in the air. Where was the Camaro? She sat up and unbuckled her seatbelt. Pain squeezed her temples. A manicured lawn stretched along twenty-foot trees. Fresh mulch and new flowers surrounded the wraparound porch. Dread poured into her gut.

"Take me home." The dryness in her throat made swallowing difficult.

Thom perfectly navigated the drive, as he'd done thousands of times during their marriage, in what used to be Sandra's Mercedes. His rough fingers moved her hair off her face. "No. I'm not taking you out to no-man's-land after you've had a panic attack." The garage doors opened with loud motorized clanks, and they entered the dark interior. "Besides, I thought you'd like a hot bath." He turned off the engine, lifted her hand and placed a kiss in her palm.

A hot bath? Sandra expelled the breath she held, grateful tingles of awareness didn't zing where Thom's lips left his mark. The noise in her head screamed and clamored but made no sense. Every part of her body ached. Raz and Paris needed her. *What am I doing here?*

Thom's thumb stroked the back of her hand. "I don't want to fight."

Sandra's stomach churned. Thom's change of heart wasn't normal. Forgiveness was a bad word in his vocabulary.

He eased back in the driver's seat but didn't release her hand.

"There are enough bedrooms. You won't see me. I'll keep my hands off."

"I want to go home." Her desire to flee and her need to find answers tore Sandra in two. Her head throbbed. She opened the door, but when she jumped out of the SUV, her heavy legs slumped onto the running board.

Thom rushed around the front bumper and slid his arms under her knees. Their breaths fogged the early morning air. "You might still be light-headed." He gathered her close, and his scent once again permeated the space. "You need rest."

Every inhale contained a citrus tone, and Sandra's unwanted attraction to him returned. Her arms clutched his neck against her will, and warmth flooded her stomach.

Thom made a moaning noise of satisfaction. He carried her over the threshold.

Mind against emotion battled within her, and knife-like stabs bombarded her head. Her arousal around Thom was madness. The unwelcome desires became stronger the minute he carried her through the front door. She couldn't resist him, and was a prisoner to his touch. The cravings shamed her.

Sandra traveled through fog. Acid rolled in the pit of her stomach. She had seconds to reach the bathroom.

Thom narrowed his eyes, and a furrow appeared between his brows.

"Put me down." Sandra pushed against his hard chest. Her feet hit the floor. Her legs pumped in a race toward the downstairs bath. She slammed the door behind her and emptied the contents of her stomach into the toilet. Her body shook. She cleaned up the mess and walked over to the sink. Grateful Thom's arms weren't around her any longer, she washed her hands and rinsed the acid from her mouth with tepid water. Wishing she had gum or candy to take away the bitter taste, she remembered gum was in her purse. *I have no purse, no identity.*

"I'll be okay. Just calm down and think," Sandra whispered. Her hands shook as she locked the door.

Familiar decorations and items surrounded her. She never thought she'd see the inside of this room ever again. Shot after shot of fertility drug failures had occurred here. She trembled. Her thin blouse didn't provide warmth in the cool interior. "I'm fine." She patted her face with a cotton towel. Lifting her head, she gasped at her reflection in the familiar mirror. Large purple circles sagged under her eyes, green-tinged skin and enlarged pupils masked her face. The only part of her natural eye color was the small ring of brown in her iris. She looked like death. What had Thom done to her?

A flash of light popped in the mirror. She slapped her hand over her scream. When nothing else happened, she moved closer. Her eyes were now a warm honey shade instead of the familiar chocolate brown.

"Pull it together, Sandra." She rubbed the wet towel, with initials TJR on the corner, under her lashes, but her reflection didn't change. She licked her lips. "I'll figure out what's going on."

The whispered words echoed in the cavernous bathroom. All the rooms in the custom built house were bigger than normal, reminding her of Thom's attempt to contain her panic attacks. She opened the right hand drawer. Her hairbrush still lay inside, and she used it to tame her waves. Each pull generated a massive amount of static electricity.

Unexplainable forces bound her to Thom. She tossed the hairbrush onto the countertop. The vortex at the gas station and hospital were clear memories. Her hands curled over the edge of the porcelain sink, and the cool granite made her shiver. She needed to get back to Raz. How would she get out of here? The door bounced against Thom's heavy knock. Sandra jumped and twirled.

"Are you okay?" His chilling voice penetrated the heavy wood.

If Sandra refused to answer, she knew Thom would jimmy the lock and barge in. He'd never respected her privacy. After a quick squint in the mirror, her eyes changed back to their normal color. Her hair settled against her head, free of static. She accepted the fact she couldn't improve her skin tone. She straightened her shirt. The cream color emphasized her pale hands.

Sandra inhaled, turned the knob, and opened the door. "It must be the flu or something. I ... uh ... need to get home. I'll call a cab." She brushed her hair out of her face. Her hands still jittered.

Thom seized her fingers and brought them to his lips. "You're welcome to stay with me."

Sandra shook her head. "This isn't the time."

"I still care about you, Sands. I want to help you." He dropped her hands and rubbed the flimsy material covering her biceps.

Heat flushed her skin and flew up her chest and neck. Her thin see through shirt exposed her pebbled breasts to Thom's hungry gaze.

He placed moist lips against her neck. "What have they done to you? You're exhausted. I can't believe you had an attack."

He was right. She never should've allowed herself to get involved with Raz. She gave her all and got nothing in return.

Sandra paused at her confusing thoughts. Raz hadn't caused her condition. She couldn't think or focus with Thom's lemon zing surrounding her.

He pulled her close and trapped her in his arms. "Sleep fixes everything," he whispered.

No. I must not sleep. Glorious sleep had eluded her until now. Her heavy eyelids fell, but she snapped them open. "I don't want to." Sandra didn't dare show any vulnerability around him. His control over her body was too personal. *I don't want him to touch me.*

She scrambled away and stumbled into the linen closet. Her confused body was helpless at his touch. She focused on getting him out of the room before she lost control of her mind as well. "How about breakfast?"

Thom unbuttoned the top fastening of her blouse.

Sandra's numb fingers tried to brush him away, but her arms were too heavy. She clutched her shirt to her chest, and squeezed it together as if she were afraid he had super x-ray vision. She was grateful she wore her bra this morning, despite how tight and constricting it was. The past few weeks she hadn't preferred to wear one.

Thom's hands made a quick journey down the fastenings. The last button came undone, and he whisked away the blouse. He went to the spa and turned on the faucets. The water spray, loud and deafening, hit the bottom of the garden tub.

"Take a soak." He rubbed her bare shoulders and guided her to sit on the edge of the huge spa. "I'll make you breakfast while you relax." He pulled off her shoes and socks and massaged her feet like he used to after an exhausting day. He smiled.

Yet, joy failed to reach his eyes. *This is all wrong. Why can't I make him stop?* She pulled back her foot.

He moved higher, undid the fly of her pants and tugged at the denim.

They slid down her thighs before she found the strength to grab the waistband and prevent him from exposing her legs. She hated the fiery blush heating her face and chest. "Could you ..."

He laughed and caressed the tops of her breasts, as he always did when he embarrassed her.

He was too familiar, and she had too many uncomfortable memories. Her skin turned a rosy shade of pink. She desperately wanted to leave. Why couldn't she? He controlled her, somehow, and she despised herself for accepting his touch.

"How can you be shy around me? I've seen you naked."

"Thom, please."

He backed up toward the door with a boyish grin. "Okay. I'll go. Breakfast will be ready when you're done." His tone grew more serious. "You should eat something." He walked out of the room. Footsteps thumped down the hallway.

Why was he being so nice? Concern came from him in direct proportion to how much time caring about something other than himself would take him from his research. He'd never made her a meal, requested or not.

The inviting bath tempted her aching and cold body. Sandra was tired of struggling. She didn't trust Thom to leave her alone in such a vulnerable state. Steam floated above the tub, and the water called to her. His scent hovered around her, and she desperately wanted to erase it. Removing her jeans, she walked over to the vanity. The chair fit under the doorknob. Again, she turned the lock. Inside the linen closet, she found her favorite soap and shampoo. One of her favorite cotton T-shirts was folded neatly on the lower shelf.

Is Thom too lazy to clean out this stuff, or has he been expecting my return? A sweaty heat wrapped her body in moisture, which emphasized the citrus odor hovering in the room. She wrinkled her nose. *The stink is awful.* After grabbing the towels and soap, she set them on the edge of the bathtub. She removed her bra and panties then sank into the blissful hot water.

The sudsy foam of her shampoo ran over her face. She scrubbed away Thom's scent and touch. The water soothed all of her aching muscles. Lilac soap intoxicated her and deepened her relaxation. She rinsed and soaked. Her hands tingled as she moved her arms in the warm liquid. Small jets of water beat against her hands and legs. A deep breath filled her lungs with warm steam, but she couldn't shake the headache. She opened her eyes, and a pleasant ambient light reflected off the white tiles. *What a wonderful way to spend an afternoon.*

Sandra sat up. Water splashed over the sides of the tub. What in the hell was she doing? She was wasting the day away while Raz and Sean dealt with Paris's illness alone. She pondered the light reflection. It wasn't the sun. The bathroom faced the west side of the house, and dawn had peeked over the horizon as they'd entered the drive. The reflection in the mirror showed the light came from her eyes, and a sheen of water coated her exposed body. She wiped it away. A few streams spurted off in random directions, but the majority of it stayed glued to her. The light in her eyes faded. The water dropped into the tub and onto the floor with a heavy splash.

Fear spurred Sandra into action. She shook her head to remove her foggy thoughts. What was going on and what had Thom done to her? These types of hallucinations had to be drug induced. She toweled off and pulled her jeans back on sans underwear. The blue material of her T-shirt clung to her chest, tighter than she remembered, but the material was warmer than the see through blouse. Besides, her aching breasts protested the donning of her bra.

Padding to the kitchen, she figured the only way to get information out of Thom was to play along with his game. She remembered Dr. Nazier's cunning facial expression at the hospital. They were up to something. Without a phone or car, she had to plan carefully. Thom would trap her here.

She watched him from the kitchen entrance. At the stove, he flipped an egg onto a plate. Coffee gurgled in the pot beside him.

She sat on one of the bar stools.

He added toast and set the plate and a coffee mug in front of her. He poured the java into her cup.

"Why are you doing this?" She blurted.

Thom's movements slowed. He filled his own cup and spooned in exactly two tablespoons of milk and one of sugar. "I realize this seems odd—"

"And why were you at the hospital?" Her interruption would drive him crazy. She didn't care. The habit was one of the many faults he'd listed about her failure as a wife, but she needed answers.

Thom sighed in what could only be exasperation. He inhaled a deep and slow breath. The motion brought her attention to his chest. He wore what used to be one of her favorite T-shirts. It was tight and black with a thin collar on the crew neckline. The fit emphasized his muscular pectorals, still sexy as hell.

We're over! Why am I noticing these things about him right now? She scrubbed her face with her hands.

There. The lemon scent, faint under the breakfast odor, buzzed in her nose. Was it the drug? Had he piped a gas into the central air of the house? Her guesses didn't make sense because a gaseous drug would affect him, too.

He pulled the pan of bacon from the oven and set it on the stove top. "I was doing a favor for Dr. Nazier at the hospital."

The bacon obliterated all the smells in the kitchen and attacked her gut. She scrunched her nose as queasiness got the better of her. *Oh, yuck. That bacon is so offensive.* She lifted the coffee cup closer to her face to help cover the scent. "I thought you'd be working with my virus this weekend. Like a kid in a candy shop."

Thom settled his hand over hers on the island counter.

A small flicker of static electricity traveled up her arm, similar to what had occurred at HUP in her office. The neediness of desire from earlier thankfully stayed away.

"What's wrong with your research?" Thom asked.

"Nothing. I wish I hadn't given it to you." She shook off his hand and sipped her coffee. The caffeine purred along her nerve endings and eased her headache.

"Why did you?"

"Something else is more important to you than my little plant viruses." She lifted a forkful of eggs to her mouth. Her stomach protested. "Maybe what, or who, caused my panic attack?" She pushed back the plate, lowered her uneaten forkful of food and gave him a direct stare. "Who are they?"

Thom smirked. He leaned closer. "What they are is a secret."

"Something was going to happen before you came into the room." She focused on her legs to hide her gaze from his suspicious one. He didn't need to know whatever she'd experienced in Paris's room had already happened. "I ignored your warning. Am I in danger now?"

"If you only knew what was going on."

"Then tell me," Sandra begged. Thom loved it when she did.

His gaze flickered over her with a softness that irritated the piss out of her. She pleaded again. "Please, tell me. What were you doing at the hospital? Does your reason have something to do with your psychic experiments with Paris? You send me that email, and tell me you love me, but nothing's changed. How can I trust you when you're hiding something?" Light-headedness overcame her, and she swayed on the stool.

"Slow down." Thom grabbed her shoulder. "Since when do you deem psychics as existing?"

Sandra cleared her throat. Would he trust her? If he didn't … Raz had been desperate to get them out of the hospital. Would Nazier drug them, too? Her windpipe closed, and her eyes burned. "I couldn't tell you at HUP."

Thom narrowed his eyes, and his grip on her shoulder tightened.

Tears filled her eyes and blurred his face. Would he suspect she wasn't telling the truth? Sandra whispered, "I … Paris was controlling my mind. She made me help them when I didn't want to."

Thom's eyes rounded, and his mouth gaped. "Not possible."

She wiped her face with a napkin. "Then why couldn't I leave them? I was terrified, but if you hadn't shown up, what would've happened? This is why I didn't believe you when we left. Paris failing your experiments meant I was imagining everything." Sandra waited for him to call her on the lies. She'd no idea what experiments he might've performed on Paris, drug-induced or not. His unfocused gray eyes stared at nothing. She imagined him going through his mental checklists on what he might've missed.

"Paris and her people are dangerous."

Sandra's heart stopped.

"We don't know what her son is capable of, but if Paris can hide her abilities from the testing ..."

"A little boy is dangerous?"

Thom pulled her from her seat.

She dug in her heels. "Where are we going?"

"You want to know the truth, don't you?"

Sandra hesitated, but the only answers she had right now were zero. The facts couldn't be that bad. She had no faith in Thom's research. If he thought Paris hid something from him, he couldn't have much tangible evidence. She'd keep what happened in the bathroom to herself. Her visions were obviously drug reactions.

Thom led her to her familiar backyard greenhouse. Morning frost covered the frozen blades of grass in a white sheet of ice. Walking across the yard soaked her bare feet. Anxiety stroked her neck, and her body turned into a giant goose bump. He replaced the glass panels of the atrium with sheets of plywood and turned her beautiful sanctuary into something ugly and gross. "What have you done?"

"You'll love it." Thom preened like a kid showing off his macaroni necklace. "We won't have to beg for funds anymore. We can do whatever we want."

Once she entered the greenhouse there'd be no turning back. Sandra moved forward, even though she knew what she'd see would devastate her. The false garden sucked her soul into a black cave. A pinprick of light flashed.

At her hesitation, Thom jogged to the extension cord dangling from the roof. "What was I thinking?" He plugged it in, and the single bulb lit the room.

An arctic breeze filtered between a broken section of plywood and played with her wet hair. She clenched her chattering teeth. The primitive lab spread through the entire structure. "Did you steal equipment from the university?"

Thom laughed. "No need. I have all the supplies I can request, no questions asked."

"From who?"

While neat, solutions and bottles littered the benches. Syringes filled with liquid sat next to a metal table. Laptop computers lined a slab placed between two sawhorses. Extra cords and wires connected to unfamiliar machines.

Thom sat at a computer and opened a file.

Sandra edged closer and examined the notes over his shoulder. It was her research, but different, and geared more toward people instead of plants. *What does he predict will happen? Plants and humans can't infect one another.* She skimmed the file, and her gaze fell on the referenced drug, Z-211. The dates coincided with a timeframe not long after Sandra met Paris. What caught her eye next was life expectancy after taking the initial drug dosage at the recommended rate. *Human trials on unsuspecting patients?* Thom had recorded giving Paris twice the recommended amount.

The dirt floor tripped her exit. She ran out into the yard, and the frozen blades of grass cut into her feet.

CHAPTER TWENTY

SANDRA'S LUNGS BURNED. Her bare feet pounded the ground and slapped onto the driveway as she neared the garage. Rounding the east side of the house, she entered the code into the security pad. The garage door didn't open. She didn't believe Thom had changed the code, but she couldn't get it to work. She beat the plastic casing. He hadn't changed the password in five years. What had made him do it now? She checked for the spare house key hidden under the third rung of the trellis. Right where she'd left it. The click of the key into the lock made her push on the door. Dashing to the interior garage entrance, her wet feet slipped in the entryway. She hopped into the black Mercedes SUV and pushed the start button. She pushed again. Nothing.

Sandra growled out her frustration. She forgot she needed the key fob to start the vehicle. Her head banged against the steering wheel. How many seconds would she have before Thom found her? Ten? Five? A spare set of keys was in the den. She touched one foot to the cool cement floor and listened for any hint of noise. Silence. She sprinted into the house. The welcome mat abraded her feet. She skipped across the hall and skirted around the leather chair in the den.

Think … The keys are in the wooden treasure chest on Thom's desk.

She flipped the lid and stared into the empty box. She pushed and shoved the papers on the desk but found nothing.

Her finger bumped the mouse, and Thom's computer came to life. Sandra stopped and stared at the colorful background image. He modified the external security pad but didn't think to secure his files? She shook her head in disbelief. He never used a password on his systems no matter how many times she told him to keep his research secure. Had he changed the garage code to keep someone out, or keep someone in? A chill entered her veins.

She sat in the chair and pawed through the drawers again. They were filled with flash drives and post-it notes, but no keys. The brightened monitor tempted her to take a peek at its contents. A glance at the screen chilled her body. A filename popped out on the desktop, fertility_tests. Her finger hovered over the mouse.

If he's still testing, so what? She clasped the black plastic. *Who would he be testing? Damn it. I don't have time for this.*

She clicked.

"Where in the hell are you?" Thom's voice boomed from the back entrance.

Sandra grabbed a USB drive and shoved it into the port. She captured the entire container of files and dropped them onto the removable media. The few seconds it took to save the data became an eon. She yanked out the drive and shoved it into her jeans pocket. Then she trotted over to the entrance and hid behind the door.

Lemon scent tickled her nose, making her want to confess every detail about Raz and Paris. *The drug must be coming from his pores. I only smell the citrus when he's close.* A spark arced from the doorknob to her finger. She pressed lightly against the mahogany door. Peeking out the sliver between the wall and hinges, Sandra searched for movement.

Thom walked into the kitchen from the back entrance of the house.

The hand over her mouth cut off her air, and every muscle in her body tense. Warm breath hit her ear.

"Don't be scared. It's me, Ms. G." A low, masculine voice rumbled behind her.

The man's other hand gripped her hip. She looked back and recognized her student. A five o'clock shadow covered Zach's young face. "What in the hell are you doing here?" she whispered.

"I didn't know you were back with Dr. GQ."

Sandra pushed away his hand. "I'm not," she hissed.

Zach shrugged and pulled at the wrinkled picture of Bill Murray pointing on his T-shirt. The caption read, *"You're Awesome!"* "I wouldn't have come if I'd—"

Sandra placed two fingers over his mouth and checked the hallway. She crouched and awkwardly dragged Zach with her. The thump of Thom's feet raced toward the main bathroom.

Sandra couldn't risk Thom hearing them and mimed her words. "We have to get out of here."

"You won't tell anyone, will you?" Zach whispered in her ear. "It's just a Six prank. No harm."

Zach had no clue of the danger they were in. She pursed her lips and kept her tone low. "Leaving a calling card on my office door isn't subtle."

Zach laughed under his breath. "That's the point." He swung his backpack over his shoulder. "GQ has had it coming for months. I've been waiting for retaliation."

Sandra narrowed her eyes, but her lips twitched as her snicker tried to break free. "Instigator." She didn't understand the rivalry between Zach and her ex. It'd been going on for three years. Zach loved the fact they were divorced. She wasn't technically on his side, but his pranks entertained her. "Do you have a car?"

He shook his head. "Nah. A buddy dropped me off."

"I don't have a key to the Mercedes. We need to get out of here."

"You don't need one."

"Yes, I know I don't actually need a key." *Thanks, Mr. Obvious.*

"I can hack it. Code is my natural language. An antenna will do the trick." He pulled equipment from his bag.

Sandra's head cocked to the side. His statement was odd, but the prospect of having transportation out of here made her disregard the phrasing.

Zach blushed. "I was going to take it to the university lot. Maybe paint it pink or soap it. Hadn't decided, yet."

Sandra grunted. "I'm driving. I don't need Six reasons for you to get arrested for carjacking."

"Grand theft auto."

Sandra rolled her eyes. The hall was empty. She sprinted into the garage, with Zach on her heels. She got behind the wheel.

Zach jumped in to ride shotgun, and he performed his hacking antenna magic on the vehicle.

Sandra placed her finger on the pushbutton starter of the Mercedes, and it purred to life. She reached over her head and pushed the garage door opener on the visor. The massive rectangle of aluminum lifted to the whirr of the engaged motor.

Thom burst through the entry door.

Sandra slammed the gas pedal and clipped the half-open door. It crunched under the pressure of the large vehicle and flew out onto the pavement. She executed a three-point turn in the L-shaped driveway and gunned it down the path.

Zach's gleeful tone worried her. "The Six keeps it real. Thom needs to be kept on his toes like this. Are you two fighting? Are you taking back what's yours?"

"It's complicated." A glance in the side mirror reflected Thom's foot chase. She peeled out of the driveway. Stray pieces of loose gravel from the gutter flew behind the Mercedes. A red sedan with black-tinted windows blocked her exit. She slammed on the brakes. The seatbelt pulled her back into the optimum crash position. A second passed. Sandra caught her breath and glanced at Zach.

He white-knuckled the dash. "Friends of yours?"

"Nope."

"Go around the back of the house." Zach tapped the console.

"What?"

He jerked his thumb behind them. "Cut through the side yard."

Sandra glanced in the rearview mirror. "Drive in reverse? Who do you think I am?"

"I've seen you drive on campus."

Smart-ass. Apparently, Zach had more faith in her then she did. She put the car in reverse and pressed the pedal to the floor. The wheels chirped a second before traction control kicked in.

"Can't have any fun in a Mercedes, anymore. Pft ... traction control. I can't believe Dr. GQ didn't turn that shit off."

"Why do you think I ended up with the Camaro?"

The greasy yard tested her confidence. Yet, she navigated around the house like an expert stunt driver. It was all adrenaline now. Zach directed her behind the neighbor's house. They reached the highway with a skid and two near-accidents. Sandra spun the car around and pushed the gearshift into drive.

The red sedan tailed.

Zach braced his lanky body against the dash. "Care to tell me what's up?"

Sandra weaved in and out of traffic, but eluding the red sedan was impossible. Her paranoia kicked into overtime. A Chaser was after her. Why now, when she'd been separated from the group? It made little sense.

Zach sat calm and focused.

Too calm. Sandra said, "Someone's after me."

"Really? What for?" At her sharp stare, Zach screeched, "Watch the road."

Their vehicle lurched off the shoulder. Sandra swerved back onto the highway.

"Any ideas on how to lose this guy?" Sandra weaved around another SUV on the two-lane thoroughfare. Soon, she'd enter a no-passing zone when they approached the hills.

Zach licked his lips, hands on the top of his head.

"Cut the crap. You're a master at getting out of trouble. Why would this be any different?" She monitored the side mirror. The car was two lengths back but kept pace, despite her erratic weaving in and out of traffic.

Zach smiled. He concentrated on the back window.

"I'm uncomfortable with this."

The pleasure on Zach's face exposed his lie. A half-smile appeared on his lips, and his eyes danced with amusement.

"Are you running from the law? What the hell is going on?" A buzz came from his backpack, and he pulled out his cellphone.

"I need help, or we're both toast."

Zach swore at the phone and texted a swift reply.

Sandra swerved around another vehicle. "Hurry. Lives are at stake, Zach. Like ours." Her next attempt at passing failed, and metal grazed metal as she sideswiped the oncoming truck.

Zach's tone changed, and his face became hard. "A hidden road is up ahead. We can lose them."

Of course, Zach always had an exit plan.

More text messages dinged. His head snapped up. "Fuck me. What in the hell did you do?"

Sandra blinked. Did he just change personalities? Without the smile on his face, the kid before her turned into a man. "I didn't do anything. And watch your mouth—"

"Keep your eyes on the road, Ms. G. I don't want to be kidnapped by a Chaser."

Sandra's skin became cold, and her ears rang as the blood fled her extremities. A hand joined hers on the wheel and steadied the SUV.

"You *can* trust me." Zach made quick finger taps on his smartphone. "At the top of the next hill is a trail that can't be seen from the highway. When we crest the hill, brake then make a hard right." His voice was calm and controlled. "We have to get more cars between us."

She pushed the pedal to the floor, and the speedometer approached seventy, too fast for this winding road.

Zach kept his gaze out the back window the entire time.

She came up on several cars and passed them. The dotted line turned a solid yellow again. They were in the hills. She went around another car and pulled back in line before a truck smacked them. Her heart galloped. They weaved around an S-curve.

Zach turned forward in his seat. "Past the sign up ahead, then make a hard right."

Sandra slammed on the brakes and maneuvered around the billboard. She swore the Mercedes lifted onto two wheels. Afraid they would roll, she tensed for impact, but the heavy machine righted itself on a grass-covered path. Tree limbs scratched both sides of the vehicle. Rocks flew up and banged against the underbelly. Thom's baby was getting the shit beat out of it.

"Easy. You did great. Stop behind the large pine ahead."

She parked the vehicle on the other side of the tree and shut off the engine. The sound of their heavy breathing filled the silence. She faced Zach.

An excited smile stretched over his face. "Hot damn, woman. You're my getaway driver, any day."

"What now?"

"Now, we walk."

"Walk? Some fast talking is in order."

Zach got out and walked down the hill.

Sandra stared after him for a few seconds. She could either follow, or take her chances back where they came from. He probably knew more than she did about what a Chaser was. Dirt and stones cut into her tender feet, but she caught up with him. She'd left everything behind. Not that she had anything at Thom's house, but the sense of only having the clothes on her back troubled her. "You know what's happening to me, don't you?"

Zach chuckled. "Happening *to* you? You landed in a pile of shit without a hose."

"Our car chase was too routine to you. I need answers."

Zach continued down the hill, making his own path in the underbrush. "I like you, Ms. G, always have."

Lacking shoes, Sandra trailed him the best she could. This man wasn't the lighthearted student she'd known for three years. Dare she call Zach a friend? She liked him and enjoyed his antics, but she'd still been his teacher. What had removed her rose-colored glasses? She'd been too wrapped up in her own world and hadn't seen the deceit surrounding her.

"You need to stay away from assholes." Zach snickered.

"What're you talking about?"

They'd reached the bottom of the hill. Zach trudged through a stream.

Sandra found a path of rocks. She jumped from one to the next and successfully avoided getting her feet wet in the cold water.

He stopped.

She smacked into his back.

Zach cocked his head. "I would've been able to keep you safe. Oblivious, but safe. The Six was formed for that reason."

"You were guarding me?"

Zach turned and grabbed her arms. "I wanted to keep you from what's going on right now, right here. How could you go back to an asshole like GQ? Never mind. Don't answer. Cameron wants you back at HUP."

"I'm not back—" She stomped her foot. "Why am I explaining myself to you? My private business is mine. You've got a lot to answer to for what you were about to do to Thom's car." She banged her palm against her head. "Thom and I aren't even close to what's important right now."

"Small amusements. I need them, or I'd get bored on this mission."

"All the Six pranks on campus were because you were bored?"

Zach shrugged and smiled a devious smile.

The pieces fell into place. The way Cameron had acted around Raz and Paris. Raz's reference to his past in the military. "Raz and Paris. They're your mission. You're not a student, are you?"

"I knew you were pretty smart, but that's classified info. I'm sure Cameron can tell you more. As of two minutes ago, I have orders to transport you back to HUP."

CHAPTER TWENTY-ONE

SANDRA STEPPED ON a rock and winced. She hated the outdoors. How long would they be in this horrible forest? Numb from the falling temperatures, the pain in her foot was insignificant after her next step.

Zach's pocket buzzed. He removed his mobile phone and held it to his ear. "Where are you?" A cloud of vapor escaped his lips. "Amber, the purpose of a rendezvous point is so we can find each other." He raked his hand through his short dark hair. "It's not my fault Cam gave you babysitting duty. Deal with it, and get your ass here ASAP. I'm freezing my balls off."

Zach's hardened soldier facade took Sandra by surprise. His acting abilities impressed her. Which Zach was the real one? The one before her was a stranger, but the harmless prankster no longer fit him, either. One shiver, then two, chased each other down his neck.

He's as vulnerable as me in this hell-just-froze-over woods. Sandra rubbed her arms.

Zach pulled his pack from his shoulders and fished for a canteen. He offered it to her.

One glance down, and every filthy word Sandra knew, and some she didn't, exploded from his mouth.

"Where in the hell are your shoes?"

"As you recall, we were in a hurry earlier." Sandra grabbed the water and gulped a quarter of it down.

Zach unzipped several pockets of his bag and found a roll of duct tape. He lectured her like a wayward child.

Sandra pursed her lips. "Yeah, I get it."

Zach arched a brow, and embarrassment prickled over her face. He dug around the forest floor and pulled a large piece of soft bark from a tree. He snapped it in half with a quick thrust of his thumbs and motioned her to the ground. "Sit."

Sandra bristled. She wasn't the child here. Right? Yet, her feet were cold, and the numbness became an ache at every cut and scrape. After another defiant drink, Sandra sat in the dirt.

"Why were you at the ex's house?" Zach asked.

The ground was dry. Sandra smacked the earth from her hands and cleared her throat. "Why were you there?"

Zach snorted and tee-heed.

Sandra's head snapped up. *There's the Zach I know.* In the easygoing way of his, he elaborated.

"To steal his car. The bastard gave me a C this semester." He removed an intimidating knife from a zippered pocket.

Sandra didn't take her gaze off it. He carried that monster in his backpack? He was a kid!

Zach cut away the bottom edge of his shirt, exposing a ripped stomach. *Oh, wow. He's definitely not a kid.* The eye candy was nice, but taut muscles reminded her of Raz's splendid body, and another obvious fact right in front of her nose. How could she have mistaken Raz's soldier strength for anything else?

Sandra held the cloth Zach nudged into her hand. "Why care about Thom's stupid Mercedes? You're not just a student."

"I take my studies seriously. Might as well get an education out of my time here. Especially when nothing exciting is going on." Zach tapped his skull. "Got to keep the mind sharp." He cleaned her scrapes with the leftover water. "The wounds are shallow. They'll be healed by tomorrow." Winding the ripped fabric of his T-shirt around her arch, he dressed the injuries.

No one intentionally wanted to attend Thom's classes. "Thom's lectures are that stimulating?"

Zach chuckled. He tied a firm knot at her ankle. "GQ often slips up and provides intel."

Sandra shivered. Before today, she would've never matched Thom with secret intelligence. What had she copied to the thumb drive? "Did you see the mad scientist laboratory he created in the backyard?"

"The greenhouse is on observation." Zach formed the pliant bark around her foot and wrapped it in duct tape.

His creativity was remarkable, but without a doubt, this wasn't the first time he'd assumed the role of medic with limited materials. "How much observation?"

"It's classified." He reached for the remaining bark. "Your feet might still be cold with these temp shoes. At least they'll be dry and protected until we get to base."

Sandra inspected the new shoe. "Interesting creation."

He shrugged and got busy on the other foot. "You still in love with GQ, and you don't want to tell me?"

So much for an attempted subject change. Sandra didn't want to discuss Thom, and definitely not the weird attraction to him she hadn't been able to break at the house. The horrid chemistry she experienced with Thom was gone now, but was it gone for good? She cleared her throat. "Thom made me leave the hospital."

Zach tensed. His brows scrunched together. "He forced you?"

How much should Sandra tell him? "Raz is still there." The events at the house faded like a dream. They hadn't been real. Thom had drugged her. Her receptivity to him made sense now. "I had a panic attack. Thom took advantage of it to get me out of the hospital." Sandra had seen the reality of Thom's experiments in her greenhouse oasis. She stood. The flash drive gouged her hip. Awkwardly testing her ability to walk on the bark shoes, she weighed the pros and cons of trusting Zach with the information on Thom's experiments. Remembering Nazier's insistence that Thom test her churned up the acid eating away her stomach lining. "Why would he do that?"

"Leon should've gotten you out." Zach returned the supplies and zipped up the bag.

"He was there. Why didn't he?"

"Chaser exposure was too great."

Sandra replayed the events at the hospital. When she'd blacked out in the waiting room, she and Sean had been alone. Leon could've helped them leave then gone to warn Raz and Paris. There had been enough time well before Thom came anywhere near them. Was Zach suggesting hundreds of Chasers were at the hospital who would've waited patiently for Paris to receive medical care before capturing any of them? Something wasn't adding up. "Is Thom a Chaser?"

Zach continued along their original path by the stream. "We aren't sure what your ex is."

Sandra tailed him. Her shoes allowed her to make faster progress along the trail. Leon had given off bad vibes, but none came from Zach. She had to trust her instincts.

They neared a small shelter, and a woman dressed in black-and-green combat gear emerged from the door.

"Amber, you made it. Congrats."

Amber threw a bundle of clothes at Zach's face. "I only brought one set, *mi amigo idiota*."

In two seconds, Zach had his arms in the long sleeves and the fabric over his head. He tossed the green camo jacket to Sandra.

"What were you thinking?" Amber asked.

Her annoyance was evident in the sarcastic lilt to her voice. Sandra's head snapped up, but Amber ignored her.

Zach tucked a pistol into the waistband of his jeans. "That your sense of direction is ridiculous."

"So funny. You've moved on to plan X instead of plan B."

At Zach's sly smile, a few dozen swear words blasted from Amber's lips along with a hefty dose of Spanish. "Thom will realize you're M83 if you keep tormenting him, *estúpido*," she hissed.

"Never gonna happen."

Amber eyed Sandra from head-to-toe, and Sandra put on the jacket. The threat in Amber's eyes chilled her more than the air ever could.

"Thanks for ruining my day, *pendejo*."

Sandra stuttered. "I—"

Zach laughed. "The insult was directed at me. Amber gets sour when she has to babysit."

Sandra jutted her hip. "I'm an adult. Neither of you have to—"

"You're not even wearing shoes. You need supervision." Amber walked around the shelter on high alert. She concentrated on the woods, her control that of a seasoned hunter.

A tremor danced down Sandra's back. "I had no choice about the shoes."

"Oh, yes. Running from your precious Thom." Amber jerked her head in Zach's general direction. "Has she come to realize her womanizing Thom caused this mess? I'd love to blame it on her. Cameron says she's an innocent bystander."

Sandra shook her fist. "I'm still in the dark. Zach won't explain."

"If you used your intelligence, no one would have to. The answer is right in front of you."

Sandra bristled.

Zach checked another pack at Amber's feet. "Give her some slack, Am. Let's get out of here before the idiots chasing us wise up."

"Are they really chasing us, or was that a reason to get me out here alone?" Sandra asked.

Zach and Amber froze. They both spun with open jaws as if *Sandra* were *estúpido*.

She trusted no one. "How convenient you were already at Thom's house."

Amber turned and approached Zach with a predatory gait. "At his *casa?*"

"Classified mission."

Amber cocked her head.

Zach shrugged. "It was fate."

Amber pulled back her arm. The smack of skin and crunch of bone broke the silence.

Sandra jumped.

Zach staggered back from the punch. The smirk, accented with a split lip, spread across his face.

"That was fate, too." Amber grinned.

He spat blood at her feet. "You might've chipped a tooth, woman."

Amber harrumphed. She rubbed her knuckles on her jacket. "They're weapons of minor destruction." She laughed, but quickly sobered. "You and your classified shit constantly risk our exposure. You're supposed to keep Six activity at the university."

"Thom hasn't a clue about me. You, on the other hand, are screwed because I told him *all* about you."

Amber shook her head as Zach ducked into the shelter before she could dish out more physical punishment.

The flash drive burrowed into Sandra's hip as she caught the bag Amber threw at her. *Tell them about it.* The ridicule thrown at Thom suggested he was their enemy. She forced her fingers to stay at her sides. *Not yet.* The coat provided much-appreciated warmth. She pitched the bag over her shoulders and threaded her arms through the straps. She shoved her hands inside her coat pockets. *Wait until I see Cam. I'll give the drive to him, only him.* Her skin fluttered as circulation and heat returned to her arms.

Zach came out of the shelter with additional supplies. "Am has a Jeep down the trail. We'll be warmer in a few minutes."

Amber and Zach entered a hidden path.

Sandra froze like a deer in headlights. Did she dare follow them?

Zach popped his head back out the path entrance. He flicked his hand in the direction they came from. "Thom attached a GPS tracker on the SUV. They've already found it by now. You want to stick around and verify?"

"Then why steal it?"

"The point was for him to find it, but then my orders changed."

"It's the Jeep, or stay here," Amber called from within the underbrush.

Sandra sighed. Her eye ticked. Amber needed to butt out. Sandra didn't want to stay here, but going with them sounded just as pleasant. "I still need answers, Zach. Who can I trust?"

"You can trust me." He disappeared.

Sandra jogged into the forest and left the last remnants of civilization behind.

Zach picked up the pace.

The trail grew dense with thick brush, and she was grateful the coat protected her arms. The back of the Jeep came into her line of sight. Tires poked out under tree limbs.

Zach stepped over a fallen log.

She climbed over the tree and wiped her dirty hands on her jeans. A step forward had her colliding with his back.

"Crouch down," Amber whispered in her ear. "Don't make a sound."

Together, they moved onto their haunches.

A man dressed in military gear emerged from the evergreens.

Sandra's heart pounded, and she was grateful the camo jacket helped her blend into the backdrop. The trees were dense, but the sun filtered in and cast shadows on the ground. The three of them were invisible because the soldier, his face painted in black and green, had disappeared in the blink of an eye wearing similar clothes. If they'd been three seconds later, they never would have noticed him hidden in the trees. As he continued to move through the forest, she couldn't make out the outline of his body. Sandra kept her gaze glued to his weapon so she wouldn't lose sight of him.

Amber held a finger to her mouth.

Sandra nodded. No sound emerged from her lips.

Zach and Amber exchanged a short series of hand signals.

Clack. Clack. Clack.

A small scream erupted from Sandra.

The man jerked and fell.

Sandra held her hands over her ears to muffle the eruption. Small puffs of dirt and tree limbs flew into the air from every direction. They were surrounded. Sandra couldn't catch her breath. *Oh, no. Am I having another panic attack?* She closed her eyes. She visualized an open beach, sunlight and waves, sand and warmth.

Had they returned fire?

Someone cried out.

The noise died and became faint in the distance. Sandra opened her eyes.

Amber kept her eye pressed to the scope of her gun and monitored their surroundings.

Zach held his cell in his hand.

Sandra caught the text messages in her peripheral vision and leaned in to read them.

ZM: *Rendezvous pt compromised. Advise.*

CM: *Damage?*

ZM: *2 teams. We're safe.*

CM: *ID if possible. Continue transpt.*

Sandra surmised *transpt* referred to her, but nothing indicated where they were taking her.

Two more men walked through the destruction, guns at the ready.

"Base," a soldier said into a headpiece. "We've cleared section J."

The second man crouched and checked the victim's pulse. He nodded to his partner.

"Request permission to follow scout."

"Granted," a voice crackled from the communications device. They left.

Seconds, or minutes, ticked by. Sandra couldn't tell.

Amber scoped the area.

Every muscle in Zach's body tensed.

"We're clear," Amber said.

Sandra didn't believe Amber, because she never lowered the rifle.

"I'll check casualties and report." Zach entered the battlefield.

Sandra grabbed his arm. "Zach, no."

"The area is clear." He removed her hand and whispered, "It's okay, Ms. G."

Amber jumped to her feet.

Fear paralyzed Sandra's body. She didn't want to leave their safe hiding place, but once Amber stepped away, Sandra stuck to Amber like a cocklebur.

Zach searched one of the fallen soldiers. "No identification on this one. Special ops, for sure."

Amber swept her rifle through the woods. Tensed. Focused.

Zach moved on to the other fallen soldiers.

Where had they come from? A slight movement caught Sandra's eyes. A fallen soldier had moved. Maybe he wasn't dead. Sandra scrambled over, dropped to the ground and checked for a pulse. A faint spark of electricity arced between them. She closed her eyes, and warm waves of energy flowed along her arm. Superhuman strength entered her muscles.

"What's she doing?" Amber asked, horror in her voice.

Calm entered Sandra's body in stark contrast to Amber's angry heat. The man jumped and twitched under her hand. She couldn't stop herself, the movements involuntary. The energy built in intensity and glowed with unnatural light. She waved her other hand over the body. A weightless aura settled over them like a cocoon. She opened her eyes. A soft glow came from her hovering hand. Perpetual static electric sparks emanated in every direction.

"Her eyes have changed," Amber said. "What's going on, Zach?"

"How the hell do I know?" Anxiety had elevated the pitch of Zach's voice. "I deliver her to HUP. End order." He circled Sandra and the fallen man.

Sandra couldn't make a sound in explanation.

"We have to go. She'll compromise headquarters." Amber bounced from foot to foot.

Zach wouldn't disobey his orders. Even as Sandra's pretend student, Zach followed through. He lifted his phone.

"What're you doing?" Amber asked.

"This is too big, Am. I have to inform Cameron."

There. The flickers of energy still coursed down Sandra's arm where she touched the body. A flash of pain slammed into her face and exploded into a kaleidoscope behind her eyes. She reached for her head and moaned in agony.

Amber pointed her rifle at Sandra. "She's the enemy. All along, she's been working with Thom. Can't you see what's going on?"

Zach blocked Amber and pushed the muzzle to the ground. "Your prejudices are influencing you. Thom's the enemy, not Sandra."

"This display indicates she's a Zenith. Chasers are using Zeniths and their fake Nexus connection as infiltrators, now. Bring her back to base, and *todos estaremos muertos*. Dead."

Sandra scrambled back from the lifeless figure. She rolled in the leaves. Her hands still zapped from the connection. The man lay still. Had she jump-started his heart only to let him die again?

"We have orders, and we follow them," Zach said.

Sandra gasped. "I'm not working with Thom." Her throat burned. She pushed past the raw ache. "I don't know what he's been doing."

Amber stepped closer, to do what Sandra wasn't sure, but thankfully Zach held her back.

Amber shoved away Zach's arms. "Then why did you give him your research?"

Sandra stood and caught her balance. She jabbed Amber in the chest. "What about my research?" Why did everyone care about what she was doing?

Zach separated them.

Amber had a cruel twist to her lips. "We know all about what you've been doing."

"I gave my initial developments to Thom to get rid of him from my life, but at the house, I found out he's responsible for Paris's sickness. I have to go back to Center Medical and help her." Sandra's body shook under the effort of bringing her emotions and physical strength under control. She was a vibrating machine focused on releasing the toxins coursing through her body. Lemon scent oozed from her hands and made her retch. She was still reacting to Thom's drugs. The powerful hallucinogenic made her mind spin.

Zach helped steady her. "Cameron wants to speak to you." He pressed the phone to her ear.

"Sandra, are you all right? Did Thom hurt you?"

Sandra languished in the calming effects of Cameron's voice. The impulse to debrief him infused her mind. She struggled to tell him what the soldier knew. "He's here … Ta … Ta …"

"Thom is there? Did he inject you?"

"Taft," she croaked out.

Amber and Zach looked at each other. "Is she bat-shit crazy?" Amber asked.

Zach tried to take the phone from Sandra's hand, but she held on tight. The impulse to relay the message repeated in her head. "Soldier 5892349. Order. M83 cell destroy. Taft initiated infiltrators."

"What?" Cameron inhaled sharply on the phone. "Did Thom tell you that?"

"No, the dead soldier did." Sandra released the phone to Zach.

He spoke briefly then hung up.

Amber went over to the fallen soldier. She checked his wounds and pilfered through his pockets. Trotting back to them, Amber threw the dog tag at Sandra's duct-taped shoes. "You have some explaining to do."

Sandra picked up the metal tab and rubbed her finger across the raised numbers. The same identifier she'd given Cameron embossed the surface.

Chapter Twenty-Two

RAZ PULLED INTO the university drive. He couldn't shake his anger. The Chaser dart kicked in along with the expected paranoia. Sandra's betrayal salted the already oozing wound. *I can't trust anyone, but I have to trust Cameron.*

Chaser tranks were among the most powerful ever made. The Nexus light emanating from his hands faded to a shimmer. A human would've passed out in the garage. A normal Sixxer would've been slowed enough for capture. Only Transors resisted the drug … to a point. Exhaustion would be difficult to beat down. Chasers wouldn't stop until they found him.

Raz glanced in the backseat. An amethyst blush highlighted Sean's cheeks, but sparks no longer emerged from his fingertips. He startled awake. Bloodshot eyes stared at Raz in the rearview mirror for a split second. They still held the Nexus glow.

Instead of the M83 bustle Raz expected, HUP held a yellow calm. He passed row after empty row of the parking lot. They had a greater chance of not getting caught here than on their own. At least, that's what he kept telling himself. Raz parked close to the building.

Sean climbed out, and the metal chuck of the shutting door echoed like a sledgehammer hitting concrete. He held his teddy by the arm, and the little bear's foot dragged on the pavement.

The campus was too quiet. The way Cameron spoke, a swarm of M83 soldiers would be purring along the buildings of Hamilton University. Raz and Sean walked up the stairs to the front of Sandra's building.

Sean's fingers grasped Raz's hand. "Will the Chasers find us here?"

"Cameron has an anti-NEU." *It should conceal our power and Nexus energy.*

Sean dragged his feet. "The man at the hospital … I didn't like him."

Raz helped him up the steps. "Neither did I, but we can have a render here without worrying about him."

Sean stopped, eyes rounded. He hopped in a burst of energy followed by a Nexus vibrational release. "We need Sandra, Daddy. Do you think they'll hurt her like they did Mommy?" His words came out in a rapid fire. He tugged on Raz's hand. "Let's go back and get her."

Sean echoed Raz's own worry for Sandra. Although, remembering her deception stifled any remaining concern he had for her. No one was innocent when fraternizing with Chasers. *With the enemy.*

At the top of the stairs, Raz crouched to Sean's level. The breeze ruffled his hair. Even the Nexus illumination in his baby browns were like his mother's. Raz's eyes stung. Paris's sacrifice was still a needle-like burn in his lungs. *So stupid.* Hadn't she known how much they needed her? Raz brushed tear tracks from Sean's face. "We can only trust each other now. Do you understand?"

"But, Daddy—"

"I'll find out what happened to Mommy."

Sean nodded. He took a hesitant breath and struggled to control his emotions. "I want her back. Do we have to leave everyone?"

"I hope not, buddy. We need Cameron's help."

"How can he if he's a bad man?"

The door burst open. Cameron motioned them inside. "Don't linger." He jogged to Sandra's office.

Raz and Sean ran behind.

Cameron gathered a stack of notebooks and Sandra's laptop. "Chasers are bad. I'm not a Chaser, kid. But that doesn't mean some aren't around." He cupped Sean's chin. "Shit. He's still reacting to the render."

"The anti-NEU will hide it. You need to remove the sensor. Now."

Cameron removed what looked like a kid's character sticker from his shirt. "When you're tagged with one of these suckers, renders are taboo." He moved Sean's head from side to side. "At this level of activity, the anti-NEU isn't likely to hide your excess energy. You said the render failed. The circle is open. There should be little Nexus signature left." Cameron snagged a cloth shopping bag from the back of the door and handed it to Sean.

Sean stuffed his bear down his shirt. The head and arms flopped out the top. He struggled with the floppy material of the bag.

Raz helped by pulling the edges of the sack wide. "Our Nexus energy and circle connection is sporadic. Paris altered our connection somehow. I don't know if she was able to because of the drugs or her illness."

Cameron filled the bag with his bounty. "You should've told me Sean was still pulsing. I'll have the team take Sandra to Omega's new HQ instead of here. Damn it." He pulled a cell from his pocket and dialed on speaker. "Amber?"

"Yeah, *pendejo*?"

Amber's voice dripped thorns.

"Where did you think I went, on vay-cay?" Her voice echoed in the office.

Cameron laughed. "Sweetheart, is that any way to treat the love of your life?"

"In your wet dreams, soldier."

Amber didn't take any shit from Cameron. Raz liked her immediately.

"What's the problem?" she asked.

"Rendezvous point B. Our road trip north is canceled."

"Affirmative, boss," she said.

Cameron swung the shopping bag over his shoulder. "Communicate our location change to the team, and meet me at our secondary rendezvous point at 1100 hours."

"Copy that. Out." The phone went silent.

How did Omega have Sandra and not the Chaser? "You captured Sandra?" Raz asked.

Cameron jogged down the hallway. "Captured? Zach picked her up this morning. Come with me. I'll use a second anti-NEU to make sure Chasers don't detect your residuals. One unit should've been enough to dissipate your render energy, but I'm doubtful, considering Sean's condition."

With every step along the hallway, the drugs from the dart weakened Raz's ability to communicate with the Nexus. The extra energy Paris had given him wasn't enough to bring him back one hundred percent. "We're not going anywhere until you start talking. Paris was highly energized before she died. Sandra's position is suspect. We aren't following you, or anyone, anywhere."

Cameron stopped and waited. "Sandra's fine. We'll pack up then I'll give you details."

"You have five seconds."

Cameron shook his head. "I guarantee Chasers are getting closer, and one of our anti-NEUs is old. It's built on outdated radiant technology and isn't always reliable in a closed circle. We don't have a lot of reasons to use those devices anymore."

Outdated radiant technology? Only radiant heat could deflect a NEU. "An energy transfer will take five minutes and stabilize Sean. We aren't leaving until I can do it. The anti-NEU can hold that long." Raz stood his ground. Would Cameron call his bluff?

Cameron opened a janitor's closet and removed a handheld device from a toolbox. "You and your circle have been lucky. An entire government division is devoted to Sixxer identification. In fact, as brilliant as humans are, they called it the Six ID division. Detection of Nexus auras has become pretty advanced since Sean was born. Did you think you'd hide forever? We have anti-NEUs that work in a pinch, but we're also fighting advanced NEU devices just on the market. Those are nasty bastards. If Chasers suspect the university is a hub, they'd already have the place surrounded. That's why renderings are on the strict no-fly list."

Raz took a gut check. Fighting against Chasers with a broken circle, a recent dart and advanced technology screamed foolishness. He trailed Cameron down the stairs to the basement level. "Don't I have clearance? Debrief me." Cameron was ignoring Raz's suspicions of Sandra working for the enemy.

Sean skipped beside them.

Raz scooped him up into his arms and swayed. He caught his balance before Cameron noticed. "Why are you hesitating?"

Cameron paused. He studied Sean like a bug he didn't want to touch. "I've never been around a Sixxer child. I don't want to scare him."

"Sean can handle himself."

"Mm hmm." Sean nodded his bobble head in affirmation.

Cameron stared for a second then nodded, too. He fiddled with the device in his hands. "Hope this works. We have to hurry in case the other unit failed."

Raz widened his eyes and tensed. *That small thing, no bigger than a cell phone, is the other anti-NEU? I'm not surprised it can't contain our collective energy.*

Sean squeezed his neck.

Raz didn't understand how the tiny machine deflected the Nexus surges of two Sixxers. "What's Sandra's position?" He placed a hand on the wall. He concentrated on each inhale, and he'd be damned if he let Chaser darts bring him to his knees. They weren't enough to take him out.

"Are you all right?" Cameron asked.

"Tell me what's going on." Raz moved forward. He winced at the pain in his shoulder. It radiated outward in a spinning web intensified by Sean's weight.

Cameron glanced at Raz's shoulder. "They fucking darted you. We have to get the hell out of here."

Raz grunted. "It didn't stick." He didn't mention more than one had glanced off his body. The shoulder dart had been the deepest one. Raz touched the wound. He had pulled the pin out, but sticky blood seeped through his shirt. About three, maybe four, darts had penetrated his skin and created surface wounds. Cameron didn't need to know how weak he was. "You want me back in the Corp. Give me intel." His arms shook, and Sean slid out of them to the floor. Raz would have to trust Cameron to keep them safe.

"Paris was a target from the moment you set foot in Angelville." Cameron said.

Impossible. Raz would've sensed Omega's observations, because the team watching Sandra equaled the team monitoring him. "She was under surveillance for a year?"

"Under our watch, not Chasers, until about twenty-four hours ago. You and Sean weren't verified targets until last night, when you arrived at Center Medical. It's been on the comm."

They rounded the now-familiar basement corner, and Cameron swiped his badge at the lab entrance.

"M83 is targeting Sixxers?" They'd never been hidden.

Cameron entered his code and opened the door. "Sixxers working for the enemy. According to released intelligence, Paris had always been listed on General Taft's inventory. They were waiting for her to show up on grid."

Which happened when she went to that fucking Chaser for psychic studies. What had she been thinking? What had she been planning?

Cameron set the anti-NEU on a table, and a steady ping emanated from it. "For the past twenty-four hours, General Taft wanted Paris alive, but Chasers hadn't officially filed her mark." He cast Raz a sharp look. "Still haven't."

"General Taft wouldn't have let our circle linger for a year." Especially one with a Transor. "Paris has to be marked now after her capture. Chasers mark captured Sixxers alive or dead."

Cameron shrugged. He made short work of counting the lab inventory.

Raz conserved energy as Cameron hurried around the room pilfering supplies.

"Considering how badly General Taft wanted Paris, I found it odd a team didn't descend on the hospital. Leon reported only a few Chasers," Cameron said.

"Chasers were plenty upon exiting," Raz said dryly. He couldn't gain more intel by himself. If M83 wanted Raz, they had him now. He had to make Paris's death right. She'd clearly detected her father at the hospital. She wasn't marked. Dr. Nazier wanted her presence kept a secret from General Taft. Omega and Cameron were his only link back into M83 so he could find out why.

Cameron made his way around the lab and came back to the table with the anti-NEU. He made an adjustment to the device and gathered more computer equipment and notebooks. "M83 has been observing Chaser activity at HUP for years. M83 placed your circle on observation eleven months ago, once we determined Paris's entry on the target list. No engagement."

"Why the no engagement order?"

"You and Paris both have a reputation with M83. Paris's recent interactions with a Chaser were suspect, as well." Cameron finished his heist and made a beeline to the coolers.

Raz followed. The numeral thirty-nine was stamped on the surface of the door Cameron entered.

He moved a tray of specimens, flipped open a hidden panel, and entered a code. A small square in the wall popped open. At the release of the handle, half of the cooler wall disappeared.

Raz noted the massive size of this operation, but found the limited crew outside of M83 protocol. "How long has the Omega team been here?"

Cameron sighed. "Classified. I was under the impression you could fill me in on why Paris was of interest. We've been ordered to evacuate headquarters, and all base units until we determine the infiltrator level."

"Sean can't be exposed to any infiltrators in his current state. Isn't HUP a safe harbor?" Raz stumbled against the threshold and reached out to Sean.

Cameron narrowed his eyes. "Do you care about Sandra?"

The threat was back in Cameron's demeanor. Raz bristled. *I never wanted to care.* Why was Omega so interested in Sandra's safety?

"Daddy, we have to help her." The sparks were back in Sean's fingertips. They flashed in the bear's little black eyes. A render would bank their Nexus energy, and Raz couldn't do it without Sandra, or a lot of time and rest. The effects of the tranquilizer made the room spin in slow motion.

"Something has happened to her," Cameron said.

Raz would've taken a punch to the chest better than the blast of Cameron's news. Had the render done something to Sandra?

The vibrations in Sean's body came back full force. "I didn't hurt Mommy, Daddy. I promise. I told her to wait, but she lost my hand."

Cameron bent and ruffled Sean's hair.

The boy choked back hitched sobs.

Cameron's gaze pinned Raz to the wall. "Sandra is safe, but we're out of our element. Is there something you need to tell me?"

Sean sobbed.

Cameron furrowed his brows. "It's an intricate web. We need all the help we can get."

"Sandra is my second mom!" Snot bubbled from Sean's nose at his outcry, and he swiped his jacket sleeve, Sandra's jacket, over his mouth. "Mommy said it was all right for me to do it. That it wouldn't hurt her."

"It's not your fault. We didn't know she was a Chaser, buddy." Raz patted Sean's back, but he knew the gesture wasn't enough to take Sean's confusion and grief away. He was dealing with situations way beyond his maturity level.

"Sandra isn't a Chaser." Cameron marched inside the bunker, gathered supplies and weapons, and packed a military duffle. Each thud of metal on fabric echoed off the basement walls. "In fact, she knows little about any of this."

"Sandra left with one of General Taft's go-to guys. I only know him by sight. She knows more than you think. She's a Chaser." Raz recognized Cameron's lack of surprise at this revelation, and he found his reaction odd.

A thoughtful expression came over Cameron's face. "Thom's the go-to guy? Fuck me. I didn't see that coming. If he's the go-to guy, the mighty general would've taken your sorry ass months ago."

"Have you heard of Dr. Nazier?"

Cameron's head snapped up. "Go on."

"He's Paris's father."

"Impossible. Nazier isn't a Sixxer."

"Paris was … she says adopted, I say taken as a baby. I'm sure you can imagine for what. Her empathic power sensed Nazier's presence at the hospital."

Cameron leaned forward. "Confirm you saw him." He rubbed his neck then stepped back.

Raz crossed his arms over his chest. "Why should I?"

Cameron laughed. "We've been monitoring Thom for years. He's in charge of nasty Sixxer experiments, but he hides his affiliation with General Taft well. Almost too well. We suspected he was working on his own, possibly with an underground anti-alien terrorist group. Wacko humans out on an alien-hunting mission. Now we know who the leader is."

"Nazier." Raz examined the gear on the table and noted what

Cameron had deemed essential enough to take. He prepared for battle. "Sandra left the hospital with a Chaser. She waited with the three of us until there was no denying what we were. Our plight went to shit after that. She's working with Nazier. Sandra fooled you, Cameron. Infiltrators deceive the best of us." *Even I failed to see the game for a second time.*

Cameron shook his head. "The man she left with is her ex-husband, Dr. Thomas Robins. It's why we've kept such close tabs on her. He's using her research for Sixxer experimentations we haven't discovered. His connection to Paris isn't a coincidence."

All Raz heard was *husband*. One Sandra had never told him about. All the air left his lungs. "She's married to a god-damned Chaser?"

"Divorced. I wished she'd filed sooner, but you know how stubborn she is. We've been keeping surveillance on her for years." Cameron rubbed his chin in cold calculation. "Now the connection between Paris and Dr. Nazier is clear, it's why they targeted her for a mark. They wanted her alive to continue the experiment." He jerked a first aid kit from a shelving unit and other items scattered to the floor. "Because of Sandra's past relationship with Thom, and her current association with your circle, she'll be next. General Taft will find her."

Sean's hysterics filled the room, and a force shoved Raz and Cameron back against the table.

Cameron fell to the floor.

Raz stopped the second ball of energy Sean threw toward Cameron. The Nexus surge couldn't be disguised by an anti-NEU.

Cameron didn't blink.

Because he knew exactly what he saw, or because he didn't have a clue?

Cameron didn't fight back. "What have you done? Why is Sean so protective of Sandra? She's not Sixxer, she'd be a control for Thom and Nazier."

"I helped her be my Mommy," Sean's tiny voice said.

Raz slumped. The tranquilizer engulfed the last of his power.

"What's he talking about?" Cameron asked.

To Raz's knowledge, no other Sixxer had ever attempted to render a human into a circle. Raz had done it twice. Unsuccessfully.

"Sandra's aura is binding with our circle."

Cameron narrowed his eyes, and his lips twisted in disgust. "You included her in a render." Pulling himself off the floor, he walked to the second table containing medical supplies. With efficient movements, he checked the labels for amounts. He placed the first aid kit into his backpack with slow movements.

Fury churned under his calm facade, and Raz didn't understand why.

"Do you have any idea what an unfinished render will do to Sandra?" Cameron asked.

What? Others humans had been in a render? "I won't be fooled again, Cameron. Paris brought an infiltrator into my circle which killed my parents. She was the one to convince me to render Sandra." *I don't know why I listened.*

Cameron picked up a water bottle and splashed the back of his neck. Loathing marred his face. "Some days, I hate my job. You're not getting a choice now. Stunts like this aren't approved by M83, whether you're in the Corp or not."

Chapter Twenty-three

SANDRA'S HEAD POUNDED with each rut the Jeep bounced over on the rough trail. She needed sleep. The choppy ride, along with Amber and Zach's incessant bickering, had her considering survival odds if she jumped out the back. The soft top couldn't be difficult to remove.

Zach waved his hand emphatically. "I'm telling you. There's no way one of your Aliens could beat the Terminator. He's a freaking robot, not to mention a killing machine."

Zach's logic was sound.

"Aliens have acid for blood, *estúpido*. A Terminator can't survive acid. Aliens are *born* killers. Literally." Amber shredded Zach's logic with a precision knife. She down-shifted as they drove along a steep incline.

"They're aware, not dumb machines."

Zach argued in a petulant tone.

Sandra couldn't stay silent anymore. "Unless it was Terminator versus Predator. Then Predators would win. There's no competition. I mean every Terminator bites it in the end."

Amber and Zach froze.

Blessed silence filled the vehicle. Well, if that's all it took to shut them up, she would've commented on their movie discussion earlier.

Zach twisted to face Sandra. "Didn't know you were a Predator fan, Ms. G."

Sandra cringed at the title. "Please don't call me that."

Amber jerked the wheel.

Sandra smacked her head against the side panel of the vehicle.

Amber snickered. "No one asked your opinion. You can't introduce another character into the discussion. This was clearly about Terminator versus Aliens."

Zach shook his head. "Uh. Yeah. Sorry, I agree with Amber on this one."

At least they agree on some things. Will this ride ever end?

Zach launched into another tirade.

Obviously Amber didn't like her. Sandra rubbed her hands over her face. She had so many questions for Cameron, ones pointless to ask the two in the front seat.

Classified is Zach's favorite word. Is the term also Cameron's favorite? As soon as they arrived at their destination, she'd tell Cameron what had happened at Thom's then give him the flash drive. How many hours had been wasted while Paris declined in the hospital without Sandra there to help her? The sun flickered through the canopy, highlighting the tops of the trees surrounding them. The sun's position indicated midday, at least that's what Sandra told herself. She didn't have a watch.

They drove up a steep gravel drive. The thick underbrush formed a wall on both sides of the trail and gave her heart a brief claustrophobic jolt. The next bump bounced Sandra so high her head grazed the ceiling, and she landed hard on the seat.

A building came into view, and Amber pulled into a flat area big enough for the Jeep.

Zach exited the vehicle. He folded down the seat for Sandra and held out a hand. "Don't let Amber get to ya. She can be a real bitch."

"Heard that, asshole," Amber said.

Zach's smart-ass grin lit up his face. His golden eyes twinkled. They always had after he'd come up with crazy ideas for The Six pranks. Sandra had shot down every one of them but secretly wished he'd perform them behind her back. She wondered when the soldier would return. His bi-polar personality had her on edge. Sandra jumped out, ignoring Zach's offer of assistance. "Where is everybody?"

Zach shrugged.

He obviously wasn't offended by her cold shoulder.

He shut the door. "This used to be a children's summer camp

years ago. It's base while we evac HUP. Like a resting point until another HQ is determined."

"HUP hasn't been abandoned, just temporarily evacuated," Amber said.

"We'll be here overnight. The first building is a sentry point and supply storage." He pointed to the right. "Cam will be in a smaller building, Command and Control, along this path. I'll take you there once we unload supplies."

Sandra considered making a run for it, but she'd get lost. Trees surrounded them. Camping and navigation never were her strengths.

Amber hauled equipment from the back of the Jeep into the sentry building.

Sandra hovered next to the vehicle, but curiosity got the better of her. The path was right there. She was so close to Cameron and answers. If she waited any longer, she'd collapse from sheer exhaustion.

Behind her, Zack and Amber argued over another movie trivia controversy.

Sandra rolled her eyes. They were acting like children. She set her gaze forward. The path beckoned. Adrenaline kicked her heart into full speed, and a surge of strength filled her body. Tingles spread along her arms to her fingertips. She traversed the path as Dorothy had followed the Yellow Brick Road. The forest swallowed her, but turning back wasn't an option. Another, smaller cabin came into view as Zach had promised. Boarded-up windows, peeling paint and the broken roof screamed dangerous. She stopped. *I have nothing to be afraid of.* Sandra removed the bark-constructed shoes from her feet. The remnants of Zach's T-shirt were still wrapped around her arches. She padded semi-barefoot onto the porch.

Sandra recognized Cameron's voice. He murmured through the window out of sight. The muffled words were indistinct. Here was her friend, her confidant. If Cameron had ever cared about her, he'd have to prove it. The door glided open without a hint of sound. She passed a table filled with donuts and snacks. Her stomach rumbled, but her hunger wasn't enough to stop her. Cameron stood beside another table pushed against a wall with a row of windows above. Papers and computers covered the table along with an assortment of junk food and drinks. A living area behind them consisted of a futon and two mismatched chairs. The room was homey, in a college-dorm way.

"What am I looking at?" Cameron asked.

A massive soldier sat in front of a laptop, his back to Sandra.

Weird vibes ran up her spine. Cameron and the soldier stared at a computer screen containing familiar lab reports. Her stomach fluttered. Had they stolen her research? Cameron's buddy shifted in his seat, and she saw a familiar tattoo circling his bicep. *Leon?*

He pointed to the results. "The first set here are the lab results from Sandra's blood sample."

Her breath whooshed out. When had he taken blood samples? She'd remember getting stuck in the arm, no matter what had happened to her since.

Cameron tapped the screen. "Was she infected with the Xnix-624?"

"She's clean. The virus test came back negative. For both of them."

Of course, I'm not infected with a plant virus. Paris wouldn't have been infected, either.

Sandra hated learning Raz had been right. Cameron used her research without permission. She had been his friend and colleague for seven years and never suspected his deceit.

Cameron crouched over Leon's shoulder.

She listened for information on what other testing they might've done. The glucose meter couldn't possibly have such analysis capability from a single drop of blood. Paris hadn't even been tested by the meter.

Cameron tapped the edge of the table, which he always did when he couldn't put the pieces together. "She's not a Zenith, then. I don't understand why she had symptoms. Coincidence?"

What's a Zenith? Amber called me the same in the forest. Sandra didn't dare move. She made no sound to distract them. She stood within the answer zone.

"Oh, shit." Leon sprang upright in the chair, his back ramrod straight. "You aren't going to believe this."

Cameron stood and examined the charts. "What did you find?"

"She's pregnant." Leon answered in awe.

Sandra stepped back and tripped over a folding chair. She

grabbed it before it fell to the floor. Her mouth went dry, and she couldn't swallow. *Calm down. They're not talking about me. I've been off fertility for months.*

Leon continued reading her tests. "About nine to twelve weeks, based off human hormone levels."

Her hand splayed across her stomach. How many times had she felt nauseated and lightheaded in the past few days? A smile curved her lips. Joy flooded her body and soul. She wanted a pregnancy to be true, even though she didn't believe them. No. She'd accepted a long time ago she'd never have children.

"It's her ex's," Leon said.

Sandra pinched the edge of the chair so tightly pain shot up her fingers. *Cam won't believe Leon. Will he?* She shook her head, mirroring Cameron.

"It can't be," He quietly said.

"Who else? It can't be Raz's. A Sixxer and a fucking human, pardon the pun, can't have children." Leon folded his arms behind his head and leaned back. He weaved his fingers together against his black ponytail.

Sandra had no one else. Raz was the father. *If it's true! I have no proof I'm pregnant. I need facts.* Sandra denied their conversation. An accidental pregnancy rated as high as the chances of landing a spacecraft on a comet.

Cameron leaned in closer to the chart.

Sandra would find a logical explanation. *I need to see those tests!*

Oh, my God. Sandra couldn't breathe. *How will I tell Paris?* Her hand flew to her mouth, and tears blurred her vision. A child would end her friendship. Paris would hate her.

"This is fascinating data, Leon, but I need a point. ASAP."

Leon sighed. "I'm getting there, or you can read this stuff yourself. I won't always be around for you."

"One can only hope," Cameron said.

"Ass."

"I do my best. Please, continue."

What were they talking about now? Sandra had missed part of the conversation as she ran through scenario after scenario in her mind on how to tell Paris about the baby.

Leon opened several reports with multi-colored graphs. "Ok, I'll explain all at once. Try to follow along."

"You're a dick. I analyze this shit in my dreams." Cameron pivoted and locked gazes with Sandra.

Zach burst through the back door and clutched her upper arm.

Sandra barely registered the touch.

Zach's shoulders dropped in relief.

"A knock would've been nice, Zach," Leon called without turning around.

How had Leon known Zach entered the room?

Zach rubbed his forehead. "Tell that to your spy. She was here long before I was."

Leon lurched to his feet and stared. They were frozen in place.

A pregnant woman terrified these grown men. "Your analysis can't be true, Cam." Sandra was so quiet she could barely hear herself. The tears spilled onto her cheeks and dripped off her chin. Her lips wanted to smile, her voice wanted to laugh, but her heart pounded in fear. The joy bubbling in her chest wanted to shout to the world, but Cameron's facial expression carved her heart into a hideous jack-o'-lantern. He ran to her so quickly her head spun.

"You can't tell him."

"Of course, I'll tell him." Years of bottled-up joy spilled out in her words. She held nothing back. "Do you understand what this means? It's a miracle."

"Yes." He caught some of her tears, but too many fell. He kissed her forehead and enfolded her in his arms. "He can't know. Not yet." Cameron pulled back and held her face. "I told him about Thom, but you both need to be debriefed. Give me time, or we might lose him."

Cool air settled over Sandra. Was Cameron telling her a child, Raz's child, would push Raz away? "What … what did you tell him about Thom?"

Cameron's hands fell to his sides. "Everything within clearance. Especially, your ties to his research at HUP."

Sandra gasped. "My ties? I don't have research ties to Thom. I never did."

"He doesn't trust you." Cameron leaned a hip on the desk.

She swayed.

"But he will. I need time," Cameron said.

Sandra was going to throw up. Thom had a classification level? Did she have a classification level? *Raz thought ... he couldn't ... he wouldn't.* She whispered, "Did you tell him about the fertility?"

"I'll leave those details to you, but I did mention you divorced Thom."

Zach snapped his fingers between their faces. "I hate to break up the reunion, Cam, but what did you and dick weed tell her?"

Zach appeared more relieved than angry. Sandra almost felt sorry for him. He must've seriously feared she'd run away. They didn't know her as well as they thought they did.

Cameron dropped his arms and went back to the computer console. "This isn't the reunion we need to worry about."

Sandra mourned the loss of Cameron's concern. He should've celebrated with her, happy for the good news after all this time.

"I'm tired of you." Amber came into the room, bitching as usual. "*El burro sabe mas que tu.* It's a good thing you didn't run away."

Cameron raised a palm.

Amber shut up.

"Leon, would you go get Raz and Sean and bring them here? We'll debrief everyone."

Leon nodded and gave Zach a friendly punch on the shoulder as he left.

Cameron sat on the futon. "Are either of you familiar with Sixxer pregnancies?"

"Sixxer?" Sandra asked.

Amber laughed. A big smile spread across her face. She leaned toward Cameron. "You expecting?" she whispered.

Zach guffawed as he gave her a high-five. "I'm not your baby daddy, either."

Cameron held out his shut-the-hell-up hand.

"Our tests indicate that Sandra is pregnant."

Zach once again became the serious soldier. All humor drained from his body. He scrubbed at his five o'clock shadow and then raked his hands through his hair. The strands stood on end. "Ms. G can't have kids."

"Don't call me Ms. G, Zach. This isn't about Thom." Sandra

walked to the oversized chair perpendicular to the futon and sat. Her hands shook in her lap.

Cameron had his elbows on his knees. "Thom is a big part of what's going on."

"Don't accuse me—"

"The child belongs to Raz," Cameron said.

Sandra snapped up her head. "This child belongs to me."

Everyone's shocked faces turned toward her.

Cameron's gaze darted around the room, and he waited until their attention was back on him. "Raz admitted they included her in a render."

"Son of a …" Zach bit off the gluttony of swear words. "That's why she could get signals from the dead guy."

Sandra was like a child who didn't understand what the adults were telling her. "You're using terms I don't understand. Are you worried about the viability of the pregnancy? Trust me, I am, too. Not once in five years had I even come close. Twelve weeks. I should've suspected …"

"Sorry, but we aren't an effing maternity ward." Amber stood beside Sandra with a plate of goodies and handed it to Sandra.

Sandra hadn't noticed Amber had left the conversation. Now, Amber sat beside Cameron and crossed her arms over her chest all judgmental.

Cameron nudged Amber's arm. "This changes our mission. We know it's possible, now."

"You've no proof the baby is a Sixxer." Amber's skepticism had Leon nodding his head.

Sandra didn't understand how a child caused this much discomfort and alarm. "It's a baby. Why are you so freaked out?" She bit into a donut. Oh, the delicious cream and powdered sugar tasted heavenly on her tongue.

"Zach, I want you to bring up the data we have on Sean Donovan. We need to know the who, what, and how about Sixxer children." Cameron barked the order.

The BBQ potato chip was half-way to her mouth. Sandra stilled her hand. Maybe it was better to keep the pregnancy from Raz for a little while. This baby would destroy his family.

Amber narrowed her eyes at Cameron, and her upper lip curled. "You're still hung up on the kid having power. Come on, Cam. The kid is six years old. Skills don't develop until Sixxers are in their twenties."

"First priority is to debrief Raz. No one is to inform him of the pregnancy until I say. M83 wants him back." Cameron's voice commanded. "Get the data on Sean and get it ASAP. Sandra has survived an open circle render, read a dead soldier and provided intel from that soldier. This is bigger than Omega. M83 suspected natural fertility between our races, and now we've found evidence. Protect this information with your lives, ladies and gents."

The sinking in her gut she'd had when she first entered the room came back full force. "Amber already thinks I'm stupid, but I need you to spell it out for me. What's happening? You know, besides me having a baby?"

"You're bonding to the Nexus. Raz's render, along with the fact that you're pregnant, suggests your body is changing faster than normal for a human, or a Sixxer."

Zach offered an explanation with an excited grin. Just like he did in class when they learned something new. Sandra wasn't sure she liked being an educational opportunity.

"Like when we go through elevation?" Amber asked. Zach nodded, and Amber paled. "I don't see how that can happen. *Ella es humana.*"

Sandra hiked over to the snack table. Her stomach rumbled. "Human?" She snickered. "You keep saying the word *human* like none of you are."

Everyone shut up. The silence became uncomfortable.

Sandra's attention left the food and focused on the group. She cocked her head at Cameron.

He shifted on the couch, rested his hands on knees, and leaned toward her. "We aren't."

Chapter Twenty-four

WOODLANDS SURROUNDED THEM and created a fantastic hiding place, despite the mid-day sun. The cabins of the abandoned children's camp served well for a base location. Raz admired Cameron's choice.

Sean trailed his fingers along the sloping evergreens at the edge of the path. He made his teddy bear fly over the branches. They walked behind Leon on the narrow path. Behind them stood the building where the two of them had waited. The vegetation hugged the structure until it disappeared. After several minutes, only aged trees and new undergrowth crowded around them.

Raz kept his cool. The effects of the tranquilizer still slowed his reactions, but the fog had disappeared. His shoulder still ached, but he ignored the pain. Amber and Zach had returned and waited at the main building. Time for Cameron and his team to talk. If Omega had been observing his circle and Sandra, why hadn't they engaged when the Chasers got too close for comfort? Why sacrifice a fellow Sixxer circle when the risk of discovery was so great?

Sean skipped ahead of Raz, but the heavy brush stopped him.

Leon spoke over his shoulder. "We'll clear these branches, and the control cabin is ahead."

"Why didn't you help us at the hos-petal?" Sean asked.

The bundle of tree limbs fell from Leon's hands in a jumbled heap. He arched his brow, and his lips curled into a nasty interpretation of a smile.

"You were with a Chaser's ex-wife. I wasn't going to be responsible for bringing her to HQ."

Raz grabbed an armful of foliage and moved it aside. "Cameron informed me he cleared Sandra long before we arrived at Center Medical."

"*I* haven't cleared her. Cameron likes to form useless attachments to humans. His behavior is stupid." Leon squeezed through the small opening they'd uncovered.

The control cabin appeared as though an invisible force field had been removed. Raz described the building more like a rundown piece of crap than a place of command.

A large belly laugh threw back Leon's head. The gem in his ear twinkled. "I guess the same can be said about you and human attachments."

If Raz hadn't been dealing with the remaining effects of multiple darts, he would've punched Leon in his smug face.

"Sandra is nice," Sean mumbled.

Raz laughed between clenched teeth. "Accusing me of being a human sympathizer doesn't hurt my feelings." *Wait until I'm at full capacity and then let's see what's so funny.*

Leon chuckled again, and his feet thumped up the steps. "All too often, humans become Chasers."

Raz strode through the doorway. Sandra stood there like a vision holding a plate of food. Her creamy skin was stark against her dark hair and the heavy military jacket she wore. Her freshly scrubbed face emphasized the grime of escape coating his body. His anger tapered to nothing as his desire for her sparked along his body.

Powdered sugar clung to her upper lip, and she clutched a half-eaten donut in her hand. A dazed expression covered her profile.

His body responded, and his need for her erased his every thought.

Zach and Amber stood in military stance behind the couch.

Cameron sat in front of them.

Sandra gestured to Zach with the donut still in her hand. "Are you serious? This is a big practical joke, right? Funny on the teacher."

Zach stroked the back of his head. "No joke."

Sandra stepped closer to the group. "It's not funny."

A tease of lilac shampoo floated to Raz and flared his nostrils in desire. The automatic reaction stunned his senses. He no longer cared about Sandra's past. Touching her and kissing her consumed him. He wanted to make her his.

Field dressings wrapped her bare feet.

"Are you hurt?" Raz asked.

Sandra locked eyes gazes with him and sucked in a breath. "My injuries are minor. Scrapes. I just didn't' have any shoes to wear."

Raz looked around at the still forms in the room. "What are you all waiting for? Find her something decent in supplies."

Zach hurried into the kitchenette to a storage cabinet.

Her color looked good, but gray shadows outlined her eyes. Her lips parted as though to tell him something, but she held back. The heat in her eyes socked Raz in the gut. His blood rushed south, and he stifled the urge to adjust himself. *I am in control.*

"Sandra!" Sean slipped around Raz and Leon. He launched himself at Sandra's legs. Half of the plate's contents in her hand squished between them. The other half scattered to the floor.

She wrapped Sean in a bear hug and lifted him off his feet.

Zach lunged around the sofa and peeled Sean off her. "You shouldn't pick him up."

Sandra's eyes rounded at Zach's warning, and her face blanched.

She set Sean on his feet. He ran over to the table loaded with junk food and snacks.

Raz's gaze caught hers.

She looked away and focused on Cameron. "Raz is finally here. Let's talk. Who are you? What are you?"

Cameron crossed his arms. "We're Omega Unit. Part of a covert military operation called M83 which comprises a race of people not native to this planet."

"You've given her clearance?" Raz yelled. He cracked his neck and relaxed his shoulders so his power wouldn't explode.

Sandra bit her lip and stifled her laughter. "Aliens?" She stepped closer to Zach and Amber. "Like the bullshit you were talking about in the Jeep?"

"Don't you know the difference between movies and reality?" Amber smarted.

"Apparently not." Sarcasm eked out of Sandra with little effort.

Leon swaggered over to the kitchenette and snagged a bear claw from the box of pastries. "Taft's men dubbed us Sixxers to differentiate our sixth sense, the Nexus."

Cameron walked to the small bank of computers. He addressed Raz. "New developments demanded we inform Sandra."

Raz moved to stand beside her and he hated how she tensed at his approach. So he stayed back. Would he be able to touch her again? *For fuck's sake, why do I want a Chaser so damned badly?* Because despite what Raz told Leon, there wasn't a confirmation Sandra wasn't an infiltrator. "You going to let me in on these developments, Cameron? She's associated with a Chaser, and you're giving her intel?"

Amber shifted her stance. "I agree, *pendejo*. She's not to be trusted." She plopped her body on the futon and picked at her fingers.

"I told you." Sandra mumbled around a bite of donut. "My research isn't mixed with Thom's. He has used my formulas in his pharmaceutical studies, to no effect."

Sean trotted over to Sandra and gave her a plate loaded with snacks which they devoured together.

"I don't mix my research either, *bruja*. I always get my job done." Amber pointed her fingers at Leon like a gun, fired and blew on her fingertip.

"Braggart," mumbled Leon.

"Don't disrespect my girl, asshole." Zach jumped back, landed an elbow in Leon's side, and grabbed him by the neck.

"You wish she was your girlfriend, like every other female you see," Leon grumbled under Zach's chokehold.

Amber sat back, eyebrow arched. She didn't appear impressed with the defense of her honor.

"Ladies," Cameron scolded. "This isn't the time for your bullshit."

Amber rolled her eyes. She joined Cameron at the computers. "I don't believe she married *el bastardo* but had no idea what he was working on."

Sandra rolled her eyes right back. "Everyone on campus laughs at Thom's psychic research. I'm surprised he keeps getting funding." She licked the sugar off her lips.

Raz studied her posture. He wanted her to be innocent so damned badly, but the past kept intruding on his dream of a perfect future with her. "A well-placed front. No one would take him seriously. Therefore, his experiments were under the radar. He must've salivated over Paris's empathic ability."

"Her power is what tipped him off." Cameron opened a laptop and logged into the security screen.

"If Paris had told me what she was doing, then we'd be long gone. Chaser or not." Raz paced along the edge of the couch. He stared at Sandra. "Why didn't she tell me?"

Sandra shoved a blueberry muffin in her mouth, lowered her gaze to the floor then her eyes shot back up to Cameron. Around a mouthful of food, she said, "Zach says you have the greenhouse on observation. What is Thom using it for?"

Cameron tapped the keyboard, fingers flying over the letters. "He studied Paris there. It could be where he infected her. We aren't entirely sure."

Raz froze. "He keeps his experiments close."

Sandra brought her hand up to her mouth.

Cameron checked the progress of the info he sent to M83.

Raz would've done the same. He didn't know whether to be pissed off or impressed at how fast protocol returned to him.

Cameron drained a soda. "He's in deep, Sandra. Thomas Robins is a contracted scientist for the military. He has been studying Sixxers for the past fifteen years. He uses the ridiculous study of psychic ability to distract humans from the truth."

Sandra walked closer to Raz and stopped two inches from him.

A play of emotions filtered across her face. Would she be able to accept the truth? Flecks of gold shimmered in her eyes.

"You're a part of this team?"

"I was an M83 operative before I met Paris."

Her gaze bounced from his hair to his eyes to his mouth. She examined every inch of his body.

Raz fought the urge to squirm under her observations but tingles of Sixxer power zapped his nerves. Did she see the alien within him? Did it disgust her?

"You look human." She caressed his chest.

Her palm ignited more sparks of fire along his muscles. Raz inhaled the sweet fragrance of her hair. His T-shirt was a useless barrier against his desire for her. She didn't stop her determined examination of his alien body.

"You feel human." Her fingers petted and rubbed him.

She obviously didn't care they were in a room full of Omega soldiers, and neither did Raz. He bit back the moan that bubbled to the surface.

She leaned into him and buried her nose against his chest. "You smell human." She tilted back her head, and her gaze danced over his face. "But, you aren't."

"I never was," Raz whispered.

Cameron called over his shoulder. "What happened at the rendezvous point doesn't happen to humans, either."

Sandra's eyes widened. "I'm not …"

Raz touched her face. "What happened?"

A jolt of Nexus energy flashed and floated between them. Her eyes responded with a flare of honey. With a quick inhalation, recognition illuminated her face. She'd seen this energy before. She must've refused to believe it was real, as any sane human would. Raz pulled her closer in the hopes her body would respond to him, as well, but the fatigue in her movements stopped him.

Sean also swayed where he stood.

Cameron cleared his throat. The team stared at the two of them, confusion on their faces. Had they never seen the Nexus like this? M83 trained Sixxers on how to use their power and the association of that power to Nexus energy before placing them into the field. Was it so surprising because Sandra was human?

"Sandra communicated with the Nexus during an inspection a few hours ago," Cameron said.

His words flipped Raz's world upside down. The render worked. *I can close the circle.*

Sean yawned. "We'll be too tired, Daddy."

Raz swiveled his head in Sean's direction. Had Sean read his mind? *No. We're punch drunk from sleep deprivation.*

Zach crouched in front of Sean. "We'll be okay. We'll leave tomorrow after we've slept."

Cameron stood, and the team huddled around him. "We'll rest. It might be the only sleep we get for a while." He gestured to Raz's shoulder. "The render will have to wait until you're healed."

Sandra pulled back her head and spoke to Cameron, "There's no way I can sleep now. What's happening to me? What are you?" She twirled back to Raz. "How do you look and feel human, but aren't?"

Sandra's heat surrounded him. He cupped her face, and whispered in her ear, "Don't be scared.

"I don't understand."

"Your energy is a pulse inside me." Raz placed her hand over his heart. "Here." The Nexus was an experience, and explaining the energy to humans, who weren't supposed to have a connection, challenged him. "It pulls us together, but an open circle can make a Sixxer lost."

"I'm not a Sixxer."

No. She wasn't. Raz scooped away a dollop of frosting lingering on her lip.

Sandra flushed and melted in his arms.

Raz pulled her tight, not a millimeter of space separated them, and kissed her. He no longer cared who saw. In fact, he wanted everyone to see. He savored the taste of her lips and the softness of her mouth. Any second she'd push him away, outraged at his need, and afraid of the alien he now was in her eyes.

She returned the kiss with hot blazing lust.

"Zach, you're not shocked at the PDA going on here." Amber's voice was a background buzz.

"None of us should be, after that blast of Nexus in the face," Cameron said.

Zach snickered. "I hope they remember we're here, or Sean will get an early education."

Raz jerked up his head at the mention of Sean. Sandra's rough breath turned him on even more, but he couldn't give into it, to her. Nexus energy strained toward Sandra. The tendrils of light wrapped around her, wanting to close the circle. The bond was never this strong with Paris. His gaze met Sean's again, and realization dawned on his tired and stressed brain. A cold chill ran over his skin. *She doesn't know.* His stomach heaved. His hands trembled. The temptation to delay the inevitable repulsed him. He was a coward. His emotional distancing from Sandra allowed her to step back.

She brushed her hair out of her face and smoothed her clothes. She unzipped the heavy military coat and threw it toward the couch at Zach's head. "Behave yourself. I don't appreciate your smart-ass comments."

Zach threw up his hands. "Me? Control your own hormones, woman."

Sandra raked her fingers through her hair.

Every toss caused her addictive scent to float around the room. The unfamiliar T-shirt pulled tight across her chest, and Raz's mouth watered at the sight of her full breasts straining against the material.

She licked her lips. The Nexus had a sampling of her aura and enhanced it. Energy surrounded them both and fed Raz's desire for her. She was his.

Sandra turned her attention to Zach. "Did you see anything at the house?"

Hunger pains got the better of Raz, and his stomach growled. "What house?" He perused the goodie table and focused on the conversation, not Sandra. Distraction was always beneficial in calming the Nexus … and lust.

"My old house." Sandra waved her hand in Raz's direction, but her attention was on the crew.

Leon joined Cameron at the computer center. "We were talking longer term exposure."

Sandra stepped closer. "I haven't been around Thom, except for the occasional HUP activity, since the divorce. Almost a year. He must've drugged me at the house."

Raz swiveled from his position at the table. "Drugs? He was trying to kidnap her."

Zach shook his head. "I would've have sensed drugs or been under their influenced at the house and neither occurred."

Leon pulled up reports from the laptop and dragged them to a big screen in the center of the equipment. "Thom might've subjected you to his Sixxer experiments at HUP."

Raz followed. He read the computer screen over Leon's and Cameron's shoulders. The experiments were well documented and extensive. The detailed notes on Paris made his blood run cold. Had she been an active participant or another victim?

"Omega has records about your fertility treatments. Without Thom's research, we don't know how the drugs and viruses might interact," Cameron said.

Fertility? Raz raised his voice. "The what?"

"During their marriage, Thom gave Sandra his own tailored cocktail of fertility drugs."

Leon volunteered information Raz hadn't expected. Wild jealousy engulfed Raz. "You have children with a Chaser?"

At the same time, they said, "No."

Sandra glared at Cameron. Her face turned green, and she rubbed her stomach. "His own cocktail?"

"Thom has been working with Chasers for a long time. You had no idea because he made sure you didn't," Cameron said.

Cameron hadn't stopped Thom. The betrayal cut Sandra to the core. "But you knew?"

Cameron nodded. "Collecting information is my job."

Sandra's head snapped up. Her nostrils flared, and a stripe of rose crossed her cheeks. "I confided to you my struggles getting pregnant, and you just sat back and watched Thom experiment on me?"

Cameron jumped out of his seat. "Omega had eyes on you the entire time. If there had been any danger, we would've stepped in." He rubbed the back of his neck and stared into her eyes. "Sandra, the experiments might be why you've had a success ..."

Sandra's eyes grew round.

What wasn't Cameron saying?

Sandra circled her arm around the room. "What else do Thom's drugs have to do with this situation? With Zach being my student? With Raz? Paris? Thom wasn't trying to get Paris pregnant. He wouldn't have given her fertility drugs."

"No." Cameron leaned back and balanced the chair on two legs. "M83 had Raz and Paris on observation, because they were hanging out with you. Our Omega team wasn't to engage until relationships were established."

Sandra gritted her teeth. "Seven years of watching me, Cam? Are you still confused on who the bad guy is?"

Cameron threw his hands in the air. "You would've been free if you hadn't gotten mixed up with Raz."

His clenched teeth couldn't compare to the burning anger he saw raging inside her.

"Thom performed experiments on me before I ever saw Paris or Raz. Why?"

Leon stepped between them and led Sandra to the desk chair. "Thom used you as a control for various other drugs, other viruses he researched."

Sandra refused to sit.

Leon shrugged. "He had the means of testing them on you at HUP without your knowledge. He's been searching for a Sixxer for a long time, and Paris was a goldmine."

She clasped the back of the chair and brought her other hand to her mouth. "For what?"

"For the virus he infected her with." He turned to Raz. "The first successful virus that disrupted the Nexus connection."

Sandra gasped. "My virus, Xnix-624."

"Explains Sean's unstable aura. I need to close the circle." How would Raz get Sandra's willing participation when her discovery of Sixxers, of aliens, was fresh? Raz understood Cameron's subtle head shake. The mention of a render at this point wouldn't turn out positive.

Sandra paced five quick steps back and forth in front on Cameron. "When I came in, you and Leon indicated I was clean. You tested me for the virus," she accused. "You expected Paris to have Xnix-624 when I brought her to HUP. You're not making sense. My virus doesn't infect people. It's a ridiculous statement. Why did you let us go if it's so dangerous?"

"We aren't just people, but Sixxers. He modified the virus somehow so that it can infect a Sixxer," Leon said.

"She held out a thumb drive. "Would Thom's personal files explain how he did it? Because I still don't think infection of any of us in this room is possible with *my* virus."

Amber grabbed the potable device.

"It contains Thom's fertility research. I copied files from his computer, and I think the drive definitely contains info on his fertility drugs, but I also copied experiments with current surrogates and other files that were on his desktop. They could be anything he's working on. Some of the files might correlate to the virus research and studies you think Paris was exposed to. They might at least give us a link. Thom had a habit of cross-referencing his materials."

Amber and Leon moved around the computers in a surge of activity.

The stunned expression on Cameron's face would've been amusing, but Raz salivated over the thumb drive, too. He couldn't take his gaze off it as Leon copied it to one of Omega's systems. The drive might hold the secrets to discovering and fighting Paris's disease, and how to protect his son.

"I collected your research notes and laptop from HUP." Cameron stumbled over his words.

Sandra spun on a toe. "Why?"

"Thom was using your work to develop additional viruses and drugs." Cameron pounded his fist on the table. "His hidden usage of your stuff is why I let you leave. With him in the building, I couldn't risk his suspicions if he was monitoring you."

Raz saw the wheels spinning in her mind. Sandra was searching for a solution without having facts. He didn't understand how her research could've been used against Paris, but the thumb drive was life to Omega, to him.

"The flash drive contains what I think is fertility testing he'd have done to me, too." Sandra swallowed and straightened her shoulders. "If it contains information that will help Paris, I'll find it. Give me my laptop, and I'll start analysis right now."

The commotion in the room stilled.

Cameron moved toward her like she was a wild gazelle about to leap away.

"You should rest before we do anything else," he said.

The ache in Raz's stomach returned. He couldn't hide any longer.

Sandra's gaze skimmed each one of them. "We shouldn't waste time. Where is she?"

"Paris didn't make it," Raz whispered.

Sandra whipped her head around.

Raz waited for her to fall apart, but the connection with his words hadn't been made.

Her eyes narrowed. "That's okay. Leon will take the team back to the hospital. If you had to leave her there, then she'll just be monitored. Thom will think we've left. There's still time to get her out."

The desperation in her voice cut Raz's heart to shreds. She turned to Cameron. "What anti-viral can we give her? You've seen this infection in Sixxers before, right? I'll examine Thom's notes while you're gone. I might be able to suggest some things to counteract the virus."

"She's not at the hospital, Sandra," Cameron said.

"Mommy," Sean cried.

Sandra scrunched her brow.

Sean ran from Zach and wrapped his arms around her legs.

She held him to her and brushed his hair with her fingers. Her gaze bounced between Raz's and Cameron's. Uncertainty clouded the chocolate depths. "Her father took her?" Her voice shook.

Raz held out his hand.

Sandra refused to take it. Sandra didn't move a muscle.

The air, heavy and dark, pressed into Raz's skull. "Paris is dead," he whispered.

Sandra stilled. She didn't cry. In fact, she didn't do anything.

Had he spoken, or had he said the words in his mind? What should he do? What should he say?

Cameron walked up behind Sandra and rubbed his hands over her shoulders. "Sandra."

She shrugged him off in an angry twist. She stepped in front of Raz.

"Sandra, you're my Mommy now," Sean whispered. "She's a part of you now. Every time I take your hand her Nexus is a light I feel."

The disgust on her face threw Raz off-kilter. Didn't she want him and Sean when they had no one else left? Mixed emotions warred inside Raz's body. His need for Sandra, for her acceptance and caring didn't make logical sense. He didn't need a human to make him whole.

The crack of her hand reverberated in the room, and pain exploded along the side of his face. His cheek turned into a hot wildfire of prickling needles. Raz caught his breath. He blinked at Sandra, and the fury in her eyes sparked the Nexus to come alive in her body. Eyes of honey brilliance billowed out a ray of power, of hatred, directed at him. The Nexus was magnificent on her body.

"You had one job to do." Her voice cracked, and her words were cold, hard. "One fucking job, Raz!"

Everyone in the room held their breath.

Sean pulled at Sandra's raised arms and clenched fists and babbled.

Raz couldn't take his gaze off her. He'd failed her. She'd never forgive him.

Her fists hit his chest, his stomach.

He accepted each blow as the punishment he deserved.

"How could you!" She raged. She reached out for Sean. "Why did you give me this? I didn't want a new life like this," She whispered.

Zach and Cameron lifted her off her feet, and she kicked her legs and screamed.

Raz found the ability to move and followed. He touched her face and neck with an easy touch but forced her to look him in the eye. "We were almost out," he whispered. "The exit was so close."

"They tranked him. Their options were gone," Cameron said.

No. Raz gave up too soon. He should've gotten Paris out.

The Nexus enfolded Sandra, cocooning her in a blue glow.

Everyone in the room gasped.

Raz wanted Sandra as much as the Nexus did. Was it because of Paris's death, the open circle, or something else? His all-consuming need for a Chaser's wife made little sense. Instead of her betraying him, he was the one who had wronged her.

Sandra's eyes were dry.

The anguish on her face cut Raz to the bone.

Between clenched teeth, she said, "Take your hands off me."

Raz froze. He had to make her understand. "Listen to me."

"I can't think when you touch me. Please. Go," she whispered.

Her words hurt more than any slap ever could. Raz's throat burned. Sean was right. They were losing everyone.

Leon's hand slammed into Raz's chest and propelled him away. "Let her grieve. You knew telling her wouldn't be easy."

Amber held Sean. "I'll give you some advice, Raz. Close your circle, or every Chaser in a fifty-mile radius will be on us."

Chapter Twenty-five

SANDRA PACED AROUND the room and formed mental jigsaws from the pieces of Thom's research and M83 information she'd been given. She teetered between believing Cameron and committing them, or herself, to a facility for the mentally ill. Aliens that appeared human? *Aliens aren't real. Not like this, not hiding among us!* Secret military groups the average person had no clue about? *All of us have our secrets.* Herself a victim of medical experiments performed by her ex-husband? *Thom isn't evil. He's an asshole, but not vicious, right?*

The internal questions spun around and left her dizzy. Her hands splayed over her belly.

What was the truth? Raz had told her so many lies. Leon had convinced Raz to give her space, which Sandra found hard to believe. Leon must have voodoo alien power to force Raz out of the building. Yet, he had a dejected look about him when he left that confused her. Blaming him for not getting Paris out of the hospital had been wrong of her. Fighting Thom had been impossible. What if they all had been exposed to the same drugs as her that took away their control?

She remembered the odd awareness and responsiveness her body had with Thom at the house, and a small tremor vibrated through her. If he had known she was pregnant with an alien's baby ... She shivered.

Cameron hugged his arm around her shoulders and brought her back to the present. He escorted her to the table of computers and monitors.

She staggered onto a flimsy folding chair, and it wobbled on two legs.

"Whoa." Cameron caught the back. "It'll be okay."

Sean snuck under Cameron's arm, inched as close as possible and slipped his hand into hers. "Not crying is okay, Sandra."

Amber gave her a foam cup filled with water.

The cool liquid quenched her thirst. Sandra placed it between the keyboard and monitor.

Sean's fingers tightened around her hand. His swollen and red-rimmed eyes contributed to his lost expression.

For a few seconds, Sandra held her breath. The hell with not holding him. She'd been picking him up all night at the hospital. She grasped his hand and pulled him tight into her arms. Her throat compressed. She squeezed her eyes against the sting of tears. Zach couldn't use the jaws of life to pry them apart.

Someone brushed the hair from Sandra's face. Through blurry tears, Sandra saw Amber standing before her.

Amber stroked her hair. "You need to decompress, *bruja*," she whispered.

Sandra sniffled. "I just need a moment."

Cameron pulled up a second chair. "You're strong, Sandra, but there's no need for it here."

Sandra refused to fall apart in front of Omega. How long had they watched her, judged her? She was weak in their eyes for unknowingly contributing to Thom's research and allowing him to harm the people they'd sworn to defend. Not knowing didn't equate to not being responsible. She'd promised Paris she'd protect Sean, and crying about her death wouldn't safeguard anyone.

Sean pulled his hand from hers but wrapped both arms tight around her neck.

She pulled him into her lap. His donut-sweetened breath warmed her ear.

"Can I call you Mommy, now?"

A sharp pain twisted inside her chest. Sandra kissed Sean's cheek and held him close to her heart. The windows above the table faced a canopy of trees. The camp was hidden.

Sean turned his head onto her shoulder. "I miss her. A lot. Who will take care of us now?"

Sandra didn't know. She'd never been a mother. Did she have the strength to heal his emotional wounds? Thom had stolen her research and used it to break alien bonds. Sean's bond. Her studies were for the good of mankind, not destruction. If anyone physically hurt the boy in her arms, she'd go on a murdering rampage.

"Where did Daddy go?"

Amber reached out and gently chucked Sean on the chin. "He's been added to rounds for perimeter check with Leon. The activity will help calm him down."

Sandra reached out and bumped the mouse with her fingertip. Thom's research files came to life on the monitor. Her gaze skimmed over dates and recordings of medicine dosages for Paris. She leaned closer, clicked on more files, and saw documents marked with Paris's name, followed by notes on infection rate. He had combined research materials on his desktop with the additional computer in the greenhouse. Thom's betrayal cut a deep and open wound where she thought he couldn't hurt her anymore.

Her gaze darted to Cameron. "Time is the enemy, right?"

Cameron glanced at Amber than back to Sandra. He shook his head. "We leave in the morning. You've been up for over twenty-four hours. Yours and the baby's health are more important."

"Shhh." Zach ducked his head to scan Sean's face. "Kids are little recording devices. We don't want him to say anything to Raz."

Yet, Sean talks to the baby. Could he talk to Raz like that, too?

Sandra looked down and Sean's eyes were closed. "He already knows. Do you think the Nexus allows Sean to talk to the baby?"

Zach and Cameron exchanged glances and shrugged.

"An ability like that is new to us. We aren't sure what Sean can do. He's really too young to have power or be able to utilize the Nexus the way he does." Cameron scrubbed his face. "In your condition, rest is more important. We can fill you in on details later."

She pointed at the window. "I won't sleep during the day. We have the entire afternoon. You need to fill me in so I can get started."

Amber leaned a hip on the table and crossed her arms. "On what, *bruja?*"

Zach paced behind her.

"I'll figure out what killed Paris and destroy any connection between my research and Thom's." Sandra stared into Cameron's midnight eyes. "If what I've developed harmed Paris, or hurts another Sixxer, then I have to fix it." She glanced at Amber and hugged Sean closer. "I have to stop it."

Amber harrumphed. "Good luck, *chica*."

"You can't save the world, Sandra," Zach said over her shoulder.

She pointed to the monitor. "All of this determines my baby's health. Got to keep the mind sharp, Zach." Over her shoulder, she squinted at her former student. "In my condition, the sharper the better, don't you think? You've been in my classes. I won't stop digging until I find an answer. What if I contract Paris's illness—" She choked on her word choice and lowered her tone. The lump in her throat made speaking difficult, but she couldn't keep silent. "The illness Paris *had*. I have to know what I'm up against."

Zach studied her and rubbed the five o'clock shadow on his jaw. "Yeah. Sandra's right. Her brain needs an upload." He wandered over and punched a code on the keyboard.

Amber grumbled. "That's classified, King of Classification."

"So is your love life."

Amber bounced to her feet, mumbling Spanish under her breath. "I'm doing a perimeter check. Have fun with your lessons."

"She's constantly hot and cold," Sandra said.

Cameron scratched the back of his head. "You've no idea. Where do we start?"

"Raz said he'd have to close the circle. What does that mean? You can't be much different from humans, or I wouldn't be in the *delicate* state I'm in. I can't believe this is happening. I'm in a dream."

Cameron reached over and grabbed two snack bags of pretzels setting on the end of the computer table. He handed her one and gave Sean the other. "It's a lot of intel for you. Take your time to digest."

"I want more information, not less."

"Every Sixxer has a natural power or ability that is like an energy signature. When we approximately reach our mid-twenties that power forms." Zach stood beside her and leaned over the console. He brought up a few documents on his screen. "Here are some medical texts that might help you understand."

"Is that what's happening to me? I know you joked earlier, but something is happening to me."

Cameron nodded. "The Nexus is accepting you as a Sixxer without having a power."

Zach sat beside her. "Which is opposite of what happens to Sixxers. We develop our power then the Nexus energy attaches to our change and allows us to control our abilities better, among some other aspects." Zack lifted his hand, palm up, and a network of light briefly illuminated the lines running from his wrist to his fingers.

Everything I've seen had been true. "Where does this Nexus come from?"

"The energy is all around us." Cameron pulled up a document on a second computer screen. "As you can see, the DNA of a human and a Sixxer is almost indistinguishable."

Sandra examined the document. "These slight changes don't translate into an alien species."

Zach tapped the screen. "Similar here, yes. Makes sense considering how much alike we actually are. If you look at the numbers below, you'll notice the percentages on this measurement are much lower in Sixxers."

Significantly lower – how's that possible? Sandra blinked. Was the data correct? The numbers didn't explain how Raz manifested the trails of light that'd flown toward her at the gas station. "My baby is already exposed to the Nexus. Will he or she be alien?"

Zach sat to her right and pulled up additional files on his computer. "My assumption is your baby is a Sixxer. The Nexus would trump the human DNA in favor of building the baby's aura."

"Will my baby be safe? Healthy?"

"Jamie likes you," Sean mumbled under his breath before his head sloped to the side.

Sandra looked Cameron in the eye. "Tell me what I should be doing for this baby."

Cameron munched on a cookie he snagged from a stack beside his workstation. "Zach is our expert in Sixxer pregnancies."

Zach pulled Sean's sleeping body from Sandra's lap. "I'll lay him on the futon. He needs as much sleep as he can get. We'll keep him close. His attachment to you is strong."

Sandra nodded, watching as Zach carried Sean and his teddy to the couch and covered him with a blanket. She appreciated Zach keeping him close and had a feeling that Raz wasn't far from the building either. She just knew in her gut he wouldn't leave Sean blindly in the care of others after losing Paris. She moved back to the computer and the complex research. "This is why you were so good, and also so bored, in my classes."

Zach chuckled. "Once you dig into this, you'll be bored with classes, too. The Nexus is something external, but biologically inherent to us. Sixxers have studied it for decades." Zach paused for a second and swallowed. "You not being a Sixxer … The longer you're exposed to the Nexus; the more modification will occur. Your energy gain has already begun. The way you communicated with the fallen soldier before we arrived at camp suggests none of this pregnancy will be normal in human terms."

Change my … what? DNA? She was in an alternate dimension. "Being around M83 and Raz exposes me to the Nexus. What if I'm not around all of you?"

Cameron shook his head. "The Nexus is around everyone, even humans. We can't escape the energy once we are through elevation. You can't either because of the baby. He's already hooked into Sean's energy connection."

Sandra placed her hand on Cameron's arm. The hopeless acceptance in his tone was awful. What had happened to him?

Cameron stared into her eyes. After a few seconds, he cut off the vulnerability written on his face. He went back to his task of bringing up file after file of scientific studies of Sixxers, both by M83 and humans.

Zach brought up several documents containing advanced mathematical analysis of Nexus research. "The baby was your catalyst. The Nexus won't leave you now."

Sandra poked around the files Cameron and Zach had given her access to, along with Thom's notes. She had difficulty working through the biology of the Sixxers and their connection to the Nexus. M83's texts on alien physiology was magical mumbo-jumbo. How can an external energy *decide* to accept someone? "Where have you put my research documents?"

Cameron swiveled to the left. "Here's your laptop. I haven't had time to transfer any of the files."

This will take weeks, if not longer, to devise something useful. How long will I take to decipher the fundamentals of Sixxers' biological processes, let alone how the Nexus communicates with them? I'm not sure I understand what the Nexus is right now.

Sandra raked her bangs off her forehead. "This will take a while…"

"It already has." Cameron swigged from a soda can, scrunched his face and stuck out his tongue. "Yuck, it's flat."

Zach whistled. "Here's something interesting in Thom's files." He scrolled down a paragraph. "His original virus, Xnix-624, consisted of a biological specimen he harvested from an ordinary strain of human flu virus. He controlled it by using a nano-computer."

Sandra couldn't believe it. "Xnix-624 has been my virus from the beginning," she whispered, checking the notes Zach referenced. "The possibility Xnix-624 could be modified in such a way is beyond my knowledge."

Zach whistled. "It's right here in black and white."

That technology was in its infancy, laughed at as being plagiarized from science fiction films. In no way could Thom have bioengineered something so powerful from her research. "A nano-computer requires a team of programmers. Thom doesn't have access to such a group."

Cameron speculated. "Are you sure? General Taft or Nazier could've funded another project outside of HUP. Let another team program the toys and allow Thom to focus on the virus." He read farther. "He used your research to manipulate the virus into releasing protein destroyers. With the nano-computer, the virus could be programmed to attack specific portions of a Sixxers DNA, corrupt their protein structure and make the connection to the Nexus nonexistent."

Sandra was fascinated by the discussion. This technology could skyrocket her research into something beyond imaginable. "This is similar to what I was working on for plant viruses. The nano-computer is a brilliant idea. Technology I wouldn't have thought of, since the field is out of my area of expertise. I can't even fathom how it's possible to do so. You both said after infection the connection to the Nexus is then disrupted or broken. How do the waves of smoke form? If they don't appear, does that mean the Nexus bonds were disrupted?"

"You can see the Nexus? Surrounding Paris?" Cameron asked.

"No. I saw it near Raz then again at the hospital when I fainted. I was convinced I was hallucinating."

Cameron spoke over Sandra's head to Zach. "Do you think it's because of the render?"

"The render was done after they got to the hospital. Paris was included."

Cameron used his hands to hammer a drumbeat the countertop. "This means energy changes occurred in Sandra from the moment of conception." He tapped the keyboard while he entered several notes into a document.

"Or before," Zach mumbled. "Sandra could've been accepted by the Nexus because of her time spent with Paris, or because the bond she's developed with Sean."

Cameron got up and skipped to the snack table. He picked up random pieces of food and popped them in his mouth as he hopped around the room. "She has a natural ability to visualize the Nexus."

A warm tingle entered her chest. "You find it odd I can see the Nexus smoke?"

"Things about the Nexus don't … appear to follow the laws of nature," Cameron ambled back over. "Humans see nothing physical when interacting with the Nexus. The lack of a visual energy cue is why so many of them fear us. Our power and energy is unpredictable and mysterious. You might be part of a select few who can see the Nexus in visible form. Then the baby enhanced your ability."

"So, I'm changing in more ways than one," Sandra mumbled to herself. Not only would she have to deal with the bodily changes that came with pregnancy, but she'd have to figure out how these Sixxer enhancements would change her. For good? *Sounds like it. DNA modification, remember?*

Sandra noticed a section of Thom's report. A brief scan of the notes turned her blood to ice. "So, you haven't explained what a circle is. Raz was very concerned about it."

"It's a method of bonding Sixxers together so they can use the Nexus energy to enhance their natural power."

"Is Omega a circle?"

Cameron munched a handful of potato chips. "No. It's considered a waste of power for M83."

Sandra stole a few chips from Cameron. "Am I in a circle?"

Zach placed a hand on her arm. "It won't harm you. In fact, the baby might be safer if you're in a render and brought into Raz's circle. It'll focus your Nexus power and make the circle stronger."

Sandra pointed to the screen. "Unless Thom's virus is contagious between Sixxers of the same circle."

"What?" They both asked.

Cameron rushed over to the monitor, read the report, and swore a few thousand times. He crumbled up the bag of chips and threw it against the window. "The amount of time we have is shrinking before all Sixxers in a render contract the illness. This is a pandemic. Zach —"

"I'm already on comm."

Chapter Twenty-six

SANDRA SAT UP on the single bed, disoriented from her deep sleep. A hint of daylight teased the edge of the window and chased the shadows around the single person lodge. Raz's cinnamon scent lingered on her shirt, but he wasn't there. Her body tingled from the dream. The vibrations had started not too long after he left the control cabin. They continued off and on throughout the night, along with the sexual dreams. Her breasts ached. A flutter of need quivered in her stomach. The kiss from yesterday had awakened her senses. Her desires didn't want to remain dormant any longer, no matter what crisis was on the horizon. The thermal blanket fell to her waist. The cold air should've penetrated the thin fabric of her T-shirt, but waves of sensual heat swirled around her. Omega had little information on the side effects of the Nexus accepting a human. Add a pregnancy to her changing body, and her hormones took over.

Cameron and Zach's discussion about her and her research popped into her head. The three of them had argued for hours on the possibility versus probability of a plant virus infecting a Sixxer or a human.

If I accept these people as aliens, have I gone crazy? What proof do I have other than a virus that infected Paris, but no one else? Which indicated Paris was the alien, or logically the one more susceptible to the virus than the rest of them. Yet, the light and smoke were visual markers that something about these people were different than her, at least for the time being. Her change was coming.

She'd reached a point where her eyes wouldn't stay open any longer, and Cameron had led her to this tiny cabin for blessed rest.

Although, Raz hadn't been far from her thoughts. After her head hit the pillow, she'd fallen into a fitful sleep. How had morning arrived so quickly? The furniture in the room materialized as the light grew stronger. The one-room cabin had a single bed, a chair and a dresser.

A nervousness rushed through her, and her dream from moments before was now a distant memory as one hundred ideas bombarded her mind. Sandra paced around the room. She rolled on a pair of socks and shuffled her feet into the old shoes Zach had found in the supply cabinet. Other M83 units had left a hodgepodge of items behind in the main cabin. The salve Leon had given her had healed the cuts rather nicely. Zach had called him healer, instead of medic, of the team. She understood quickly that M83 didn't fool around with paltry human medicines and cures.

The air was crisp, and she rubbed her bare arms. After a quick trip to the outhouse, Sandra shivered in the morning fog. Two other cabins were clustered by hers. One was similar in size to hers, and the other a larger structure. Their quiet and dark nature didn't fool her. Someone from the team monitored her every move. They wouldn't track her like a wolf on a hunt for seven years then forget about her here.

Can I trust Cam's team? I have no evidence I'm pregnant. No testing. I have Leon and Cam's word I'm having an alien baby. I've had symptoms I could've imagined. I suspected I was pregnant before and examined every possible imaginary symptom. Each test had been negative.

Sandra laughed. Her musings were ridiculous. A scientific explanation existed. If she was pregnant, the baby was human. An alien race couldn't procreate with humans. Therefore, the only conclusion is they were human, all of them. *Why say they aren't?* She focused on the path to the control cabin. She tiptoed through the fog-infused woods. Her mind raced with too many questions. The experiment files were waiting for her. She'd find answers.

Sandra opened the door to a welcoming warmth. The futon was empty. She expected Zach and stopped in her tracks.

Raz sat at the kitchen table.

Her palms became sweaty, and her heartbeat galloped in her chest. They were the only ones in the building. She closed the door against the cold air. "Where's Sean?"

"I put him in the big cabin. He was exhausted. Too much foot traffic in here. I didn't want him to keep waking up. He's been through a lot in the past few days. I'm at a loss on how to help him emotionally, but at least I can make sure he's sleeping well. I have a connection to him. The open circle makes it weaker than normal, but it's still there. He's safe."

Sandra nodded, relieved. She didn't like both of them away from the boy. Observing how tired Raz's eyes looked and the scruff on his face, she knew his spoke the truth. He'd been up all night making sure they were all safe. "Did you get any rest?"

The clean scent of soap filled the room.

"Some. Zach was here for a while before he rotated on perimeter check." Raz scooped up a duffle from the corner of the room. "Here are clothes and a few personal items. Amber found them in the leftover supplies." He shrugged. "They're not much, but hopefully you'll find a few comforts inside. M83 makes sure units have a few luxuries."

She accepted the bag of clothes.

Raz opened a door off to the right of the kitchen. The essence of cinnamon and … apples flowed out of the space. A tiny bathroom, with a dreamlike shower, was nestled inside. Sandra debated if it was too small. Although, she'd risk a panic attack for the hot rush of water on her skin.

Raz laughed. "You should see your face. I'm surprised one of the team didn't show you this last night."

Sandra shuffled her feet. Her mouth opened, but no words could express her excitement over being able to wash her body in *hot* water.

Raz pulled the door wide. "You can leave this open or cracked if you want to take a shower. There's plenty of hot water. M83 might appear to be roughing it in the wilderness, but the comforts of life are spared no expense for us. I used it a few hours ago. You'll like the multiple spray shower heads."

The promise of a body spray called to her weary muscles. "I can't go in there."

Raz crossed his arms over his chest. "You're craving a shower."

She smiled. "You know me pretty well."

"I'll be in the main room. Take your time. You'll be fine with the door open. Rotation isn't for another two hours."

He entered the control room as though he wasn't thinking about her getting naked in the shower. Maybe he wasn't. Maybe she was the only one with an active imagination. A vision of him in this room, rubbing soapy water over his massive and muscular body, brought a wave of heat over her midsection. One she remembered well from yesterday. After checking Raz's location, she entered the room before she could talk herself out of it. She left the door half open to afford her some privacy and lessen her anxiety at the size of the room. Rummaging through the duffle bag, she found a bar of soap, Lilac Breeze scent, and two changes of clothes, along with toiletries. Her heart softened. Raz had to have found the soap for her. He hadn't smelled like lilacs when he passed. Raz's scent was manly and had a faint hint of cinnamon, like the air of the room, but better.

His spice smells good enough to … Take a shower and get him off your mind!

Sandra turned the faucet to hot and adjusted the temperature to a degree below scalding. The main control building was warm, but she couldn't shake the chill she'd gotten from the walk outside without her jacket. Steam filled the room. She pulled the curtain far enough to leave openings on either side and stepped under the heated blast of heaven. Raz certainly had found a way to warm her heart.

The yucky urges she'd had at the house nudged the back of her mind. Thom's demand for a bath had taken her control away and left a glacier inside her heart. She washed away the disturbing memory. *Would Thom sway me now that Raz is outside in the next room?* She soaped her hair and pushed her face under the stream of water, erasing the recollection. Thom wasn't here. She needed to act like it.

A rumbling stomach quickened her speed, and she reluctantly finished. She could spend all day in this shower. She donned another pair of jeans and a T-shirt from the bag. After combing her hair, she plaited it into a braid to keep the waves tamed. Another belly growl drove Sandra to the small propane stove on the kitchen counter. She studied the folded metal box. Last night it had been set up. *It's not rocket science, only a camp stove.*

"Do you want breakfast?" Raz asked from behind her.

Sandra jumped. Her face heated at his presence. *My face is warm from the shower. Nothing else.* She cleared her throat. "I don't know how to work this. Coffee would be wonderful."

Raz stood, made quick work of opening the stove, and attached the small container of propane to the side. He opened a cabinet, pulled out a coffee pot, filled it with water and set the canister on the lit burner. He turned to face her.

A spark of light arced between them. Sandra gasped and backed up two steps. *Find the science.* The unknown quantity of the experience overwhelmed her.

Raz held out his hand. "Don't be scared."

"This phenomenon makes little sense. None of this does." Sandra ignored his hand. She didn't want to touch him and allow the out-of-control power to zap along her nerve endings. She didn't want to think about her dreams of him, and how her new Nexus energy aroused her further.

Raz turned back to the stove. "You were never supposed to find out."

He'd have left me before I even knew I was pregnant. Telling him about the baby was on the tip of her tongue. Why couldn't she tell him? Who made Cameron her leader?

I'm not M83. I don't have to do what Cam says. Does he want me to keep the baby a secret because I'm not pregnant?

Sandra stepped as close as she dared to Raz. "Do you have any idea how crazy this makes me? Can we be near each other without this spark?"

He lifted the pot off the burner and shut off the fuel. "The render at the hospital broke our Nexus connection and left the circle open. These random sparks won't go away until we perform a render and close the loop. Our Nexus energy has a way … to escape."

She remembered the reactions of the others during and after their kiss. The electricity that'd exploded at the touch of Raz's lips hadn't been normal. Omega's reaction suggested the arcs weren't normal even according to alien standards. This distraction wouldn't do. She had research to review and viruses to pick apart. She threw back her shoulders. "My intentions are to work this morning. I can get a lot done now that I have a clear head." She pointed to the steaming pot. "And coffee."

"I'll leave you to it."

"What're you doing here? Why aren't you sleeping?" She carried a steaming mug into the living area.

"Cameron requested my reinstatement into M83 before you arrived. I was bringing myself up to speed."

She settled into a chair and woke up the computer she'd used the previous night. "You've missed a lot?"

He sat at the station beside her. "So much can happen in seven years."

Don't I know it. Sandra settled into a similar pattern she used last night on searching through Thom's research. His OCD came out in his recordings. Would Omega have deciphered his cryptic notes as easily if she hadn't been here? The code T6 appeared frequently and she couldn't place what he meant.

"We're lucky to have electrical power so I can work." She cocked her head at him. "How is this place so state-of-the-art in certain areas and falling apart in others?"

Raz laughed. "That's the beauty of M83. When a team needs resources, they find a way to make it happen." He shrugged. "I'm comforted that some things haven't changed since I've been out."

Sandra understood him perfectly. "Without change there's little progress." Searching through the notebooks, she discovered the one she needed was missing. "Drat. I forgot my journal where I recorded Thom's codes. I'll go to my cabin and be right back."

She stood at the same time Raz did. His manly scent overwhelmed her senses. Was her association of him to cinnamon candy making her crave him, like the craving for chocolate? "You don't have to follow me."

"We should talk."

Sandra hated that phrase. It was one she remembered well from her marriage. A list of her faults would follow or stats on how much she'd failed at a particular task. *Stop. This isn't Thom.* They needed to discuss a lot of things.

Sandra led the way back to her cabin. The temperature had risen one or two degrees with the sun, but in the chill air, she regretted leaving her jacket. She'd bring it back to the control cabin, too. "What happened at the hospital? Why did you let Thom take me?"

Raz grabbed her arm and forced her to stop. "You were out of control." His words came out in a stream of frozen vapor. "The render had gone horribly wrong. The circle weakened us then I recognized your ex's face. Every delay you caused to our departure popped into my mind. I thought you were working with the enemy."

Sandra gasped. She swallowed the lump in her throat. "How could you …"

Raz ignored her, dropped her arm and marched toward her cabin. "The render failed. You were hysterical and you left with a Chaser. Nothing I did stopped your panic, nothing except *him*." A muscle in his jaw twitched.

Sandra's heart pounded. He was more pissed at the fact Thom eased her distress than at the assumption she was a traitor. "What changed your mind? What convinced you to trust a Chaser's ex-wife?" She spat the words, offended he'd automatically concluded she was out to destroy him and his family.

"I called Cameron."

And Omega filled you in on my life.

Raz walked the path in front of her.

This conversation wasn't over. Sandra ran after him and blocked him at the door of her cabin. "And just like that? You believed Cam when you wouldn't waste two seconds with him yesterday?"

Raz leaned into her.

His sweet candy breath rolled over her face.

He stroked her cheek. "You had left with a Chaser. Paris was dead. I had to do what was right for Sean."

The panic attack had gripped her hard. "The render must've caused my panic attack. It was unlike anything I've ever experienced. The room was dark and tight. The light had disappeared. Something powerful had closed in on me. It mesmerized … and terrified me."

An arc of light bounced from his fingers.

She jerked back. Sandra stepped inside the cabin.

She crossed the room to her jacket and the notebook she'd left on the dresser. The room condensed into a miniature version of the cabin she'd left a few hours ago. The pressure of the render came back in a horrible rush. Her breathing increased. "I'll have to go through that again, won't I?" *Am I tough enough to experience such heaviness on my body again?*

Raz entered the room and pulled her into his arms.

She tensed, but the energy from earlier never formed.

He caressed her shoulders. "The render defines the boundary of our circle. The Nexus will protect you. Paris had been right all along about you."

Which meant she'd be a part of a circle and susceptible to the virus. So would the baby. She backed up a step and bumped against the edge of the dresser. Her camo jacket slid over the side and pooled onto the floor. Would the open circle be enough to prevent the virus from attacking her? She needed more time to understand how to fight this threat.

Raz dropped his arms to his sides. His shoulders slumped, and deep grooves appeared besides his mouth. He snagged her fingers into his hand and massaged them with the lightest touch. "I'll do anything now to keep you safe. Paris … Paris was the reason for my parents' deaths."

His voice wasn't a whisper, but it was low and … naked. Sandra didn't want to hear about their past together. The pain inside her bled her dry and mutilated her memories of Paris.

Raz dropped her hand. "Her lies started the day I met her and continued until she died in my arms. Until I let her die."

Sandra pushed from the wall. "No. You don't have the capacity to stop a virus. You had to get out."

Raz shook his head. "I was thinking about … My distraction led us right to them. I broke us apart and made us weak."

Sandra reached for him and stepped on her jacket. She was so damn cold. The chill bumps on her arms had her in a constant state of trembling. Had she driven herself into the middle of Raz's family and torn them part? "You were together."

Raz whipped his head around.

Those light eyes of his were like hooks snaring her within their grip.

"Paris turned fragile. I led her and Sean into danger. A broken circle is the first method of Chaser capture. We have to fix it."

"I'm not yours," she whispered, but the baby connected her to the circle now. She had Raz's blood running through the veins of her unborn child.

"When I met you …" Raz rubbed the stubble on his cheek. "You want to know if I loved her."

No! No! No! I don't want to know!

"How could I love someone who took everything in my life? I loved her in the beginning. Once I gave her my heart the Nexus connected us. She was used and manipulated, but what she did to my parents destroyed my emotional bond with her." His gaze met hers. "Yet, we had already made a new life. Months later, she gave me *my life* back, my reason for living, in the form of a precious baby. I've survived for Sean. I kept her safe for him."

Sandra caressed his cheek. His words said one thing, but his body said another. He had loved Paris. Would she ever understand the complex relationship he'd had with Paris? Could Sandra accept it? Even after Paris's death, Sandra was jealous of their past, of the connection he described between them. His eyes held a pain she feared would never go away. She hugged him. It was the only thing she could do. Her throat was tight and breathing hurt. Paris was gone and the pain between both of them was almost unbearable. She pulled his body close.

Raz wrapped his arms around her.

His warmth chased the cold from her limbs. Tears stung the backs of her eyes but wouldn't come to the surface. Had she led Paris to her death? If she'd let them go, and not insisted they go to HUP, would Paris still be alive? His arms tightened around her, stealing her breath.

He sank into her body and leaned on her for strength.

Sandra stumbled back into the wall, but accepted the support the solid surface offered.

"I never forgave Paris for what she did. I don't expect you to forgive me for killing her." His voice was a low and gravelly in her ear.

"My research killed her," Sandra rasped.

"No." He rained kisses over her face. "My selfishness ended her life. I never trusted her, and that lack of trust made her keep secrets. I won't keep the truth from you. When I saw you yesterday, I wanted to hold you so badly. I've been miserable all night without you."

Dreams of him had tortured her all night, too.

Raz's warm breath flowed over her neck and collarbone. "I'm so sorry."

Those words unleashed her tears. Sandra heard her own guilt come out in Raz's words. Struggling to hold back sobs, she didn't want the pain, or the grief, to consume her. Her emotions were too much. She wanted to erase the sorrow from her life. Her love for both of them filled her heart. "You're holding me now." She turned her face, and their lips grazed. "Hold me tighter." An actual spark ricocheted from where they touched.

Raz groaned, pulled her closer and deepened the kiss. His tongue, hot and possessive, invaded her mouth.

Her T-shirt was a pathetic barrier separating them.

He pushed her against the wall.

The shock of the movement opened her eyes. His focus and intensity on her sent a pool of volcanic lust straight into the core of her body. Was this right? Should they give in to their lust when they had so much baggage between them?

He turned her head to the side and nipped her neck.

She moaned. Too many emotions raged a battle within her.

His hands found her breasts, and he massaged the aching flesh. He moaned. "You're not wearing a bra. It's so hot, so sexy. I've been imagining what might be under this shirt for hours while you sat and worked."

His words sent her heart into overdrive. He was fighting himself as much as she was fighting herself. He found the stiff peaks of her nipples, and she gasped at the pleasure of his touch. Sandra wanted the electric trails of fire to follow wherever Raz caressed her. She didn't want to think or analyze anymore. "Take it off," she demanded. The shirt was too confining, too abrasive.

Sandra hadn't expected her command to spur Raz into unbuttoning her jeans. He pulled them down to her ankles. He flipped off her shoes and yanked her socks from her feet. Cool air on her naked skin competed with Raz's hot breath along her stomach. The slick heat of his tongue caressed the apex of her thighs. She cried out and clutched his hair.

Raz's hand stroked the back of her legs and clutched the globes of her ass. He tugged her body to his mouth. "We're done hiding," he said. "I want you. Everyone will know you're mine."

Sandra's legs threatened to give way. She leaned against the wall but slid a few inches before Raz caught her. Yes. She didn't want to hide anymore. Everyone would know her claim on this man. This Sixxer.

"This lilac essence on your skin has been driving me insane for hours," He whispered. "When I found that soap, I knew it'd drive me crazy, but I had no concept, until now, on how it'd wreck me. On you, the scent tantalizes. I want you to mark me with your scent. I want them to smell it on me, and to know I've touched every inch of you."

A blast of arousal encased her body at his words. Raz sucked her puckered nipple into his mouth, and fireworks exploded behind Sandra's eyes. "Yes. Oh God, yes." She moaned. "Take me quick and fast. I don't want to wait." He flew her to a high she'd never been to before. Clutching his shoulder, she yanked his shirt until it glided over his head and onto the floor.

He lunged to his feet. Hooking an arm under her knee, he lifted it over his hip.

Her body responded to his hard erection as he ground against her center. His response was welcomed, but she wanted more. His jeans still separated him from her where she needed him the most. Her hands flew over his bared chest, taking in every curve and hard muscle. He was beautiful. She undid his pants and pushed them past his hips as far as she could reach.

Raz's penis sprang free, and he leaned in to kiss her.

Again, his hard length intimately teased her where his tongue had just been. His steel flesh pressed into her. He moaned into her mouth and gyrated his hard sex against her wet heat. If his arm hadn't been holding her leg, then she would've melted into a puddle on the floor.

His other hand jerked up her shirt and thrummed the stiffened peak of her breast before pinching it.

A quick suckle of the nipple into his mouth left her breathless. She pulled his hair, not to make him stop, but to express the need to have him inside her. Now. "Don't make me wait a second longer."

He placed another kiss to her tingling breast, bent his knees and lifted her into his arms. He spread her legs and held her weight as she leveraged herself against the wall. His cock nudged her opening.

Her lower body bucked against him to get closer to the pleasure. Trapped against the wall, Sandra couldn't move her hips very far.

Raz had control, and he entered her in one quick thrust then stilled.

His heat and his spicy scent were all her mind could process, but she wanted more. His mouth tangled with hers, and he thrust inside her again and again. The hairs on his chest teased her breasts, and the rhythm vibrated the walls.

The dresser beside them bounced.

Sandra concentrated on the pleasure of each point where their bodies touched, gaining more and more, tighter and higher until she couldn't hold it inside anymore. Her release burst from her body in a mind-blowing orgasm that left her legs weak. Her lungs gasped for air as she floated outside her body in an exquisite dance. Her muscles, inside and out, quivered in a performance she never wanted to end. She was falling, or was she coming down from the most natural buzz she'd ever experienced? She opened her eyes. They were both on the floor in a heap of arms and legs.

The sounds of the room intruded upon her bliss. The small clicking of the dresser echoed as it slowed its rocking. Raz's heavy breaths filled the room. She heard a murmur of laughter outside the window. Her face burned.

Raz caressed her jaw and dropped a gentle kiss to her brow. "They recognize you're mine now. I'm not ashamed of how much I want you. I won't hide."

Raz's possessiveness comforted Sandra in an odd fashion. Did she belong to him now? What did alien ownership mean? He'd given his trust freely. She must do the same. Yet, she still needed to tell him her secrets. Was her past enough to send him packing, or would the circumstances only force him to stay and repeat history?

Chapter Twenty-seven

NEXUS ENERGY PULSED through Raz. His Transor rhythm oscillated in an unnatural beat. Spheres of light cascaded down his arms. An unbearable heat built in his fingertips, and they glowed with white-hot light.

Sandra trembled beside him. A layer of sweat coated her face and neck.

Was her exhaustion from their recent lovemaking or her body's attempt to absorb the Nexus? Raz hugged her close and caressed her back.

Sandra hissed. "Your touch burns."

Raz removed his hands but not his lips. He kissed her neck. Her low moan brought back a surge of desire. The fire in his hands flared again.

Sandra yanked away from him. "You're too hot."

Raz struggled to hold on to his meager energy connection so the heat wouldn't affect her. The open circle was discharging his electrical field, and he couldn't reach the essence of the Nexus to command the charge. If the circle was closed, Sandra could accept his touch without pain. He willed his body to internalize the heat and temper the pulses of light. He reached for her.

When she flinched away from him, the movement cut him to the core, even though he knew it was involuntary. "It's all right, now."

She gritted her teeth and nodded. She stared at him for several moments. Her braided hair was askew. The dark plait ran over her collarbone and down her upraised T-shirt, covering one exposed breast.

Her unbound flesh drove him insane. Damn. She was so gorgeous like this, strong and vulnerable, and willing to trust him.

Raz cupped her chin.

She closed her eyes. No energy flames touched her. She sighed into his hand. Opening her eyes, the now honey-gold irises danced over his chest.

Everywhere her eyes gazed was a physical caress as the new Nexus energy in her surrounded him.

Sandra spread her hands over his stomach and ran the pads of her fingertips over each dark wound she discovered. "What are these?" She examined the largest one on his shoulder.

"They're from the tranks."

Sandra curled her legs underneath her and sat up. She smoothed her shirt, and her panting slowed into a normal breathing pattern. She wrinkled her brows. "How did you leave the hospital after so many?"

The remnants of the dart wounds were red and inflamed, but the pain had faded. He'd almost forgotten about them.

A light blue glow followed the path of her caresses. The swirling pattern of energy ghosted along his skin. He loved her touch but held his breath in awe at the unusual Nexus presence within her.

Frowning, she pulled back her hand.

The uncertainty in her eyes squeezed his heart. "Don't be scared. Please."

Sandra leaned forward. She hesitated centimeters from his mouth.

Raz didn't push and allowed her to close the distance.

She kissed him. The low Nexus hum changed frequency. A glow of heat and power formed between their lips. The spark nipped her tongue. Sandra jerked back a few inches, and her bangs covered part of her face.

Raz lifted her chin. He tucked an errant strand of hair, fallen from her braid, behind her ear. Lilac-scented shampoo filled his nose, and the Nexus tingled in his fingers.

A full body shiver went through Sandra's frame. "What's happening?" She ran her hands over her arms. "I feel overheated and on edge, like my skin is ready to burst." Her brown eyes alternated between milk chocolate and honey.

"I think you are going through a Sixxer transformation, but I can't be sure. Your reactions aren't quite the same, and I'm guessing they are different because the circle wants to close." The Nexus surrounded her and highlighted her beauty. The vision left him breathless. Once they were out of Omega's watch, Raz would make love to her long and slow. Their fast and furious technique had its benefits, but he wanted to treasure her. He wanted to never let her go. "I must fix the broken link in Nexus energy. Your panic attack occurred before I could finish the render. The heat between us is residual energy. It makes communications with the Nexus unstable until it's bound to the circle again."

Sandra stood on wobbly legs. She pulled her pants back on then smoothed her hair into place. "Does the Nexus always produce a Sixxer's energy?"

Raz shook his head. "No. A Sixxer's power is different from the Nexus energy. A render protects us and allows The Nexus to amplify our individual power."

"Why doesn't the energy come from Cam, or anyone else in Omega?" She asked.

"They've never formed a circle. I don't understand M83's strategy for denying them the Nexus. Renders increase a Sixxer's ability to heal."

Leaning her hands on top of the dresser, she peered over her shoulder.

Honey light flared in the depths of her eyes.

"The Nexus couldn't heal Paris," she whispered.

Raz wanted to deny what Sandra said, but she was right. The Nexus had failed Paris. Why?

A spark of light burst on her fingers and dimmed.

Nexus aura hovered around her, never entering her, but created a corresponding hum inside his body. He glanced at his fingers. A blue cloud of Nexus energy surrounded his hand. Gentle offshoots spun around each finger, and the vibrations purred along the back of his forearm.

Raz lowered his voice. "Paris's life force is still a separate essence in our circle."

Sandra's startled gaze met his. "Paris is dead."

"Her energy still amplifies the unstable elevation Sean's

experiencing and has to be reabsorbed."

"How can there be a life force when Paris is dead? She either is or isn't," Sandra said.

Raz scratched his head.

Sandra's eyes widened and followed the movements of the Nexus energy flowing from his fingers.

"Our bodies die first, but the Sixxer's power essence remains. Some have theorized the Nexus is nature's way of helping us cope with the trauma of grief without using our Sixxer powers to destroy ourselves or the circle in our emotional pain."

Sandra took two steps toward him. Her arm stretched out to touch him. Light waves ran up her arm, and she drew back. "Paris is this light?"

"Yes."

Sandra closed the distance between them and grasped both his arms. "Then she's still alive. If we go back and find her, you can—"

"No." He shook her shoulders. "I can't bring her back to life."

A crinkle formed between her eyes. "Then why is the energy still available? You could resuscitate her."

Her eyes were glowing embers of fire. How would he stop the direction she was heading? Her speculations only led to more heartbreak.

She clenched his shirt and pulled him toward the door. "Like what I did to the soldier. I could bring her back. The Nexus has given me the gift of life. I'll endure the pain again to heal her body."

"Shh." Raz went through every checklist in his brain on how to calm Sandra.

When the Nexus light had left Paris's eyes, she touched him and gave him her Nexus energy forever. How could he make Sandra understand the exchange?

"Sweetheart." He cupped her face in his hands. The Nexus still pulsed and glittered. The blue haze reflected off her tears. "Breathe. Please. Sixxers have immense power, but nothing living can bring back the dead. She's gone."

"I brought him back." She choked on a sob.

Her hot tears burned his hands. "No Sixxer on this planet or another can bring Paris back. Her body can no longer sustain the

Nexus or life. She passed her energy to me so I could get Sean out of the hospital. His mother's energy can't linger in our circle without hurting him. The energy leaves an opening that makes us vulnerable. Our circle is weak and getting weaker. I'll find Sean, we'll finalize the circle and close the holes. Paris's residual energy will be shared among the three of us."

Sandra turned away. She wiped her face with the edge of her shirt collar. A haunted expression remained on her face, and she absent-mindedly chewed her fingernail. An energy signature flickered at the base of her spine, and the light traveled up the back of her neck to the top of her head.

Raz didn't understand how the Nexus illuminated her so readily, even without a closed circle. He touched her arm.

She turned to face him. "According to Thom's research, the virus was designed to infect a circle."

"A circle isn't a person."

Sandra tapped her chin and looked down as though gathering her swirling thoughts.

"Thom discovered a unique characteristic within each circle. He called it a heat signature, but when I correlated his experiments, temperature variations were minor. He was referring to a render. The virus finds a weakened host, breaches a barrier within the circle and infects the other members when a render is performed." Her gaze flew up to his. "Have you or Sean been feeling sick? Are you having any of the same symptoms Paris had?"

"Son of a—" Raz grabbed his shirt and pulled it over his head. "They were developing the virus as an infiltration mechanism. Put on your shoes. We need to tell the team."

Sandra found her discarded socks and pulled them over her feet. She toed on her shoes. "Zach and Cam got on comm last night when we came across the data."

Raz's body cooled from the fear at how vulnerable they were. Sandra's Nexus energy didn't have an easy explanation. If her changes impacted her vulnerability to the virus, she was in the most danger of infection. She didn't have the Nexus to protect her until the circle was closed.

She snapped the pen from the front of her notebook and wrote a series of codes on a blank page. "I need to review Thom's results again and find out what the difference is in his successful experiments versus the non-successful ones."

Raz finished putting his clothes together. "Neither I nor Sean are sick. Sean's energy is unstable because of his age."

"How old should Sean be before he can use the Nexus?"

Raz had promised no more lies, but what can of worms would he open once Omega found out what he and Sean were? "Sixxers don't go through elevation, the process in which we develop our Sixxer power, until they're in their mid-twenties."

Sandra arched a brow. "You don't think his *elevation* occurring when he's six is cause for worry?"

"It's not because of the virus."

"Then what's causing his change?"

"I don't know, exactly." *This technically isn't a lie. I don't know why he's in elevation.* "He's the first Sixxer child I've ever been around."

"You've never been around kids?" Sandra opened the cabin door. In her enthusiasm to get to her computer, she walked out into the cold air in her T-shirt.

Raz grabbed her jacket from the floor. They wouldn't come back here. He draped the fabric over her shoulders. "From now on, carry your belongings. We might have to leave quickly."

Nodding, Sandra threaded her arms into the sleeves.

Raz followed her along the path to the control cabin. The temperature hovered at its current freezing state. He wanted to return to M83, re-joining was necessary to fight for Sean. If he helped Omega, he had to go against his instincts and provide Sandra details about his race and his past.

"My parents believed Sixxers could no longer have children. Young Sixxers, including myself, were in despair that our race was dying. When Paris told me she was pregnant, the news was bittersweet."

Sandra stopped.

Raz ran into her. He latched onto her wrist to prevent a tumble on the path. Her heartbeat thumped madly under his fingers.

She turned and cocked her head to the side. "That can't be true.

Zach has an extensive amount of knowledge regarding Sixxer pregnancies."

Raz promised to tell Sandra the truth, not Omega or M83. "I don't believe the children he's been exposed to are true Sixxers. How do we prevent Sean from getting the virus?" He stared into her soft brown eyes. "Or prevent you from getting the virus? Is there any information in the research you've reviewed on its effects on humans?"

"I've yet to find any. Leon says I was a control because the virus doesn't affect humans."

They bounded up the stairs. Sean sat at the kitchen table. His bear sat beside him. Cameron and Leon stood behind him, talking in hushed tones. Zach and Amber monitored the computers. Raz's and Sandra's footsteps clipped over the entrance. Four pairs of eyes stared at them.

Raz wasn't known to blush, but after several arched brows, smirks and throat clearings, a burst of heat coated his cheeks.

Sean placed a donut and a pancake on his plate.

Raz ruffled Sean's hair. "Don't any of you believe in protein around here?"

Zach and Leon snickered.

"Grow up, guys," Amber said.

Sean held up his pancake. "Try some, Daddy. They're good. Just like Mommy would make us."

Raz picked out two muffins with nuts and handed one to Sandra. Junk food was better than thinking on an empty stomach, and the nuts would give them nutritional protein. "Sandra told me the virus attacks a circle."

Cameron snapped to attention and narrowed his eyes at Sandra.

She gave a slight shake of her head.

Was there something else they had discovered in the research?

Cameron packed up a cooler and a reusable grocery tote with non-perishable food. He handed both containers to Leon. "Zach informed M83. We're waiting on orders. Give Leon your bags." He picked up a coffee mug from the table.

Sandra scooped up her bag from the bathroom floor. Seeing Leon give a gimme gesture, she handed over her sack.

Leon carried the supplies and duffle through the main living area and outside.

They were packing up. Sandra wouldn't have any time to work again until they were at the next location point. Raz didn't want to wait that long. "Have you sent the information files?"

"Only verbal confirmation. No files have been sent." Zach called from his desk.

"I think you should hold off."

Amber pushed off the computer table and postured. "You don't have the clearance level to make those decisions."

The backdoor banged shut at Leon's return.

Cameron drank his java. The steam rose in a lazy pattern over his face as they crowded into the living area near the computers. He nodded at Raz. "You make good coffee." He covered his yawn with his mug. "Withholding electronic information is against protocol."

Raz popped the last of his muffin into his mouth. "From what Sandra explained, Chasers are attempting to infiltrate Sixxer circles with the virus. You already told me the infiltrator level in the area was high when Sean and I got back to HUP."

Leon crossed his arms. "How would a virus that disrupts the Nexus lead to infiltration of a circle? M83 doesn't allow renders anymore, so the infiltration wouldn't be at a level where any useful intel could be derived."

The decision was crazy. Raz technically wasn't M83, but who in their right mind would put so many Sixxer soldiers at risk? Cameron hadn't told his team the three of them would have to render again to close the open circle. Did Leon have a concept of an open circle? His fresh face wasn't old enough to have ever participated. Raz cautiously said the next words. "Any breach of the Nexus leaves us in a very dangerous situation. Not to mention Paris's death left my circle wide open. It should be closed immediately to protect Sandra."

Sandra paled. She stuttered and stumbled to the bank of computers. She sat and accessed a computer. After several deep inhales, her composure returned. "Let's not get too rambunctious about a render until I've looked more into the mechanisms of the virus. M83 might have more research."

"I'm sure Nexus energy won't hurt you," Raz said. "Not after what happened this morning."

Zach snickered. Cameron shot him an evil eye.

Sandra twittered. Her face turned pink. "I'm not worried about me." Her gaze bounced between Raz and Cameron.

Raz had made a promise not to lie, but Sandra wasn't following his lead. They were keeping something from him, and that pissed him off.

Cameron held out a hand. "Slow down. Sandra's right to be concerned. M83 stopped renders for a reason."

Raz fumed. "As a way to control you." Each member of Omega had a casual and relaxed air around them. No one believed him. Seven years was plenty of time to create a major culture shift in the organization. The prevention of renders reeked of insanity. Paris had been brainwashed, and so had Omega. *Who here is on my side?*

Chapter Twenty-eight

AN OBJECT GRAZED Raz's neck from behind and hit the floor with a muffled thump two feet from Sandra. Warm liquid trickled down his collarbone. He flew across the room and yanked her from the chair. Charges of blue light rose from his fingers. They wrapped, armor-like, around her arm.

Amber ran into the kitchen and pulled Sean to the floor. She crouched beside him, shielding him with her body. She grabbed her sniper rifle and scouted out the back window.

Leon scrambled over to Zach and slammed his hand over the blood gushing from Zach's leg. Zach dropped from his seat, and Leon dragged him under the computer table for cover. Leon searched for the first aid kit perched on top of the desk, found it, and dressed Zach's wound.

Raz rubbed his neck. His fingers came back blood red. Pings cracked throughout the room as shots hit metal and wood. Had the Chasers found them because of the open circle, or because of the communication Zach sent to M83? M83 base camps and point locations were guarded secrets.

Sean mentally cried out, *Daddy!*

Fingers of silver smoke jettisoned from Sean's arms and rushed to the perimeter of the building.

His power blasted Raz in the face.

Sean connected to the Nexus and blitzed like an uninitiated Transor, chaotic and deadly. Sean's age and lack of formal training saved this group from his Transor destruction.

Bullets ricocheted everywhere. Food sprayed onto walls and

furniture splintered, shooting other deadly weapons their way.

Raz opened his body to the Nexus, and every muscle became infused with strength. The only way to stop Sean's blitz, and his own, was to accept the energy inside himself. He no longer feared Sandra would die from the energy wave. This morning proved she handled a Nexus surge.

He regulated the slow amplification of his power. The heat and vibration hummed low in his spine. The Chaser darts had weakened him more than he suspected.

Sandra squeezed his waist, and the light of her Nexus connection built between them. The pain in his neck no longer registered.

Sandra pushed his chest. Her eyes glowed with honey sparks.

My God, she's beautiful with the Nexus blossoming around her.

She stared at his neck, mouth agape.

The wound must be worse than he'd imagined. "We have to get out of here," he shouted over the chaos.

Cameron was at the kitchen door, pistol in hand.

Leon applied pressure to Zach's left thigh. Blood painted Leon's fingers crimson. Omega hadn't tapped into the Nexus, so the energy couldn't repair the injury. Leon would mend Zach, he obviously had Sixxer healer power.

Leon picked up the weapon beside him and fired over the computers. Bullets sailed out the broken bank of windows. Others embedded into the wall.

Amber kept Sean close, despite the wild energy surrounding him.

Would Sean hurt her?

She swiveled around to reload, her back leaning into the wall. Her eyes danced with green fire.

Omega won't render, despite how close they are to the Nexus energy. They won't use it!

"This is what I saw," Sandra mumbled. She pointed at the mist flowing from Sean and the eerie light surrounding Amber.

Raz leaned in.

Her rosebud mouth pressed against his ear. "This mist was at the gas station. The color was different, but it's the same substance."

She saw my true self and still followed us. "It's Sean's Nexus power. He's out-of-control."

Sandra nodded.

Only the three of them utilized Nexus energy. Raz controlled the light and heat in his favor. Each Omega member signaled their power, but none of them enhanced it. They fought in their vulnerable state, stronger than a human, but weak against Chaser bullets.

If they only knew what they're capable of, we wouldn't be sitting like toy ducks in a kiddie pond. We'd have the advantage if Omega acted like the aliens they are.

Unfortunately, the odds without a render were, at best, fifty-fifty. The energy pulled from deep inside his gut. His Nexus connection was still off because of Paris's death and the residual effects of the Chaser tranks, but the cork wouldn't hold with the constant gunfire.

Cameron cocked his pistol and popped his head over the windowsill for a few seconds before ducking back inside. "I need answers, people! What the fuck just happened?"

Amber hopped over to the second kitchen window.

Sean followed, glued to her feet. The teddy bear was in a death grip in his hands.

Broken glass littered the floor, but with so much visibility Omega defended their position. Amber scouted the forest. "Keep me loaded, and they're history." She fired random shots then hunched below the sill. She motioned toward Zach with her chin. "Leon, if you don't keep him alive, you'll have me to deal with."

"No worries, Am," Zach said through clenched teeth. "Nail the bastard that shot me."

Leon had a free moment and examined Zach's wound again. He pulled bandages and pills from his pockets. "Damn it."

Zach eyed the bottle of pills Leon yanked from a cargo pocket. "Why does seeing that make my stomach flip?"

"It's bad, man." Leon tapped two pills into Zach's hand.

Zach shook his head. "Fuck it." He downed the medication.

Taking drugs? M83 soldiers didn't take medication for wounds. It dulled the senses and their ability to connect. To take meds was pure madness. Why wasn't Leon using his power? Raz held on to Sandra. He glanced at Sean. Tendrils of energy emerged from Sean's small body. He shook under the onslaught of bullets and power. His clenched jaw held the yells and screams inside, but silent cries generated dozens of tears on his cheeks.

The team didn't stop fighting, oblivious to the little boy beside them ready to explode.

They had to get the hell out of there.

Sandra crawled closer to the futon. She hooked her arm in the strap of a fallen backpack and rummaged inside.

Raz was proud of her. Her instincts were that of a survivor. "I thought you said this was the safest place?" He shouted to Cameron.

"Sorry, man. I'd say I'm only human, but we both know that's not true." More shots sounded, and the tinkling of broken glass hit the hardwood floor. Cameron fired a few shots and crouched low. "Get your asses over here."

"Sean, crawl toward us." Raz wanted Sean right beside him. He'd been able to prevent his own blitz in the hospital, but controlling his and Sean's would be tricky. The open circle vented out excess energy, their saving grace.

"I got him," Amber yelled. "Worry about yourself." She continued to place cover fire. "Nothing will get to him over here." She gave a thumbs-up sign.

Sean huddled in a ball, his hands over his head.

Bits of woods and fabric smacked Raz in various places. He followed Sandra behind the couch toward Cameron. Raz's body took the full brunt of the shrapnel. Brief flickers of pain zinged at every impact. Soon he wouldn't feel any pain. The blitz was upon him. He didn't resist. His family needed him. Omega needed him. Past training kicked in. The residual after-effects of Paris's death kept Raz's blitz hovering at the brink, like a rollercoaster stuck at the top of a hill, waiting in eternity for the free-fall.

On her belly, Sandra scurried closer to Cameron. She held up a pistol. "How does it work?"

Cameron checked the clip, loaded a round and turned off the safety. A smirk covered his lips, he handed the weapon to Sandra and arched an eyebrow at Raz. "Make sure to aim at the enemy."

Sandra nodded, unaware of the taunt.

Raz surveyed the living area.

Leon dug the slug out of Zach's leg and bandaged the wound.

A clip hit the floor as Cameron reloaded. "Leon, can you round up the most critical laptops and destroy the rest?"

"Time's a bitch, boss." Leon tore the medical tape with his teeth and finished the second dressing.

Zach moaned as he moved in and out of consciousness.

Leon crawled out from under the computer stations. He yanked the cases off the table. One punch to each of them broke the outer casing and the motherboards. He pulled the hard drives out and beat them to a pulp.

Raz watched in disbelief.

Leon ripped the electronics in two with his bare hands without the magnifying effects of a render.

Raz only had that amount of strength after a blitz.

"Raz, I need your help," Cameron shouted above the discordant sounds.

Focus! He banged his head with his hand. *I'm acting like a rookie Transor.* He pulled Sandra toward the back door.

She held the gun with the muzzle pointed to the floor.

Was she prepared to use it?

Raz caught Cameron's gaze. "What do you need me to do?"

"I'll open this door while Amber, Leon and I give you cover fire. I need you to get the Bronco. It's old, but it runs and has our supplies from HUP." Cameron handed him a set of keys. "It'll be a squeeze until we can find something else, but we'll fit better than in the Jeep."

"You want me to go out there?"

Cameron nodded.

Raz wasn't stupid. He wouldn't leave unarmed and get shot. He'd lose control. "What'll you be doing?"

"Saving our asses." Cameron shoved the keys into Raz's hands and motioned toward Leon. "How's it coming, Lee?"

"We're good. I got the big systems destroyed. How will we get the others out?"

"You volunteered. I'll carry Zach while Amber gives us cover."

"Hand me a gun. I can still aim." Zach reached out.

Amber placed a weapon in his hand. Then she reloaded, readying for their departure. She looked at Raz. "You better get moving, or we're dead." She handed him another pistol.

Raz got into a crouch. This was happening. He'd wanted to get his circle the hell out of town. Instead, he had to run into enemy fire, get to the Bronco and back to the control cabin in one piece, without the blitz to help him.

"Go, now!"

Raz ran faster than he'd ever run in his life and dodged bullets. He didn't understand the attack. General Taft always captured. He'd been out of the fray so long Chasers' goal was eradication. The Bronco sat behind the sentry building, and Raz dove toward the front bumper.

The adrenaline inside him pumped Nexus energy through his veins as though it were his life blood. He inserted the key in the ignition. His hands shook. A flash of light flared in the rear-view mirror. His eyes had a Transor glow.

Shit. Glowing eyes. Not a flash, but a steady Transor light.

Sandra wouldn't be able to take it. She hadn't had time to come to grips with the existence of aliens. This might send her over the edge. He couldn't waste time worrying about it. He put the Bronco in gear, mashed the gas pedal and drove the short distance to the cabin.

Cameron waited at the door. Sandra and Sean were huddled behind him. They hopped in the front seat. Cameron had Zach's arm over his shoulder. Zach limped to the Bronco. Leon burst out the door with three laptops and a stack of files clutched under his arms.

Cameron helped Zach into the backseat. "It'll be a tight fit and mighty uncomfortable, but we'll deal." Sandra held Sean. Cameron jumped in the front and lifted Sandra onto his lap.

A growl of displeasure escaped Raz's lips. "Keep your hands to yourself, Cameron."

Leon and Amber hopped in the backseat.

Cameron laughed then commanded, "Drive north."

Raz gunned the Bronco again and went through the gears to gain speed.

Amber shot turret-style out the back passenger window. A shower of gunfire pelted the Bronco.

Raz created distance between them and the camp, bumping over the pothole-ridden road.

"Open the glove box, and hand me what's inside," Zach mumbled.

Sandra reached in with unsteady hands. She pulled out a small metal box.

Cameron chuckled and passed the control to the occupants of the backseat. "This will be cool."

Zach pushed the top button and Leon cried out beside him.

Raz smelled smoke.

"What the hell?" Zach shook the small box and banged his palm on it.

Raz glanced in the rear-view mirror.

"God damn it, Zach," Leon shouted. He patted the smoldering embers on his pants. One laptop eked wisps of smoke.

"Sucks to be you right now." Cameron grinned.

A litany of curses flew out of Leon's mouth.

"Must be a frequency overlap." Zach fiddled with the box and pushed the button again.

The Bronco lurched forward. Raz struggled against the force pushing the Bronco down the gravel drive.

Sandra slid off Cameron's lap and wedged herself between the manual shift and Cameron's body.

The blast echoed through the valley. In the side mirrors, flames shot above the trees and engulfed the sky in black smoke.

"Hell, yeah!" Leon pumped his fist. "Let the motherfuckers try to find us now." He punched Cameron in the arm. "Why didn't you tell me you rigged the place?"

"You'd have wanted to push the button." Cameron smirked.

Amber snickered. "So true." She sat, more relaxed, but still on guard.

Raz glanced to the right, which brought Sandra's wide eyes and exhilarated flush into view. She wasn't scared of Omega or of the danger they'd escaped.

She laughed with Cameron and Leon. Her gaze strayed to Raz's, and her smile faded.

He shifted his vision back to the road in front of him.

She leveraged her left foot under the center stick and straddled the shifter. Her entire left side settled against him.

His hand was inches from the center of her body.

She still held the pistol in her hands.

Raz didn't think she'd fired one shot. He grabbed it and flipped the safety.

Sandra's hand brushed his temple. Her warm breath floated over his ear in a promise he willed her to keep.

Chapter Twenty-nine

LATE AFTERNOON SUN fell in the sky, along with the temperatures. The Bronco was ready to call it quits in the face of such primitive surroundings. A cold front had moved into the area. *Is Omega prepared for it?* Sandra shook her head at the stupid question. *I'm thinking about a secret alien military. If they aren't prepared for weather, then I'm definitely in a dream.* She didn't know their location and didn't have skills to navigate out of here by herself if she had a map.

Deep forest surrounded them. Pockets of heavy vegetation and underbrush scraped along every side of the vehicle. They'd left the slightest resemblance of civilization behind hours ago.

Coasting to a stop half-way down a hill, Raz pulled the emergency brake, and the vehicle rocked in place.

"Out of gas and no quickie mart in sight." He laughed.

Zach's meds and wounds made him delirious. The maniacal sound irritated Sandra because it fit the situation perfectly.

Leon reached into his pocket and dispensed two more pills to Zach.

He chewed the pain medicine. His grimace suggested they tasted worse than awful. The risk of infection out here was high. He needed full medical attention.

"Give me a team assessment, folks," Cameron said.

Leon hopped out of the backseat. "I got a few wings, but nothing serious. Zach's holding on. He'll be in and out for a while."

Cameron grunted. "Secure a perimeter. We must cleanse ASAP."

Leon clapped Zach on the shoulder. "Sleep tight."

Zach's eyes lowered even as he nodded to his unit mate.

Leon then entered the brush and disappeared.

Cameron arched a brow. "Amber?"

"Not a scratch."

Sandra pushed Raz's head to the side. "Raz has a wound on his neck."

He shook her off. "It's superficial."

"Your clothes are soaked in blood."

They tumbled out of the vehicle. Raz, and everyone else, ignored her. The uneven ground tilted them on the incline.

Amber swung her rifle over her shoulder. "Protocol, Cameron. We go to the e-loc."

Cameron gave a sharp shake of his head. "We set up camp for the night." He opened the Bronco's doors and loaded his body with supply bags. "As soon as Leon confirms, we'll set up a cleansing unit. In Raz's and Sean's state, the sooner the better."

Amber chased Cameron around the vehicle. "You've never gone against M83 protocol."

He threw folded tarps behind him near the rear bumper. They landed with a thump on the ground. He sighed and raised a quizzical brow to Raz.

Raz nodded.

Sandra paid more attention to the interactions between the two men than between Amber and Cameron. Something wasn't right. Their first encounter at HUP, Raz and Cameron were two spitting cobras. Now, they agreed with one another and consulted each other on order confirmation. Why? Yes, Raz admitted to calling him at Center Medical, but a total reversal in opinion wasn't like either of them. Sandra touched Raz's arm. "Wouldn't it be better to keep moving?"

Sean shuffled his feet. He stuck to Raz like Gorilla Glue. "I want to go home, Daddy."

His energy mist had evaporated, but the ghostly sheen to his face made Sandra's heart ache. She didn't think she could continue on with Omega if they kept lighting up like a rock concert's pyrotechnics at every snap of a twig or break of a falling branch. She'd talk to Raz. They'd create a plan to get out of the forest and go back to Raz's original strategy.

Don't be stupid. There isn't any witness protection. We're out here on our own. I'm pregnant. Raz is wounded. An ache pulsed in her shoulder blade. She rolled the shoulder to ease the tension. The attack had shaken her more than she cared to think about.

Amber tripped around the front of the Bronco, still trailing Cameron like a lost kitten. "Yes. Keep moving." Her head shook like a bobble-head. "I agree with Sandra."

"I'll tweet the masses." Cameron rolled his eyes.

Why's he being such a dick? Sandra wanted to get back to indoor plumbing, and her electric blanket, as fast as her feet would take her. Now she'd have to figure out how to use a gun, determine what a render would do to her and how to stop a mass Sixxer pandemic. The weight of the world crushed her body.

"We're too vulnerable out here." Amber kicked the side of the Bronco.

Raz squeezed Sandra's shoulders. "We're far enough away for a safe campsite setup. The e-location, or agreed emergency rendezvous point, could be compromised. Staying hidden in the forest will buy us time to figure out how Taft discovered the children's camp."

Cameron scooped the tarps from the ground and handed them to Raz. "Find a serviceable area here to set up shelters. Sean, you can help by gathering any large pieces of dry wood you can find. Take them where your dad tells you."

Raz bent to Sean's eye level. "Stay where I can see you, okay?"

Sean nodded. "Like when we went camping with Mommy?"

Raz looked at Sandra and the pain etched on his face broke her heart.

"Exactly," he said.

Sean wandered about eight feet from them. He tied the bear around his neck again.

Sandra didn't blame him. She didn't want to be out in this creepy woods by herself, either. She'd love it if a teddy bear could make her feel safe.

Sean searched the ground for branches and sticks.

Cameron pointed to Sean and murmured under his breath, "Is he okay?"

Raz's shoulders slumped. "I'm not sure how to help him through Paris's death."

Sandra wove her fingers in his. "Let him talk about her and ask questions."

"The Nexus does make this process easier, but no less painful." Raz trotted over to Sean and directed him on what to search for.

Amber stomped around the supplies Cameron offloaded. "How can the e-location be compromised?" She narrowed her eyes at Sandra. "We're exposed because of you." She glared back at Cameron. "Staying here is bullshit."

Cameron grabbed Amber's arm.

She jerked away.

Cameron went into what Sandra dubbed Commander mode.

"Am, Zach's injured. I need you to set a perimeter with Leon. You're not just a grunt. Think for a second. Your eyes protect Omega. Raz and I'll set up camp."

Amber clenched her teeth, and iridescent waves ignited along her jaw. She spun away.

Here come the fireworks again.

Cameron ran after and stopped her march. "We don't have enough daylight to reach a populated area, let alone the e-location. If Chasers or Thom have set an extraction for us as we leave the hills, then Sandra—" His gaze landed on Sandra.

A chill ran through her.

"Sandra's exposed to the virus," Cameron whispered.

Possible exposure, and no confirmed infection, Cam. Sandra kept her musings to herself. The extent of contamination wouldn't be determined without a laboratory and a lot of time—neither of which they had.

Amber relaxed but didn't lose her angry expression. She inhaled and brought determination back into her body. "Message received."

The urgency and excitement that had flooded Sandra at the news of the pregnancy returned. Before all hell broke loose at the children's camp, Cameron had been relieved at the discovery she hadn't told Raz about the baby. She couldn't keep news from him much longer when he kept insisting on a render. Yet, the act unlocked an automatic entryway for the virus to infect her and her unborn child.

Leon had saved several computers. Of course, that didn't mean they contained any useful information. How long would the systems be functional in the woods?

Raz trotted back to her, but addressed Cameron. "Is your second okay?"

Cameron nodded. "She's with us."

They took turns bringing the limited supplies, thrown inside the vehicle during their escape, from the Bronco to the campsite. In the backseat, Zach came in and out of consciousness. His leg was bloody and swollen. He needed a medic, preferably a hospital.

Would a Sixxer go to a hospital? They must have facilities to care for their sick or wounded.

Raz carried Zach to their primitive setup.

Shivers ran up and down Sandra's spine. Damn. She wanted to keep running. Was the general they kept talking about chasing them, or had Thom attacked them? Thom was a bastard, but Sandra couldn't comprehend the level of hate he must have to harm other people.

She was ashamed for not knowing. For not guessing what type of man he really was.

Cameron walked up the hill with another arm full of supplies.

"Let me help." Sandra caught up with him.

"It's the last one." Cameron dumped his haul on the ground. He gathered the leafy and evergreen-covered branches Raz and Sean had collected. Trotting to a small grouping of tall maples, he placed them in a pile.

Raz chopped down bigger limbs with a wicked hatchet he'd found in the vehicle. Cameron spread the soft branches on the ground.

Sandra hovered behind him and Raz.

Cameron turned. "Staying out of the way would be helpful. I don't want you to get hurt."

Raz raised his eyebrows at the comment.

She'd given Raz a piece of her mind both times he'd suggested she wasn't capable of doing physical labor. Besides, Cameron should know better than to say something like that to her. "I can handle setting up a camp—"

"Not in your condition," Cameron said.

Sandra's heart stopped, and her gaze flew to Raz. She held her breath.

He shrugged.

She caught his smug look before he turned his back to her.

"Cameron's the boss, but I wouldn't take his shit."

He wants me to get into a fight with Cam. No questions were asked on Cameron's reference to *your condition.* Raz was enjoying her discomfort. He even thought it was … funny? Damn it. The BFF going on between him and Cameron grated on her last nerve.

Raz handed her the stack of packaged tarps. "Hold these. Before you ream Cameron a new one, we need to set up the shelters before nightfall." He cut down another young tree and peeled off the shoots and leaves. He assembled it over two notched branches and tied each end to the poles with twine. Raz leaned the frame against the tree. He grabbed a tarp and unfolded it over the structure with the shiny surface face down.

Cameron made a sound of agreement at Raz's actions. "Three tarps have a heat shield. Makes sense to use them for the longest wall of each shelter. They'll reflect back the occupant's heat during the night. Temperatures will get mother-effing cold tonight." He pulled the fabric tight across the upper log and secured the camouflaged exterior to the frame Raz had just made.

Before Sandra's eyes, he created a tent wall.

Raz made four additional notched poles for the two other reflective tarps. He cut trees for the shelters without direction from Cameron. Raz knew everything Omega was supposed to do in this situation.

Yeah, because he's a soldier, too. An alien soldier.

Sandra was the only one out of place. The only one in the group that didn't belong. Even her child was alien. *Do I believe that?* What would happen when she told Raz?

Cameron and Raz made additional frames and left them bare of tarps.

Cameron paused beside her. "What're you going to do?"

He carried the wooden constructions under his arm like they weighed about as much as a puppy. Sandra gaped at him, but his question brought her back to reality. How would she protect herself,

Sean and the baby from the virus or Chasers?

Cameron cocked his head. His gaze flicked from the packages in her hand back to her eyes. "Are you going to place tarps on the other structures, or not?"

Raz nodded, even though Cameron wasn't speaking to him. He tapped the items in her hands. "We'll have a B & B set up pretty quickly."

Sandra tore open the plastic coverings and unfolded the fabric. It was lighter than she expected.

Sean bounced on the three evergreen mattresses Cameron had spread out beneath each tree.

The beds looked uncomfortable. Sandra didn't care if it was for an emergency, she'd take a cot or blow-up mattress over this contraption.

"Are we camping here?" Sean asked.

"You got it, bud." Raz showed Sean how to stack the branches evenly, but their accommodations wouldn't be a Hilton.

Sandra followed Cameron and accepted the knife he offered. Mimicking him, she cut strips of twine to tie the coverings to the posts. She had to do something. "Give me another gun, Cam. I can hold my own. Help keep Sean safe."

Raz tilted his head to the side. He eyed the knife in her hand from tip to handle. "You don't need a gun."

Sean picked up a branch, and a flash of amethyst colored his cheeks. What surprised Sandra was how much actual gun power Omega carried when Raz had only himself. Raz and Sean seemed to have built-in guns. The other Sixxers didn't.

Cameron scoffed. "Sweetheart, you're crazy. You've never held a gun in your life before today. Back at base, we needed all the firepower we could find. A nervous trigger won't help us out here. Do you want that on your conscience?"

"I need to protect myself."

Sean skipped from shelter to shelter and tested each bed. "This one isn't soft enough." He ran to get more branches and tested it again.

Cameron trimmed leaves and bark off several shorter branches. He carved one end of each stick to a point. "A team of soldiers will protect you. We might be out here two or three days. Raz will teach you how to handle the equipment later. Right now, camp set-up is priority. We're cut off from M83. Last night's communication was the only way someone found us."

Sandra shuffled from foot to foot. "I have to go back to HUP. I'll have access to the lab and run Thom's research through vigorous testing. Find out what he's been up to in his backyard studio."

Cameron shook his head. "You'll have to do it here with what we salvaged. HUP is compromised. We're not going back."

"We need to determine the infection rate of the virus. We need to keep testing Raz and Sean to make sure they don't show symptoms." Sandra tugged Cameron's arm.

He stopped what he was doing. His gaze bored holes in her skull. He twisted his hand and pointed his knife at her like an extension of his finger. "You think you can figure out what's going on all by yourself? M83 has been scrutinizing General Taft, your ex and men like them for decades." He threw a handful of the stakes to Raz.

Raz narrowed his eyes and flexed his biceps at the threat against her. His fists clenched around the sharpened stakes in his hands.

Cameron lowered the blade. "At ease, soldier."

Raz pulled Sandra behind him, placing himself between her and Cameron. Light flared in his eyes. "I am at ease." He used the sharpened sticks to secure the loose edges of the tarps to the ground as if they were tents. "We need to get Sean out of this area. Find a safe place for a render. We can no longer avoid the protection our circle will provide."

Cameron shooed Sean from the bed of branches and assembled the walls of each shelter around the trees. "You can't render. We no longer have tech for protection. The energy will be like a flare to our attackers. When we're done setting up camp, a cleanse will act as an anti-NEU."

A flare? Sandra couldn't believe what he'd said. *Is Cam high on something?* "Like the blow 'em up job at the previous camp wasn't a beacon?"

"By the time they find us, the Nexus will protect the team." Raz tied the two walls of the first shelter together. It created a v-shaped enclosure against the tree. Placing more branches over the walls camouflaged it among the vegetation. He moved onto the middle and biggest hut and did the same. This tent formed a u-shape and resembled a tiny imploding wigwam.

"Omega won't be in a render." Cameron pushed another set of stakes into the ground at the farthest tent. One wall leaned against the tree, and the space inside was tight.

Sandra didn't want to contemplate crawling inside that shelter.

Cameron walked back to the stack of cut tree limbs. "We'll be here until first light, at the least. Let's get more distance tomorrow and determine if the e-loc is safe. Then we'll contact M83 for info. You can render with Sean then. Amber and Leon have set a good perimeter."

Cameron handed Raz and Sandra bundles of the brush. They both covered the tarps with the scavenged branches. The shelters disappeared into the underbrush. No one would discover the huts unless they were right next to them.

A cold shiver ran up Sandra's spine. *Like how the soldiers faded into the forest during my magic reading of the dead guy.*

Raz grabbed a canteen from a pack and gulped the water. "I don't think Taft attacked us. I think Nazier and Thom are working on their own and sent a small unit to flush us out."

Sandra fit smaller branches into the sides of the shelters. "What's Thom's motive to come after Omega? They wanted Paris, didn't they?"

"She wasn't his goal," Cameron said.

Raz leaned closer. "Who was?"

Sandra smelled a hint of sweat mixed with the cinnamon scent that always hovered around him.

"I understand, now. Thom doesn't have you." Raz's voice tickled her ear. He took another drink from the canteen.

Cameron arched an eyebrow. "He declared his undying love to you at HUP."

Raz sprayed water out of his mouth.

Sean jumped out of the way.

Sandra grabbed a sleeping bag from the supplies and asked Sean to unroll it inside the third dwelling. "Thom won't throw away his research to convince me to come back to him." Sean would barely fit inside, let alone anyone else.

Sean crawled out and stood.

Cameron nodded at Raz. "I agree with your boyfriend in this case. Thom's main concern has always been you, Sandra."

She felt the blood drain from her face and swayed. "Your reasoning makes little sense. I'm not alien."

Cameron shrugged. "He's invested a lot of time and effort into you. With the fertility drugs. Having you as a control. If he no longer has you available, then his work will mean nothing, and he won't be able to repeat any of his experiments."

Raz grasped her upper arm. "Why does he want you so much?" A flush of anger spread across his face.

Sandra didn't care for his jealousy. "I don't know how Thom thinks, and I don't care."

"He wants what he can't have." Cameron covered the first hut with the last of the underbrush and threw two sleeping bags inside. "You two can use this one. The sleepers are good down to thirty degrees, but Leon said it's going to get colder than that tonight. Snuggle up. I have two more sleepers rated at a lower temperature. The kid and invalid get those. They'll sleep in the largest bungalow."

"Heard that, asshole," Zach mumbled. "I'll be on watch tonight."

"I want to sleep here." Sean climbed into the biggest one and snuggled into the sleeping bag.

"Yeah." Cameron shook his head. "Zach isn't on any watch tonight. His leg hinders movement. So he gets more space with the kid." He leaned toward Raz. "He's getting pain meds tonight. The middle shelter is between yours and whoever is resting from perimeter watch. We'll tuck the two most vulnerable of the group inside."

Sandra motioned between herself and Raz. "Sean can stay with us."

"No. I'm not taking any chances with the three of you running off into the night then having to drag your asses back here. Besides, the two of you won't fit in the first structure, and I doubt Raz wants to snuggle up to Zach. Amber, Leon and I'll rotate on perimeter until dawn. The smallest shelter will work for one person, and rotation will keep it warm."

"I don't like it, but Cameron is right." Raz rubbed the back of his head. "We'll keep the weakest members of the group in the center. If we're attacked, then we can defend them."

Sandra couldn't help the little sigh of relief that shuddered through her. She wouldn't have to sleep in the tiny hut. Although, sleeping with Raz was giving her a different kind of anxiety. How eerie that Cameron had guessed her idea of making their get-away when they'd first stopped here? She was always two steps behind this team of soldiers and at their mercy.

Raz helped Cameron carry Zach to the largest shelter and covered him with a sleeping bag.

Leon lumbered up the hill and whistled. "Damn quick moves, team. I'm impressed with the digs."

"What's our status?" Cameron asked.

"A small stream, more like a ditch, isn't far from here. Amber and I scouted about a mile radius. It's quiet, almost too quiet, but we're confident a cleanse will dissipate any remaining energy we have from the attack at the children's camp."

Cameron smirked. "Excellent. You and Am going first?"

"Amber is finished. I'll hold watch while you rotate. The station is already set up."

"I won't like this," Raz grumbled beside Sandra.

Leon laughed.

Cameron slapped Raz on the shoulder.

The glee on his face bothered Sandra.

Cameron nudged Raz in the direction Leon had come from. "It's for the best, in your case. The energy at camp was stunted, but here it'll be available to any NEUs out there."

Sandra followed them both.

Cameron stopped her with a hand on her chest. "One at a time."

"What're we doing?" she asked.

Leon snickered, and Cameron failed to keep the humor off his face. "Time for your cold showers."

Chapter Thirty

SANDRA STOPPED A few feet in front of Amber. She imagined how large her eyes were, and an incredulous expression was probably permanently etched on her face. How could any of them blame her after seeing the contraption they called a shower? "I'm not getting in that thing."

Amber tapped her rifle. "Don't make me go Rambo on your ass. We've all done it. You're the last holdout."

The shower erected in front of Sandra was a single stall tent big enough for one person to stand inside. Why did Omega keep insisting she go inside these little freaking enclosures? She examined the heavy plastic bag, similar to a canvas canteen, attached to the support at the top of the tent. The sack had a miniature shower nozzle attached to the bottom. Amber had already filled it with water from the stream, which was about ten feet away. Why did they have this tent, and not any actual tents big enough to sleep in?

Sandra noticed Amber's damp hair. The dark locks floated around her head, and a clean fresh scent hovered around her. She'd been the first one of the team to jump in and take a freaking cold shower, in the woods, in almost freezing temperatures.

A full body shiver quaked through Sandra's body. She'd never make it as a soldier. "Do you realize the temperature?"

"Quit being such a pansy and get in." Amber's frustration was evident in her tone. "Don't linger. Just cleanse."

Sandra picked up the duffle bag containing the extra clothes Raz gave her at the children's camp. The bag weighted her arm. A prickling sensation fluttered across her back. "Amber?"

Amber turned and narrowed her eyes. "What?"

"I'm not sure I can go inside." Sandra hated the wobble in her voice, especially in front of Amber. She hadn't yet come to terms with the fact she'd have to sleep in a tiny enclosed space.

Amber stepped up beside her, and together they studied the facilities. She shrugged. "Could you walk inside and do what you had to for your baby?"

Sandra swallowed. "Yes."

Amber softened her voice. "That's all you need to focus on. Besides, you don't have to zip the door closed. You'd be warmer zipped, but it's not required. In fact, we're lucky we had the shower in the supplies. Our exit was too quick. With enough time, we could've grabbed the portable water heater and tents and been living the dream out here in this human paradise."

Sandra pursed her lips. "A portable water heater?"

Amber laughed. "*Bruja*, M83 isn't bare bones like a human army. The women don't tolerate living in squalor for months or years at a time. M83 has money and resources that aren't tied to any government entity so we can demand what we want. And we get it. *Always.* We have teams of soldiers like Zach who come up with new gadgets all the time to satisfy our comfort levels."

Sandra dropped the bag. "Yet, I get the pleasure of being naked and vulnerable right now. I'm sure, so you can jeer at me? You have the other comforts hidden?"

Amber bent over and loud whoops and snickers echoed around them. "I hate this survivalist shit. If I'm hiding stuff from you, I'm hiding it from myself. I'm here so no one else jeers at you, princess. Like I said … privacy is at a minimum in a unit. We're very lucky to have this cleansing facility. I'm not here to guard you like Cameron thinks. I'm here to keep the horny bastards away."

The smirk on her face was foreign to Sandra, but she liked this side of Amber. "Why do I have to do this?" She could write a book based on the facial expressions flickering over Amber. Was a shower top secret, as Zach would've said?

Amber sighed. "The attack put too much stress on the unit. At the camp, we had an anti-NEU." She waved her arm around the trees. "Out here there isn't anything except us."

"You're talking about the light I saw on each of you, and the mist around Sean," Sandra said.

"And the light on you. We cool the Nexus energy attached to us to dim our internal light at night after such an intense fight." Amber pinched her lips together. "Not much daylight is left. You better get in there before it becomes a dark tent."

Sandra used her counting and breathing technique to calm her nerves and entered the shower. The door had a zipper, like Amber had said. It draped a little and provided privacy without being enclosed. For years, Sandra had wished for control over her claustrophobia, but she'd only decreased the panic attacks in familiar surroundings. Now she had more to think about than herself. She ran her hand over her stomach and continued the deep breathing. After a few seconds, Sandra no longer heard her guard. "Amber, you there?"

"Yes, *pendeja*. Hurry." Amber's voice came from the left outside wall of the shower.

Sandra breathed a sigh of relief. "Why do you act like you don't care?"

"I don't."

Sandra found the same bar of soap she'd used at the children's camp and a small towel in her bag. She undressed and placed her dry items outside the door on top of the duffle. The shower head hung over an aluminum bar, and she turned a valve to release the water. The cold water hit her, and she squealed. Five seconds was Sandra's limit, and she turned off the nozzle. The soap lathered well and scented the tent with lilacs.

Amber shuffled outside the tent.

Sandra hastened her shower. "I'm curious. What does the cleanse actually do? From what I noticed during the attack, the Nexus acts like electrical energy. Water and electricity don't mix."

"It isn't electricity. The Nexus taps into the nervous system. A cleanse with water and soap muffles the connection. The technique isn't perfect, but it helps."

Sandra washed the soap from her body and hair. Her entire frame shook with attempts to warm itself while she rinsed. She squeezed water out of her hair and rubbed the towel over her limbs. The cotton square wasn't big enough to wrap around her torso, but at least it dried her frozen body. She pulled on her clothes and the military coat, seeking any warmth she could find.

Sandra straightened with pride at the pleased expression on Amber's face. A fallen tree became a seat while Sandra rolled on her socks and shoved her feet into warm shoes. She finger-combed her hair then wove it back into a braid. It'd take longer to dry, but she couldn't stand the icy strands against her neck.

Amber stood in front of her and had stowed the disassembled shower in her bag. "Ready?"

"I know you care."

"You're such a know-it-all—"

"No one else cared about Sean like you did when Raz couldn't get to him."

Amber shook her head and twisted her jaw. "Just my training. Don't get your panties in a wad." She stomped off toward camp.

Sandra didn't tell her she wasn't wearing any panties, and if her response was M83 training, they all would've swarmed Sean like POTUS. Her chest burst with comfort that Sean and Jamie had someone else to keep them safe. Sandra had difficulty thinking of any other name to call the baby. Jamie suited him. She headed back toward camp and crossed her fingers in the hope of a warm fire.

Cameron was placing rations into the rotation shelter when they entered the campsite.

Amber tossed the shower onto the main supply pile. "Now that's settled, I'll go back on scout duty with Leon."

Amber left.

Cameron nodded and walked back to the main collection of supplies and sat.

"Why isn't there a fire?" Sandra asked.

Cameron patted the spot beside him next to the cold fire pit. "No campfire until morning. We've got self-heating meal packs so we don't need one, and it'll give away our location."

Sandra shook her head. All she wanted was warmth. She was cold and damp, but the thought of a hot meal made the lack of a fire bearable. Checking on Zach in the middle shelter, she pulled back the limbs covering the entrance and peeked inside.

In the dim light, Zach hadn't moved in position. He was where

Raz had left him. His chest rose and fell in steady movements.

The meds Leon had given him had him out like a baby, or how she thought a baby would sleep. She tugged the door back in place.

Sean stood behind her. He reached out. "Mommy used to tell me a story and sing to me at bedtime."

She pulled him into the biggest bear hug she could manage. He smelled like cookies and linen-scented soap. "I think I'm up for such a very important task, but I think we're going to eat first."

"Okay."

Cameron shuffled packs of ready meals inside a container and selected four. "Tell me why you're so important, Raz."

Raz was stretching his arms and back while pacing between the shelters. "You wanted me back in M83. Didn't your commander give you my stats?"

Sandra was tired of their posturing. She arranged the sleeping bags in the first shelter like she was decorating the White House. The extra wall provided more space to maneuver in, but the cramped enclosure would test her control over her panic attacks.

Sean helped her decide the best way to maximize heat was to spread an extra tarp over the tree limbs and then zip the two sleeping bags together into one blanket for them to sleep under. His camping experience was endlessly useful.

"I want to sleep in here with you and Daddy. I'm scared."

Sandra threaded her fingers through his soft hair and kissed his forehead. "I do, too, but Cameron won't let us. He thinks we'll run away."

"We should. I don't want to be here."

Neither did she. "Keeping you in the center makes you the most important person here."

Sean wrinkled his nose. "Zach's there, too."

"Well, he has a bad leg and Cameron knows that you can protect him."

Sean gave her a stink eye. She never had been very good at telling tales.

She focused on the beds. Thinking of her and Raz in this tight space elevated her body temperature. "The shelters are bunched together, which means you'll be close to Raz and me. Once we're sleeping, you can come over here any time you want."

"Okay."

They crawled out of the shelter and into Cameron and Raz's conversation.

"There's no backing out of it now." Cameron's voice was low and deep. "You've been hiding information from the team, and you better spill. How dangerous are you? How much power will you have after you complete your render?"

Sandra didn't stop her sarcastic retort. "What other secrets are there, besides you being aliens?"

Raz drank from a canteen. He stood across from Cameron, hulking over him in a display of dominance. "My information is above your security clearance."

Sean plopped on the ground beside Cameron.

Cameron handed him the meals and dug a spoon out of the bag of camping silverware he snatched from one of the supply containers.

Sandra wandered closer. She wasn't sure who'd win the pissing match.

"The Nexus formed around Raz and Sean during the attack." Cameron spoke to Sandra. "When Raz went out to get the Bronco, he had a definite muscle mass modification. His eyes changed, and by more than a normal Sixxer reaction. It occurred the moment Zach was hit." He pointed at Sandra. "You were in the Bronco. You saw what happened."

"I saw a lot. None of it made sense. You told me back at the children's camp the mist or smoke was what few humans could see of the Nexus." Sandra recognized the ready meal Cameron prepared. Thom had a brief period of living off the grid a few years back. She'd refused to go camping on his week-long treks, but he'd insisted she learn how to prepare the ready meals. *Had he been expecting us to run like I am with Omega?* She sat next to Sean. His teddy bear had gotten a shower, too. Sean had wrapped a towel around him.

Cameron poured water into the sleeve containing the meal pouch and waited for the heating element to warm the food.

Thom had been eccentric. Hindsight brought a clarity to his actions Sandra hated. *I'm such a blind fool. Everything Thom has done pointed me right to this other world.* "The mist happened at the hospital, too. Isn't that the alien part? What all of you do?"

Cameron shook his head. "I don't know what the fuck the mist was. It's not natural. When you said you saw something, Zach and I assumed you were talking about an aura signature. That's not what surrounded Raz." He heated an additional meal for each of them then selected one for himself.

Raz squatted and picked up meal. He opened the steaming contents and handed the package to Sandra.

Black bean aroma and the smell of chicken broth had her crinkling her nose. Her stomach rolled. *Can I eat this stuff?*

She grabbed the spoon Sean held out. "Your power can't be cleansed, can it? Can Sean's? Are we just waiting for Thom to find us?"

Shoulders slumped, he sighed and faced Cameron. "I'm a Transor."

Cameron straightened his spine. His face lost color. He rolled the beef stew around his mouth like it was mud. "Bullshit. Transors don't exist."

"I have to be careful, or I hurt people," Sean whispered then dug a spoon out of the baggie and ate his meal.

At the scent of beef teriyaki, Sandra wrinkled her nose and coughed into her fist.

Cameron laughed. His white teeth flashed in the dim light. "He isn't one, either. What shit are you trying to pull, Raz? Are you supposed to be the mad prophecy come to life? No one in M83 will believe that."

Raz bumped Sean's shoulder. "You haven't hurt anyone."

Sean's eyes were wide. "I made Sandra's nose bleed. I hear thoughts."

Sandra hugged him. "You didn't make me do anything. None of this is your fault."

Cameron's dark gaze flew from Sean to her. He nodded at the pouch in her hand. "You better eat."

Raz grunted. "I haven't believed I was a part of a prophecy since I was Sean's age. That's a story about the return of our race, but the sad fact is our race is dying a slow and painful death. Transors are rare because Sixxers are having difficulties having children."

She grimaced. The food was unappealing. "What is a Transor?"

Cameron tilted his head and sighed. "A Sixxer who has a pure connection to the Nexus. The power is difficult to explain. Elevational training for Sixxer Transors theoretically allows them to control Nexus energy at their will without a render. Although, renders would make them stronger, physically and energetically." He glared at Raz. "I repeat, they don't exist."

Raz fished a spoon out of Sean's bag and sat cross-legged opposite the three of them. "We can't risk Taft finding us. Or him finding Sean. I'll teach him how to control his Nexus aura."

"Sean's too young to be a Transor." Cameron coughed. "If they existed, Sean wouldn't go through elevation for at least another fifteen years. Two mythical creatures right here with Omega. All the while we're being hunted by the biggest dill weed in the state."

Sandra wondered which dill weed Cameron referred to.

Sean bounced. "We need to keep Jamie from the bad guys, don't we? Mommy said I had to be brave and be a big brother now. Does the prof of sees say I'll be a big brother?"

Sandra choked on her bite of chicken with black beans and rice. She bumped Sean's arm and subtly held the package out to him.

Sean grabbed the meal from her hand and spooned out a bite for himself.

He ate like a starving lion who'd been prowling the savanna for weeks.

Around a mouthful of food, he said, "He was scared before, but now he's okay."

This was the second time Sean acted like he could communicate with the baby. Was such a thing possible?

Raz squinted one eye, and his eyebrows drew together. "Who are you talking about?"

"My baby brother. The one Sandra's gonna have."

CHAPTER THIRTY-ONE

SEAN'S WILD STATEMENT coursed through Raz's body like poison. His jaw slackened, and his mouth gaped open.

Sean smiled a toothy grin.

Sandra coughed in an uncharacteristic manner, and Sean patted her on the back. She recovered and sipped her water, but the strange fit had Raz remembering how the illness affected Paris in the same way. The coughing bouts had marked the beginning.

Sean bit his lower lip. "Are you okay, Sandra? We're excited to be camping. Jamie thinks the tents are cool. They're made of trees."

What was Sean up to? Confusion after a failed render wasn't out of the question, but an imaginary brother was pure attention-getting. No brother existed. Years ago, Raz had broken off romantic ties with Paris. This must be Sean's way of grieving. Amethyst mist smoked his dancing eyes.

He grinned again, but at Raz's lack of amusement, his smile faded. He ducked his head and ate in an unbearable silence.

"You're very important, Raz." Cameron chewed another bite of his beef stew. He pointed at Sandra then at Sean. "We've been sucked into the vortex. Fighting against it isn't wise. We work together to keep everyone safe."

Raz blinked at Cameron's words. He'd ceased to exist for the minute lag between conversations. What was he talking about? Raz wasn't fighting against anything.

Don't be mad at me, Daddy. The message from Sean entered Raz's mind.

A tingle spread at the base of Raz's neck and flowed down his arms to the tips of his fingers. The energy was unlike the spark of a blitz, or the link between him and Sean during a render. Sean had engaged the Nexus as a Transor and communicated with Raz. He'd suspected Sean's power had grown, but now he had proof inside his own head.

Cameron swigged from his canteen. "Both of your sons need protection."

"Sean doesn't have a brother," Raz choked out. His fingers became numb from the forces emanating from Sean. Raz dropped his MRE. He would've known after the render if there was another child. The Nexus would've connected them.

Sandra sat with her head tilted and widened eyes. She opened her mouth to speak and closed it quickly, but she repeated the movement several times. She finally whispered, "Hopefully, in another twenty-eight weeks, Sean will be a big brother." A warm color spread across her cheekbones. She glowed. A shy smile turned up her lips.

Sean laughed. His excitement at the prospect of a sibling was a tangible wave of heat.

Is it because we're both Transors that his energy is hitting me without a render? Raz tried to focus on Sean and Sandra at the same time and failed. He calculated in his head, twenty-eight weeks. Human gestation was placed at forty.

The baby, if it was a Sixxer, could've communicated with him via the rendering. Why hadn't he sensed it at the hospital?

"I'm guessing the baby will go through the normal gestation time for me, but we aren't sure," Sandra said.

No. She's human. There isn't a child.

"Zach might have more details on the baby's development when he wakes up. He's learned about this topic on deep missions," Cameron said.

An ache blossomed inside Raz's chest and down to his stomach. *A baby isn't possible. We can't produce a child.* Yet, knowing there was a chance she could be pregnant made him yearn for another child.

Sean bounced beside her.

The Nexus connection between the three of them ... no, the four of them, heated Raz's limbs, his spine. Sean's laughter echoed inside

Raz's head. He raised clenched fists to his temples, but he dropped the heavy arms back to his sides. Invisible energy from Sean turned Raz's hands into fifty-pound weights.

Maybe the emotion isn't from Sean. Where's it coming from? The open circle prohibited Raz from pinpointing the source of the joy within the circle's fluctuating electrical energy. No boundary was present. A spike of doubt fluttered across his shoulders.

Sandra's lips drooped, and her eyes lost a hint of their sparkle.

The desperate need to render the circle whirled inside Raz's body. Chaos warred within the Nexus signatures of all four of them.

Then the Nexus sucker punched him. All the air left his lungs in a whoosh. The child was theirs. The unreality of how they'd created life didn't matter. Sandra's face held a nervousness and a want for this child. Was Raz guessing, or was the Nexus allowing Sandra to communicate across the open circle? Raz wanted the baby with every fiber of Nexus energy running in his blood, but procreation was impossible between humans and Sixxers. Right? Sean had already bridged the gap between Sixxer and human by communicating with the baby. The bond between Sean and Jamie was obvious. When Raz closed the circle, would he and Sandra have the same connection? A bond a Sixxer hoped for, but one that rarely happened. His heart pounded.

Negative scenarios played in his mind, now. If the situation were true, Chasers had created Hybrids. Sandra's ex must know about the child, and he attacked the camp. Thom wouldn't stop until he captured her.

Cameron tossed his empty ready meal in a trash bag. "Thom fucked up this mission for us. A simple observation has turned into a mole hunt inside M83."

"An infiltrator?" Raz asked. External threats were easier to deal with right now. At least, Raz had protocols to follow. Sandra's pregnancy had no rules.

Curiosity got the better of Sean, and he reached for a box of ammo beside Cameron's leg.

"Uh-uh. You're not to touch any of this. Stay close to Zach tonight. Wake him if you hear anything weird. If you can't wake him, get Raz or scream for us. Got it?"

Sean nodded.

Cameron double-checked his gear. "Our location had to have been leaked via the comm message Zach sent regarding Sandra's discovery of the viral infection path. The mole, or double agent, is within M83. Chasers don't assign infiltrators into field positions anymore. The nixing of renders within the Corp stopped that practice. General Taft has to be targeting civilians now."

Cameron cracked his knuckles then shuffled through the supply bags. He gave Raz a gun and a box of ammo. He handed another one to Sandra. "I had intended on giving this to you, but I don't want Amber or Leon to know.

Raz popped the slide with a quick snap and checked the chamber of the gun. Loaded. He stuffed the barrel in his waistband and the ammo in his back pocket. "What was the message sent to M83?"

"Confirmation Thom's research specifically tested if an infected infiltrator could spread the virus inside a circle." Cameron leaned forward. "Once he finds out about Sandra's render, her pregnancy and the potential for virus infection, he'll do anything to get his hands on her."

Sean's power dissipated, and Raz regained control of his body. He stretched his neck and allowed the new information to penetrate. The risk of infection, if Thom's research was right, would be with Raz's circle. So far, Paris had been the only one with symptoms. The potential of virus infection was another convenient means for M83 to declare renders off-limits. "Do you trust your team?"

Cameron stretched out his legs in front of him. "Yes."

His hesitation would've gone unnoticed by anyone else, but Raz saw the slight twitch of Cameron's eye. *Cameron has created a foolish plan he's keeping to himself.* "The traitor is inside your team."

"We'd be captured if that were the case." Cameron arched a brow.

Sandra and Sean finished the last of the ready meals. Although, Raz watched Sandra give most of hers to Sean.

"How long has Sean been telepathic?" Cameron asked.

Raz snapped his head back toward Cameron. How had he sensed the connection? Raz rubbed the back of his head. No. Cameron sensed nothing. Omega had no sensitivity to circular bonding. The instinct had been driven out of them. Sean spoke to the baby through

Raz's specific circle bonding. "The last few months, for sure."

Sandra paused in her clean-up efforts. "Sean reads minds?"

Raz nodded. "Within our circle." He rubbed his face. How would he keep the four of them safe? "Are you sure gestation be the human equivalent of forty weeks?"

Cameron sighed. "It depends on Sandra's Nexus energy. Thom's details on the fertility experiments never resulted in a pregnancy for Sandra. Zach thinks there could be accelerated growth, or a greater Nexus transformation, within her. Without access to M83's central lab, we have no way of understanding the development of the baby."

The experiments. Fuck. What impact would Thom's shit have on the baby? On Sandra? Was she really innocent in knowing about Thom's experiments? Raz knew in his heart she'd never hurt a child. Yet, she was too happy. He expected that reaction for a human child, but her face showed no signs of trepidation or worry. *This is an alien child. The Nexus is changing her physically, and she's not freaking out. Paris had gone totally berserk about being pregnant.*

"Daddy?" Sean hugged Sandra close. She rubbed Sean's back, and his son basked in the offered comfort.

"When did you find out?" Raz asked.

Sandra cleared her throat. "Yesterday, when I arrived."

"How's it possible?"

At Sandra's blank stare, Cameron said, "M83 thinks Thom's fertility experiments on Sandra made it possible—"

"You told M83?" Raz shot to his feet and paced to a nearby tree. "Now the mole and General Taft know she's pregnant!" The last rays of the sun filtered through the trees. He ran his fingers through his hair and pulled until the pain smarted.

"Mommy said I'd have a new Mom. I want to have a Mom." Sean blubbered on about Paris. The initial happiness in the open circle degraded into fear. *It's happening again. The running. The hiding.*

Sandra squeezed Sean closer. Her eyes shimmered from brown to honey. "I can tell you're not excited about the news, but we need to be careful about a render. The virus could infect the baby or Sean. We have to be safe until I can find out more."

"Not excited?" Raz barked. "Are you flipping nuts? You're trying to convince me you're ecstatic about having an alien baby! Let's get on the page called reality."

Sandra reared back. Her face paled.

Raz wasn't fooled. "What a coup for you to have an alien child at your whim to experiment on."

Her ghost-like face crumpled in the twilight. She choked back tears. "Stop talking."

"Did you already know what we were?" He couldn't stop the accusations.

"Stop talking, right now!" She pulled Sean closer.

Being forced into another situation where he had to run and hide brought back his anger at Paris.

Sean's head swiveled from Raz to Sandra and back again.

Raz grabbed a low hanging branch and ripped it from the tree. Sean's loyalty should belong to him.

A moan came from the second shelter. "Can you keep it down?" Zach called out. "Your shouting is destroying my beauty sleep. Does anyone have any water?"

Sandra jumped to her feet and grabbed a full canteen.

Always to the rescue, isn't she, my little alien saver?

Cameron snickered. "Love on the rocks. It takes two to make three. Doesn't it, Raz?"

Raz snorted. The combination of miracle and nightmare was lost on Cameron. "When was the last time you've seen a Sixxer child other than Sean?"

"Never. A soldier doesn't get many opportunities to visit the nursery."

"Because there aren't any. Sixxers haven't been able to have children in decades."

Cameron tilted his head and pursed his lips. "Amazing, isn't it? You'll have two."

Sandra helped Zach out of the shelter and wrapped his arm around her shoulders as they walked back to the camp circle.

Zach was milking his injury. A Sixxer never took this long to heal, medication or not.

Raz shook his head. *How did we produce a baby?* "Sandra is human."

She straightened her back in one fluid movement.

Zach was a helpless prisoner to her shifting. He stumbled to the ground in a flare of pain and expletives.

Sandra's upper lip flared into a snarl. "Are you suggesting the baby isn't yours?"

"It isn't mine." Zach chuckled.

Raz growled. He was two seconds away from twisting Zach's body into a pretzel. Of course, no one was on his side. The Nexus glow around Sandra's head was interpreted as a halo whenever an Omega member glanced at her.

Sandra glared. "Answer me!"

"No." Raz threw the limb in his hand into the trees behind him.

Cameron held out his palms for calm. "Sean can connect to the baby. Parentage is obvious. The more important question is, where do we go from here?"

Raz looked out into the dark trees. "Chasers will do anything to find me or Sean. General Taft will wet himself knowing two Sixxer Transors exist."

Cameron handed Zach a hot meal. "We've been watching Sandra and Thom for seven years. She has no clearance and is off the suspect list. She's not the enemy."

Sandra gasped. "You've been watching me for *seven* years? How?"

"The team placed several surveillance cameras around you and Thom, especially at HUP. The painting in your office is one of them," Cameron said.

Sandra's face turned a sickly grey color. "Why me?"

"Your association with Thom made M83 nervous."

Sandra stepped away from Cameron.

"Sandra, this was our job. I knew you weren't working with him."

Zach scratched his face with the end of the spoon he'd grabbed from the plastic bag. "Chasers have been experimenting with Sixxer fertility, just like Thom, in the lab. Paris must've been a part of this strategy from the beginning."

Sandra pulled Sean into her arms. "They're experimenting on children?"

"In the lab." Raz snorted. "Those children aren't real."

Sandra stepped back from Raz, dragging Sean with her. The physical distance was only a few inches, but the emotional distance placed miles between them. "Not real? Why wouldn't the kids be real?"

Raz strained to hear Sandra's questions. Without a Nexus connection, Chasers could experiment with fertility all day. They'd still get human babies. Lab kids weren't Sixxers. "They're artificial. They'll never speak to the Nexus." He waved his hand at Zach and Cameron. "Has this information been buried for the past seven years? They have no Sixxer power or ability to render into circles. They'd be useless as infiltrators against M83, and we'd sense they weren't Sixxer children."

Cameron stood. "Zeniths have gotten better at connection. They infiltrate from inside a circle, and most can easily connect. You wouldn't realize it until it was done. Their children might also have this ability."

Zach sat forward, winced and grabbed his injured leg. "Damn. That's why they stopped M83 renders. The children Raz is talking about aren't the children General Taft has now. A lot of strange shit happens." He ruffled Sean's hair. "Like kids who go through elevation at a young age and spikes of Nexus power without renders with other Sixxers. General Taft is building his own infiltration army that can connect to the Nexus artificially."

Raz's pulse skipped a beat. Sean had early elevation.

Sean wrapped his arms tight around Sandra's waist.

Sandra stared off into space.

Raz didn't like the ashen sheen to her skin. She blended into the approaching shadows, and entered an internal place Raz couldn't to reach.

Her gaze met Cameron's, Zach's and finally penetrated Raz's. "Thom didn't want someone else's child." Honey flashes of Nexus light engulfed her eyes. "I can't … couldn't." She blinked against tears. "The fertility treatments became too artificial for him. I suggested adoption, but Thom wanted a *real* child."

Zach pulled her shoulders toward him. "Artificial children isn't a literal term. Chaser labs are different—"

Sandra cut him off with a flick of her hand. Her gaze never left Raz. The Nexus fever in them wrapped around his body. The open circle played havoc with his control of his Nexus power.

Sandra swallowed. "What happened between you and Paris is your business. What happened between us was good. It was loving, and none of you will take this joy from me. This *reality*." She cradled her stomach in a way only mothers did. "So many years I tried to have a baby. Each and every failure was a cut on my soul." She grunted. "I guess Thom did me a favor by giving me his drugs."

Raz touched her arm. "Don't you dare thank him."

"I'm grateful he decided I wasn't worth his time anymore. The endless parade of women right in front of my eyes, in front of colleagues. My reputation was in shreds, not to mention they knew why."

Cameron reached for her. "Stop talking. He's not worth this."

Sandra stepped closer to Raz and ran her finger along his chin.

She came back to him, which sent a flutter of hope into his heart. A zap of Nexus heat came from Sandra's hand and jolted back his head.

Her fingers trembled. "I love you. I want and love this child with every cell in my body. Alien. Human. The only way anyone will take him from me is to pry him from my cold, dead hands. Artificial or not. Real or not. We're not leaving Omega until I find answers."

CHAPTER THIRTY-TWO

THE SUN RACED toward the horizon. Puffs of vapor formed wispy clouds with every outward breath. A two-foot chasm separated Sandra from Raz. His accusations opened a wound on her soul. Twilight tried to sneak between the leaves, but the tree canopy blocked all traces of light. He avoided her with a precision she found disturbing.

Was this how Paris always felt at his cold shoulder?

Shadows engulfed them. Her eyes took the nighttime cue, and a weariness entered her bones, but she didn't want to sleep. Chilled from the cleanse, she rubbed her palms together. The friction gave her a small amount of relief from the frigid temperatures. She feared her toes had frozen solid.

Cameron helped Zach into the second hut before handing a headlamp to Raz.

Raz's belief that Sandra would harm her child, or any child, twisted a spoon in her heart. The promise she'd made to Paris was at the forefront of her thoughts. Sandra would do whatever was necessary to keep Sean safe. Cool night air wrapped around her. She shivered and zipped her jacket to her chin.

Why'd Raz say children who aren't conceived naturally weren't real children? Their baby was a result of drug assistance. She must've misunderstood him. If not, how would he view her fertility attempts and failures?

Raz waved her over to the shelter.

Sean sat inside his sleeping bag with droopy eyes. "Will you tell me a story like you promised?"

Sandra smiled. "I'm not sure if I know any good ones, but I'll give my best." She told him a story her mother told her as a child. When he asked for a kiss goodnight, she felt warmth blossom in her chest. She loved this child.

She wished him sweet dreams and walked back over to Raz. "He's ready to say goodnight."

Raz hugged her tight. "Thank you. He needed a mother's tenderness tonight. Don't worry. I'll be able to feel his Nexus energy right beside us. I'll know if something happens to him."

Sandra nodded.

He crawled into the shelter and spoke to Sean in low tones.

"Omega is trained to sleep lightly. Any of us will wake at the slightest movement." Cameron raised his voice. He stood a few feet behind Sandra rummaging in a sack.

Sandra rolled her eyes. "Unless you have a GPS hidden in the supplies, I couldn't find my way out of a paper bag in this forest."

Cameron passed a hands-free lamp to Sandra. His gaze followed Raz.

Raz helped Sean snuggle into the shelter's sleeping bag. He tucked the blanket around Sean and his teddy bear then kissed them both.

A large yawn came over Sean before he closed his eyes.

A corresponding yawn had Sandra inhaling, too.

Cameron shrugged. "My announcement was for Raz's benefit, not yours."

Sandra laughed. "Raz is ex-M83. He's been through the same training you've had."

"Raz has been out a long time. He's a soldier, but his training doesn't compare to Omega's. Makes me wonder why he left."

The only logical reason for Raz leaving M83 was because of Paris and Sean. The fear Sandra had for her unborn baby was astronomical.

Raz caressed Sean's face and kissed his cheek again. He backed out of the shelter and hid the entrance with branches.

"Do you think he'll run?" Sandra asked.

"It's a possibility." Cameron touched her arm. "You need to stay with us."

She nodded, but she wouldn't leave her family. Raz, Sean, her and the baby—they were a unit now.

Cam's forced separation between Raz and Sean must make Raz crazy with worry. Sandra couldn't stand it. She wanted Sean as close as possible to her and Raz.

Sandra stared Cameron in the eye. "He won't leave."

"Because of your love confession? It won't keep him here."

Was her love enough for an alien? She was furious with Raz, but what she said was the truth. She loved him. She loved Sean. Recognizing the obvious bond between parent and child made her crave a family. Romantic love … was something else.

Sandra focused on her fascination at discovering the differences between humans and Sixxers. The scientific lure protected her heart in case Raz couldn't love her back. *Hopefully, I'm strong enough, like Paris.* She placed her hand over her belly. "You've watched him with Sean. He won't leave his children behind."

Cameron elbowed her arm. "The man needs to figure out how to use birth control."

Sandra's small burst of laughter brought her out of her musings. A smirk curled her lips at Cameron's smart ass comment. Serious situations forced Cameron to joke. Another yawn attacked her. She brought her hand to her mouth and hugged her arms against the chill night. "I'm curious what alien birth control entails. Perhaps we can have that discussion in the morning?"

Cameron chuckled with her.

Raz trotted over to them. They stood around the cold camp fire. She'd be so much happier if there were flames in the ring of stones, but understood why they all had to sacrifice that luxury. Sandra didn't look forward to sleeping, not only because she'd have to share a bunk with Raz, but because she wanted to work on an anti-viral as soon as possible. Another wave of cold air brushed past her shoulder, and her arms generated a thousand goose bumps in response.

Cameron swung an arm around her shoulders and squeezed. "Once you're in the shelter, you'll warm up fast. Get some rest."

The wind picked up, and a cold breeze flew over her. Tremors fluttered along her spine. "I'd love to get my hands on the research tonight."

Cameron shared her love of problems and bounced on the balls of his feet. "I'll give you the laptop with Thom's stuff on it. Make sure you don't drain the battery. I can't help tonight, but we'll collaborate tomorrow."

Sandra clapped her hands. The thrill of exploration surpassed her longing for sleep. "Yes." She placed the extra headlamp on the ground and glanced at Raz. "Are you staying up?"

"No. When you get the computer, find a pack of granola and water. You need to eat and stay hydrated."

Sandra was ready to smart off.

Cameron interrupted her. "He's right. We might be out here for a few days. You need to keep up your health."

Despite the danger, Sandra resented the orders. "I'm not an invalid, just pregnant." She huffed and stepped over to the supplies. "I can take care of myself."

"Yeah, I know," Cameron whispered. He blocked her and ran his hands along her arms.

Here was her missing friend.

"By the way, congratulations. I'm happy for your chance at motherhood."

Sandra turned into an emotional basket case at his words and blinked back the quick rush of tears. "Thank you."

He cocked his head. "I'm also ecstatic the baby won't be Thom's little brat."

Sandra giggled. Cameron had a way with words. She was also happy the baby was Raz's. Her outburst had been the truth. She kissed Cameron's cheek.

He pulled back.

The smirk on his face let her know he had mouthed something or made a rude gesture at Raz behind her back. One she wouldn't have approved of. She glanced over her shoulder.

Raz narrowed his eyes.

What thoughts ran through his mind? Sandra was too chicken to ask him.

The supplies were nestled on top of two plain tarps. Once they were down for the night, Cameron would pull the corners of the tarp together and tie it to an overhead limb. Thom always said it was to keep critters out while everyone slept on his treks.

Cameron pointed out the correct laptop. She picked it up and tucked it under her arm.

Reviewing the research tonight would help her relax after all the stress. Puzzling out things before bed allowed her mind to work out details in her sleep. Upon waking, she'd have several ideas in her head ready to discuss with Cameron. She couldn't wait to get busy. She walked back to the camp ring and Raz. "I'll sit out here for an hour so you can rest." The suggestion was stupid. She'd be a popsicle in an hour, but she knew Raz would be asleep by the time she finished.

"There's room inside our shelter," Raz said. "You can sit up by the door. It will be more comfortable."

She arched a brow.

"I won't bite." Raz smiled. "Promise."

"You're mad at me."

"I'm disappointed at the situation, but not because of the baby."

Cameron bundled up the supplies. "There's my cue to exit." He crawled into the single.

They were left alone, or as alone as possible, surrounded by M83 soldiers. Sandra had forgotten Amber and Leon patrolled. They'd faded into the background, doing the job they were trained to do. She clutched the laptop to her chest. "I'm sorry this has happened to you. Again."

"I'm not." Raz touched her arm. "I was out of line earlier."

Butterflies entered her gut and formed a dance party. The small, dark shelter loomed in her vision.

Raz crawled in and turned on his headlamp. He held his hand out toward her. "If you have an attack, we'll figure out what to do together."

Sandra nodded. He witnessed her fears without her saying anything. Was she placing too much emphasis on his recognition of her habits? She hoped he loved her, too. Yet, feared her thought was a wishful musing.

Raz lay down and Sandra crawled in beside him. She had enough room to sit by his feet, and she had just enough space around her to push any feelings of tightness aside. The enclosure was quite cozy inside. The heat shield and branches warmed the air a few degrees.

She pulled the large branch over the entrance to enclose them. Their body heat would soon raise the temperature even higher.

"Will you be okay with the lamp off?" Raz asked.

A breeze tickled Sandra's hair. Panic didn't burst like a soap bubble in her gut, which surprised her. Perhaps because the walls weren't solid or permanent, and she could sprint out if necessary. "The laptop emits plenty of light."

Raz flicked off his headlamp and plunged the hand-built tent into darkness.

She turned on the computer in her lap. Blue electronic light filled the shelter and outlined Raz's body.

He stared at her intently.

Sandra cleared her throat. "You don't mind my working?"

"Do what you need to. I want to find Paris's killer."

She cleared her throat. "You're looking at her killer. My virus caused her death."

"No, you didn't kill Paris. She was my responsibility. I thought running would keep us safe. Discovery was inevitable."

"I developed this virus. It's the one Thom based his research on. If not for me, then you, Paris and Sean would be safe somewhere else far away from here."

"You can't control Thom, like I couldn't control Paris." Raz removed his jacket and shoes. He folded the coat and placed it behind his head. His large body settled into the sleeping bag. His foot ran along the outside of her thigh, and she jumped from the unexpected contact. Shifting, she made room for Raz to stretch out, but they both couldn't be inside the tent without touching.

Sandra cleared the sudden lump from her throat. "Are we safe tonight?"

"General Taft has always feared Transor power."

"Raz, talk to me."

He eased up on his forearms. "Chasers can't penetrate M83's network. It's secured by the Nexus. Cameron is right. The mole is inside M83."

"Then the leak is from a Sixxer. An infiltrator?"

Raz fell back into the covers and folded his hands behind his head. "No. Infiltrators are human. We call them Zeniths. They undergo modification in order to gain Nexus energy. Their false connection used to be easy to identify. Maybe they've gotten better at Nexus manipulation in the past seven years."

Sandra touched Raz's leg. "You said Paris infiltrated your circle. She was a Sixxer."

"Yes, she was a Sixxer. Nazier brainwashed her into believing our circle harmed humans. She asked to become a member of our circle. My parents agreed. She brought the infiltrator to their house. We assumed he was a Sixxer, and when we rendered him into the circle, the human disrupted the Nexus bond."

Sandra snatched her hand back. "Exactly what I did at the hospital."

"Not the same." He sat up. "The Nexus reaches out for you because of the baby." He paused for a few seconds. "The infiltrator died. My parents died. Paris's coma lasted for three days." He stroked her cheek.

Sandra tensed and jerked away her head. The room shrank. "Paris didn't want to kill you. She loved you."

"Paris intended to leave before she found out she was pregnant. With an adoptive father like Dr. Nazier, she feared what he'd do to Sean." Raz rubbed the back of his neck. Then his words came out in a rush. "Nothing stopped her except her fear Sean would be harmed. I left the Corp after my parents died. I couldn't trust anyone. Sean became my priority. We ran from that day forward. We're still running." He grasped her chin and turned her head toward him. His eyes glinted in the electronic light. "Humans are vulnerable to the Nexus energy. It's why the artificial children can't create a bond. The Chasers are manipulating something they don't understand."

"They're still real children," Sandra whispered.

Raz tensed and shook his head. "They're Chasers from birth now."

"What if they aren't? Won't our child have power?"

Raz brushed a strand of fallen hair behind her ear. "Our child won't be a Zenith. He can communicate with Sean through the Nexus. He'll be a Sixxer."

Silence fell. Sandra was unsure how to respond to Raz and Paris's past. The Paris Raz described wasn't the one Sandra had known.

The quiet stretched on, and Raz settled back on the sleeping bag.

Sandra didn't have long until the shelter would be too cold to work. She opened several files and reviewed the research notes.

Raz cleared his throat. His eyes glowed in the dim light. "Paris's essence blinked out when we left her."

Five agonizing seconds ticked by. She waited patiently for more specifics about Paris's death. Her need for details overwhelmed her, but she didn't pressure him for more. *If he tells me what happened, will it help me understand?* Sandra placed her hand on his foot.

"We'd made it to the parking garage." His voice was grave. "The render filled her with strength. She was so high on energy I couldn't keep pace." He groaned and rubbed his hands over his face. "A Transor couldn't keep up with her. Sean was at a blitz precipice. I had to stop it. Then Paris collapsed. She gave me what was left of her. That's how I know she wasn't the enemy. She was on our side."

Sandra didn't know what to say, and after a while, she thought it best to not say anything. Minutes passed. Raz's deep breaths filled the shelter. She focused on the backlit screen.

I need to use the time I have. She started the arduous process of sorting the various facts of Thom's fertility and virus research. She focused on her work for some time while making notes on possible connections.

A shuffling noise caused her to look up from the computer at Raz's form. The two separate sleeping bags were zipped together into one bed. Why had she listened to a six-year-old? It'd be very snuggly in there.

Before she crawled into the sleeping bag, she had to confirm for her sanity's sake that Raz was asleep. Several times, she stopped typing and waited for sounds of movement from him. Raz hadn't shifted in the sleeping bag for ten minutes. Only his steady breaths filled the space. Sandra wouldn't be able to keep her hands off him if he were awake. After his heartfelt confession of what happened to Paris, Sandra didn't want to experience any rejection if she touched him.

Focus on your work.

Her eyes got blurry, and she glanced at the battery indicator. Thirty percent power was left. She had so much more to read and analyze. Her icy fingers typed her final notes for the night. A shiver fluttered down her back.

"You should come to bed."

Raz's voice startled her from her concentration. Her heart beat tripled. She'd have to snuggle up to his very warm and awake body.

He pulled back the top edge of the covers. "This shelter is warmer inside than outside, but it's still damn cold in here. The night will get colder. Warm up under the sleeping bag."

His voice dripped along her limbs like hot oil. She licked her dry lips. *It's only sleep.*

Sandra shut off the laptop, removed her jacket and shoes, and crawled in beside Raz. She used her coat as a pillow like Raz had done earlier. Once she settled under the covers, Raz pulled her tight into him, spoon fashion, and his hot breath chased the cold off her neck. She sighed, encased in the pleasure of his arms. His Red-Hots-candy exhale spread arousing goose bumps over her skin.

He inhaled and pulled her closer. His arm wrapped around her middle.

She ran her hand along his forearm.

"Your hands are freezing. You should've come to bed sooner," He whispered in her ear.

"My fingers are cold from typing. I have poor circulation or something, unless it's ninety degrees outside."

"Did you make any progress?"

His voice was a low rumble. The combination of the dark and his sexy voice spread delicious vibrations along the back of her neck and made her ability to concentrate on his question difficult. "I'm getting a feel for the research right now. No progress will be made until I'm in a laboratory."

His lips grazed her skin, and his tongue licked the spot behind her ear. "Can you stop the virus?"

Sandra wiggled her hips, but the tight space settled her bottom closer to him.

He moaned.

She stilled. The evidence of his erection pressed into her behind.

"I can't keep my hands off you." His hand squeezed her hip and slid down to her core. He licked the shell of her ear. "I don't want to, either."

Sandra couldn't think of anything other than his large body behind her, and the wonderful sensations his mouth created on her skin. She shifted under the blanket onto her back. She had to stop him. Didn't she? The movement brought her lips within millimeters of his. Her breath hitched. "I was waiting for you to fall sleep."

"Sleep is impossible while hearing your breath and inhaling your perfume. Lying here, I remembered how good you tasted. How I made you moan, and how much I want to do it again."

She couldn't get enough air. Excitement teased along the nerves of her arms, her breasts. Her body responded to the memory of his mouth sucking and his lips licking. Anticipation of a repeat performance heightened her arousal. She saw nothing in the dark, but the spatial perception of his nearness drove her crazy. The shift in their positions brought his hand along her midriff, and his fingers settled under the curve of her breast. She was very aware the thin T-shirt separating her breasts from his fingers.

An unseen energy sensitized her nerves. The slightest tilt of her head, and ... "I want your mouth on me again, too." *What? I shouldn't be asking for more.* Raz didn't trust her. She didn't want him. *Liar. I do. I've always wanted him.*

"This is a dangerous game we're playing, Sandra."

She squeezed her thighs together.

Raz traced the curve of her face with his other hand.

Pin prickles of heat erupted along the line his fingers sketched down her body. Sandra feared giving in to his passion, and her fears were coming true. Her breathing hitched, and her breasts, achy and sensitive, pressed closer to his warm, calloused hand. Her body pulsed from arousal and from something else.

"Does the light hurt you like before?" His fingers fluttered over her eyelids, brushed her cheeks and stroked her lips.

"No." Her tongue darted out. She tasted the tip of his finger.

He moaned. His other hand palmed her breast, and his thumb teased the hard peak.

"Kiss me," Sandra whispered.

He settled his forehead against hers. Low quivers of pleasure radiated out from every place his skin met hers. Raz's lips sipped at hers, teased and coaxed hers to part, but he maddened her by not deepening the kiss.

His hand stilled on her chest over her heart. "Being with me will bring you misery."

"No. Being with you will bring me joy." She settled her hand over his.

"It's the truth, Sandra. The life I've lived hasn't brought happiness to anyone."

"You know that's a lie. Sean is proof." She ran her fingers through his hair and brought his mouth to hers for a gentle kiss. "What we have is good. You're the first positive thing in my life in a long time, and I'm fighting for you."

He held her close. "We'll be running forever."

Sandra gave him another kiss. She'd follow him to the ends of the earth and back. To Mars and back.

He wouldn't let her deepen the kiss.

You're mine, alien. All mine. I'm not letting you go.

A weariness settled into Sandra's bones. How did the present moment keep getting lost in the past and shadowed by an unpredictable future? "Forget about the past. The future is far away from here. Right now matters. I can't describe the joy I felt when I discovered I'd be the mother of your child. My life won't be as I've imagined. I don't want what I've imagined."

Raz let out a sigh. "We have now."

Was his exhale one of relief? She nodded in the dark, knowing he couldn't see but convinced he'd sense the movement. "If we have to run tomorrow, okay. Tomorrow is hours away. When will we get another chance?"

Raz laughed. "Another chance?"

She wrapped her arms and then her legs around his body.

He ground his hard erection into the center of her and tucked his face into her neck.

She wanted her clothes off. Now. "I don't want to resist our attraction. I can't. I want you. The need for you builds inside me every day."

Raz pulled back. "The Nexus is bonding us."

She tightened her grip, but Raz kept his torso away. The cool night snuck between them. Sandra didn't like it. She loved him, no matter what happened. The vibrations she experienced earlier skipped along her skin. They chased away the cold and her cowardice. No more waiting for Raz. She'd take what she wanted, and if he rejected her, so be it.

Sandra grabbed the bottom of her T-shirt and slowly, but with steady determination, lifted it up her midriff. A soft haze followed the removal of the fabric, like her skin oozed light. Over her head the shirt went, and her breasts lay bare beneath him.

Raz choked on a moan.

Sandra skimmed her hand over her breast. Her finger grazed the pebbled nipple. "Kiss me."

Raz's soft lips landed on one peak then the wet heat of his tongue and mouth swirled around her flesh. He plumped the globe with his hand and suckled her.

A sharp wave of arousal shot down to her core. Her hands were on his face, sliding along the back of his head. She yanked and pulled his hair in time with the movements of his lips as he loved on her breast. The warm glow increased in intensity and cast faint light within the shelter.

Raz raised his head and his eyes glittered with fiery blue passion.

A flush painted his cheeks. "You're changing. Your power is growing."

His alien nature, in the mist of his desire, sent shivers of lust down her spine. *This is what it's like to belong to an alien. To a Sixxer.* Sandra loved his possession.

"You're so beautiful." He caressed her from her neck and collarbone down over her breasts, lightly pinching the stiff peaks and lower to the waistband of her pants. He manipulated the button open and unzipped them. They loosened around Sandra's hips. An urgency entered her body. She gripped the material to push off the binding clothes, but Raz blocked her. His kiss landed an inch below her belly button. The glow increased. Sparks of light fluttered around the low ceiling like they were making their own lightning show.

"Easy. Tell me if anything feels uncomfortable," Raz shushed. "It's like unwrapping a gift. I want to savor it."

Of course, he'd be a slow un-wrapper instead of tearing at a present as fast as possible, as she did. His words made her so hot and ready she bit her lip to keep back the long moan she wanted to shout. "I want you inside me."

He half-laughed and half-moaned in her ear. "Oh, my little alien saver. You have no idea how much I want the same, but I want our loving to last this time."

Oh, how will I survive the torture?

Raz rolled to his side and pulled her with him. His hands slipped between her jeans and her backside. He caressed her bottom with slow intent.

Is he memorizing every curve? His fingers touched her slick core, and her body jerked. He thrust his hips between her legs. She didn't want to stop, but she had to get rid of her clothes. His finger slid along her folds. She couldn't stand the teasing. He kissed her deep and hard. His tongue entered her mouth in time with his hand flexing into her heat. The touch wasn't enough. She needed a more-thorough caress. She moved a leg over his hip, and the tightness of her pants trapped his hand close to her, pushing his finger farther inside.

Raz kissed her. "You're so wet. I want to touch you all night."

A full body flush warmed her from the top of her head the tips of her toes. Raz wanted slow, but she couldn't take it. She wanted, needed, him. All of him. Hands flew over the hard planes of his chest and stomach. She kissed and sucked his salty skin as her hands freed his hard length from his pants. He filled her hands, and she undulated against his thigh, against the fingers inside her body.

"You're going too fast, my love." He pulled away.

She rolled on top of him. The upper half of her body bare, the lower half in agony of wanting to be bare, but trapped inside her jeans. The faint glow in the shelter pulsed around them. *Is the light coming from me or Raz?*

"Help me take my pants off." She squirmed in his arms, but he wrapped them tighter around her. She'd never seen Raz like this. His eyes held a cerulean hue. They flashed and mesmerized her. The possession in the depths of his eyes made everything fade away. He focused on her completely, and tingles spread from the top of her head to the tips of her bare breasts. The illumination in those blue eyes pointed out his alien ancestry. No human man would ever devour her with his eyes in such an all-consuming need.

He bent his head and caught a nipple in his mouth. His attention was that of a starving man given his last meal before execution. The sounds of pleasure and animalistic grunts fed her own desires. Soft sighs and gasps filled the shelter.

Their breaths fogged the cool air. Sandra had forgotten the cold temps. Her body was on fire from the inside.

Raz licked her puckered nipple. "I need to taste you."

Sandra didn't recognize Raz's deepened voice. Pure man, and so goddamned sexy she wasn't sure she'd come out of this experience with him alive.

Two seconds of confusion were followed by an understanding of what he wanted. She studied the shelter, plenty of room for their current position, but not a lot of room to move around in. "How?" Her voice didn't even sound like her. It was sultry and low, half-whisper and half-sigh, desperate to agree to anything he said.

Raz's smile was pure devil and full of satisfaction. He pushed her thighs until she lay flat on top of him instead of straddling his beautiful body like she wanted to.

She moaned at the loss and wiggled her hips as he pushed the material off her body. Teasing nudges of his hard shaft rubbed her body, and she shoved his jeans down farther so she could rub her wet heat and swollen flesh against him.

A few quick thrusts against her, and he stilled. He prevented her thighs from falling back around his hips. He slipped her to the side.

She feared he'd stop making love to her, but he ran his hand down her thigh. He brought both her legs up toward his chest so her legs and torso were in a V-shape. A gentle nudge on her shoulder had her spinning one-hundred-eighty degrees. Before she registered what plan he had in mind, she was flat on her stomach, face and lips inches from his very prominent cock.

He grabbed each of her legs and pulled her back toward his face.

Her center was millimeters from the heat of his mouth. Sandra couldn't see what he was doing, but the anticipation of not knowing thrilled her more than she thought possible. His hands went under her stomach, and he lifted her until she was on her hands and knees. His penis swayed under her chin.

His fingers stoked her slit, back and forth to her clit, teasing the bud with light touches. Settling his palms on her backside, his thumbs parted her and a hot tongue traced the same path his fingers had. "You taste like heaven."

Sandra lost control. Her arms and legs weakened. She fell forward while Raz held her bottom in place. She couldn't think. Glittery sensations of pleasure encased the lower half of her body.

Her hips fell into a pattern of seeking his tongue and lips. She gave a dance of unpredictability, never knowing what he'd do next. Sandra panted and licked dry lips. She was so close to coming, but the teasing onslaught to her body was delicious. She wanted it to last all night. Raz's cock nudged her face. She licked her lips again. In the dim light between their bodies, a bead of moisture ran from the tip of his sex. She couldn't stop herself from sipping the decadent treat. She rose up and suckled the tip into her mouth. The scent of man and sex made her want more.

The vibration of Raz's moan rumbled against her. His tongue plunged deep inside her.

She sucked his tip again and brought more of his cock inside her mouth.

His strokes against her became harder and stronger. Tension rose within and pulled her muscles taut. Her release was close. How she had lasted this long was a mystery. A small ripple fluttered over her. She let his cock slide from her lips. "I'm going to come."

Raz doubled the speed and intensity of his ministrations.

Sandra stifled her moans. She went down on him and sucked him deep into her throat. His moan against her, and the tensing of his body at his own pleasure, sent her over the edge. Raz suckled the bud of her clitoris, and wave after wave of pleasure crashed through her body, surrounding them with light and heat.

The hot spurt of his own release hit the back of her throat, and she reveled in her ability to pleasure him. She collapsed alongside him. Their panting filled the small space.

Raz sat up and dragged her with him until they were face-to-face. He stared into her eyes and kissed her lips. His eyes still flared their eerie blue. "I'll never get enough of you." He ran his hand through her sweat-dampened hair.

Her braid had been destroyed in their passion. "Is it always like this?"

Raz cocked his head.

The heat of a flush filled her face. "Making love with aliens."

Raz laughed and pulled her into his arms. He laid them back down on the sleeping bag and covered their cooling bodies. "I've never experienced anything like that before. Not in my entire life. The Nexus was all around us, a part of you. I think you are now a Sixxer."

"It's impossible."

"I'm starting to believe nothing is impossible."

Chapter Thirty-three

SANDRA AWOKE AT the first hints of coffee and wood smoke tantalizing her nose. Raz's strong arms held her close. The sleeping bag was a pocket of heat, and she didn't want to leave the cocoon of safety. Vibrations hummed along her arms and pulsed at the back of her neck. *Is this the new me? Am I now an alien?*

She sat up in the darkness of the shelter. The cold penetrated her skin. Chill bumps rose on her arms. She reached for the headlamp and clicked on the button.

Raz didn't stir from the deep sleep that'd overtaken him in the late hours of the night. She couldn't help but notice his hair was deliciously mussed, and she remembered all the hard muscles of his body. Had making love again been wise with so many unresolved issues between them? What had happened during their encounter should've frightened her, but for the first time in her life, she belonged to someone. The Nexus energy still zinged along her spine. Did every Sixxer experience the Nexus like this? Sandra caressed Raz's face. She eased her sore body from the sleeping bags and pulled on her clothes. Grabbing her jacket, she clicked off the light and pushed aside the evergreen door.

Cameron sat beside the camp fire, ablaze with crimson and black embers. A glorious heat penetrated her clothes and warmed her body. He extended a cup of coffee. The flickering flames wrapped him in an otherworldly glow.

Sandra lumbered to her feet, giving her body a much-needed stretch. She pushed her arms into her jacket and zipped it to her chin. The cup, another welcome warmth, penetrated her hands. The tingle in her spine from her new energy connection bloomed along her back. She sat opposite of Cameron and inhaled the rich and earthy brew. "What happened to the no fire rule? Your coffee addiction is putting our lives on the line."

Cameron grimaced. He gulped the beverage in his hand, despite the waves of steam rising above the top.

When he didn't laugh at their secret coffee addiction joke, she observed him more closely. Tight lines bracketed his mouth and pale skin surrounded his eyes like he hadn't slept at all.

He pushed a fallen log back into the fire with his boot. "We haven't seen activity all night. Daylight comes in about an hour."

"Do you have a plan?"

Cameron shrugged. "Plans are for pussies." His eyes crinkled as his humor returned.

At least, he was attempting a counter-joke, but something was wrong. Her fingers tightened on her mug. "I don't really know you."

"You do." His eyes lost their small sparkle. "The original plan was getting you, Raz and Sean to the new HQ."

Sandra tasted the black brew. It held little sweetness and huge amounts of flavor. Perfect. "What's the new plan?" Cameron didn't fool her. He had plans scheduled years in advance.

"Raz will perform a render with you as soon as he wakes up."

Sandra cleared her throat. A vibration flowed along her fingertips emanating from the inside of her body. The buzz wasn't unpleasant but unnerving. Did she have control over it, or was her human body only a passive mechanism? "Do you think a render is wise right now? A deadly virus is at large. We don't have time to work out details before we leave."

"We're not sure if the virus killed Paris. At this point, hesitation is dangerous."

Sandra stared into the black liquid in her cup. Then her gaze met his above the rim. "Not sure? What's going on, Cam? The virus obviously destroyed Paris's Nexus energy. Thom has extensive notes on its effects. I'm not losing this baby."

Cameron threw a stick on the fire. He stared into the flames until the fire consumed the wood and turned it into a glowing black charcoal. He flicked his gaze back up to her face. "The longer you're a part of this life, the easier trading one risk for another becomes."

"This risk is too great." She caressed her stomach. Cameron knew what was at stake. "Plan B is a render?"

Cameron shook his head. "Omega is against a render, but the decision is mine. We're on to Plan X now. Only two letters left before we're screwed," he whispered. "The render will protect the baby the most. Zach was up a few times during the night. He agrees with me."

Cameron's flat statement chilled her blood. The low, achy hum expanded at the back of her neck. "What's happened?"

A faint crunch of leaves broke the silence behind her. At the edge of the campfire, Amber wove through the branches and into their conversation. "Does this *bruja* never sleep?"

Cameron stood and dumped the dregs of his coffee into the fire. It sputtered. "She's bonded with Raz's circular energy, which keeps her energized. I'm no longer surprised by it, but it's one of the reasons we're in this bitch of a mess. She has to be a Transitional to be able to change from human to Sixxer without Zenith enhancement drugs. M83 has confirmation of such instances. Report?"

Amber sighed. Her breath exited her lips in a cloud of white vapor. "Sean's not within the perimeter. Leon and I have searched for an hour."

Sandra's heart stopped. She dropped her coffee cup on the ground. "What?" Refusing to believe Amber's words, Sandra crawled on hands and knees to the largest shelter. Pulling back the door, she saw Zach slept inside. The campfire highlighted the deep purple half-moons under his eyes, a stark contrast against his face. Flinging the second sleeping bag aside, Sandra already knew it'd be empty. No Sean. No teddy. Over her shoulder, she inspected Amber and Cameron's casual conversation. For a team of Omega's reputation, their lack of concern was offensive. "How could you not see him leave?"

Cameron squeezed his eyes shut. "Tell me again, Am. Take the 'Sean's not within the perimeter' part out."

Sandra ran back to the fire pit. "Why didn't you immediately tell me he was gone?" The panic in her voice scared her further. Where could Sean be?

"We thought he was exploring, like kids do, *bruja*."

"A six-year-old in the middle of the night after an attack on us? In the scary-ass woods? Are you both crazy?" She circled the campfire, searching the barely visible edges of the gray woods. *What am I doing? I can't see him in the dark even if he is there.* The first hint of daylight peeked between the frost-covered leaves. She turned back to face Cameron and Amber. "Now I believe you've never been around kids. You both say the stupidest things I've ever heard."

"Sean is a powerful Transor. He's young, but he can't leave without being detected by anyone," Cameron said. "Unless he hid his power from us."

Sandra pounced on Cameron. How can he be so calm? Not knowing where Sean was hurt her stomach. "Why are we standing here doing nothing? My little boy is missing!"

Zach moaned. A few seconds later, he poked his head out from his shelter door. His drawn and tight face had lost the relaxed air he'd had when asleep.

"Zach, give me intel," Cameron demanded.

Zach yawned. He scrubbed at the five o'clock shadow on his face. "I'm still buzzed from the pain meds, but because of my superior intellect and savvy knowledge—"

"Humility suits you," Amber said.

Zach narrowed his eyes. "Because of my expertise in computer systems and networks, and Sandra's attunement, I detected an aura and figured out a general location where Sean might've ran off to."

"When?"

"About thirty minutes ago, but the meds put me out again."

"Great work." Amber clapped her hands. "Let's pack up."

Zach limped over to the fire. "Not so fast, hot shot. We're sitting on a time bomb here."

"What in the hell does that mean?" Amber flung her arms in the air and threw camp supplies into her bag. "Doesn't matter how difficult it'll be. We find Sean, the sooner the better."

Cameron grabbed her bicep. "I can't allow Zach to send any transmission in case it might be intercepted."

Sandra swiveled her head back between the three of them. Why were they arguing about whether to follow Sean's trail or not? "We don't need to send a message. Zach found a trail, we just have to follow it." She trotted over to Zach and clutched his shirt. "We have to leave now. Sean's out there alone. Standing here isn't acceptable, and you know it." She stomped toward Raz's shelter. He had the Nexus at his disposal. He could find Sean, somehow. She reached the door.

Zach hooked her arm and shook his head.

Sandra suspected the ashy green tint to his face wasn't from his injuries.

He jerked her away from the entrance. "Remember if I tell you, I'd have to kill you? In this case, it's true. My secrets will compromise hundreds of people, Sixxers and humans alike. If leaked to General Taft's people, we're all dead. By all, I mean everyone. Our team. Sixxers in hiding. The humans helping us."

Hot tears ran down Sandra's cheeks. "What does your secret information have to do with finding Sean?"

Zach bent down to looked her in the eye. "One wrong move, Sandra, and none of us will be alive to find Sean. The men we came upon when Am and I extracted you were a Taft unit. He's searching and clearing this area."

She didn't understand and shook her head. "But Cam said there's been no activity."

Zach clenched his teeth, and the muscles in his jaw rippled "That doesn't mean they aren't watching us or waiting for an opportune moment."

Cameron cleared his throat. "Raz is our biggest weapon and defense right now. Once he finds out ..." He leaned closer and spoke in her ear. "He'll destroy the team and any chance of discovering our leak or Sean."

The enormity of Raz's alien power finally clicked inside her brain. What Raz would experience wouldn't be human panic about a missing child, but an Transor's wrath at their separation and the individuals responsible. If Omega didn't think through Sean's rescue, they'd be captured by General Taft or her worthless ex-husband.

A shuffle and snapping twigs made them face Sandra's and Raz's shelter. He crawled from under the brush and stretched like Sandra had done when she woke. Telling him about Sean would be a delicate dance, but it'd be okay. Their bond was stronger now, and once he calmed she could talk to him.

"You must conduct a render with Sandra," Zach commanded.

Sandra just barely prevented slapping herself in the forehead. Zach had a knack for misinterpreting the meaning of subtle.

Raz gazed at each of them around the camp. "Good morn to you, too. Interesting demand. I need fuel first." He sauntered over to the pile of supplies and searched for food. He called over his shoulder. "What's for breakfast?"

Can I have you for breakfast? Sandra's lack of focus troubled her. *Out of sight, and I'm a normal human woman. In sight, and Raz sends my hormones skyrocketing.*

"Hell. I'm starving, too." Zach rubbed his stomach. A loud growl from his belly filled the air.

Cameron popped his neck. "We … I believe a render with Sandra will strengthen the group."

Raz was too relaxed. Sandra thought he would immediately sense that Sean was missing because of their circle, but he acted like there were holiday camping.

He eyed the fire. "I'm surprised Zach isn't healed. This is where M83 risks your team, Cameron. Is the area clear? Is Sean still asleep?"

The continuous drone at the back of Sandra's neck shifted in tone.

Cameron peered off into the ravine a few feet from the camp. "Our two-hour rotations found the surrounding perimeter quiet. The attack at base wasn't subtle or a lucky find. Someone knows where we are, and they're waiting."

Zach stumbled closer to the campfire and mumbled for water. "What in the hell did Leon give me last night?"

Still in exit mode, Amber packed the supplies. "Only what you deserved for getting shot, *pendejo.*"

Raz found packages of granola and handed one to Zach. "A render will advertise our location. You find an anti-NEU you didn't know about? If you did, that's great. The cleanses are worthless. Getting kicked by Sean all night will make you feel like shit, too. Why didn't you wake him up?"

"Extra Nexus energy is more important right now than technology." Cameron spoke without taking his gaze off the valley below. "A Transor's son needs specific training to control his aura.

He's very dangerous when he's too young to understand all the threats. Yet, he can put up a worthy fight."

Amber slapped her leg and guffawed. "Nice try, Cam. I thought you lost your sense of humor on this mission."

Cameron pinned Amber with his midnight gaze.

Her laugher died.

He rubbed the back of his neck. "Raz has been hiding for seven years. What Sixxer can stay off the grid for so long? Especially one in General Taft's sights?"

Amber snatched her own package of granola from the box and popped a handful of the mix into her mouth. "Every Sixxer knows Transors are fairytales. You're telling us a real life prophecy is among us?"

Cameron laughed. "A lot of tales are becoming truth the past few days."

Raz stilled and narrowed his eyes. "Why are you all insisting on a render? The virus hasn't been cured since last night."

"Like I said, a Nexus connection is more powerful than technology."

Raz flexed his biceps. "Are we as good as captured?"

Cameron tensed and so did Sandra.

"Sandra generated harmonics as soon as we discovered Sean was missing," Cameron said.

"What? Someone came into our camp?" Raz bellowed. He raced to the shelter just as Sandra had done moments before.

She caught up with him and watched him tear the structure apart. "I looked there first. Do you think he's hiding in the trees?"

Cameron shook his head. "No. I don't know what happened, but there is no indication that anyone other than the team has been in the area."

Raz scanned their surroundings. "Sean wouldn't run off by himself."

His chest heaved up and down and the panic on his face was enough to throw Sandra into another fit of tremors that ran through her body.

With leftover coffee, Cameron doused the fire and kicked dirt over the embers. "He ran away. The only connection we have is a weak vibration from Sandra that's signaling his aura. The Sixxer power could be from her or the baby. In either case it's a way to trail him."

Raz choked on his granola and threw the package to the ground. "We have to find him. Where's the trail?"

Sandra gasped. "You're relying on me? You're insane. How's that even possible? I know nothing about tracking." She couldn't believe she was the one with the ability to find Sean. Her transformation to Sixxer power was new and couldn't be reliable. The stakes were too high. "Raz can determine his location—"

Zach picked up his laptop. "We'll find him. A render will help us find him faster by amplifying Sandra's new power."

Sandra's heart skipped a beat. She watched Raz carefully.

Every one of his muscles tensed. He held himself back. He held the Nexus back. "I can't sense him, Sandra. I should have known he wasn't in the camp. Can you feel his aura?"

She shook her head, and a tremor went through her body. "Is the sensation I'm experiencing from me or Sean? I have no idea. My heart is literally skipping beats, but everything is changing so fast I don't' know what it means."

Raz's eyes flickered a weird, mesmerizing dance of light, becoming brighter than any light she'd ever seen. The Transor everyone talked of emerged from the man in front of her. She squinted against the pain. Once again, a fluttering of vibration tingled along her spine.

Similar pulses echoed off Raz's body in heat waves. Fingers of smoke snuck around his feet and legs. The sapphire edges sparked with white energy. "We don't know what happened. The Nexus will force me to protect my remaining circle." The clouds above the trees crackled with the energy Raz added to the surrounding air. Layers of lightning flashed above them.

"Raz?" Sandra called. *The render will happen now.* She waited for the oncoming panic attack. She was scared, but also grateful that Raz would close the circle so he'd regain his connection to Sean. "What do I do?"

Cameron turned as the light hit his face.

Amber backed away from the camp, gun at the ready, and her free hand shaded her face.

A wave of swirling blue and silver light flowed from Sandra's hands. Her body shook as the waves turned into bursts of energy. Raz changed before her eyes, his body became bigger and more threatening as the tendrils of power surged around him. They came toward her in a flash of light.

"Don't fight it," he called. "The shield will protect you. Once completed, the Nexus will give you more focus."

His words came to her as though he were hundreds of feet away.

"Make it stop." Sandra collapsed onto the cold ground. She held her stomach and braced for the energy to hit her, but a rush of strength infused her muscles and coated her entire body.

All at once, a discordant number of sounds and voices entered her mind. The tips of her fingers glowed like they had with the fallen soldier, but this time the sensation was forceful, purer.

Amber lowered her gun. Her jaw dropped.

Leon ran into the camp but stopped on a dime, eyes wide.

"I can't stop it," Raz called out. "The Nexus has taken over my circle."

"Team, disengage," Cameron commanded.

Sandra was astonished they all retreated by widening their semi-circle around them. If they were afraid of what might happen to them, she closed her eyes in acceptance that she might not come out of this blast of energy whole. She only hoped that Raz could use the energy to protect the baby and to find Sean.

His light display faded within seconds. The massive growth of his muscles remained, and the supernatural glint in his eyes flared every few seconds. He stepped toward her.

She couldn't move, couldn't look away. The alien before her was true to his nature. He controlled the energy and light surrounding them with expertise and precision. The closer he came, the more sparks of heat spread over her skin, but like the previous evening she felt no pain. Her fingertips swirled with her own enhanced power, and Nexus energy danced along the ground.

Raz bent down and helped her to her knees. His hands cupped her cheeks.

The wonderment on his face stunned her. She searched his glowing eyes. "What's happening?"

"You're the most beautiful thing I've ever seen. You've no idea the power the Nexus has gifted you with. Paris was right."

Sandra clutched his shirt. "But this has happened before."

"Never. I wish you could see yourself." He placed a light kiss on her lips. "So damned sexy. You're glowing." His eyes darkened and narrowed. "Taft and your ex will fight to the death for you. To take you from me. The shield wants to protect you." He raised her hand and observed the subtle vibrations that ran along her arm. "Your power can talk to Sean. I'll have to figure out how we can use it to find him."

Tears sprang to her eyes. She would get their little boy back. "I thought this communication with the Nexus wasn't possible unless we closed the circle with a render?"

"A shield isn't supposed to be possible. The Nexus must've recognize the baby's energy during my blitz."

Sandra stood. Deep breaths steadied her nerves. "When I collapsed, I heard voices. I heard the words in my mind like I did with the fallen soldier, but I've only touched you."

Raz hugged her. "You weren't in elevation before. What did you hear?"

She pulled back. "Someone wants to draw us out. They're using Sean to do it."

Omega surrounded them.

Turning back to Raz, she whispered. "Can they hear us?"

"No. If they come any closer, the Nexus will attack them. If they had their own circle, they might have a chance against me, but not without one."

Sandra grasped his hand. "I think someone in Omega is a spy."

CHAPTER THIRTY-FOUR

SANDRA SAT IN the passenger seat of the Bronco. Cameron had moved them back to the vehicle, away from any part of Raz's shield. Although, Raz contained the initial threat and now controlled his Nexus energy.

Sandra propped open the vehicle door with her foot. Sunlight had arrived and rays of light brightened the forest.

Cam's afraid of me, too. I can sense his fear through the Nexus which is mind boggling. She tugged Raz's hand on his way past her. The light in his eyes had yet to fade. Her extremities were lead after Raz's render, but she now carried a visual aura which clung to her body. She glimpsed her reflection in the window. Honey-golden light flashed back to her. The same light that'd appeared in Thom's bathroom mirror.

I'm afraid of myself. What'll happen if I'm near Thom again?

Raz dipped his head, and his crystalline eyes focused on her.

Before, his eyes illuminated from within, but they had still resembled human eyes. Now his eyes *were* blue and white light. Shocked at their otherworldly brilliance, Sandra stared. "Will the humming ever stop?"

"When we're safe." He brushed strands of loose hair behind her ears.

The power that'd surrounded her and Raz had lasted an hour. Omega hadn't heard them or touched them until it had dissipated. For most of that time, Sandra had battled Sean's and Paris's voices in her head. The tones echoing off her body replaced their whispers.

"Do you think Sean is hurt?" she asked.

Raz gave her a sharp shake of his head. "After the blitz, I'd know if he was hurt. He's scared, but you have to remember he has the Nexus energy, too. Any threat to him and he'll use it. I'll have a corresponding flare."

Cameron returned from a perimeter check and commanded the team to pack any supplies they could carry.

Sandra admired his determination in finding Sean, and while she trusted Cameron, she was pissed he hadn't protected their boy. *Which one of them betrayed us? Sean is now at the mercy of Thom, or worse, Dr. Nazier.*

Her breath puffed out before her. "How much time do we have?"

She prickled in awareness as tension bounced from one group member to another. Her harmonic amplifying ability, and Raz's perpetual energized state, made everyone wary. Yet, she knew their behavior wasn't different. Her awareness of the Nexus had increased tenfold with the shield. The team kept their distance from the two of them, but of course, didn't let either one of them out of Omega's sight.

Raz ground his teeth. The muscle in his jaw twitched. "A day. Twenty-four hours, at the most until his trail will fade."

"How will we—"

"I'm done with Omega orders." He brought her hands to his lips and kissed her palms. "We follow them out of the woods and make our break. No one in this team will stop us from tracking and finding Sean. No one."

A spark of light and a small pressure wave from her harmonics leapt from her chest. Raz stepped closer to her knees and nudged her legs apart. He leaned in and kissed her until her toes curled. "Steady waves, baby. The flow between us will be difficult to fight with you in elevation. Try to focus on Sean's aura to help keep your power constant. It's the only way to get Omega on our side. Any bursts will keep them on a higher edge than they already are."

"Can you help me keep the power manageable?"

"I can try, but my techniques might make us too aroused. Your pregnancy and elevational power are irresistible to me, especially since I have Nexus energy flowing through me." He pushed her braid over her shoulder, and it cascaded down her back. Using his breath, he teased the cold skin of her neck. Raz chuckled when she arched into him.

She moaned her pleasure. Wired and over-sensitized only mildly described her conscious state.

Raz nibbled on her neck. "As much as I want to do this all day, teaching you how to control the bonds between your Sixxer power and Nexus energy is imperative."

Heat skimmed along her face. "How can I do that and still use it to communicate with Sean? We can't let this distract us."

"I won't let us get sidetracked. I'll stick with Cameron, or whoever is leading. Physical distance between us will help, but you have to find a way to calm your power: deep breathing or visualization. Zach can help you focus the waves on Sean with whatever tech device is he's tinkering on."

Sandra bit her lip and nodded.

At the far edge of Omega's packing activity, Zach slapped together a tool. The intent of the device would make her body a tracking device.

None of them knew the extent of her Sixxer broadcasting ability. Far beyond her magic trick of communicating with the fallen soldier two days before, she now could communicate with her circle from miles away. Her mind spun, and the immediate transition into a Sixxer terrified her.

Raz stared into her eyes with his calming gaze. His physical presence was the only thing grounding her right now.

"We'll find him." He brushed his lips across hers.

A spark of energy flashed between them and warmed her skin, but it zapped her strength even more. She sat straighter and forced herself to appear stronger. Although, her mind and body wouldn't cooperate. If she couldn't cope with current events, she wouldn't cope with an infection outbreak, either. After such an explosive render, the virus must've been released among them.

Raz removed his coat and wrapped it around her shoulders.

The double layer of outerwear helped ease the ice in her veins. She protested, but he shushed her. *Am I shivering?* She couldn't tell, but the temperature was too damn cold out here for him to be in a T-shirt.

"The blitz will keep me warm for hours," He whispered. "The burst of Nexus energy should've done the same for you. You might need more time to absorb the excess energy, then you'll be toasty. Once we determine Sean's location, I want you to stay with Cameron."

She shook her head. Behind Raz, Leon and Amber finished packing and hauled their bags onto their backs. The animosity etched on their faces touched Sandra like a cold, invisible mist.

Raz squeezed her arms. "Damn. You're getting weaker every minute." He pulled her into his embrace again.

She loved the connection and never wanted to break it. The other hum, the one that infused her with passion, teased her everywhere they touched. "No. I'm not leaving you."

"Omega hasn't been prepared for this. Our separation from them is more detrimental than any other decision we make right now. We'll use M83 technology to our advantage and conserve your power. Zach can use your harmonics to track Sean. But, like I said. If we have to leave, I'll get us to Sean."

"What if the spy realizes I can sense them?"

"He or she doesn't," he whispered in her ear. "Keeping your secret to ourselves is the best shot we have of Sean being in our arms again."

The words made her hands shake. She'd have to pretend she didn't suspect any of them. Were the lives of her children being sold to the lesser of their two enemies? How could the traitor possibly be Cameron? Or Amber? She hissed low, "I'm not a soldier or a trained spy."

"They have M83 training, but none of them know what I'm capable of. They can't read your mind."

His hand caressed from her forehead to the hollow of her throat. A trail of comforting sensations flowed over her face. Her eyes skid shut. She wanted him to kiss her, and have him bundle her in a cocoon of safety and love.

"Two minutes for departure. Wrap it up, Raz," Cameron called to them.

Sandra's eyes shot open. The luxury of security was no longer an option.

Raz placed his forehead against hers then stepped back a few inches. The closer they were, the more nervous Cameron became. Raz tilted his head toward Cameron. "They don't know how their bodies will react to danger within the Nexus connection so they retreated from the shield. There's something else, something more powerful going on. My blitz should've injured them, but they're unharmed. Perhaps, once we complete a render they won't be able to escape the Nexus protective force."

Sandra sputtered. "That wasn't a render?" *What sort of power do Sixxers really contain? No wonder humans are horrified.*

Raz held out a hand to her and helped her from her perch. "The Nexus burst was a shield for my circle, and a blitz to counteract any threats. The blitz sent out Nexus energy waves in an attack formation. Omega left us alone because of this and the energy dissipated, but somehow they were able to stand just outside the reach of those waves."

"Yet, your Transor blitz made Omega very nervous." Sandra brushed her hair out of her face.

"My lack of reach made *me* nervous. They watched us for a year. I had no clue. If they'd been working for General Taft, then I'd either be dead or tucked away in a lab somewhere for people like Thom to play with."

Sandra cringed. "A render will make me stronger?"

Raz walked them over to his bags. He hunkered down and finished adding supplies. "Not just stronger. Everything will be enhanced. When I went through elevation, my focus was spot on, my thoughts always clear. I sensed every threat to my circle. I could prepare in advance for danger."

She crouched beside him and caught the jacket as it slipped. "Why didn't you blitz before this morning?"

"The partial render and the darts weakened my connection."

She stood and grabbed his shoulder when she lost her balance. Everything happening hinged on Raz's ability to keep his circle intact. Devising a method to disrupt the connection was a perfect way to infect Sixxers. The render was their defense and Thom took their only safety away from them. *Raz's circle is still open because of me. I'm hurting the people I love.* "Let's have a render now."

He swung his pack over his shoulder. "We need Sean to close the circle."

She pushed her arms into the sleeve of the second jacket. "You said the darts made your power weak. Are you still?"

"No. The tranquilizers disrupt the Nexus connection, and they slow us long enough for capture without permanent damage. But I was almost at a blitz state when they darted me, so I was able to retreat with Sean."

Sandra moved her hand to the places on his chest where she'd seen the wounds at the children's camp. There had been so many. Hovering near a wound, a tiny glow of light wrapped around her finger in a swirling pattern. *Can my new power heal him? Take away his pain?*

He clasped her hand and brought it to his face for a nuzzle. "Transors can resist the darts, to a point. I didn't tell Cameron how many hit me. I didn't heal fast enough. The open circle wouldn't allow me to link."

She had seen the evidence of the attack on his chest, but hadn't counted. "How many darts hit you?"

Raz hesitated. "At least ten. I didn't react to the drugs. Only a Transor can fight them. By now, someone in Taft's team, or Nazier, has already guessed I'm Transor."

Cameron called to them, again.

Raz pulled her behind him and they joined the group. A bundle of supplies sat at Cameron's feet.

"Don't say anything about carrying your weight, Sandra," Cameron said. "Focus on keeping up and staying alive."

Zach stepped beside her and held out a two-inch strap attached to a small triangular-shaped piece of plastic. "This is an augmenter. I'll tie the strap under your chest, and Sean's aura will show up on my tracker." He tapped his wrist.

Sandra removed both of her jackets and fastened the device around her body. She shivered uncontrollably in the cool air.

"I'll be quick." Once the augmenter was in place, Zach's watch pinged. He grinned. "Got him."

Sandra rapidly put her layers back on.

Omega rounded up their provisions, and the team formed a line.

Following Zach, they marched along the trail supposedly leading them to Sean.

They hiked for hours. The temperature was as freezing as it'd been last night. Where in the hell were they? Cameron set a grueling pace, bounding ahead of Zach with either Leo, Amber or Raz then coming back to check progress and tracking the line.

Sandra had a difficult time keeping up. She blamed her exhaustion on the pregnancy and on the constant trembling as her harmonic waves communicated with Zach's augmenter.

Raz alternated between checking on her and running ahead to talk to Cameron.

She would've liked to hear what their discussions were about but had a sinking feeling they were figuring out ways to coddle her in *her condition*.

Amber paused and stared back at Sandra. "Try to keep up, *bruja.*"

Sandra stepped forward and slipped on dead leaves in her struggle up the hill. She narrowed her eyes. Her mood grew more rotten by the second. "Suck it, Amber." She rubbed at the spot along her side and under her breast where the augmenter chafed. Her T-shirt was a pathetic cushion between the device and her skin.

Amber laughed. She continued her forward march. "Sandra is like a child with her new elevation."

She loves my pain and isn't on my side. Perhaps the female bonding and concern over the kiddos is her way of gaining my trust, because she shouldn't be trusted.

Leon and Zach chuckled. Passing jokes among their threesome had become their favorite activity the last forty minutes.

They don't even know what my elevation is, do they? Has a human ever experienced this before? Snap out of it, dodo bird. I don't know what elevation is, except that it's unnatural for kids and humans to experience. I'm the odd carrot in the basket. "Maybe one of you could educate me on my power and changes so I don't drag you down the hill with my next slip."

Leon sidled close. "I'll signal to Cameron for a short break."

"No. I'm okay." *Aren't I?* Her palms were sweaty and trembling. The granola they'd had for breakfast was a distant memory. Her belly growled about every ten steps. She ignored the stabbing tingle in the small of her back. Its needle-like poking made her twinge. She raised her head. Leon's hair was now loose around his shoulders, but every so often the gem in his ear caught the light. Sandra raised her hand to block the sunlight and his jewelry from blinding her. "You're a healer, right?"

Leon's eyes crinkled, and he held back a smile. "I'm the assigned medic."

"What should I expect?"

He raised a brow.

"The truth. Not a joke you tell to Zach or Amber."

He snorted. Leaning down to her level. "They aren't that funny," he whispered.

Sandra laughed. "No, they aren't." She relaxed beside the large male Sixxer. Leon worked so hard at keeping them healthy and injury free. Could someone with that much compassion turn around and sell a child to a madman?

Leon slowed enough to match her shuffle-like stride up the inclines of hill after hill. They'd eventually have to go down, wouldn't they?

He shrugged. "Elevation is a very emotional time for Sixxers. No matter how many descriptions are given, the experience is nothing as expected."

"I can't prepare?"

"Out here? Probably not."

Sandra sighed.

Leon bumped her arm. He heaved his large frame up the side of a steep grade. "I'm assuming the changes are no different between you and I. Sixxers are indistinguishable from humans until elevation. Unfortunately for you, elevation is happening quickly."

Sandra grasped a tree root sticking out of the side of the hill and hoisted herself up the steep trail. *If they've always had this power since their early twenties, and the ability comes on slowly over years, why haven't they had a render? Have they been in Omega since before their metamorphosis?*

She reached the top of the ridge, but a wave a dizziness slammed into her. She swayed backward.

Leon snatched the collar of her coat.

Being woozy was a classic symptom of pregnancy, along with dehydration and the extra stress of the hike, hit her all at once. Complaining about the pace because of the baby would make Omega stop. Sandra didn't want to stop. She had to get to Sean. *I made a promise to Paris.* How could she keep a baby safe when she couldn't protect a six-year-old boy?

Sparks of electrical energy flickered off her fingertips at random intervals. This energy inside consumed her.

Raz trotted toward her from the front of the line. He'd never lost the residual pulsing in his eyes from the shield. Had he just now sensed her distress and near fall?

Cameron emerged from the trail following Raz. The physical dome of the shield had disappeared, but Raz said the trigger could go off at any moment. Whenever threats against Sandra occurred, the shield projected Nexus energy to them to increase their power. Why wasn't the Nexus strengthening her?

She couldn't control anything about herself anymore. Her human body was rejecting this alien energy. She didn't have what a Sixxer had to process the Nexus. Her scientific mind understood this. In no way could she change into something else at a biological level. Yet, the Nexus was inside her blood, surrounding her body, and in every touch from Raz.

With each breath Raz exhaled, puffs of air froze before his face. His muscular body radiated heat waves. The black T-shirt molded to his chest.

Sandra wished she had the energy to put those muscles to good use. Pulses throbbed low in her abdomen. *Don't get distracted!*

He ran to her and didn't stop until she was in his arms.

She couldn't hold back from him anymore. Each touch, no matter how much she craved it, drained her strength. She leaned into him for support.

"Are you all right?" He ducked his head so their eyes were level.

"I'm fine." She wasn't about to tell him otherwise.

"You're sweating. A lot." Raz pulled a cloth from his pocket and wiped her face. "Cameron, we need a break."

"No. I don't want to stop." Sandra moaned and forced her feet to move.

Raz stayed right by her side.

If she stopped, she couldn't force herself to walk anymore. Once she found her tempo, she'd be fine. "Go faster … the closer we get to Sean. Get him back. I want to review my notes as soon as possible …"

Cameron was beside them. "Take a breath." He held a canteen to her lips. "Drink this."

Would her research stop the spread of Thom's virus? She'd have to re-engineer and start from scratch, but if she failed, more was at stake than the deaths of a few plants. Raz could sicken and die. Cameron and his team. Her.

The baby.

"Sean's trail passes a supply point a few miles ahead," Cameron said.

Miles? Sandra's last amount of vigor left her, and she sagged against Raz.

"We can't afford to go off-course. Not when she's like this." His rough voice surrounded her aching head.

"It's Amber's secret crib, or the location was secret until about ten minutes ago. Zach verified we're on a direct path back toward the children's camp. We drove too far to make it there on foot. Amber's place has a vehicle, food and ammo."

Sandra moaned into Raz's shirt, but she couldn't force her vocal cords to work. *No one else knows about it? Why would Amber have a secret place?* Short stabs of white hot discomfort vibrated across her lower back. Sandra couldn't determine if the pain was a result from her elevation or from the virus infection. She tapped on Raz's arm. She said the words so low she was tempted to believe she communicated with Raz telepathically. "Sean is everything."

They hunkered to the ground.

Zach consulted his GPS watch and augmenter sensor. "The coordinates are true. If Sean is at the children's camp, someone drove him there. Sixxers aren't men and women of steel. They can't fly."

Cameron and Raz stared at each other.

"We must go to Amber's," Raz said.

Sandra sat on the ground. The effort to crouch was overkill for her muscles. "How long will the detour delay us?"

"Forty minutes to get there at this current trek," Zach said. "Thirty minutes to find our jewels and pack up."

Damn. "That's too long." *I can't keep up.* They'll be even farther behind Sean because of her.

Zach sat, too. He stretched out his injured leg, but he was favoring it less and less as the day went on. "We'll easily make up the time with a vehicle and Sandra's driving."

She weakly chuckled. "You're funny."

Cameron leaned over and held Sandra's face.

His hands were hot coals on her skin.

"You look like shit."

"Thanks." She rolled her eyes.

He turned back to Raz. "What were Paris's symptoms prior to the hospital?"

"Nothing like this. The blitz was too much for her."

Sandra raised a weak hand. "I needed to rest. I'm already better."

Cameron turned her face side-to-side. "Zach, what happened at Thom's house? Did he give her anything?"

"She ate breakfast, but so did he."

"I didn't eat anything."

Zach continued over her interruption. "He didn't drug her."

Leon threw a chocolate bar and a package of peanut butter crackers at Sandra's feet. "Human women have morning sickness and extreme tiredness about this time. This could also be from her elevation. Her exposure to Nexus energy stimulated her changes."

Relief whooshed through her. Yes. Morning sickness explained her constant upset stomach. The dizziness and fatigue were from the pregnancy itself, but something gnawed at the back of her mind. Had Thom drugged her at HUP or the house?

"The lemons." Her heart thumped in her chest. "At Thom's, I constantly smelled lemons. He could've been developing an airborne virus. He used me as a test. Injections require a face-to-face dynamic. Difficult when attacking the enemy." Sandra replayed her reaction to Thom. His drugs had created that awful desire she experienced. She whispered, "There was also an ..." Her face heated. Swallowing the lump in her throat, she had to tell them. Would Raz still touch her after she said the words? "I had an attraction to Thom at the hospital, and later at the house. He had some kind of control over me."

Each Omega member rounded on the other and shrugged.

"What's she talking about? Was she acting funny when you got there?" Leon asked.

Zach shook his head.

"This happened before I saw Zach. I took a bath." Sweat broke out on her palms and under her arms. She didn't want to tell anyone what happened but knew she had to tell the team what Thom was capable of doing. "Thom tried undressing me."

Raz turned her shoulders so she faced him. "Whoa. Whoa. Whoa. He undressed you?"

"He attempted to, yes." Raz would break their connection after this confession. She closed her eyes. She didn't want to see the disgust on his face once he realized she'd been unnaturally attracted to her ex-husband but attracted to him all the same. If she'd stayed—*No, don't think about that possibility.* Shame coursed through her. "I didn't want him to. I smelled the lemons, and I couldn't stop him. He made me ..." She spoke around the lump in her throat. "He made me want him."

Cameron swore. He sprang to his feet. "Zach. Leon. Is this in any of our fucking intel?"

Silence answered him.

Raz tightened his hold on her shoulders.

Cameron's back was to her. Why wouldn't he face her?

"Did he hurt you?" Cameron asked.

"No."

Raz leaned his forehead against hers, and he wrapped his arms around her tight. "I'll kill him, Sandra. I never should've let you leave the hospital."

Tears sprang to her eyes. "What if he had made me do something? Would you have believed me that I couldn't stop him?" She caressed her stomach. "Would you have still wanted me, after?"

He tilted her face up to his. "Would you have forgiven me for not keeping you and our children safe?"

Her sobs echoed around them.

Raz pressed her against him and squeezed her tight. He rained kisses over her face.

The Nexus leaped to the surface of their skin, and at that moment, Sandra knew he would never leave her.

Amber cleared her throat. "As touching as this is … What. The. Fuck?" The sarcastic lilt came out of her mouth, shattering the moment. "How's it possible for a human to control another human? Sixxers can't even do that."

Raz pulled back. "Mind readers can manipulate the Nexus to force others to do what they want." The light in his eyes brightened. "Did you say you smelled lemons?"

Leon sat beside her. His hand cupped Sandra's forehead, and he flashed a light into her eyes. "Any drug given to her then would be worn off by now and was probably meant to relax her. Get her to cooperate. Mind readers do not exist. There hasn't been one recorded Sixxer in M83 history with that type of skill."

Sandra stilled as Leon continued to examine her. "I thought the lemon odor was weird. The house frequently smelled like lemons. Thom was obsessed with them. The scent never faded. I never suspected he'd create a drug that resembled the odor. I didn't … I … resisted him … somehow. I can't remember if it was him I was attracted to, or something else. Then, in the bath, the water stuck to me, and I saw the Nexus light in the mirror."

Amber said, "*Dios mio!* Is she delirious? Her eyes are dilated."

"I got out of the bath. My eyes glowed, but it went away."

"The energy in your eyes was residual from the render at the hospital." Raz sat on the ground and pulled her onto his lap. "At the end of the render, a citrus odor permeated the room." Raz looked at Cameron then Zach. "This isn't good, guys. Lemons must signify Thom, which suggests he's a Sixxer."

Zach slapped his knee. "Son of a … He's a Zenith, Cam. He's been experimenting on himself. He has an artificial connection to the Nexus and to Sandra."

Amber rose. A frown dragged her lips south. "We'll hurry to my place." She held the semi-automatic at the ready in her arms, the strap loose over her shoulder. Amber's hard-as-rock personality surrounded her like additional armor. She brushed her dark hair out of her eyes.

Cameron agreed. Break was over, and they needed to move. The trail opened and the number of trees thinned. After about twenty minutes, they reached another ridge. Sandra could see the interstate in the distance. The terrain as they got closer to Amber's wasn't as difficult to hike, but the effects of cumulative fatigue wore Sandra down.

Amber slowed, walked beside her and handed her a canteen. She shook the contents of a package in Sandra's face.

Sandra accepted the water and what she suspected was a pack of granola from Amber's rations.

Amber smiled. "Guarantees in life don't exist, *bruja*. We've been exposed to the virus if Thom created an airborne deployment. Any fear of the sickness is useless at this point."

The fear her baby would die drove Sandra. How could Amber be so casual? "Thom made a backyard lab dedicated to creating a killing machine." Unfortunately, his research was brilliant. "I'm not afraid of him. I'll stop him."

Amber laughed. "Very stupid move."

"Thom reacts to fear. When I stood up for myself, I was able to leave him for good." Sandra glanced out of the corner of her eye at Amber, envying her confidence. "You don't think I can fix this."

Amber shrugged. "You're either an asset or detriment." She matched her stride to Sandra's. "If you can win, *chica*, I'll make a path for you."

A tone of Sixxer power blasted through Sandra's stomach. She tightened her muscles in defense against the pain. "You're being way too nice."

Amber smirked. "The truth?"

Sandra nodded.

"I don't like you."

Sandra lifted her water bottle to her lips and rubbed an arm across her forehead. Sweat rolled off her body, but she trembled from the cold temperatures. "Then why the tender care? The offer?"

Amber fixated her gaze off into the distance.

She didn't appear aware of her surroundings. Staring into the past, perhaps? Sandra didn't think Amber would answer her.

Amber came out of her reverie. She flicked her hair back with a toss of her head and rounded each shoulder in a stretch. She stuck out her rifle to block Sandra. They stopped. "Because, *bruja*, mothers have to stick together to protect those too small to protect themselves. That's all there is to life."

CHAPTER THIRTY-FIVE

THE RIDGE THEY traversed followed a main highway. Sandra couldn't see the road beyond the tree line. Every few minutes, she heard a car pass by. It wasn't the interstate, since it lacked the steady drone of cruising vehicles, but she couldn't be more grateful for this small sign of civilization. She ached from head to toe. Every few steps, the twinge in her side stabbed her. Concentrating on Amber's back, she shadowed her. *We must be close to Amber's house for them to leave me at the tail end of the line.*

Cameron jogged toward them. He reached Sandra and slapped her on the back. "Doing okay?" He raised her chin, studying her face.

Sandra shrugged. The scent of pine needles, and what she could only describe as the smell of spring, floated from Cameron.

Amber pushed them apart, and the springtime floral note saturated the air. "She's fine. Leave her alone."

Amber expressed her concern for Sandra's well-being in heartening tones, but then followed her mothering by a suck-it-up, be-a-solider message Sandra found infuriating. This dual personality had lasted for the past ten minutes, further exhausting Sandra.

Cameron whistled.

Raz emerged from the front of the line and trotted back.

After a rest at Amber's secret hideout, she'd be herself again.

Raz gave her much-needed TCL. He kissed her cheek and swung an arm around her shoulders. His awkward hold threw her off-balance. She fell backward, but Raz steadied her.

He nuzzled her hairline. "It's been a long hike. I'm proud of you."

"Thanks," Sandra whispered. Raz's sweet cinnamon pheromones

drowned out the forest scents. She soaked them into her body like a lifeline. She was proud of herself for finding the strength to make it— both in body and mind—and for keeping up with this physically fit team. Unfortunately, the journey had just begun. *Will I find strength in the Nexus to help me locate Sean? Do I have the experience necessary to cure a virus in an alien race? Is it impossible to do both, or either one?* The burden sat heavy on her neck. Raz's nearness, although welcomed, brought back the high tones of her vibration. They shook her body. Blobs of crystals floated around her eyes, and the edges of her vision went black. Sandra didn't fall unconscious, but she'd reached her limit.

"Is she getting worse?" Cameron rushed to her.

Raz scooped her into his arms. "I'll carry her the rest of the way."

He cradled her close to his chest, his comforting embrace surrounded her.

"We aren't far," Amber said. "Down this ridge and we'll be home."

Leon and Zach backtracked to their positions. Zach stopped them and unzipped Sandra's jacket. "The augmenter isn't working anymore."

Yes, I want to go home. "I want to save Sean," Sandra mumbled. "I promised."

Raz tightened his hold. "We'll have a meal and sleep soon."

"Yes ... a few minutes of rest." She craved a two-hour nap. She was so tired.

Zach finished his cursory evaluation of the augmenter strap. "I'll have to work on this when we get to the house."

Raz rubbed his cheek against hers. "I'll keep you safe."

Amber scanned the woods.

Yeah, like you kept Paris safe. Sandra opened her eyes wide. She tensed. She'd heard Amber's thought as clear as Zach and Leon's conversation. *Had to be my imagination. How can I hear thoughts of Omega team members?*

"She shouldn't be this weak," Leon commented. His brows were pulled so tightly together the expression gave him a comical appearance. "Sandra, are you okay? Are you having any pain?"

"Tired," she sighed.

Amber pulled Leon back. "You forget she's still human. Let's get her to the cabin. She'll be fine. A warm belly and a bed is what she needs."

"Am, she's pregnant with a Sixxer baby. She shouldn't be tired," Zach said.

Sandra wiggled. "I can walk." *Probably not, but I hate showing weakness in front of the team.*

Raz nuzzled her hair. "Not gonna happen."

Sandra snuggled into his arms, and she didn't want him to let go of her. She was grateful, this time, he'd ignored her. She might not have been able to take one more step forward. They made their way down the hill. Amber's house came into view. It was a freaking mansion of a cabin situated mid-way on the opposite slope, overlooking the valley they crossed. The rustic, original exterior was surrounded by a wrap-around porch and nestled in an enclosure of trees. A two-story addition tied into the main part. Two old and rusted vehicles were parked under a carport. *I hope those aren't our rides out of here.*

Leon hiked down the slope. "Holy shit. You win the lotto?"

"There's an effing hot tub on the deck." Zach snickered. "It's her old boyfriend's place."

Amber extended her foot and tripped Zach. His face ate the forest floor. She kicked him when she went by. "It's *your* old boyfriend's place."

Cameron and Leon laughed.

Zach stood. "Not funny."

Sandra smiled. "Too bad no one recorded that fall."

Raz's voice rumbled in his chest under her ear.

"Zach could've won one-hundred thousand dollars on America's Funniest Videos with that move then bought his own cabin in the woods." He passed Zach and continued toward Amber's homestead.

They walked through the lowland and up toward the cabin stairs. Sandra craned her neck over Raz's shoulder.

Zach dusted himself off and hopped on one foot behind them. Favoring his injured leg, he yelled, "You wouldn't like my version of a cabin in the woods!"

Sandra laughed and turned her head back around. Amber rolled her eyes and trotted up the steps. She unlocked the front door.

Raz paused at the top. He walked closer to the corner hot tub. "Too bad we don't have time to use it."

Yes, too bad. Raz all wet and steamy in a hot tub would be a tragic sight, for sure.

They entered the main room and were met with heat, furniture and blessed electricity. Sandra relaxed. No more tiny tents to deal with. A fragrance of warmed buttercups teased her nose once she was inside the living area. The original house was small and quaint with a dining room table off to the left, and a stone fireplace on the opposite side of the coffee table.

Amber opened all the blinds in the two rooms, providing a clear view of the valley and surrounding forest. "Continue through the kitchen. The house has five bedrooms and two full baths in the additional. Use what you need."

Raz nodded, but placed her on the couch. He pulled a blue-and-white wool blanket from the back and covered her before sitting at her feet. "Leon. Zach. You need to figure out if Sandra can continue. As the medic of the team, and with Zach's previous missions, you're the ones with the most knowledge here."

Sandra grabbed Raz's arm. "I've worried you for nothing. I'm not used to so much exercise, and I've read being pregnant takes a lot out of someone."

Zach crouched beside her. "Raz is right. We'll set up a computer station and charge the laptops so I can work on the augmenter. If we get a clear signal, we won't need Sandra to go with us. Raz can extract Sean easily. Amber, do you have access to M83's network here?"

"Absolutely."

Cameron surveyed out the windows. "I haven't authorized comm, yet."

Amber smiled. She opened a box on the coffee table and lifted a small device—an electronic tablet on steroids. "We can get out, but they can't get in. How'd you think I kept this place a secret?"

Zach whipped his head around. He snatched the device from Amber's hands and opened the interface. "How did you get an M83 network blocker?"

"You're not the only one with access to classified information."

Leon trotted to the kitchen door offset to the right of the massive fireplace. "My medical opinion? Sandra is dehydrated and should eat. Classification not needed."

Cameron piled their supplies in the corner. "Get busy, Zach. I'll expect a debrief in fifteen."

Zach turned with wide eyes. "I can't provide any of you with classified information, especially not Sandra."

Cameron threw a backpack onto the floor. "This mission's priority has been blown all to hell! Classified doesn't mean shit right now!"

The room fell into silence. Leon froze in the kitchen doorway, a sandwich held to his mouth. A plate with another sandwich was in his other hand.

Zach set the network blocker on the coffee table.

Will his secrets expose him as the leak, or give the spy more leverage? Sandra met Raz's gaze.

His thought entered her mind. *Wait.*

Her arms trembled from the chill racing over her. She'd mentally spoken, and he'd answered.

Zach rolled his neck and raised his hands to his forehead. "I wasn't on R&R five months ago. My trip was a top-secret mission to discover what technology General Taft's organization was developing. I wasn't sure if I would make it back alive." He laughed. "Didn't want to worry any of you."

Amber shook her head.

Leon laughed. "We never worry about you."

Cameron gripped the back of the couch with white knuckles. "Why'd you take the risk without us?"

"I figured I'd get ten weeks of relaxation." Zach shuffled back and forth. His fidgeting appeared involuntary. He found the bags holding the two laptops they'd taken with them. One had Thom's data and Sandra's notes. The other was the one Zach used to manipulate his gadgets.

"Tell us what happened," Amber commanded.

"It wasn't pretty. Definitely out of the definition of R&R. I'll still get my leave from M83 when we're done here in Angelville. Have you seen the augmenter strap?"

Sandra patted her ribs. "I'm still wearing it."

"Oh, yeah. Well, I'll get these plugged in to charge. What's our next move, Cam?"

His stalling techniques were classic. Sandra had never seen him so agitated. What had he experienced that was so bad he didn't want to talk about it?

Amber gathered his laptop and set it on the coffee table with painstaking movements. "Where were you?"

Zach hunched his shoulders. "Mexico. I was at the site lovingly called The Cemetery."

Amber gasped. "You're lying. Stop making stuff up."

"It's no lie, Am."

Leon choked on his sandwich.

Sandra waited for Raz's reaction. His face was as confused as hers probably was.

Leon's long strides brought him to the dining room table. Placing the plate on the wooden surface, he raked his hands through his hair. He slapped a chair back on the second round of his pacing. "No one has been able to get inside that facility."

"You don't want to go there, either. Any identified or marked Sixxers are Chaser meat, or dead. I couldn't blow my cover ... I couldn't help any of them." Zach's gaze emptied of all emotion. "It's a fertility lab. That's how I know about ..." He swung his arm toward Sandra.

Raz retrieved the food for Sandra and handed it to her. The sandwich was peanut butter and jelly. She devoured it. Her hunger took precedence over the tension unfolding in the room.

Amber clenched her fists. "God damned fucking Taft. When I get my hands on him, I'll make him wish for death!"

"It's where you learned about the Sixxer pregnancies," Cameron said in a deadpan voice.

Zach nodded. "I went in thinking the purpose of The Cemetery was to strip Sixxers of their Nexus power. Like what happened to Paris but without a virus infection. Instead, I found a facility dedicated to the artificial insemination of both humans and Sixxers with genetically-altered embryos to determine if our species could crossbreed. They've been experimenting for years."

Sandra pushed down the sickness churning in her stomach. The PB&J wasn't satisfying any longer. "Experimenting at the expense of children? Sean is with this evil now. We can't wait around here much longer."

Raz prevented her from rising. His lips twisted into a sneer. His eyes narrowed and flashed a white heat. "We can't fight General Taft if we're unable to reach Sean. Zach needs to get the augmenter fixed so Sandra doesn't get so tired. The harmonics weaken her. Sean's time cannot run out. I won't allow that to happen."

Do we have a working vehicle?" Cameron asked.

Amber shook her head. "I'll need you and Leon's help to get one of my old cars running. We'll be on the road in an hour."

An hour came and went. Sandra could still feel Sean's aura though her vibrational power, but Raz's connection to him weakened the longer they were here. Urging Zach to go faster in his modification of the augmenter had worked. He tinkered with the augmenter, and Sandra was grateful for the faint signal.

Raz patted her leg. "Sandra is rested and recharged, which is probably why it's working again."

Zach gave a technical discussion on the inner workings of the electronics and associated computer program. Raz emphasized the Nexus connection while Zach fell back onto the mechanical and digital aspects of the tracker.

Sandra was unable to help Raz or Zach, so she worked on her notes. After she ate another sandwich and some snacks, her urge to nap had disappeared. She re-read the data before her and contemplated getting up. Raz had insisted she limit unnecessary walking and allow the Nexus to heal her stressed and sore body. Resting had worked. The dull ache in her back left, and the augmenter no longer dug into her. Despite her body being weary, her mind was sharp and focused. Her gaze went back to her laptop. Her conclusions were ... disturbing.

Zach had commandeered one of Amber's personal computers, and the guts of the box peppered the dining room table. He smashed his finger and swore. "I'm almost finished. We won't be on foot after they get a car running. Amber wasn't prepared for a quick getaway. Probably never thought she'd have to bring anyone here." He adjusted a setting on Sandra's augmenter strap. "You should tune your signal with minimal effort, now. I've increased the sensitivity of the program and modified the strap device with Amber's sacrifice. Raz will have to give you pointers on how to channel your power."

Raz squatted at Sandra's feet. "Can you see Sean's aura?"

Sandra closed her eyes. "I don't see any light if that's what you mean. I have pulses of vibrations I see in my mind. I can feel them, too."

"That's your Sixxer power forming. Are the tones stronger? My Nexus bond will help increase your impression of Sean's aura." Raz squeezed her hands. "I can't pinpoint a location like you can."

Sandra opened her eyes. "How do we know I'm sensing Sean?"

Zach put some finishing touches on his new and improved laptop. "Other Sixxers have this ability. Your Transitional power is harmonics, and you can track those close to you. As your elevation continues, it will become stronger."

Sandra inspected the electronics on the table. Her new talent comforted her, because now she'd always find Raz and Sean. Eventually, she hoped by herself. "How mad will Amber be about her desktop computer?"

Zach's mischievous grin spread over his face. "We'll hop in the car, and she won't notice."

Raz stared out the window toward the car port. "Are we sure we'll have wheels? Time is getting wasted here when we could be getting closer to Sean."

Zach stood and popped his back. "I'll go check. They probably need a tech guy to handle it. If you raid the fridge and get the gear ready, we won't have to wait much longer after they get the cars started."

Sandra stood after the door closed behind Zach.

Raz turned. "I'll get everything ready."

"No. I've sat long enough. I need to move. Taking groceries out of the fridge won't hurt me." The kitchen was small and cozy. Sandra found a cooler and placed a few cold items from the fridge inside. She opened the pantry and discovered that Cameron wasn't the only one on the team with a junk food addiction. At least peanut butter crackers and protein bars could accompany the snack packs of chips and crackers. When they found Sean, he would love the selection of goodies. For a secret location, the room was well stocked and maintained. Amber lived here, surrounded by homeyness and luxury which Sandra would've said didn't fit her personality.

Raz came up behind Sandra. His warm hands caressed her shoulders. "I need to know you and Jamie are safe. Did you find any additional clues on infection in the data? The blitz could've acted the same way as a render and created a pathway for the virus."

Sandra feared the same, but working on her notes was leading her toward a different theory on how the virus spread. "I'm not tired anymore. Our time here has helped me to relax."

Raz kissed the back of her neck. "Don't forget to fruit snacks, cheese and peanut butter crackers, and fudge cookies. Sean will be starving when we reach him. Nexus energy makes us ravenous."

Sandra spun to face him. "I already packed them. I can't wait to get him. The team is taking forever."

"I know. We'll have him back soon. I promise."

A pulse emanated from his body and surrounded her in a cocoon of heat. She flattened her palm against his chest and realized his heartbeat resonated within her. How could his presence become a part of her?

He cupped her face and kissed her lips. "This delay makes my ability to resist you near impossible."

Desire pooled low in her stomach. Her body told her she was completely rejuvenated and ready for passion. His tongue licked her lips and she sighed. She opened her mouth for another tender kiss and a taste of his cinnamon tongue.

She stopped herself from going farther. The information she found in Thom's files … She had to find out if her projections were true. *I don't want to know, but what choice do I have?* Sandra pushed against Raz's chest.

He dropped his arms. "What's wrong?"

She gathered packages of food and exited the pantry. "Once Paris had symptoms of the infection, did she ever have a remission?"

Raz shook his head. "Her illness worsened."

Sandra spread handfuls of candy bars and single servings of dried fruit over the island. The cabinet had plenty to satisfy both Cameron's and Sean's sweet tooth. Raz would be picky about protein, so she added packs of mixed nuts to the collection. She sat on the stool. "How could you tell she was a Sixxer?" She had to tell him what she found, no matter how unpleasant. "I need confirmation so I know I'm heading in the right direction."

He was quiet.

"Did your connection with her happen during sex like with me?" She boldly asked. Raz nervously laughed.

He stepped away and rubbed the spot on his forehead. "Where is this coming from?"

Sandra shivered, despite the room being toasty warm. "Was what we experienced last night a new experience for you? The light and the vibrations ..." She jumped off the stool and wove a path around the island. "I don't want to know about your sex life with Paris, but I need to know the details of the Nexus connection. I have two viable theories on how the virus copies itself and why it only copied itself to Paris. Did something different happen between you and her?"

Raz stared. "You really want the details?"

Sandra nodded. "I want to understand the Nexus connection. How's my change different than Paris's? We both got pregnant." She licked her lips in nervousness. "With your children."

Raz paled. "Do you think I'm the carrier?"

"No, but you might be a catalyst." Her answer relaxed the tension in his frame, but she could tell he was still uncomfortable.

Elbows on the island, he scrubbed his face. "Sixxers have a unique way of channeling their power. Humans obviously can't do it. Hybrids and Zeniths haven't figured out how to do it, and I believe physically they can't."

"How is this different from a render? Zach keeps calling me Transitional. Where does that fit?"

"Transitional is a temporary term. Once through elevation, you'll be a Sixxer. We can channel our power through a process called drifting, which is a fancy term for ultra-focusing the Nexus's energy onto one particular thing. I used this technique to stop a blitz at the hospital. The downside of a drifting is that the Sixxer involved can't focus on anything else. He or she is very vulnerable because they can't break the binding until the task is finished. They are almost floating among the Nexus energy instead of commanding it. The techniques done during a Sixxer's elevation, when they're learning to control their power. Drifting is dangerous in an unsafe environment."

"Okay." Sandra sat on the stool next to the kitchen island. Raz's description didn't sound so bad. *What has him so bent out of shape?*

Raz blushed.

Sandra paused. That damned mental connection transmitted her question to him.

"Paris would drift frequently. The experience can be very ... potent." He cleared his throat. "As an aphrodisiac."

Sandra's jaw dropped. *An aphrodisiac?* "Have you done this with me? Last night?" Was she being manipulated into having sex with Raz? Was she in control of any of her emotions?

"Not since my Transor education."

Then why did she have the uncontrollable urge to touch and caress him? She wanted to rip his clothes off every time she saw him.

Raz crossed his arms. "I'd never use someone without their knowledge. It's a manipulation tactic Paris utilized very effectively. Every time she would drift, her focused energy was on me."

Every *time?* Her curiosity and perverse thrill at new knowledge made her ask, "How is the process done?"

Raz laughed and shook his head. "This is like having the sex talk with my parents. Very uncomfortable."

"Learning the details is important. I mean ... I am a scientist."

He leaned over and placed his mouth at the shell of her ear. "Drifting during intimate relations leaves a vulnerability in our power, because we're channeling the Nexus for ultimate pleasure. I say aphrodisiac, but the sensation is unlike anything a human has experienced. Drifting during sex ends one way—ecstasy. If I had drifted last night, neither of us would've been able to resist the other all day."

His description heated her blood. She'd experienced ultimate pleasure last night with Raz. Finding out their lovemaking didn't even compare to this Sixxer process—one that Paris had done *every time*— stopped her heart. She didn't want to hear any more, but she did. She wanted what Raz described. Of course, Raz and Paris had had sex. They'd created a child, but hearing how they did it more than once filled her with jealousy. Her reaction was ridiculous, but she couldn't rationalize her feelings.

Paris is also dead. How can I be jealous of a dead woman over something that happened years ago? Raz said he no longer loved Paris, but how could he forget ecstasy? A person couldn't.

Raz grabbed her hand and pulled her back into the living area. "Stop thinking."

"What?"

"I can see the wheels running full speed in your head. Stop thinking." He wrapped his arms around her and pulled her into a full body hug. His hard, strong arms encircled her back. "The past isn't right now. What I said was true. Last night … I've never experienced that before. All I do is think about you. I want to touch you, breathe you and taste you."

Sandra remembered, too. Her passion for him heated her entire body.

Raz groaned. "The light flared in your eyes just now. We need to be connected, closer."

"Are you saying sex brings the Nexus closer to us? Should we—"

He stopped her words with a kiss. His tongue swept inside her mouth, and they moaned together.

The vibrations of their moans moved deeper into her chest.

"You're talking too much. Let the energy wash over you," Raz whispered.

Her nipples ached. He pulled her hips tight and crushed her breasts against his chest. His erection pressed into her stomach. A need built inside her, and she wanted to have him again. She was becoming a sex maniac, and all without the mysterious drifting Raz described. Were the fertility experiments and drugs turning her into a raging nympho?

He backed her against the wall. The chill in her body was now an inferno. He unbuttoned her jeans. His hard fingers delved inside the material and found her wet heat. She flushed at the conflicting sensations flowing over her. Being exposed in the light of the day, with Raz fondling her in the open space, and the threat that any moment someone from Omega might interrupt them heightened the intensity of their passion. The rough surface of the cabin logs rasped against her back and snagged the thin material of her T-shirt. "Raz, I want you more than I can stand."

He bucked against her, and she wrapped her legs around him. A spark of the Nexus flared and burst between them. The intensity of energy startled Raz, but his arousal and need still showed on his face. "All I want to do is consume you. I can't imagine what we'd be like if I drifted for you."

She moaned.

"Damn it. We have to stop. This is a distraction we can't afford right now."

Yet, he leaned into her and kissed her neck then dipped his head to kiss her chest. She didn't want him to stop, but he pulled back. Her body screamed in unfulfilled desire.

"A render will temper this lust and give you a boost of strength so we can both be strong the rest of the journey. You need everything so your signal and connection to Sean isn't lost."

Sandra didn't want to temper anything. She loved how possessed she felt in his arms and anticipated her loss of control at his touch, but she also wanted to end their search for Sean as soon as possible. "Did the render make you stop wanting Paris?"

Raz pulled back. "You've misunderstood me."

"Isn't that what happened? Isn't that what you want to happen? If she kept you on a string of lust, how could you survive General Taft's tricks? We can barely focus on our search for Sean."

"Aw, hell no. That's not how it was, Sandra. I'm a Transor. Paris didn't control me. After my parents died, we only had Sean. There is more keeping us together."

Raz's eyes darkened with desire and … dare she hope, love.

He didn't speak. His jaw had slackened, and his eyes grew wide. Was he going to tell her what he felt? The door creaked behind him, but he never turned or acknowledged it.

"Aside from me, Omega is a bunch of whiny ass bitches," Zach groused. "Cars are easy to fix. I don't know what in the hell is taking the team so long to repair a machine. They won't listen, but at least among the bickering they are somewhat close to getting a vehicle running."

Sandra stepped away from Raz.

Zach focused on her and his face flamed.

What did she look like? A sex kitten? Disheveled and thoroughly pleasured, but still unfulfilled? How inappropriate considering their current mission. She straightened her shirt and walked back to the laptop. "Zach, I found something in the data you should take a look at. I was just about to tell Raz."

Zach stood where he was. "Hmmm. You have an interesting way of telling. A new Sixxer power?"

Raz chuckled.

Sandra glared first at him then at Zach.

Zach moved his eyes in an exaggerated way down to her crotch.

Following the direction of his pointing, she discovered her fly was open. Heat and tingles infused every part of her body. She nonchalantly zipped herself up.

Zach grabbed Sandra's laptop. "What did you find? Damn, the battery level is low. Is it not charging?" He wiggled the power cord.

"Raz never sensed Paris as anything other than a Sixxer," Sandra said. "Therefore, we concluded she couldn't be a Hybrid or a Zenith, but in Thom's research, he had two groups of subjects that responded differently to his experiments."

"Which tests?" Raz asked.

"The fertility research."

Zach raised an eyebrow. He focused on the laptop to examine her findings.

Sandra glanced at Raz before she continued. Being alone with Raz made her forget everything. Explaining facts and research was easier with Zach in the room. Now, she had to bring up a difficult subject she didn't want to discuss. "No participant in the first group had a pregnancy, like me. The second group ..." She hesitated then licked her lips.

The moment Zach read what she'd found his eyebrows disappeared into his hairline.

Raz's gaze met hers.

She cleared her throat. "The second group were insatiable for sex. They became almost crazed for it. Yet, the subjects in those experiments were human, or so Thom believed. Ironically, I understand now why Thom cheated on me. He had a harem of literal nymphos at his slightest request."

"Seventy percent of the second group became pregnant." Zach arched a brow. "With Thom's children?"

"I've found no indication of sperm donations, or parentage of those children," Sandra quietly said. "Although, the notes suggest Thom as being the ... male subject in question."

Raz stood beside her. "What does this have to do with Paris?"

The warning indicator popped up on the laptop screen. Zach shut down the system and closed the lid.

Sandra exchanged a look of dread with him. "Paris was part of the thirty percent of the second group. These tests were done about ten years ago. Thom and I weren't married then. I don't know if they..."

"Was there a possibility she was in a relationship with your ex?" Zach asked.

Raz swore. "No. I would've sensed such a connection through the Nexus."

Sandra sighed. "A possible relationship. Thom was pretty adamant about me not undergoing in-vitro fertilization. I would've picked up on his advanced amount of knowledge. He probably thought he'd slip and tell me about his experimentation. Thom likes to brag. Keeping me separate from any of his research, made discussions of his other women or fertility knowledge private."

Zach pounded his fist on the coffee table. "Thom was running his trials on humans. Everything points to Paris being a human. There is one way Raz could've mistaken Paris for a Sixxer."

"How can she be human one moment and Sixxer the next?" Raz asked.

Zach pointed at Sandra. "Paris was a Transitional."

Raz paced. "What? Impossible. She knew everything a Sixxer was suppose to know. No offense to you Sandra, but you don't understand anything about our race. Most humans don't."

Zach scratched his head. "Well, Transitionals can go either way. Change to a Sixxer from a human state or change to a human from a Sixxer state. The question now is, which one had she been first? A human or a Sixxer?"

Sandra chewed on her fingernail. "Because Sean was born, I'm going to guess human, like me."

Chapter Thirty-six

SANDRA SEARCHED FILE after file for the answer to Paris's biology, alien or human, assuming such details would be written in the information she'd copied from Thom's computer. She had read through various study results and old notes, but she hadn't been able to decipher them, yet. She nestled into the plush couch cushions. Thom had scanned the handwritten codes he'd scrawled on post-it notes and interpretation took time. More time than they had at Amber's forest oasis. She concluded Thom hadn't known if Paris was human, either. Nazier let him assume she was a Sixxer. Why?

Sandra wasn't even sure if any of this information would help her in her battle to figure out the mechanisms of the virus. Was she wasting her time, when she should be focusing on learning how to use her Sixxer power?

Raz sent a small burst of energy into her laptop, which charged it to half power. "No guarantee the battery will last. The Nexus doesn't respond well to animating electronics."

Sandra peered over the top of her laptop. "Then how can Zach create the tracking device we're using to find Sean?"

"He's not tapping into the Nexus to run the device. Sean's aura surrounds us because of our circle."

Zach held up his watch-of-all-trades. The one-inch by one-inch glass surface gleamed under the light. "A regular watch battery runs it. One is in the strap sensor, too. These are just instruments. I calibrate the sensitivity level for tracking. What's so cool is your power amplifies all auras and harmonics around you or ones you're connected to. Then I separate the tones. It's not rocket science or virus design, but it's something I'm good at. I'm definitely pulling out all my talents to find Sean. A kid getting taken on my watch … I'm ashamed."

Sandra pulled the wool blanket around her shoulders. He could be lying so no one would suspect him as the spy, but he seemed dedicated to making the augmenter work with her power, which they all knew lead to Sean.

She hadn't fallen back into the mind-numbing cold she'd experienced on the way here, but a slight cooling had overcome her as the fire settled into a steady flickering. Raz added logs and stoked the fire, but its deep heat didn't penetrate any part of her. "Zach, could you get an aura reading on a Transitional?"

Zack arched a brow. "Uh … Probably not. No. I take that back. Depending on which Transitional change is occurring there might be a Nexus aura available to the sensor."

Raz stood and scratched the back of his head. "I can't sit around here doing nothing. I'm going to bring the food in here so we're ready when the team gets the cars running." He walked to the kitchen.

Zach sat in the chair beside her. A wide grin spread over his face. "I'm surprised Thom didn't have these defined in his research."

"He doesn't know what a Transitional is. A lot of his stuff is also peppered with a code, T6. Does that denote Transitional?"

Zach's eyes widened. "T6 is M83 code for Sixxer Talismans. The name is a generic shorthand for our tech devices."

"Why would Thom need M83 tech devices?"

Zach popped out of the chair. "Hell if I know. I can't see where he'd have the time to disassemble tech devices to figure out how they work. Not between his research and classes at HUP."

Sandra's screen flickered and she tapped the trackpad. "Maybe Nazier wanted the T6s for something? Could they be used against Hybrids?"

"Hybrids are the children from a Sixxer parent and a human parent. General Taft and Dr. Nazier want to create Hybrids to harvest their light. Hybrids could use our gadgets. Many of them require Nexus energy to make them work."

Raz carried the groceries from the kitchen and piled the bags near the front door beside their other supplies. He made his way over to the dining table and pointed to the computer guts spread along the wooden surface. "What part of this crap do you want packed? We'll be leaving sooner than later."

Zach nodded and moved next to the table. "I wonder if Chasers in general are modifying their tactics? Find sympathetic Hybrids to come after us?" He picked through the computer parts constantly modifying his computer code and the augmenter settings.

Sandra clutched her laptop to her stomach and followed. "My child will be a Hybrid?"

Zach scrunched his brows together and twisted his lips. "Yes. I initially thought the baby would be a Hybrid. But with you being Transitional, you'll be a Sixxer before the birth, so I don't think that's the case any longer. The importance comes into play because my understanding is Hybrids have Sixxer power but are susceptible to human illnesses."

Sandra sat on a chair at the end of the table. "Another avenue for the virus to infect a circle?"

Raz shook his head. "I still don't believe Paris was human. If she was Transitional she was a Sixxer who was losing her power. The virus worked because her Sixxer essence was vulnerable."

Zach ran over to his laptop and allowed his fingers to fly over the keyboard. "We don't know for sure who her mother was. Nazier could've had her with a Sixxer, which would align more with why Raz didn't sense any difference in her power. If she were a Zenith, her connection to the Nexus would've been artificial, and that ... feels off during a render. So I'm told. Raz would've picked up on the false bond."

I thought the false energy Raz described had been from the infiltrator.

Zach gathered his electronic selections and tossed them into a paper bag. "If Paris was a Hybrid, she'd have been sick all of the time, because of her weakened immune system, not just from Xnix-624."

"She became sick recently. A few months ago," Sandra said.

Raz banged on the table. "You're wrong, Zach. Most Hybrids connect to the Nexus with no discernible difference from you or I. They live as Sixxers do. They have Nexus power and can render circles if they are taught how. It's a misconception they're easily identified because of illness." He tossed Zach's bag of junk into the corner on top of the other sacks. A clank rattled through the room as the contents spilled onto the floor. "When I was in M83 there were only a handful of Hybrids. If Chasers have bread more, we could be in the same room with a Hybrid and not know the difference, unless you have access to a Transor."

Zach straightened. "Ah, so that was your secret directive. Identify Hybrids."

Sandra made notes in her personal reference document. She cleared her throat. "Well, let's revisit Paris as a Transitional."

Raz sat opposite Sandra and Zach. "Paris was a Sixxer to the bone. Sean's power is proof she didn't have human DNA. I researched M83's database at the children's camp. No one has verified the existence of a Transitional, until Omega sends a comm regarding Sandra."

She hated playing devil's advocate. "The experiments and drug testing from Thom aren't adding up to Paris being a Sixxer. All of Thom's notes point to the fact that he knew Paris in some capacity. While I don't believe she was his lover, I think he used her as he did me."

"As a control," Raz said.

She pointed at him. "Yes, but as another human control for the virus. He wanted to find out which combination of drugs affected either of us in his separate research threads. His subject pool was small and he overlapped experiments, which is really stupid."

Zach picked up a piece of electronic paraphernalia and rolled it around in his hands. "You were a control in the fertility treatments and the virus infection?"

"Cam and I were leaning in that direction two days ago. If Paris was used in a similar fashion by Dr. Nazier, and Thom then became his student, the most logical conclusion is that Paris was initially human. Their testing was performed on humans, especially the early work. Thom followed in Nazier's footsteps, building off his current research at the time, and added his own findings over the years."

The light bulb idea slammed Sandra upside the head. *Dr. Nazier's experiments had nothing to do with the virus, or the fertility between humans and aliens, but in determining if Thom could figure out if*

Paris was human. It was all a test ... for Thom. "If Paris was a Transitional then went through Zenith alterations before or during her elevation, what changes would dominate?"

Raz and Zach both shook their heads.

"Thom broke his results into two groups," Sandra continued. "Group one had no reaction and no pregnancies. They were all human. Group two had increased sex drive, but only seventy percent had positive results. I think the positives were Zeniths."

Zach was quiet for a few minutes. "I saw a lot of nasty shit while I was at The Cemetery. Sandra's description of how Thom's drugs increased the subject's sex drive was a common occurrence there."

Sandra grabbed Raz's hand. She looked into his eyes. *Is everything happening to me a test Nazier devised to sneak humans into a circle?* "Thom's drugs only affected Zeniths. Yet, I think Transitionals fertility might've been enhanced because of their natural Nexus bond, only delayed until their transformation was completed, maybe? Zach, do you know who was affected at The Cemetery?" She wrung her hands. *Did they figure out how to impregnate any female, alien or not?*

Raz cupped her cheek. "The fertility results of the females at some research facility can't compare to your pregnancy. Our attraction to each other isn't the result of some effed-up drug, Sandra. You hadn't been around Thom for months before we met. The way Omega was keeping you close, I don't believe for a second Thom had a chance of testing his drugs on you after you left him."

Footsteps pounded up the front steps, and Cameron entered the room in a hiss of air and frigid temperatures. "Amber and Leon almost have both cars revived." He stilled when he reached the dining room entryway. His coat was missing. Black grease covered his arms. A fuel-oil odor wafted from his body and hovered around the room. "Why do you look like I ate the last of the chocolate cake?"

"Sandra found evidence Paris was also Transitional," Raz said.

Cameron scoffed, but his eyes widened. "Ridiculous."

"Nothing is impossible, remember?" Zach stretched out his leg. The wound had finally healed. How Zach could recover so quickly after their miles-long hike baffled Sandra. He draped an arm along the back of her chair. "I know Transitionals exist. The information is classified."

They all groaned.

Zach laughed his ass off. "I'm just fucking with ya. Seriously though, Raz wouldn't have access to this intel. During my extracurricular missions, General Taft captured a group of Transitionals and brought them to The Cemetery. They all had weird psychic power. Within a few months, they changed completely. They could render and control Nexus energy. I wasn't there long enough to find out if those changes were natural, or if General Taft gave them an accelerant. The women who became pregnant changed even quicker." Zach rubbed his face and shuffled his feet. His gaze darted toward Sandra. "Unfortunately, none of the pregnancies went full term while I was there."

Sandra's stomach dropped. She held up her hand and clicked through another batch of files. "The Transitionals at The Cemetery had positive pregnancies, too?"

Zach nodded.

Sandra shifted in her seat and sat on her foot. "In Thom's notes, only the Zeniths became pregnant." She spread her fingers over her abdomen. "So fertility has increased in Zeniths and Transitionals since Thom's early research." Swirls of acid churned in her stomach. She clutched Zach's arm. "What's my risk?" Flashbacks of the sharp abdominal pain a few hours ago entered her mind. She'd been given a gift that could very easily be ripped away.

"Artificial insemination was the acceptable method of procreation at this place. Your pregnancy is natural, as was Paris's."

Sandra pushed Zach's mess to the opposite end of the table and turned her computer around to face Cameron. She arranged two documents side-by-side on the screen then pointed to the first file. "Here's the booby prize, Cam. Thom infected Paris with the Xnix-624, which I developed specifically to attack plants. He claims his modifications allow the virus to break down Nexus bonds." Tapping the screen over the second spreadsheet, she continued, "Results showed that no Sixxer or human was affected."

Cameron sat next to Raz. He weaved his fingers together and crossed an ankle over his knee. "So, how did Paris become ill?"

Sandra had a hypothesis. Would they believe her? She arranged the computer files in the order she thought made the most sense and went into her university presenter mode. "Nazier was testing Thom. Nazier wanted to know if Thom could identify Zeniths, but for Paris the results for both of Thom's research projects were messed up. She was in a minority of subjects that didn't get pregnant with his fertility drugs and after several does of Thom's virus she *didn't* get sick. I don't think either Nazier or Thom knew Paris was going through elevation. If she was Transitional, and was well on her way to elevation like I am right now, what would Zenith alteration do to her? What Nexus connection would win? From the evidence in these files, I believe Raz never suspected her human side, because, by the time he met her, she already had a natural Nexus bond as a Transitional Sixxer, but was still undergoing Zenith modification."

Cameron tapped his fingers on the table. "I thought Paris was only exposed to Xnix-624."

Sandra shook her head. "Paris was a part of the fertility experiments Thom did ten years ago."

Cameron harrumphed. "She wanted to have a baby? Why?"

"Sixxers outside of M83 crave children. Her desire to have one doesn't surprise me if she was a Sixxer." Raz placed his hands on the top of his head and leaned backwards. "She was upset and scared when she found out about Sean."

Sandra rubbed her hand over the sudden ache in her chest.

"Holy shit." Zach sat back in his chair and pushed his chair up onto two legs. "Nazier wanted Paris to have the child. That's why he wanted her back."

Oh my God! Had Paris always intended to get Sean back to her father? The ache in Sandra's heart squeezed the air out of her lungs. No. Paris had asked her to keep Sean away from her father.

Raz stood, knocking his chair to the floor. "Then she *was* the original infiltrator."

Amber and Leon entered the room and walked up behind Cameron. Amber placed her hand on Cameron's shoulder. "Both cars are running. Time to go."

Leon was dirtier than Cameron, but he'd at least found a pair of coveralls that retained most of the grit. Sandra found it interesting Amber had clothes to fit a man of Leon's size. Other indications that a man lived here with her were absent.

Cameron shook his head. "Once we get Sean, we'll re-evaluate. Sandra left Thom's house with a Sixxer. He'll have everything under surveillance, and Omega flagged."

"I wished I could've pulled off my prank," Zach said wistfully. "Thom's reaction would've been priceless."

Sandra bit her lip. "The Six group was all of you, wasn't it? You never used the group for studying."

Amber high-fived Leon. "I'd take all the credit, but Zach walked the tightrope many times. I thought he was stupid. Although, the pranks from Omega right under Thom's nose proves he isn't as smart as you think he is."

Zach chuckled. "Remember that time we broke into the mail room in his building and put peanut butter between his packages?"

"Good times, sir." Amber smiled.

Raz raked his hands through his hair. "He knew a unit was watching him and acted dumb in order to divert Omega's attention."

Leon whistled. "Hell's bells."

Sandra read her notes and nodded. "Thom's research is funded by General Taft. Yet, all of his reports are addressed to Dr. Nazier."

"Nazier has always been a sneaky bastard." Amber cracked her knuckles.

Zach brought his chair back to the floor and tapped the keyboard. "Nazier used what he had available."

Raz pulled Sandra out of her chair and held her close.

She breathed, despite the air being squeezed out of her in the bear hug.

Raz eased the pressure, but not the embrace. "General Taft hasn't discovered Sean. Nazier handled all of Paris's experiments and kept them secret. Then Thom shows up, and they collaborate under General Taft's nose. Nazier wants Sean for himself. Thom is a tool Nazier uses to get what he wants."

Amber opened the front door. "Then there's no time to waste."

"There defiantly isn't. What also concerns me is Nazier finding out Sandra is pregnant," Raz whispered.

Cameron paced the floor. "There's a bigger threat. The number of Sixxer kids born in the last two decades is zero. It's why Taft has such a fascination for Hybrid children. Raz can procreate, naturally, with two humans turned Transitional."

Sweat broke out on Sandra's neck. Nazier's fascination with Hybrid children sickened her. "Is the augmenter working? Sean can't be away from us any longer." If the group was captured, then Thom and Nazier would have a Sixxer stud, and a human brood mare for their devious experiments.

"Like it or not, team, this is a war." Cameron turned to Sandra and led her over to Zach. "Can you link to Sean, now?"

The Nexus light flared in Sandra's arms, and her harmonic connection to Sean echoed within the room. Zach's augmenter erupted into a frenzy of beeps.

He smirked. "I like this new Sandra. Built-in GPS."

Chapter Thirty-seven

RAZ GROUND HIS teeth together. They were packed into the VW van like breakable cargo wedged between bubble wrap. The bright green color, inside and out, hurt his eyes and was obvious in the extreme. They had left the 1967 Cutlass in a warehouse parking lot outside of town with half of their supplies. Navy blue in color, the Cutlass would've been low key in this wealthy part of Center, especially as night descended.

Bringing Sandra so close to Thom, and possibly Nazier, endangered them all. She had old neighbors who'd recognize her and possibly notify her ex. Cameron didn't even attempt to hide her from view.

The only thing saving Cameron from Raz's temper was the coming evening. Twilight hid anyone inside the vehicle. The poor decision-making of the team made Raz foam at the mouth, but he was outnumbered. This plan, so far, hadn't brought them closer to his son. Sandra even agreed to this dumbass proposal only because Zach's watch kept emitting the amplified tones of her power. Did they know for sure that was Sean's aura?

Raz rubbed his chin and tightened his arm around Sandra. The third row seat kept them somewhat secluded, considering six people populated the bus. He spoke in quiet tones only he and Sandra registered. "Can you sense Sean nearby?"

She shook her head. "The humming is low." She raised her hand. Her fingers no longer trembled from her aura-tracking ability. "Could I be imagining the tones? They're very different from the ones I had at Amber's place."

Raz shook his head. "Your harmonics are weakening. Zach can't determine Sean's exact location under these conditions. This entire plan will fail." *How will I find Sean and keep Sandra and my unborn child safe?* He'd have to sneak off with Sandra and continue to HUP without Omega's help.

The augmenter had indicated Sean was at the university, and then five minutes later, it had pointed to Thom's backyard torture chamber. For the last hour of their journey, Sandra's sensor had bounced back and forth. Her Sixxer power had weakened the farther they had driven into the subdivision. As soon as they'd entered the neighborhood, a steady but faint signal appeared. He pulled her head closer to his and kissed her above the shell of her ear.

She shivered and pulled back. A glow of light illuminated her eyes.

Raz loved seeing the evidence of their bond on her body. He whispered close, his warm breath fanning back into his face. "Zach is leading us right to General Taft."

She shook her head. "No, the spy can't be Zach."

"Someone is."

She bit her lip in what Raz called her concentrating expression.

Her gaze met his. "What might help me clarify the signals?"

Raz had doubted Sandra's rest had revived her Sixxer power. No amount of food or sleep would fix the problem. A render was their best option for energizing her, but he couldn't close the circle until they found Sean. She needed a boost in Nexus energy. He'd use Omega for one last purpose before taking back control.

"A render will stabilize your power. It'll disperse some of Paris's residual energy equally between the two of us. If Omega joins, we'd become even stronger." Raz would steal whatever he could from the others to make Sandra stronger.

She nestled into his chest. "Don't we need Sean?"

"This will be a new render with Omega. We'll have another after we find Sean."

Her breath puffed over his neck and tickled him.

"I'll do it with or without Omega. Won't the spy refuse?"

Leon pulled the van over to the curb and parked.

Sandra stretched her neck over the top of the seats. "We're about a street over from Thom's house." She pointed. "I can see the garage between those two houses."

Zach turned and placed his hands on the back of the middle seat. A wide, goofy grin spread over his face. "I can see our getaway tracks."

Raz stayed alert. Activity around the house was minimal, but Thom had kept his research quiet, according to Cameron and Sandra. Amber's old VW van kept them warm, but if they stayed here too long in a running vehicle, suspicions would arise from the neighbors. The VW wasn't the typical Mercedes traveling this neighborhood. Raz had dealt with crime watches before in the various suburban locations where they'd hidden. The outcomes were never positive.

Amber checked her ammo. She reloaded her rifle then the pistol hidden in her cargo pants. "How will we get inside without suspicion? Thom and Nazier are waiting for us to show up to *ta-da* rescue Sean. We don't know if the augmenter is accurate."

Amber mirrored Raz's every question and assumption. Although, thinking alike on a few points wouldn't make Amber, or anyone else, enjoy Raz's suggestion. "I have a solution."

Four heads turned toward him.

If they don't agree, Sandra and I will break away. I won't walk into Thom's castle without an energy boost.

Would a render give Sandra the strength she needed? At this point, Raz would take the risk. Sandra's findings were too convincing. Paris being a Transitional had blown his mind. Paris's empathic and psychic abilities must've allowed her to guess at Sandra's elevation changes. Why else insist on including Sandra in the hospital rendering? Transitionals weren't mind readers, but rumors have hinted at their ability to form mental links. Sandra's nose bleeds, her intuitive trust or mistrust of people within Omega, and tracking Sean's aura pointed to her transformation.

I can hear Sandra in my head, sometimes. Sean speaks to me without a link, as well. All without a render. Paris could do the same. Hiding from the world made me blind. I'm no longer shutting my eyes to the truth.

Raz studied the soldiers in front of him. *Which one will refuse the Nexus energy?* "I can form a new circle with Omega. The render will boost our power and give us an advantage against any darts or bullets heading for us. It will extend Sandra's Nexus bond and focus the augmenter."

Zach and Leon shook their heads.

Raz prepared to reason with the team. They needed to listen. "The augmenter isn't accurate enough at the Sandra's current energy levels."

"The hell you will render any of us." Amber bristled.

"Am, calm down." Cameron placed a hand on her shoulder.

His attempt to head off disaster appeared to work.

Sandra scooted into the corner of the seat.

Raz hated the loss of heat between them. "The render will dissipate Paris's energy. If Sandra is a Transitional, and we're this close to Sean, a render will allow him to telelink with her. Hell, I should be able to telelink with him and leave her out of the danger, but I can't."

Zach bounced from the center passenger seat into the aisle. After tripping over Amber's legs, she shoved him away, and he fell onto the third seat. He opened his laptop then configured settings on his tech watch. "Knowing if we should be here would be extremely helpful."

Amber pointed at Raz. "You aren't a part of Omega. You've been bullying your way into command for the majority of this rescue mission. I don't trust you. We have no anti-NEUs, and I can *guarantee* Thom and Nazier have them everywhere." She narrowed her eyes at Sandra. "Thom is her ex. We haven't been followed. She's been communicating with him this entire time. It's been too quiet, and she's led us back here. Seems too convenient."

"I want Sean back," Sandra cried. "I'll go to the university alone if I have to in order to find him."

Raz appreciated the sentiment and emotion behind Sandra's statement, but he wouldn't let her risk the baby or herself for Sean. No. Way. In. Hell. They were his responsibility, and he would fix this mess. He pulled her onto his lap and hugged her tight. He'd die for all three of them.

Raz had embraced Sean's life the moment he knew Paris was pregnant. He'd never rescinded his promise, not to Paris, and he wouldn't with Sandra and Jamie.

Raz jerked up his head, which grabbed Amber's attention. Her green eyes flashed an automatic Sixxer warning, but she couldn't harm him or Sandra with his shield in place. "A render will verify if we're being driven into a trap."

Zach shrugged. "What we need is a SAFE."

"A what?" Raz asked.

"Secure Anti-NEU Frequency Emitter." Zach continued to pound the keys of his laptop.

Raz leaned forward in his seat. "How is a SAFE different?" The amount of new tech M83 had developed in the last seven years boggled his mind.

"The SAFE can actually hide our energy with a barrier, and it can pinpoint all the NEU locations surrounding us."

Cameron turned in the front passenger seat. He shook his head. "The one SAFE we had was the one I took from HUP. It was destroyed at the children's base operations. We'll have to risk a render without any anti-NEU."

Amber rummaged in her pack.

Cameron scooted to the edge of his seat. He tapped Amber's leg. "Raz's idea is a way out of this mess and will make Sean's extraction easier."

Zach snorted. "You're not seriously considering this plan, are you? Go against high command? You'll get us thrown out of M83."

Raz's gaze met Cameron's. *Damn. He's trying to figure out who the spy is, too.* Out of the three remaining, who was the traitor?

"We can't trust him, Cam," Amber said. "M83 doesn't want us to render and form circles. The virus is my main concern, but human infiltrators can't be sensed."

"I'm not an infiltrator," Sandra spat. "How may infiltrators develop Sixxer power?"

Leon flipped through a deck of cards he'd pulled from his cargo pocket. "Amber has valid reasons to argue with your idea. Especially with a circle-infecting virus on the loose. I don't want to get sick, either. What makes you think the render won't drain our energy?"

"You're Sixxers," Sandra said. "Paris went through Transitional elevation. Nazier convinced her to go through Zenith alteration. There's a link I haven't discovered, but I think because of the Zenith alteration the virus could infect her. Thom never recorded a full-blooded Sixxer as developing any disease state. If he had, Thom would have no need for a garden lab or a reason to capture anyone within M83. He'll deploy Xnix-624 at a large scale in an airborne state. Either we're all infected, or my pregnancy, or perhaps even my Transitional state, is preventing an infection."

"Or a carrier," Leon said. "Raz could be one."

Cameron picked up a fallen card from the floor. He laughed. "Nudie cards? Where did you get these?"

Leon smirked. "My secret stash."

Raz surveyed their surroundings. If the mole was within the team, then his suggestion of a render would become news in a matter of seconds. Right now, they were out of options. Would Cameron step up and go against his M83 commander? Something about what Sandra said pricked his memory. The missing link. The reason Paris was the only one, Zenith or Transitional, to become ill.

Cameron tapped a pattern of beats on the back of his seat. "Sitting here isn't getting back Sean. Raz's only circle is still open. There wasn't a way for the virus to spread."

Sandra nodded. "Cam, you're on to something. The circles have to be active. Paris was exposed to the virus when their circle hadn't had a render in months, and she became sick. The virus attacked her system because she had no Nexus energy."

Zach scrubbed his face and moaned. "The lack of a render was making her Zenith alterations her dominant energy source."

Raz remembered what he'd overheard at Center Medical. "Do any of you know what Z-211 is? Thom and Nazier were discussing giving this drug to Paris at the hospital."

Sandra's brow wrinkled. "As a treatment?"

"Thom had given it to her during his psychic study. He didn't say how," Raz said.

Cameron pinched the bridge of his nose. "Her Zenith power was dominant by then. Zenith characteristics and power must be the infection pathway. Z-211 is thought to disrupt Nexus energy, but her dual powers were making it ineffective until some catalyst."

"None of us are Zeniths. A Transor shield would be more effective than a SAFE against an unknown like this," Raz said.

Amber's face turned red. "We're not—"

"Back down, soldier. You aren't in command of this unit." Cameron faced Raz. "We'll be surrounded by Chasers before your finished."

"The more Sixxers in the circle, the more powerful a Transor's shield."

Raz could almost see the wheels spinning in Cameron's mind. His hesitation about a render wasn't because of Raz or Sandra. Something had Cameron wary. Could it be possible at Cameron's age that he had never experienced a render?

Raz pointed to Zach's watch and Cameron's phone. "Once we are a circle, we could use the Nexus link to communicate with each other instead of relying on technology."

"Zach, can you pinpoint any actual NEUs in the area?" Cameron asked.

Zach hopped in his seat like a kid. "On it."

He attacked his laptop with gusto.

Cameron pointed at everyone else in the van. "I'm not asking. This is an order, but remember there's a child's life hanging by a thread, and possibly many other children in danger if we do nothing. One being Sandra's baby."

Amber sat up straight and swallowed.

Leon's face turned green.

Zach acted nonchalant, but tremors shook his hands.

They're scared. No one in Omega had a clue about the render process. These young soldiers had never been rendered. Cameron was an unknown. Raz might create the biggest fuck-up of his life. The act would be easy if they were all Sixxers. If the spy was an infiltrator, he'd have to use all his power to close the circle. He'd deal with the consequences, as long as he found Sean and kept Sandra safe.

Zach's head popped up from his laptop. "A NEU signal is close. A two-mile radius from Thom's property. If we get any closer to the house, Raz will light up that sucker like a neon sign advertising a strip joint."

Raz tipped his imaginary hat. *Touché, Zach.* "We passed an abandoned strip mall. Is it two miles from here?"

Sandra nodded. "About three to three-and-one-half miles. I used to run it."

Amber raised her brows.

Sandra blushed. "This was years ago."

Raz slapped his hands together. "Good. No need to advertise the render in front of Thom's face." That was too ballsy, even for him.

Leon turned the key in the ignition.

They entered the empty strip mall and rounded the back of the complex.

Zach scanned the area. He nodded. They jumped out of the van's door and maneuvered to the back entrance of a store.

Cameron popped the lock.

Amber flanked him, and they scouted for several minutes. "The area is secure. Let's keep our equipment close." They trotted back to the door and unloaded some of the supplies from the van. Protocol was to always keep something close. Just in case.

Leon folded his arms across his chest. "Now what?"

"We'll find a clear space." Raz lead Sandra into the abandoned store. They moved around old boxes and junk until they created an empty section on the floor.

Raz observed each of their guarded faces, including Sandra's. He rubbed her shoulders and lightly kissed her. "We'll be all right. The render will help you find Sean with your Sixxer tones."

"What happened at the hospital is fresh in my mind," she whispered.

He pulled her close. The second kiss to her lips was gentle and as tender as he could make it.

"Break up the sappy shit over there." Amber tapped her foot. "If we're going to do this, we best hurry."

Raz sighed, but Amber was right. "Form a circle."

"Should we hold hands?" Leon asked.

"Are you kidding me?" Amber grouched.

Zach tilted his head in an annoyed fashion. "Are we in kindergarten?"

"Quiet." Cameron motioned for Raz to continue. "The show is yours."

He wanted his instructions to be clear and followed to the letter. He'd never executed a render with so many uninitiated. "Are you ready?" Raz's voice echoed throughout the open retail space.

Everyone nodded.

"A render *will* change you. You'll always have more Sixxer power to control afterwards. Do you know how to wield it?"

Cameron nodded. "Yes, Sixxer power control is a part of M83 training. The Nexus surge is the unknown."

"This will test every part of your training. Stand in a circle. I'll give you the two-minute breakdown of what to expect."

After reluctant foot shuffles, they created a haphazard ring.

Raz held his arms wide. "Without a Transor we'd have to hold hands, or be in physical contact. Since I'm here, standing in a circle is acceptable. You'll experience body heating. Some Sixxers experience trembling, as Sandra does, but only during the render. After the circle has formed, the shaking will stop."

Sandra clasped his hand. The vibrational waves returned to her extremities.

Her body craves the render. The Nexus glow already appears on her fingertips before I even begin the process.

"Can we break free?" Amber's gaze met Raz's.

It was full of fear and distrust. Not the best environment for a render. "Yes. Each of you can break free. The question you should've asked is if you'll want to."

Sandra clasped his hand and squeezed his fingers. Her fingernails dug into his skin. "I'm scared."

She said what the others wouldn't. He brought her hand to his mouth and placed a kiss on the back. "Once the heating or vibration begins, the Nexus light will illuminate a circular barrier around us. The more you resist it, the longer the render will take."

A murmur of unease fluttered around the group.

Cameron straightened his back and crossed his arms over his chest. "We're soldiers, peeps. Not any ordinary infantrymen, but trained M83 fighters. We're prepared for the unexpected."

The team eased a little, but their guard was up.

Raz dug deep. He pulled along the spine of his power and coaxed the Nexus energy from inside his body out to the tips of his fingers. Light fanned around his abdomen. Swirls of blue Nexus energy twisted and floated between his and Sandra's bodies. Sandra's hand heated within his own. Her skin was as hot as a fire poker, and almost as painful. A jolt of adrenaline shot through his body.

Sandra's vibrations mirrored his. They shivered in the pit of his stomach and tilted him off balance. He struggled to bring the Nexus energy back to the circle.

Sandra gasped.

Amber's head snapped up. An aura glowed around Amber and Cameron's heads. A light tone strummed in Raz's ears.

The vibration in Sandra's body increased, and her hands shimmered with light.

"Sandra glowed like that when she touched the dead soldier," Amber shrieked. "The intensity of the render is too much."

"Raz, it's overwhelming them," Leon yelled. "You have to stop!"

Amber sounded far away. Leon's long hair billowed around his face like they were in a wind tunnel. Raz turned his head. "Concentrate on the energy," he shouted back.

Cameron stumbled.

"Cam, stand up." Zach crouched. He caught Cameron around the waist.

Raz feared they wouldn't finish. "Don't break the circle. The render will finish in a few more seconds." Why was this circle so difficult to command? He'd preformed renders on hundreds of experienced soldiers before he left M83. None of those training sessions had tested him like this. An active Zenith was among them.

"Raz, hurry," Sandra pleaded.

Cameron had fallen to his knees. His face was contorted in massive pain.

Raz increased the energy of the circle.

Sandra cried out. Light and Nexus energy waves emanated from her hands and her feet. Her body lifted off the ground by a foot.

The Nexus flew around the group in the outer perimeter of the circle. At random intervals, a burst of light entered and surrounded one of them.

The energy inside Sandra surrounded her in a powerful aura. She floated higher and absorbed Paris's energy. How could he bring Sandra back down, literally, to Earth?

Glancing to his right, Raz saw Cameron on his hands and knees, gasping for breath.

Cameron held his stomach as dry heaves convulsed his body.

The opposite reactions in Sandra and Cameron made little sense. Cameron was powerful and had been the leader of this team for years.

Why's a simple render weakening him? Why's he acting as ... my parents did before they dimmed? No. It's not quite the same, but different than Paris's collapse. A bitter chill covered Raz. The open pit in his stomach became an icy, bottomless cavern. The coveted Nexus energy left a blistering heat in his lungs.

Raz's breath rang in his ears, loud and remorseful. *What have I done to my circle?* M83 kept the team at the weakest point of their abilities, just enough to survive. So many secrets. Ones Raz should've uncovered before putting everything meaningful to him on the line.

Zach and Amber stared with gaping mouths at Sandra. These Sixxers had only scratched the surface of their power. Now they saw what they could actually control. Their connection to the Nexus hummed around them and swirled in colorful patterns of energy.

"Leon, help me." Cameron gasped for breath then coughed up blood.

Sandra screamed but was paralyzed mid-air in the waves of the Nexus.

Amber rushed to Cameron's side.

Leon's head swiveled between Sandra and Cameron.

"Please ..." Sandra gasped.

Leon grabbed Sandra by the legs and sent a burst of healing energy through her. After the energizing effects of the render, Leon's healing power exploded within the room. The empty space filled with blinding yellow light. Everyone covered their eyes.

Sandra collapsed to the ground.

Just as quickly, the light disappeared. Darkness and uncertainty wrapped them in cold waves of Paris's residual Nexus light.

A smoke-like substance raced from the room.

Zach hurried to find his flashlight and scrambled over to Cameron. "Christ! He's bleeding all over the place. What in the hell did you do?" He cleared the blood from Cameron's nose and ears.

Cameron lay unconscious.

Amber made a pillow out of her jacket and rolled Cameron on his side.

Raz held Sandra. Her body was cold. She, too, was unconscious.

Leon examined Sandra's limp body. "She's been knocked out. Throw me the kit."

Zach tossed a small pack toward them. It landed with a thump near Raz's leg.

Leon's bobbing flashlight caught Sandra's face. A brilliant crimson drop ran from her nose.

"Raz!" Leon yelled. "Man, you have to let go of her."

He pried Raz's arms from her and set her on the ground. He checked her vitals and gathered meds from his kit.

What pills could possibly help her? Perhaps, something similar to what Leon had given Zach after his gunshot wound. Raz wiped his face. The tears hadn't registered until he touched the wetness. "This wasn't supposed to happen."

Amber walked over, and her precise movements reminded Raz of a black widow.

"Cameron is stable. Zach is with him. Will she make it?"

Leon fumbled the medical bag during his ministrations. "I don't know. She's human. Her core body temperature is low. How many blankets do we have?"

Raz shook his head. "She's not human anymore. She's in elevation."

Amber ran over to the equipment and brought back three blankets. "What did you do, bastard?" She spoke each word with utter care as she covered Sandra. "How is the render supposed to help us like this?"

Leon grabbed her arm. "Amber, calm yourself."

"I won't, Leon. Don't use your voodoo shit on me, either. I'm not in need of healing right now. Cameron is out of commission. Leadership falls to me. Zach?"

"Yo?"

"Are we far enough away from the NEU?"

"Fuck if I know. We should head out ASAP."

Amber removed her nine millimeter and placed it at Raz's head. "You have five seconds. Talk."

Will my suspicions get me killed? Omega had backed Raz into a corner. If they were working for General Taft, then his words wouldn't matter. He spoke clearly and with authority. "I think Cameron is Transitional, like Sandra. No one else was affected the way he was."

Amber paled. "You're a liar. Why did Sandra react differently?"

Raz would make her understand. "Sandra is pregnant. My energy will automatically go to protect her the most. When Paris convinced me to render with the infiltrator, she and the Zenith both responded oddly, like this. Their symptoms weren't exactly the same, but the Sixxers of our group are unharmed." Zach tried to interrupt, but Raz held up his hand. "Paris went into a coma. The Zenith died."

"Your parents died, too. They were Sixxers," Zach said.

Amber pushed the muzzle of the gun into Raz's skin. "Were your parents Zeniths?"

Raz slumped and dropped his head into his hands. He remembered that day like it had happened hours ago. "Their Nexus light blinked out after the render. It flickered off and on over a matter of weeks until they … were consumed by the dark. I don't know what went wrong with their energy."

Amber and Zach's jaws dropped. Amber lowered her weapon.

"Leon," Cameron quietly spoke.

His voice sounded like forty grit sandpaper scraping over wood.

Zach grabbed a water canteen. Amber's and Leon's heads swung around.

Amber rushed over to Cameron's side. Wrapping her fingers around his wrist, she checked his pulse. Her other hand covered his forehead.

He brushed them aside.

Amber was Nurse Ratchet. "His core temp is normal. Maybe it's over."

Leon placed the round metal knob of his stethoscope on Cameron's chest. "His heart rate is regular. How do you feel, Cam?"

"Like chopped steak. What in the hell happened?" He brought his hands to his head and rubbed his eyes. He pushed back his hair and spoke to Amber. "You'll have to finish this mission for me. It's an easy observation, but you can't rely on me anymore."

Amber and Leon exchanged weird looks.

Cameron leaned into a cough and stared at the blood left on his hand. "What the …"

"What're you talking about?" Amber asked.

"We have to find out if Paris is a Sixxer, and her connections to Raz."

Amber jumped back and pulled Raz's arm. "He still thinks Paris is alive."

Raz nodded. "Her essence surrounded all of you. I can't close the circle without Sean. Remnants of Paris's Nexus energy are still within my circle, and now our circle. The disorientation might last a few hours before he remembers."

Raz came over and hunched beside Cameron. He moved Cameron's head side-to-side, studying his face. "When did you change, Cameron?" He softly asked, not sure if he'd get an honest answer.

The muscles of Cameron's neck tensed, and he didn't respond.

Raz squatted. "M83 doesn't know you were human."

Chapter Thirty-eight

SANDRA BLINKED THE glue away from her eyelids. Every part of her body ached. Amber stood over her. A bioluminescence flashed under her half-closed eyelids. Sandra's heart skipped a beat then came back to a normal rhythm. She chuckled. *I must be used to her as the scary soldier. She hardly fazes me anymore.* Sandra shifted her lower body. A twinge of pain entered her back. Pins and needles brought her left foot back to life.

"She's awake," Amber murmured.

Sandra winced at the sound. "How long have you been staring? This fixation you have on me is becoming a habit, and just to let you know, it's really creepy." She couldn't make out the shapes in the room in the dim light, but the surroundings were familiar. *What the … * She rested on the hard surface of a classroom work table. Sandra massaged her temples and twisted her neck from side to side.

Zach clapped his hands once from behind Amber. They stood about a foot away from the top of Sandra's head. He rubbed his palms together. "Yes! I have a signal." He tapped Amber's arm. "Whatever happened at the end of the render blocked Nexus energy from her system until consciousness returned. Figuring out a word problem like that will get me a wearable anti-NEU device. I'd be a superstar."

"You have high dreams, sir. How strong are her current vibes?" Amber grabbed the laptop from his hands.

"The one at the top is spiked."

Amber analyzed the screen. The light in her eyes grew brighter. "The spike is there, but the intensity of her power has faded. This data isn't right. You're getting interference from an anti-NEU, or something we can't detect. She's being blocked by a device in this building."

Zach stomped his foot like a child. "I can't detect NEUs here. I've been scanning every five minutes. *Nada*. If the real deal was here, we'd see a reverse signal floating about. I thought discrepancies might be caused by a wrecker, but if that were the case, we'd be empty of Nexus energy."

The two of them entered into an argument on the helpfulness of Sandra's weak power signal versus whether or not NEU or anti-NEU devices were on campus.

They brought as much drama into her life as her biology students. No wonder Zach had fit in so well. To her right, the room was lit by a floor lantern turned to half power. To her left, row after row of student desks sat between her and Raz. He taped a wool blanket to the door. Whatever for? Sandra rubbed her face. "Are we at HUP?"

The augmenter dug into her ribs. The flexible plastic irritated her skin like it burned through her T-shirt. She raised her head and looked at her chest. The strap was in place, without signs of smoke or bursting flames. She exhaled a sigh of relief.

Amber and Zach paid no attention to her in their bickering.

Sandra reached over her head and tugged on Zach's arm. "Your eyes are weird."

A set of gold eyes, and one of green, focused on her.

Weird is too mild a description for Zach and Amber's irises. The light from their eyes brought additional illumination to the room. Unlike, the changes in Sandra's eyes, their eyes' high-intensity glare made Sandra squint, but she didn't tear away her gaze for several minutes.

Raz finished blocking the cut-out window in the classroom door. "Zach's duct tape is always handy for something." He threw the roll of gray adhesive into a plastic bin near his feet.

Cameron and Leon catalogued the contents of several storage boxes stacked near the entrance.

Raz trotted over to the table and helped her sit up. The shock of his touch was like a zap of electricity.

Several shivers jerked her body.

Raz passed her the army jacket and caught her gaze. "We found an empty classroom. Covering the door is just a precaution. Cameron assured me this building doesn't have any night classes scheduled today."

Sandra nodded. "Night classes are on Wednesdays. Tomorrow. Why not turn on the lights?"

Raz helped her swing her legs over the side of the table. "We only saw the cleaning crew, and they've already been through this part of the floor. The overhead lights would've alerted them someone was here."

She inserted her arms into the warm material of the jacket. "Did I lead you to Sean?"

Raz shook his head. "Now you're awake, Zach should have a blip on his screen."

Leon heaved a large object out of a bin. He moved it to another, but it slipped from his hands and buckled the plastic. The contents inside flattened under the weight.

"Christ, Leon! Can you be any louder?" Cameron stopped the outward flow of junk from the box. "Why don't you know what's in these damned containers?"

"I packed this shit six or more years ago. Hell if I know what's in them."

Raz zipped her jacket up to her chin. She remembered he used to do something similar for Paris. Could the chill within her body signify an infection of Xnix-624?

He wrapped his arms around her. "You've been out for a few hours. HUP was the best choice to replenish much-needed supplies and then get you to an e-loc."

She reached up and cupped Raz's jaw. The worry written on his face spoke louder than words.

"We were prepared for you to be out for some time." He choked on the words and cleared his throat. "We would've taken you to an e-loc. Cameron and I were going to come back and sweep the campus and then Thom's house. I'm not going to stop until we find Sean."

Zach pushed between them and emphatically held out is hand. "The question is: why did they collapse under the pressure of the render in the first place?" He turned his head and called, "Leon, we need a vitals check on Sandra and Cameron. We must keep monitoring them."

Leon stopped his haphazard search and swung a stethoscope around his neck. He pulled a blood pressure cuff out of a large duffle bag embossed with HUP's logo and bulldog mascot on the front.

They've been busy pilfering stuff from the labs and classrooms.

Amber leaned down to Sandra's face. "Are you in any pain, *bruja*?"

Sandra furrowed her brows. "No." Why couldn't she remember? The vibrational tones she'd had when tracking Sean were vastly different from the now almost non-existent fluctuations. "Is the augmenter useless?" A shiver ran up her spine.

Leon pointed at Sandra. "You'll have to take the jacket off."

She shrugged out of her coat. A mind-numbing chill settled over her.

"Zach's toy hasn't been working." Raz wrapped a fuzzy blanket around her shoulders.

Leon wrapped the cuff on her upper left arm. The pressure squeezed her bicep.

Raz placed his hands on the desk and leaned over. "The signal has been dead since the retail store."

Sandra gasped. Memories brought back insight. "We were inside a render. The Nexus light exploded in front of me. After that, I don't remember anything."

Raz sighed. "The render wasn't as successful as I'd hoped. It energized the majority of the team, so we still have an advantage."

Leon released the air valve, and the cuff deflated.

She shifted on her perch. "But everyone has Nexus light in their eyes. I'm confused. The render must've been a success. I feel ten times better than on our drive into Center. Although, I can't get warm enough."

Zach bumped her elbow. "Everyone has the light, except you and Cam."

Sandra's heart skipped a beat. She searched for Cameron.

He crouched by a box and waved away her concern. "I'm okay." He stood. "Leon's inventory doesn't have anything we can use. I'm confident Zach couldn't even create something from this trash."

Leon's skin darkened along his forearms, and trails of shimmering light flashed under his skin. He trotted over to his boxes. "I'm offended. I have lots of good stuff here."

"Hoarder," Amber said.

Zach high-fived her. Yet, they both pitched in to help Leon search.

Cameron walked toward Sandra in a methodical way like he was debating on what to say to her. She examined his demeanor. His tired eyes and weary face showed just how exhausted he was. *Cam needs rest. Why didn't the render boost him? Everyone else on the team is jacked up on Nexus adrenaline.*

Cameron scrubbed his hand over brow. He hopped up beside her on the table. "I'll get the other anti-NEU running." He leaned into her ear and circled his finger at the others, leaving Raz out. "These three have too many power plays going on. If we are going to find Sean, we have to do more. I'm not sure the older device will hide their Nexus energy, but it's all we have to block our signatures."

Raz straightened. "Where's the device?"

"On the lower level, near my workstation." Cameron sighed. "I can get some useful supplies while I'm there."

"Take Leon or Amber with you," Raz said.

"No one will think twice at seeing me in the lab. The only risk is running into Thom." Cameron jumped off the table and tapped Raz on the back. "I'll be quick."

Sandra didn't like this plan. Not one bit. "Why waste the time when we could be searching for Sean?"

"Getting captured won't find Sean either." Raz clasped her hand. "Unfortunately, the hard choices will keep coming. We'll balance actions between finding Sean as quickly as possible and keeping you out of any of these bastard's hands. I can't stand being away from my son, but I know we can't be impulsive."

Leon wrapped the cord of the pressure cuff around the fabric sleeve and set it aside. He blocked Cameron's exit. "Sit," he commanded. "You're not leaving until I check your vitals."

Cameron smiled. "I'm not the pregnant one. Focus on Sandra."

Leon removed the stethoscope. "As long as you let me check you out before you leave."

Cameron sighed. "Sure."

Leon walked over to where Sandra sat. He checked her heart and lungs. "You're back to normal."

She shifted awkwardly on the table. The ache in her back pulsed. "I was abnormal?"

"Very much so." He nudged her shoulder. "Lie back."

"Is the baby okay?" she whispered.

Raz squeezed her hand. "He's okay. I can feel his signature because of the render. We are more worried about you."

Leon raised her shirt over her belly and pressed on her stomach and abdomen. "We'll do a quick exam to check ya out." A spark of sickly yellow light jumped from his fingers and into her skin.

Sandra jumped at the nip to her flesh. "Ouch."

Leon laughed. "I'm sorry. I'm not used to the boosting effects of a render. Takes some getting used to."

The energy flared from his fingers and hovered above her abdomen. She glowed from within.

Cameron stood between Leon and Raz. "I might not have a healthy glow, but I'm still your unit leader. With this much Nexus energy floating around, our security is dwindling."

Raz nodded. "I agree."

"Leon, you'll have to wait until I return. I'll be back in five." Cameron trotted down the aisle. He opened the door with a whisper and disappeared.

"Stubborn bastard." Leon shook his head, but helped Sandra into a sitting position. "If nothing hurts, then I'll give you a clear bill of health."

Sandra expected to be disoriented after the energy that came into her new Sixxer body, but she really felt normal. "I ache a little."

Amber pushed Raz aside and stood beside Leon. "Where?"

Sandra looked at Raz and smiled when he rolled his eyes and swirled his finger around his ear. Yes, Amber acted crazy. "All over. It's a general soreness. I thought I'd experience something different after a render."

"She absorbed most of Paris's residual." Raz's eyes flared. "Massive amounts of power would've been physically demanding, even for a Sixxer."

Sandra swung her legs over the edge of the table. "Apart from freezing, I feel fine. My worry is my never-ending chill. Paris could never keep warm. I think I'm experiencing the first stages of the virus."

Zach brought his laptop over to the group, and set the computer beside her. He poked at the augmenter strap. "The chill is more likely from your recent elevation changes. It's common for a Sixxer to have bursts of energy followed by little output for a while." He removed the belt from around her ribs and examined the sensor. "When Leon's light ran under your skin, I had an idea. I think the augmenter would work better directly against you, under your shirt. The skin contact might provide a stronger signal to my watch and allow you to channel your power to the sensor without any interference."

Raz helped secure the device around her middle. "Will it be enough to find Sean?"

Zach shrugged. "I'm sure Amber is behind me shaking her head."

Sandra looked over Zach's shoulder. *Yes. She's vehemently shaking her head.*

"She's not in the weeds creating new sensors. We have to try." Zach paused for a second. His hand rested on Sandra's leg. He waited until her gaze focused on him. "Sean is the most important person to try for, in my opinion."

Sandra's heart burst with tenderness. Omega was doing everything they could to get back Sean. She grappled for Raz's hand and squeezed it.

Raz brought their clasped fingers to his lips and kissed the back of her hand. "I didn't agree with Cameron on the decision to come here. If Sean is here, we aren't leaving without him."

Zach twisted his arm and read his watch. "Cam's been gone a while. Do you think he's having trouble with the anti-NEU?"

Leon gathered the medical supplies scattered about and tossed them back into his sack. "Cam's trip downstairs should've been easy and quick. You don't think Thom found him, do you?"

Amber got that bored look in her eye. "Unfortunately, our Nexus communications link that was supposed to occur from the render isn't working." Her sarcasm came out thick. "Because of Zach's inability to find a NEU we don't know what's blocking our cell signals. We can't call Cam."

Everyone stilled.

Zach dug his phone out of his pocket. "Shit. I *don't* have a signal."

"I'll go check on him." Leon turned to the door.

Raz grabbed his shoulder. "I'm the Transor and have the most control of the Nexus on this campus. I'll go see what's taking so long. Besides, I suspect none of you young whips can configure this anti-NEU, considering your age."

A loud chuffing sound burst from Zach's mouth. "Raz pegged you both, but their age doesn't give them the disadvantages. They don't understand how to operate tech. I'm amazed every time they send me a successful text message. It's bizarre."

"Har-de-har-har," Amber said. "I'll go with Raz for backup. You two stay and entertain Sandra."

"Cam's probably raiding his junk food drawer," Sandra said to their retreating figures. "He hasn't had a fix in a while."

Laughter filled the room and eased a little of the building tension. They all knew Cameron as well as she did. They were a family.

Leon turned back. "I can give you a burst of Nexus healing for your aches. Once we're all back, Cam will decide our next move. You should be as fit as you possibly can."

Zach once again put all his focus onto his laptop. Sandra didn't think he'd survive anywhere without it.

She nodded at Leon's request, and he placed his hands on her ankles. The same dingy yellow light covered her skin. A sense of calm entered her, but oppressive, smoky tendrils of gas floated from Leon's torso. Before panic could set in, an easy sleep overcame her. Although, her memory struggled to pinpoint something important as she dozed. She recalled the panic and oppressive smoke that had filled the hospital waiting room a few days ago, but instead of heeding the warning, she sank further toward sleep.

The last thing she heard was Zach.

"Your healing burst didn't work on her last time. How long before her pain pills wear off?"

Chapter Thirty-nine

PISTONS POUNDED IN Sandra's head. *Not again. Will I wake up this way every day?* Had the render weakened her immune system and created a gateway for the virus to activate? *No, that can't be true. Paris hadn't been in a render for months.* Her thoughts jumped back to an earlier discussion with Omega. Anyone might be infected and not show signs with a sleeper virus. A heavy citrus scent blasted Sandra in the face. Confusion entered her mind. Had Leon made lemonade? Were they still at Amber's house?

The overpowering odor penetrated her foggy brain and reminded Sandra of Thom. She blinked open her heavy eyelids. A harsh glare of a desk lamp forced them shut. Her head ached as though from a massive hangover. *If Thom is near, I have to run!* Her taut muscles stretched as tight as bowstrings. The surface under her head crackled when she moved. She rolled to her side and swung a leg over the edge of the leather couch. Her body protested, and the jerky movements sent lightning bolts into the back of her neck.

She lifted her upper body perhaps an inch or two, and a wave of nausea slammed into her like a punch. She lay back, and her hand skimmed across the cold tile floor. *A leather couch and a tile floor? Where in the hell …* The familiar furniture registered in her brain. She was still at HUP, but somehow she was now in Thom's university office. *How did I get here?* Her heart pounded. *Who brought me here?* Amber had left the classroom. Zach or Leon had drugged her and brought her to Thom. Hand delivered to his university man cave. Why? Zach had been methodical in leading them back to HUP. Omega, Raz and her believed the augmenter connected her to Sean.

Zach fooled them.

After a few minutes, the pressure in her head eased.

Whispered voices caught her attention, but concentration eluded her. She was as drunk as an after-party bachelorette. Yet, at the same time as hung over as a frat boy before, during and after Greek week. She listened to the sounds outside of the room. The voices grew louder, but sleep called to her. The drugs in her body told her to lay back and rest. It told her to close her eyes to blessed darkness and gain relief from the harsh room lighting. Surrendering would stop the pounding in her skull.

"I won't kill her." Thom was on the other side of the door.

Sandra stilled. Her eyes popped open.

"She's a part of his circle." A second, more reasonable, voice said. "What you're doing won't work."

It's Nazier. How will I fight both of them? I can barely lift my finger.

"She belongs to me. So does the little boy. I know what I'm doing."

Thom has Sean! We're so close. I can find him. She used the Nexus and reached out in her mind. Tingles spread within her palms, and Nexus energy coiled around her forearms. Yet, she felt no link, no sense of him.

Nazier huffed out an exasperated breath. A nervous shadow danced under the door. "You won't get the grant money this way. General Taft won't support you outside of Hamilton University."

"Time to stop my romance with Taft. I can find a better sugar daddy in private industry."

Panic settled into Sandra's chest. *Why can't I remember how I got here?* What about Raz? Nausea once again bubbled in her stomach. The ache was relentless.

"The virus worked." Thom continued. "We both got what we wanted."

"You're kidding, right? Paris died. The virus is an utter failure. We can't have it killing before it spreads. Your sleeper program in the nanobot device didn't work. The other test case can't be evaluated now. The nanobot virus can't transmit Nexus information in a dead body."

Nazier didn't sound like a man who had just lost his daughter. In fact, he sounded cold and driven in his work. *All that matters to him is success in destroying Sixxers.*

The door creaked open. Thom's voice inched closer. "We have to find another Zenith to infect. Paris was so close to getting into the circle again."

I was right. Thom never knew Paris was a Transitional. Nazier is still lying about her.

"We'll use the boy for testing," Nazier said.

Sandra's heart stopped.

"We don't need to. Sean was exposed to each new strain I created. He's bulletproof. No reaction. Now that Paris is gone, we'll find a home for him for further studies."

Sandra's entire body grew cold and clammy. Her heart raced to the point of pain. She labored to breathe through the intense fear.

"Sean is Raz's brat." Thom continued talking. "He's a natural Hybrid. The Nexus protects him from infections like it does for a Sixxer. I never thought a natural Hybrid would come from a Zenith and a Sixxer."

Because a Hybrid didn't. Sean is the product of a Sixxer and a Transitional, like my baby.

Thom entered the room in a wave of sweet-smelling lemon. In the light of the desk lamp, his bleach-tipped locks competed with the dark roots. His black hair appeared to eat up the only lucent part of his body. Need entered her abdomen. *He's still gorgeous as hell. Lucifer reincarnated, and like the devil, he makes me want him.* The panic building inside reminded her of the uncontrollable terror of her attacks, but something else was underneath. Her power hummed and gave her an astonishing control over her fear.

Thom noticed Sandra was awake and stilled. He recovered and shut the door behind him. His ice-filled gaze traveled from her head to her feet. "How do you feel?"

A shiver full of both desire and disgust attacked her. "Do you care?" *Why do I want him to care? I have to get away from him so I can think. Wait ... No. I have to stay and find Sean.* The competing emotions warred inside her mind.

He set his laptop on the edge of the desk. "I loved you way too much."

Sandra snorted. "Really?"

"I expected you to be out for longer." He raked his hands through his hair. After thoroughly disheveling his pride and joy hairstyle, he shoved a hand into his pocket.

You're always falling short on your testing and expectations, aren't you? Sandra brought her hand to her nose to block the ever-increasing perfume surrounding him. "How did I get here? Do you have Raz or the others?"

"You disgust me."

Thom wrinkled his nose as though a bad odor had assaulted *him* instead of her. Sandra sat up. "Ditto."

"Since you're obviously feisty after the sedative, let's not waste time and work." He clasped her hand.

Sandra squeezed back in kind, and Thom made his typical satisfactory grunt. She shook her head but followed him like a puppy. Now, she repulsed herself. She couldn't resist him. *Why can't I fight him? I don't want to do anything he says!* They walked about eight feet down the hallway to the next door.

Thom entered his code into the security keypad. The entrance to his private laboratory opened. His fingers bit into the tender flesh of her upper arm. "I learned a lot from Paris, as did Nazier, but my first concern was how she had a kid with no one finding out until about a year ago."

"How could you?" Sandra shook her head. "You killed her. You used her to test the virus you stole from me. You've turned into a monster."

Thom pulled her inside the room. "I have the power to do anything I want."

His words rolled a blackness over her soul. The citrus odor that hovered near him increased in intensity in the enclosed space. Sandra coughed as the stench overwhelmed her senses.

He pulled her close. The heavy coffee scent on his breath blew over her face. The dark ring around his ice-blue eyes quivered before it expanded and filled the iris. A small ring of blinding light remained around his pupil. The circle of blue mesmerized her. Sensations of attraction hit her like a sledgehammer.

No!

Thom smiled. "Is this what he makes you feel?"

Sandra shivered in revulsion. He knew exactly how to force her to feel this arousal and she hated him for manipulating her at such a level.

"What does your alien command you to do?" He stroked her face. "I was willing to forgive you until I found out about the successful implantation. I never thought for a second you'd be a Sixxer breeder." He released her arms and laughed when she didn't move.

She couldn't move. Even after a render, with its healing effects and energy shots, she couldn't break free from his super human mental control.

Thom curled his lip. "Your whoring sickened me. You tossed me aside for what he offered. If you want to be his slave, then I can certainty grant your wishes."

Thom's aura scared the shit out of Sandra. *Is the Nexus power as benevolent as Raz preached?* The changes the Nexus brought her, the abyss of two renders and Thom's power to control her, emphasized the Nexus's evil side. The alien force wanted her surrender. Raz's render with her and Omega had become their enslavement. Her hands trembled. Her fingertips burned. The Nexus tore her apart from the inside.

Thom turned away.

She stepped back. *Breathe! Focus. Calm down. Thom's power turned me against Raz at the house, and here the scent of his drugs are ultra-concentrated. What can I do? How do I manipulate my energy like Raz or Omega?*

"Why are you so quiet, Sands?"

Thom's question broke her out of her trance. His back was to her, but when he turned, her body attuned to his vibrational energy. His seductive nature was unstoppable. Her feet shuffled closer to him. She needed … wanted …

In a surreal movement of graceful execution, he twisted and wrapped an arm around her. His breath, familiar yet unwelcome, fluttered hot against her ear. "Are you thinking of your lover?"

She moaned. *No. Fight him!* "Don't touch me." Her voice carried in a husky timber around the room.

He yanked her flush against him, and she spat in his face.

He wiped the mucus from his cheek and then squeezed her tighter.

She pushed against his chest with all her strength. A vibrational tone entered her arms and flowed into her hands. The pain in her fingers reached a level of agony that bowed her body backward. Nexus light swirled and circled around her wrists. Trails of white smoke slithered between their bodies.

"Fuck." Thom wrenched away. His hands were pink and blistered. His face contorted. "The son-of-a-bitch won't be able to find you." His spittle rained over her face. "No miracle rescue is on the horizon." He shoved her into a chair.

After an odd movement of his wrist, she was once again paralyzed. The plastic of the augmenter strap dug into the undersides of her breasts. She crossed her fingers Thom wouldn't find it. Zach could use it to pinpoint her location. *Right? He can track me. A signal must travel back to his tech watch.* That is if he hadn't been the one to deliver her to Thom's office.

She couldn't stop her words of bravado. "Maybe not alone, but with Cam's help, Raz will find me."

His soft laughter sent chills of dread and anxiety through her stomach. It raced along her spine. Bile rose in the back of her throat.

"My poor little Sandra. You don't understand anything. The intent was never to kill Paris. Her father definitely wanted her alive. She was such a find, so hopeful to discovering the key to unlock the Nexus." He looked at her and asked, "Do you think he loves you? Did you think your dear friend Paris had your best interests at heart?"

"You used and manipulated her. I know better than to believe any of your lies. Now you'll do the same to Sean, an innocent child."

"Wrong. So wrong." He stood before her. His fingers spider-walked down the side of her face and over her shoulder. "Sean's safe. Don't worry."

"If you hurt him, you will suffer," she said frantically.

"Oh, Sands."

She sucked in a breath. Her pet name on his lips excited her. He spoke with such love and tenderness. *Lies. He makes me do and accept everything I hated.*

He leaned over the chair and placed a hand on either side of her head. "I would've taken you back. I wanted you back. I'd have given you everything you desired."

A popping and itching sensation activated the nerves in her limbs. She worked through the pain, but the constant flares of energy taxed her strength. Rational thought left her. She narrowed her eyes. Her words were guttural. "You left me. I couldn't have children, and you deserted me."

"You're ready to give up everything for a freak of nature. Don't you get it? He's a Sixxer and wanted a good time with a human woman. He used his abilities to get into your pants. What other explanation is there? He already had a family. He can't give you what we had." Thom clutched his hands over his heart.

"You mean a child?" Sandra wanted to regret the words, but she didn't. She wanted to wound him and cut him deeper than any knife ever could. He had nothing she wanted. Thom used fake emotional responses to control her. The love between her and Raz wasn't conjured like a voodoo spell.

The dark rings in his irises consumed the narrow band of light. They turned black. "You never trusted me. I would've given you a child if you'd only been patient. I figured out how to manipulate the drugs so you'll beg me for it. From this day forward, you'll have many opportunities to have children." He massaged her neck. He brought his face closer, hot breath snaking around her lips.

She wanted to gag, but the desire to kiss him overwhelmed her. *I smell his lemon scent. Fight it, Sandra. Fight it!* "What have you done to yourself?" she whispered.

He knelt in front of her. "I've improved myself. I did everything in my power to give you a child, Sands."

"My leaving wasn't about a child, but about your betrayal. All of the women you chose over me and a family."

"The surrogates had our implanted embryos."

"What?" *He's losing his mind.* The acid in her stomach bubbled, and she swallowed past her gag reflex.

"I was using your eggs for the surrogates."

She sprang back as though burned. "I never had my eggs harvested." A cold tingling sensation ran from her stomach to her fingertips.

"Any child had to be yours, Sands. You were the one who'd been taking the Sixxer fertility drugs. We thought perhaps the embryos weren't attaching to you. A new host was the fix."

Host? She wasn't a host, but a person. "I caught you having sex with interns in this very lab."

"My high sex drive was a side effect of me taking the fertility drugs. I had to increase my sperm count. The surrogates had to undergo the same fertility cocktail so the embryos would implant. The formula affects some differently than others. Neither I, nor Dr. Nazier, has figured out why. I was a part of the small percentage of individuals who can't control our sexual impulses. If we did, we'd go mad."

Sandra's laughter rumbled from her chest in a low tone but had a maniacal quality. Had he really just said that without sex he'd go crazy? She recalled his notes. Paris's experimental group had turned into sex maniacs. Thom had dosed himself with the same drugs and hadn't been able to fight its effects. *No. He hadn't wanted to fight it. He still wants it now. With me. He's working for Nazier so he can have access to the fertility drugs. A child was his sole purpose.* The hideous realization that Thom would've used their child in his quest for Nexus power stole her breath away.

He stroked her hair. "I can see the judgment in your face. I'm only human, sweetheart. Sixxer pheromones are more powerful than you can imagine. The percentage of humans who respond can't resist, not even a tiny bit. A pure chemical reaction can't be denied. I couldn't tell you at the time because you had no idea Sixxers existed." He jeered. "You've since been educated, haven't you?"

"I've been educated on your failures. Nazier won't let you take his research."

"Nazier can go fuck himself. No one can be trusted, not even blood. The drugs are my own creation. I wasn't responsible for Raz turning Nazier's daughter against him." His hand grazed her breast. He nestled his palm over her belly. "Funny how life throws you an ace when you could only hope for a pair. We just needed to find you a Sixxer stud." He spoke into her neck. "What I have now is even better. My own little Sixxer baby to raise."

Chapter Forty

RAZ SHUT THE door to cooler thirty-nine, or more appropriately named, the door to Cameron's secret bunker. Omega assumed HUP was compromised, but nothing had been disturbed since Raz and Sandra had arrived with Paris, which made Raz speculate the attack at the children's camp had been a tip-off to General Taft and not Nazier's move.

Cameron walked the aisles, gathering items he'd left behind days ago. He dug another HUP-branded duffle bag out of a cabinet and dropped all the supplies inside.

Two other laptops joined the bag, along with a drawer of junk food that made Raz's mouth water. His hunger pains growled in protest.

Amber chuckled. "His eating disorder comes in handy, sometimes. He'll share once we get back to the classroom."

Configuration had taken them ten minutes longer than Raz anticipated to get the anti-NEU up and running. The one he held was old and full of piss. The black box, about the size of a car battery, generated a healthy motorized sound as it churned out a wave of heat. *Outdated radiant technology, my ass.* These units were the best at blocking outgoing Nexus energy and reflecting it back into the circles. The wave-like barrier coming from the device would also create a boundary that'd interfere with any Nexus Emissions Units. He breathed a sigh of relief.

Even though Sandra's vibrational quality had lowered since the render, having this small amount of protection to hide them from Chasers had been well worth the risk of coming downstairs in search of Cameron. "The output from this anti-NEU will make everyone ravenous."

Amber leaned against the wall. "I hate to admit it, Raz Donovan, but you're growing on me. Your mad skills come in handy."

"Don't get used to them." Raz held the anti-NEU under his arm. "We'll keep the box with us."

Cameron flung the duffle strap over his shoulder. He slapped Raz on the back. "I couldn't have made the anti-NEU work without you. Thanks. We relied on the newer one for years." He pulled out his phone then tapped the anti-NEU casing. "This old piece of junk gave us back cell service. I'll let Zach know we're on our way back. Am, did you notice any activity while we were in the cooler?"

"This place is a ghost town." She stood, walked beside them to the main door and stopped with a hand on the push bar. "The science behind how the NEUs and anti-NEUs work is beyond me, but I can't help thinking Thom or Nazier would've covered this campus with technology, if only in an observational capacity. Make sure no one was poking their noses around, Sixxer or human. Zach's augmenter, while specifically made to enhance Sandra's power, should've found something here. The campus is too quiet."

Raz nodded. "I agree. After Cameron left a few days ago, I was expecting a frenzy of movement here. Nothing has been touched in this lab, despite this room being Sandra's place of research. How unlikely is it Nazier didn't anticipate an M83 breach? Once he and Thom determined Sandra was with us, he would've torn this place to shreds and set up surveillance."

Only a few days had passed since Raz had been here with Paris, but the passage of time felt like years.

Cameron punched the glass door of a familiar small cabinet. The window cracked under the slight pressure, and the metal frame buckled in half. He stole the medicine from inside. The anti-NEU was already funneling power back to the circle.

Amber cocked her head to the side. "Did you just brawny your way into a coded and locked cabinet?"

Cameron examined the condition of the cabinet. "Leon isn't the only one of us who can beat the shit out of stuff without harm. I'm a bad-ass motherfucker."

Raz smiled. "The box is feeding us energy. I'm still shocked at how much M83 has limited you."

When Cameron turned, a dim flicker of light glistened in his eyes. "Is it possible Nazier didn't know Sandra was tagging along?"

Amber pursed her lips. "Thom knew from the beginning. What's the difference between Nazier and Thom? They both have secrets to hide. What one knows, the other knows, as well."

Cameron shoved the pill bottles into several of his cargo pockets. He tugged a handgun from his waistband and joined them at the door. "I've always liked how your mind works, Amber." He tapped the anti-NEU. "We have leverage with this box. Let's find Sean and get the hell out of here."

They made their way back to the classroom. As they approached, Raz slowed his march when he saw the door ajar. Nexus energy infused his muscles with power, and they expanded. The stitching in his shirt tore in several places. He tossed a grateful glance at the anti-NEU under his arm. Normally, his Sixxer power wouldn't have stayed hidden with such a reactive charge. Although, something was off. Seeing such a threat as an open and unguarded door should've sent Raz into a full blitz.

Cameron communicated with hand signals, and they eased toward the room.

Amber pushed open the door.

Zach sat on the floor by the storage container with his head cradled in his hands.

Raz secured the rest of the room. No one else was there.

Amber examined Zach. "He's disoriented, but he doesn't have a head injury."

Cameron stood as sentry at the door. "What in the hell happened?"

"Find her. Now!" Raz shoved the laptop into Zach's hands. "Use the augmenter signal."

Zach's eyes rolled around in his head. "It's not that easy." He moaned. "I'm not sure what happened … How long have I been out?"

Amber rummaged in Leon's medical bag then waved her hand at Cameron. He threw her a few of the bottles he'd taken from the lab.

She read the labels, chose one ad wrestled open the tube. "We've been gone ten minutes."

Raz slapped the pills from her hands. "When will wake up to the fact you have healing energy at your disposal at all times? The one who should rely on pills is Cameron, and his Sixxer power is returning."

Amber's eyes flashed emerald green, and a beam of light pushed Raz backward against a desk.

"You just emphasized my point, princess."

Amber pulled back her shoulders, bristling like a threatened wolf.

Raz touched Zach's shoulder, and orange energy entered Zach's body.

He jerked from the charge and came out of his stupor.

Raz nodded at Amber then tapped the computer on Zach's lap. "Get busy with the signal."

Zach pointed to the black box on the desk. "With the anti-NEU working, the closer we are to the box, the less likely any signals will register from the augmenter. We'd have to be close to Sandra."

"Work your magic, Zach." Raz was a hair's breadth away from beating every single one of them to a pulp. The last of his rational thoughts kept him from exploding into a mad beast. He looked up at Cameron. "The good news? We found the mole. If I ever see Leon again, I'll take him out."

Amber jumped to her feet. "Whoa. What's this *pendejo* saying? The room got hot, and Leon moved her. Protocol. Did you have an e-loc established here, Cam?"

"No." Cameron kept his back against the door. "I've given Leon little intel. He's working on his own."

Zach opened the laptop and brought up the augmenter's central console. "Then we have no leads on where they might be. I might triangulate a signal. Damn it. Leon has saved my life more than once. I can't believe this."

White hot light shot from Raz's eyes and illuminated the floor around Zach. "This is your fault, asshole. Coming to HUP with Sandra weak and Cameron with little Nexus energy was the stupidest mission risk of the century."

Amber puffed up her chest and got into Raz's face. "Don't blame

Zach because you can't keep your circle safe."

"Don't you get it, Amber?" Cameron's calm voice penetrated the tension. "What will happen to Sandra? What about Sean? Pointing fingers isn't getting us any closer to either of them."

She whirled, ready to strike. "Accusing Leon of being a traitor isn't right, Cam. We're a team."

"Raz and I knew there was a leak. Omega had a breach. I'm with Raz on this one. Leon's the most likely of the team to have transmitted information to M83. He wasn't around when Sean went missing. Now Sandra is missing, and he's gone again. Zach, do whatever is in your skill set to find a signal."

Amber checked every weapon on her body. She locked and loaded. "We can't only rely on tech for this. I'll start a perimeter."

Raz found his weapon and ammo in his bag. With as little instinct as Omega had in using the Nexus, Raz took whatever was useful against Chasers. "Create two teams. Cameron and I. Zach and Amber. Our telelink is still shallow, so use cell phones to keep track of the others. We weren't gone long. She has to be in the building." Sandra and Sean were his life. *I'll get them back.*

Cameron stood at Raz's side and stared at Zach and Amber. "Raz is one of us. Sandra is one of us. Leon betrayed Omega and M83, but the four us of in this room are a team. We'll work together to find our missing people."

"How will the anti-NEU interfere with the augmenter signal?" Raz asked Zach.

"It's not looking good. I'm picking up a lot of weird-ass signals. We must leave the anti-NEU here and hope its signal radius includes the building."

Cameron raked his hand over his short haircut. "The old anti-NEU is boosting our Nexus energy. Raz can telelink with Sandra or Sean if we get close."

Amber stood in her full soldier glory, a killing machine ready to kick ass. "Sandra can't control her power any more than we do. Raz can never reach her through a telelink. Both individuals have to have control over what they're doing."

Zach set the laptop on a desk and stood, stretching his neck and shoulders. "Let's find General Taft and Thomas Robins and take them out."

Cameron rubbed the back of his neck. "No, we can't kill Thom. Sandra has an unstable artificial bond to him."

Zach stilled. "Wait. Say that again."

Cameron shook his head and paced in front of the door. "You and Sandra showed me the research where Thom experimented on himself."

"Yeah, so?"

"He subjected her to Sixxer fertility treatments. He was also taking them. As a Zenith, he was playing with an artificial connection to the Nexus. All those close to him would've been bound by it."

Amber's body stiffened. Her face lost expression. "His desire for a child was absorbed by the Nexus, which is attached to Sandra's Nexus aura."

Raz pounded the desk beside him. "No. He let her go. A Zenith bond wouldn't last this long, not with her being pregnant with my son."

"Somehow, it has," Zach said. "Sandra thought Thom had drugged her, but his artificial connection has grown, which explains all the weird signals we've been getting on the augmenter."

"Shit," Amber said.

"Thom figured out how to retain his Nexus connection," Zach continued. "This will make M83 high command shit a load of bricks."

Cameron's eyes clouded over like a threatening storm. Sparks of white lightning illuminated them. "Zach, can you track the fake energy?"

Amber closed her eyes. "What about Sean? Without Sandra, we have no connection to him. I can't lose another child, Cam."

Raz whipped up his head. *Another child? Who is she talking about?*

Cameron placed his hands on her shoulders.

The act of tenderness disoriented Raz. What his eyes observed didn't fit with the assassin persona he'd come to associate with Amber, the one standing right before him. Her eyes glistened, not with Nexus light, but with unshed tears. *For my son?*

Zach moved closer and wrapped an arm around her waist. "Sean is strong. He's a survivor."

Amber came out of her slouch. A small burst of power branched out from her chest. The tendrils of green light swayed like tree limbs in the breeze. They caressed Raz's face and swirled around his head. The telelink was automatic, like Amber had done it before.

Her thoughts entered his mind. *I lost my unborn child three years ago. I won't allow any of us to lose Sean or Sandra's child.*

All of the erected walls around Amber now made perfect sense. Raz wasn't sure if Amber had been aware of her broadcast, but he'd respect her need for privacy in her pain. "If I'm in range of Sean, I'll be able to telelink with him. Once I get a clear connection with either of them, I'll blitz, and we'll be the midnight laser show on campus."

Amber focused on him. "I'll be ready."

Zach raised his hand for attention. "Thom's artificial connection might allow him to control Sandra. Hold back until we can pull her away."

Zach's watch let out a steady ping. Everyone stilled. Zach popped his neck. "Time to rock and roll. We've got something. Divide and conquer. Am and I will do a snatch-and-grab and meet you back here in twenty minutes. Trust me, this campus isn't that big. We'll find our people."

CHAPTER FORTY-ONE

RAZ DOUBLE-CHECKED his ammo. "The guns are for surprise attacks. Human Chasers should fall with a few shots unless they're doped up on adrenaline drugs."

Amber adjusted her body armor. "It's protocol."

Zach laughed and slapped Amber on the back. "Most of your stuff is *not* protocol, but your style can't be beat."

Cameron grunted. "We might need more than a few bullets to take down Thom if he has tapped into his Zenith energy. Are you ready?"

Raz stilled. He glared at Amber and Zach. This wasn't their typical engagement. "Whatever training you've had must be reconciled with your increased power. The Nexus will be at the surface, no matter what happens. If the Chasers are high, then you must go with your gut instincts. Relying on man-made guns will get you captured."

Twin flares of light responded in Amber's and Zach's eyes.

Cameron stood at the classroom exit. He pulled aside the taped blanket and peeked out of the window. "This is a precaution. There's no confirmation on General Taft's presence at HUP. Nazier and Thom are the two biggest worries."

Zach concentrated on his watch.

Raz willed the augmenter signal to improve.

Zach jerked his head toward the anti-NEU. "We'll have to leave it here. Hide it under a desk in case someone snoops around. Its proximity *is* messing with the augmenter application on my watch."

Raz grabbed the black box. He went to the front of the room and placed the anti-NEU on the table. He kicked an empty storage container with his foot. Sandra's blanket and coat were lying on the lid. He shoved the three items inside the plastic carton and pushed it under the table. "We'll cover as much space as possible. Cameron and I will start with the basement level. Zach and Amber will go to the third floor. We'll search room by room."

Cameron pushed open the door. A slight metallic click sounded as the door latch disengaged. "Two labs and a utility closet are in the basement. Let's start on the first floor then make our way down. Zach and Amber can clear the third then the second floor. Zach and I both have badges and codes to enter the lab. We'll meet at cooler thirty-nine instead of here."

Zach popped up his head from his computer. "Affirmative." He shut the laptop screen and hid the computer with the anti-NEU. "This won't do me any good. Am and I will swing by and pick it up before we head down to the basement."

They split up. Amber and Zach headed for the elevators.

Cameron waved Raz to follow him to the end of the hallway. "The first and second floors are classrooms and offices, with the second having another classroom lab. Although, it's nothing like the basement labs. Amber and Zach should be able to search it quickly. The third floor contains an administrative wing. If she's here, then we'll find her."

"You think Thom took her back to the house?"

Cameron cringed. "Another possibility. We'll verify here then continue the search back at the neighborhood."

They searched several classrooms and came to Sandra's office. Cameron went inside. He slid the landscape painting from the wall. The back popped off with a flick of Cameron's finger, and he pried the tiny camera out of the corner of the wooden frame. "You never know who might've been in here in the last few days. Zach can take a look." He rummaged around Sandra's office.

Raz kept an eye on the hallway. They hadn't seen signs of anyone on the first floor, not even evidence of the cleaning crew Zach had mentioned when they'd arrived. They were wasting time here. A pulse of Nexus light entered his chest.

Daddy?

Raz's heart pounded. "Sean's here!" he hissed. He couldn't

believe he felt his son's presence so easily. There must've been something blocking their communication.

Cameron spun on a toe. "Where?"

Raz shut the door and leaned back against it. "I heard him through a telelink."

Cameron pocketed the camera and stepped closer. "Can you reach him again?"

Raz concentrated. Sean's Nexus energy surged through him, but the clear connection he'd just had was gone. "I can't get him back. He has to be close."

How far do you think he'd be?" Cameron asked. "If he's so close, why can't you reach him again?"

"The anti-NEU blocked signals to Zach's augmenter. Sean must be behind another anti-NEU or maybe the wrecker Zach mentioned earlier."

Cameron and Raz ran out of the office and into the next classroom. Cameron watched for Chasers

Raz searched the room. "I don't know much about wreckers. The devices somehow can hide some Sixxer power, but not others." They searched every row of the lecture hall. Raz even searched under the chairs in the hopes that Sean might've gotten away and hid.

Cameron opened the storage closet. "Zach couldn't locate any other devices within the building with his laptop."

Raz raced to the exit. "Nothing is right, but something is blocking our connection. Let's move on."

Cameron grabbed his arm. "Keep your cool. We'll continue room by room. We won't fail this mission." His phone buzzed, and he glanced at the screen. "Zach has a signal from Sandra on the second floor. They will bring her to the lab. Sean must be close to us, then."

Raz inhaled a steadying breath. He was so close to having both of them back in his arms the urgency within him drove his decisions. Centering his mind, he prepared for attack. The electrical impulses flowing in his veins and along his nerves were easier to control.

Cameron displayed no light within him. The render at the old retail store had given him nothing in terms of Nexus power, and now, away from the anti-NEU, Cameron was dark again. Once Sandra had woken up, she was weak, but her power returned immediately because the augmenter worked again.

Raz cocked his head in thought. Cameron was Transitional. He was within his power and should've absorbed the energy of the render, too. Cameron should've revived his power once they'd arrived at HUP.

He opened the classroom door.

Raz pushed it shut. "Have you ever had a Nexus hum? Had light enter your body?"

Cameron narrowed his eyes. "I'm on your side, Raz. My ability isn't relevant right now."

Raz wouldn't let him open the door. "Sandra recovered as soon as she woke up. You haven't gotten one spark of Nexus energy since the render. Did you have any before?"

Cameron stared into Raz's eyes. "My elevation was unlike Sandra's. More gradual."

Raz's mind spun with the limited information he'd been able to find on M83 at the children's camp. "Why are we at HUP? What makes Hamilton University so special to Thom and Nazier?"

Raz could tell his question also spun the wheels in Cameron's head.

Cameron backed away from the door. "This university is quiet. They don't have a lot of officers poking their heads in their business."

Raz also stepped away from the door. Cameron wasn't going to leave. "Or, let's go to a bigger scale. Why is General Taft keeping them here? Thom, Nazier, and General Taft have plenty of other, bigger universities, or even private facilities, at their disposal for fertility and virus research."

Cameron scrubbed his face. "What are you getting at?"

Raz scrubbed his face and looked around the empty room. Could there be cameras hidden as Amber suggested? "They're leading us into a snare. They know they can capture us. I'm weak and they know you can't rely on your power, only ammunition."

Cameron whipped out his cell phone. Instead of texting, he pushed the call button for Amber. He held the phone to his mouth. "We're walking into a trap. Get back to the original classroom ASAP." He ended the call without waiting for an acknowledgement.

Raz pushed on the door and disengaged the latch. Voices raised in friendly banter echoed down the hallway. He held his finger to his lips.

Gun at the ready, Cameron ducked beside him.

Raz moved the door so barely a crack was visible.

Two men walked the long expanse of the hall. As they approached, the one in a dark weatherproof jacket turned on the overhead lights.

The blast of fluorescent lamps blinded Raz. He blinked through the glare.

The other man wore a business suit but was young enough to look like a kid playing dress-up.

Raz shut the door without an audible click of the latch. He leaned over and whispered, "It's Nazier, with someone I don't recognize."

"Which way are they going?"

"To the basement."

Several minutes passed. Raz surveyed the hall again. No one was there.

Cameron followed close. Raz had no doubt Cameron had his back. They were a few feet from the classroom door. A few feet from Sandra.

The elevator chimed as it stopped on the floor. Amber and Zach rounded the corner of the connecting hallway and stopped in front of Cameron and Raz. Alone.

Thom and Sandra stepped out of the opening doors.

Raz's power went crazy. Nexus heat filled his lungs, and his biceps strained his clothes as they increased in mass.

Thom pulled Sandra toward them. He came to a dead stop when he noticed the four Omega soldiers blocking his path. "Aw, sweetheart, you planned a surprise party for me. Exhilarating. Too bad we can't retrieve the booby prize inside your office."

Cameron held up the mini camera. "Do you mean this?"

Thom smiled. "Two points to Omega, but I deleted the contents this morning. You'll only see yourselves. I wanted to make sure Sandra hadn't had visitors. My hunch was right."

White heat and diffused Nexus light jumped between Raz's hands. "Let her walk over here, Thom. You've nowhere to go."

Thom tightened his grip on her. "In this building? I can go

anywhere I want."

"I can't break away." Sandra struggled, but neither Sixxer nor Nexus power assisted her. Thom clutched her arm so hard his knuckles turned white.

Zach is right. Thom can control her. Raz's energy was at full capacity, but no blitz, no out-of-control spikes of heat. What kind of advanced tech was in this building? He couldn't conceive how a wrecker could be that effective. Disruption of the Nexus like this took massive amounts of Transor and mind-reader control. The other option of a gadget preventing Nexus power nicked Raz's confidence.

He didn't like the black gleam in Thom's eyes, giving them a glazed-over appearance. All the light had been sucked out of his soul. The reaction was opposite what any Sixxer would have when channeling Nexus power. Was Thom's false connection causing the abnormality?

Raz stepped forward. "Why'd you think you could take her from us?"

"Each of you has been fooled by a master." Thom stepped back at Raz's advancement. He placed himself in front of Sandra, blocking any attempt at Omega reaching for her.

Raz mirrored Thom's hand movement, imagining he was squeezing Thom's neck. "We're a solid unit. Leon is our enemy now."

Thom narrowed his eyes.

Raz and Omega blocked the only way out.

Thom backed away toward the basement steps. He stumbled and caused Sandra to misstep and twist her ankle. Ignoring her cry, he dragged her down until they reached the lower level.

Sandra attempted to wrench free of Thom. She flung her arm toward Thom's face, but he blocked it with a flick of his wrist.

Wrapping his arm around her waist, he carried her backward to the lab entrance.

Omega had him, now. Raz and the team followed down the steps. "Give up, Thom. You're not taking her."

Thom snickered. "I already have."

Sandra undulated her body against Thom, and his hold loosened. "I'm not going anywhere with you!"

"We're going to get you out of this situation, Sandra." Cameron jogged down two steps.

Finger-like branches of energy flung from Thom's limbs. The power wrapped around Sandra in a cocoon of gray and black smoke. Thom's gaze met Raz's. "Are you sure you can trust Omega?"

Apprehension filled Raz's body. Thom's eyes hypnotized him and sent a wave of dark energy into his mind. Raz pushed away the seeds of doubt. *Leon is the traitor. The others wouldn't have stayed if they were working against us.*

"We're a team," Raz said.

Thom's black pupils were empty orbs ringed with light. "Why did Sandra come find me then, Romeo?"

Sandra kicked and squirmed against the smoke. Bursts of electrical energy flickered off her arms and hands. "No. Don't believe him." Each wave of power she generated, Thom absorbed.

What the hell? What is he? He can't possible be just a Zenith.

Thom smiled. "Can you see how pure her connection is? Her newfound Nexus control was enough to knock out your techie and send Leon running. She's been with me the entire time."

Zach stepped beside Raz and shook his head. "He's trying to mislead us. Sandra was too weak."

Raz shook his head. "Leon's hand delivery doesn't imply Sandra wanted to find you. Your delusions are extensive."

Thom sneered. "You're as stupid as this bitch." He dragged them both down another step. His eyes again flashed with gray light. "You've been fooled by both of your lovers. The techie and henchwoman behind you aren't smart enough to fool a true Sixxer, but two Zeniths working together are sure to get the job done."

Amber moved into Raz's peripheral vision. Shoulder-to-shoulder with Cameron, she raised her rifle, sighted and pointed it directly at Thom's head. "When we get done, the only bitch around here will be you."

Thom laughed. "What innocents we have. Maybe you should ask yourself why your fearless leader knows so much classified information. Cameron is always one step in front of General Taft, isn't he?"

"Nice try, asshole," Sandra scoffed. "No way in hell I'd believe anything you tell me. Raz and Amber won't believe you, either."

Amber smirked. "For once, Sandra is spot on."

Thom cocked his head to the side. "How about I know why your lover boy bleeds so easily."

Amber froze. Her head pulled back from the scope. "What are you talking about?"

"The headaches. The blackouts and convulsions at random times. Did you think we weren't watching Omega's every move? Nazier and I knew you were here the entire time." He squeezed Sandra's neck. "Although, my ex-wife's involvement came as a surprise."

Amber narrowed her eyes. She stepped back, but kept her aim on Thom. "You're one sneaky bastard, but not good enough to hide observations on our team. We would've have spotted you."

Thom's laughter filled the hall and echoed off the walls. His light-filled eyes darkened into black bottomless holes.

The hairs stood up on Raz's neck.

"Ignore him, Amber." Cameron walked up behind her. "Don't let him divide us."

"Yes, Amber, dear. Please, ignore me. It's exactly what he wants you to do. He's exceptional at deception. He lied to Sandra for years." Thom backed up to the lab entrance and fumbled with the security pad.

Sandra coughed. "No more than you."

The energy in Raz's fingers was itching to break free. His muscles flexed and strained, but the point of full Nexus control eluded him.

Thom looked right at Raz. "Ask your dear Cameron why Omega never participated in a render? Why your team has never formed a circle?"

Thom doesn't know me and Omega were in a render a few hours ago. That little piece of information will work to our advantage.

"Do you know what this crazy asshole is talking about?" Amber asked.

"M83 stopped renders," Raz said. "The decision wasn't Cameron's. I'm surprised you and Nazier didn't know that."

Thom grew more frustrated by the minutes when the keypad wouldn't accept his code. "We know Cameron can't render."

Sandra's energy shot out to Raz. *He doesn't know what me and Cameron are.* Her thoughts entered his mind, frantic and high on adrenaline.

Did her link only exist between the two of them, or did Thom have access to her mind, as well?

"Don't believe his lies, Amber," Cameron said as Amber moved away. "You can trust me."

Thom appeared trapped until he removed a university security badge from his pocket. "Cameron's headaches and shaking aren't because he's human. He's a Zenith. A willing one who was working for General Taft."

Raz snapped to attention. After discovering Leon had betrayed the group, accusations such as this would add fuel to the fire. Could Zach and Amber trust Cameron? Would Raz?

"That's not possible. You're a liar." Amber narrowed her sights.

"We discovered the missing pieces. Humans can be just like you." Thom flicked his finger and the tip of Amber's gun barrel moved up slightly.

Amber tensed and tightened her hands on the weapon. A trickle of sweat ran along her temple.

Raz watched in horror at Thom's ability to physically manipulate Amber with telekinesis.

She repositioned. "Shut your fucking mouth. I know what a god-damned Zenith is. Let go of Sandra, or I'll plug you."

"If Cameron was a Zenith, he'd be dead right now." Raz said.

Thom cocked his head. "You're all in a circle now. Oh Raz, your decision for a render was really stupid." He laughed and laughed. "This is too sweet. The render signed all your death sentences."

"Your experiments have no effect on me." Raz shuffled his feet and hoped he was right.

He tapped his badge and entered the security code again. The lab security locks disengaged. He pushed open the door. "The sleeper virus takes time to work. Paris didn't realize she was a walking time bomb."

Sandra nodded. "He's right. It's only a matter of time before all of us come down with the symptoms of the virus."

Thom preened. "We created a virus that attacks the snippets responsible for Nexus connection, but the connections are oh-so-subtle. The best methods were Zenith infection with a sleeper virus until they could be in a render. The virus didn't affect the Zeniths. They were carriers. Then M83 prohibited renders. We had to find Sixxers in hiding who knew how to render. I manipulated the virus with Z-211 so the Zeniths wouldn't die." His black gaze held on to Raz's, and he whispered, "Your family is next."

Power and anger built inside Raz. The fury hit him with such violence his biceps bulged. His pecs flexed and tore his T-shirt. Light exploded from his hands and wrapped finger-like tendrils of blue smoke around Thom's neck.

Sandra broke free of his hold but didn't move away. She couldn't. Thom still controlled her. How?

Raz lifted Thom until the tips of his toes no longer touched the floor. Just like he imagined he would. He threw Thom against the wall, and blood spurted down the paint following the path of Thom's dislodged tooth.

Thom whooped and snickered in a mixture of madness and amusement. "Paris volunteered to be changed. She wanted Sixxers dead."

"You're wrong. Paris didn't volunteer. She only wanted to get away from all of you." Raz said.

"She developed Sixxer power on her own? Like Cameron did? Omega's commander was General Taft's right-hand man about seven years ago. He volunteered for a Sixxer experimentation. A year after Cameron disappeared, Nazier discovered he was here as an M83 unit commander." Thom shook his head and mumbled. "Must've been a delayed reaction, like Paris."

Sandra shook her head. "Cam isn't a carrier."

A metallic ping echoed in the stairwell. A dart flew past Sandra's head.

"Raz, get down!" Zach screamed.

The three Omega soldiers turned their back on Thom to defend their position. He had led them into the trap.

"Raz ..." Sandra called, but her own voice came out weak and small.

Thom yanked her inside the door.

Sandra's telelink attempt hit him like a bulldozer. *Sean's close. His aura is reaching me.*

Fog surrounded his vision. *I'll link to him. Keep your power close so Thom can't hear us.*

An explosion roared beside Raz's head.

A smattering of plaster and wood particles hit Sandra's face.

Thom held out his hand. A shimmer of light, vibration, and lemon essence formed a ball in the center of his palm. The hallway reeked of the heavy smell of Thom's false power. Erratic energy cycled around his hand. Thom entered the lab. He used the door for cover and engaged the security lock.

They no longer had eyes on Sandra.

Raz pulled the Nexus to the surface of his body. He kept the Nexus close and at the ready. The shield energy was dangerous for everyone, but this battle wouldn't be won with kind words. Raz moved his hands, and a burst of light flew from his palms.

Thom's eyes widened in the cut-out window of the door.

Raz's power threw Thom back into the room. Unfortunately, Sandra arched into the air with him.

Cameron cleared the lock, and Omega pushed into the lab.

Gunfire erupted around them. Amber spun one-hundred-eighty degrees and sank to one knee.

A scream erupted from Sandra's chest. Broken glass and ricocheting bullets bounced around her. She put her arms over her head and drew her knees close to her body.

Raz yelled her name.

Cameron and Zach tossed commands at each other for better positioning.

Nazier and the young businessman were in the room and fell to their hands and knees. The surrounding chaos increased in intensity.

Sandra caught Raz's gaze. On her belly, she crawled to him.

She'd covered about ten feet before Nazier gripped her ankle and pulled her back. "They can have Raz's little brat, but yours is coming with me."

Thom and Nazier shoved her toward the service elevator at the back of the lab. They left the young man behind.

He struggled to protect himself. Several darts embedded into his arms and legs. He crouched under a desk.

Raz focused on the real threat. This kid wasn't important. He ran past the table and sent a burst of orange light toward the kid so the darts wouldn't permanently damage him. Black smoke-like strands of power encased Thom, Nazier, and Sandra. The boundary stopped Raz. *It's not possible. Thom can't create a shield.*

Sandra struggled. A dart hit her arm.

Raz howled. *Why isn't he blocking the Chasers?*

Another explosion echoed in the enclosed space. His ears rang. General Taft's unit would blow up the entire building. Raz couldn't reach her. His blitz and the shield snuffed out, but Thom's distorted power increased. Raz pulled the Nexus from deep within and sent a signal of healing orange light toward her. Healing energy should penetrate anything. In a matter of seconds, she'd succumb to the effects of the dart. The power of the circle coursed through Raz and flew across the room to her.

When the light hit her, her body bowed. Golden light came back into her eyes. She channeled their accumulative power into an energy force-field that pushed against Thom, but his dark light counteracted her Nexus pulses.

Raz connected to her long enough to link. *Come on, baby! Use the Nexus. You can fight him.*

Sandra raised her hands to Thom's chest. Each finger glowed with blue light. She laid those blossoming orbs of pure Nexus power on him.

His body flew back against the wall. A stray bullet caught his shoulder.

Nazier struggled to hold on to her, but the heat and electricity flowing inside her body burned his skin.

Thom struggled to his feet.

With a slash of her hand, glowing Nexus light cut a gash down his face.

Thom bellowed as blood squirted from his wound. He lurched toward the elevator. His hand clutched over the grisly injury.

Nazier followed him into the elevator, but two shots entered his back. He fell at the entrance. The elevator doors smashed against him as they closed.

Raz turned.

Zach and Cameron provided Amber with cover fire. She'd had

taken down Nazier and had her sights aimed on Thom.

Thom crouched and pushed Nazier out of the way, and elevator doors shut without a sound.

Sandra floated above the floor, as she had after the render. The energy surrounded her and protected her from the incoming gunfire and darts. Then she collapsed.

"No!" Raz scrambled on his hands and knees to reach her.

Cameron pulled him back. "We don't have enough cover fire. The darts will bring you down." He waved Zach over. "We'll use the Nexus to bring her back."

Raz closed his eyes and drew up all the energy he possessed as a Sixxer Transor. Omega added their own to the circle. At first, Raz just felt a slight hum within his body, as though he were riding a motorcycle. Then the sensation increased in intensity. His hands curled into fists. The light built in his hands, arms and finally reached his chest. An exploding ray emanated outward into the most brilliant light imaginable. He focused on Sandra. The circle of light grew and expanded. His tendrils of smoky energy zoomed right for her.

Cameron nodded. "Damn. I'm on a recruitment mission for M83. More Transors are needed. We have a clear path to the elevator. Once it comes back down, we'll head for the third floor. First priority: get Sean, then Thom."

Chapter Forty-two

RAZ KISSED SANDRA hard and long. The sweetness of her lips was the finest nectar he'd ever tasted. He couldn't get enough of her and didn't care about the audience crowded around them in the elevator. "I thought I'd lost you." Searching for injury, he ran his hands over her arms and back. The Nexus pulse he'd sent her downstairs had re-energized her. A tattoo of light drew an intricate golden web on her face. His hand rubbed her stomach. "Is he okay?"

She blinked back tears. "Yes. We've made it."

The elevator doors opened with a sigh. "Don't count your lucky ducks, kiddos." Cameron peered around the door. "General Taft's unit will come looking for us, and we don't have Thom's trail."

Zach wiped his arm over his face. "Hopefully, he's gone for good. If not, I'll make sure of it."

Raz noted the amount of blood on the floor, and the trail leading down the hall. "He went to get Sean."

Cameron and Amber exited on silent feet.

Raz wrapped his arms around Sandra. Cuts and scrapes marked her face. The Nexus made its way to each abrasion and filled them with light. He buried his nose into her hair and breathed in her lilac scent. "Are you okay?" He helped her step out of the elevator.

Sandra nodded. "Did your power touch me?" She raised her head and kissed him. She ran her hands around his waist and held him tight.

"I sent you healing light. Nazier and Thom must've worn some sort of blocker."

Zach touched the control panel. "I told you ... wearable anti-

NEUs are the wave of the future. I want to get my hands on Thom's device. The modifications I could make …" A spark hopped from his palm to the mechanisms of the elevator panel. The doors to the elevator remained open. He exited with a grin. "This extra Nexus-power-shit is sweet. With my mad Sixxer skills, they can't use the elevator. Chasers can still use the stairs, but at least we're at the top."

Cameron waved the all clear. The third floor of the building wasn't anything like the lower two. The elevators had opened to a short hallway connecting two separate wings.

Zach examined the augmenter signal on his wristband. "The signal direction and Thom's trail aren't the same."

Cameron swore. "We can't be sure where he is."

Amber narrowed her eyes. "Looks like we'll have to split up for an effective search."

Cameron nodded. "Each wing on this floor has a perpendicular hallway at both the north and south end. Our mobiles will keep us in contact, and we'll meet up on the north hallway. Be careful. The Chaser unit is hot on our asses." He jerked his chin at Sandra. "Good to see you back." He focused on Raz. "Can you create a shield if we need it?"

Raz nodded. "I didn't drain my power, but if there's another blocking device, then we're in trouble."

"You and Sandra, come with me. Zach and Amber have enough firepower to blast Sean out of here."

Zach motioned to the left, and Amber followed him.

Cameron led Raz and Sandra down the hall. They entered a cubicle farm and walked by row after empty row of employee cells. Dread ran up his spine. He pulled Sandra close. Were they walking into a bloodbath? Or worse, a capture?

They walked up to a set of double doors. "What's in here?"

Sandra passed the entrance and continued toward the east facing windows. "That room was built to connect the other wing for office supplies and storage." She turned and motioned to him and Cameron. "Several rows of desks are in this direction."

Raz's gut told him the room in front of him shouldn't be ignored. "Let's check it out." He opened the door.

The room wasn't filled with supplies, but with more cubicles. The employee spaces had six-foot walls surrounding their work areas, which made seeing an enemy or finding a small child more difficult than anticipated.

Cameron scouted the entrance then waved them inside.

Raz and Sandra followed. The room had little light since the overheads hadn't come on automatically. Fluorescents from the hallway behind them and, the occasional desk lamp someone had left on, created more shadows than light. The heaviness of the room made Raz uneasy. He remembered Amber's comment earlier on how quiet the building had been. Yes, the hour was late, and the office was empty of employees, but Chasers had just attacked them. Other recon units had to be searching the place.

When he spotted Amber and Zach, Raz breathed a sigh of relief, but the feeling was short lived. Zach had his gun aimed at someone. *They found Thom!* Raz rushed forward.

Amber came into full view. Her back was to them. Her shoulders slumped at an unnatural angle, and she had no weapon in her hand.

Raz slowed his gait. *That's not normal behavior for Amber.*

The three of them rounded the extra tall cubicle walls.

Zach held his position about eight feet from the entrance, and from Amber.

Leon faced her.

Sean sat huddled under a desk with Leon's legs blocking his escape.

Raz's heart galloped at the sight of his son. *Now, I have them both.*

Zach turned. "Am and I found a wrecker a few rows down from here, but I'm not sure what has paralyzed her."

Cameron shook his head. "Nexus energy is floating everywhere in this building. A wrecker would affect Leon's Nexus link and Sixxer power, too."

"I can't explain it," Zach said.

Leon cracked his neck. The gem in his ear twinkled in the dim light. "Glad you made it. I was worried."

Sean scrambled out from under the desk to his hands and knees, but an invisible force prevented him from standing or moving forward any farther.

Leon crouched to Sean's level. "I know a way out. Take my hand."

Raz stepped forward. "Sean, come to me." He held out his hand, fingers splayed and palm up. Wisps of energy charged in a wave toward Sean. They ran into a barrier right behind Amber. *Fuck! Leon has the ability to block us, too?* Energy still swirled around Raz. Leon's blocker wasn't as strong as Thom's had been.

Sean's eyes flashed purple, and a burst of white light flared on his chest.

Whatever prevented Raz from reaching Sean must've also made his sensing of Sean faint. Once Leon had learned of Raz's open circle, he used that to his advantage in taking his boy away from him. Raz noticed the bruises on Sean's arms. Rage enveloped him.

Sandra stood beside Raz. "Amber, come to us." She motioned with her hands, urging her to walk away. "Grab Sean, and come to us!"

Amber didn't move or acknowledge they were there.

Sean strained against the force holding him. He shook his head at Leon and growled.

Amber raised her head. Her dark green eyes were dim and almost lifeless. "I can't."

Sandra grasped Raz's hand.

Cameron and Zach flanked them both, weapons locked on Leon.

Leon stepped forward and wrapped his fingers around Amber's upper arm in a tight grip. "Come on, babe. You heard Sandra. Get the kid, and let's get everyone to safety."

At first, Raz didn't register the whimpers. He was so focused on Sean he didn't understand the sounds because even though Sean's eyes glittered with Nexus light, he wasn't moving or making a sound.

A little girl, about three years old, poked her head out of the cubby under the desk. She clutched Sean's well-loved teddy bear in her arms.

Daddy. She's scared.

Sandra gasped.

Amber paled.

The girl was a little moppet with springy black curls and dark skin. She also had bruises on her arms and legs which were already turning yellow and green.

A rage Raz never knew could overcome him turned his vision red. *Leon won't let us go. What do I do, Daddy?* Sean's plea entered Raz's mind.

Sandra clutched his arm and met his gaze. She heard Sean's words, too.

Leon raised his hand and made a come-hither movement.

Sandra stepped forward.

Raz's heart skipped a beat. *What the hell?*

Sandra's eyes bugged out of her head, and she grappled for Raz's hand.

He stopped her uncontrolled movements and pulled her back.

She turned and faced Leon. "How can you betray your own kind?"

Leon sneered. "Who is my kind?"

"What are you?" she asked.

Leon twisted his hand. The force holding Sean in place pushed him flat onto the floor.

Sandra screamed and ran toward the boy.

Leon's invisible power stopped her before she reached the desk and held her in his Sixxer's Nexus grip.

Raz charged. The shield once again held him back. He beat his hands against the clear shield. "You're not leaving here alive, Leon."

Leon grabbed Sandra's arm and the back of Sean's shirt. "Now I have them both." He backed out of the cubicle and down the aisle.

The shield pushed away Raz and the rest of Omega.

Son of a bitch. "He's not a Sixxer." The pieces fell together. Sandra's and Sean's inherent mistrust, Leon's desire to care for Sandra first, no matter the situation, and his continual absences. Leon was the infiltrator, and Raz had added him to his circle through the render.

Everything Raz lived for was being taken away because of another infiltrator. A flicker of Nexus energy trickled down his spine. He had to get them away from the false pull Leon wielded. Leon's force wasn't as strong as Thom's had been. Raz had to reach them. The device was so strong it broke his concentration, and his ability to hook the Nexus's energy was elusive. One thing Chasers failed to account for was a Transor's ability to use a drift to make them into a dagger of energy.

The drift was never used as a physical weapon. The bond of love and connection existed for joy and ecstasy, not harm. Raz used it as a source of power and destruction. Once he entered a drift, he couldn't stop until he consumed the Nexus energy.

Raz opened himself and his body to the Nexus. He focused all his power and strength into the action. The Nexus provided power to Sixxers, but when invoked like this it acted as a living and dynamic entity. He couldn't lose Sean and Sandra. He couldn't live without them.

The little girl, still under the desk, snapped her head up with a smile. She lifted one hand, the teddy bear still clutched to her chest in the other, and a golden shimmer fluttered along her fingers.

Leon was almost to the entrance.

The Nexus entered Raz's muscles so quickly pain burst behind his eyes.

Sandra cried out, and gold light flared in her irises.

Yes, the Nexus is helping us. Fight Leon, baby. Fight his hold on you. Let the full tide of the Nexus enter your body.

The hum within Raz shook and shimmered around him. His blitz, which had eluded him since they'd arrived, was seconds away. The energy-build escalated into something much more powerful than anything Raz had ever experienced. He controlled the Nexus, not his individual ability or Transor strength, but the life force of all Sixxers.

The little girl ran toward him.

He backed away. This much power would kill her.

She hugged his legs. Vibrations hummed within his body. The light and resonance was a symphony of the Nexus. Raz didn't understand how the girl added her voltage to his own without a render. The light pulsed around the two of them.

Daddy, I can break free of him. Sean linked to Raz.

Raz's gaze snapped up.

Sean kicked his legs and wiggled out of Leon's arms.

Leon tried to grab him, but Sean ran to Sandra instead of Raz.

"No, buddy. Come back to me. Get away from Leon. I'll reach Sandra and Jamie."

"Eyelee can help us," Sean yelled.

Sean grabbed Sandra's hand, and light erupted between them in an explosion of fireworks. Her golden eyes swirled, and the aura around her body developed a hazy blue mist. Sean stretched his other hand toward Raz. Even though he couldn't reach Sean, Raz strained a hand toward him. A stream of intense power burst from both of their hands and rushed toward each other. It flared out and lit the room. Waves of energy emitted from Sean and Sandra.

Leon collapsed, coughing and sputtering. Black liquid-like smoke spewed from his mouth.

Sandra broke free and ran to Raz.

The door burst open, and Chasers fired on them.

Zach grabbed Amber by the back of her armor and pulled her to the ground. Him and Cameron returned fire.

Raz didn't want to go toward Leon, but the Chasers behind them gave him no choice. As they passed, Leon's cold, lifeless eyes stared at them in a screen of black. They were unnatural. Several Chaser bullets had pocked his chest. Raz's enemy hadn't cared that Leon was on the Chasers' side.

The little girl ran and exited down the hallway to the opposite wing. Her small feet pounded against the carpet and down another hall. They followed her and entered a dark room. The girl was small, but clear Nexus light surrounded her. She didn't speak. She was too young to have such extreme amounts of power.

Amber raced behind Eyelee and latched on to the girl's shirt. "Slow down. If you get too far ahead, we can't protect you." She lifted the child into her arms.

The girl laid her head on Amber's shoulder. "Go," she whispered. "We must go."

"What just happened?" Cameron asked.

Sean smiled. "We completed our circle."

"That was no render." Cameron shook his head.

Sean laughed.

Raz didn't have an answer. Whatever his circle had done had never happened before. "I don't have any guesses why we were trapped back there before I drifted."

Zach trotted beside him. "Chasers used wreckers at The Cemetery to control the captured. Amber and I found the unit before Leon spotted us. I'm not sure why it worked on some of us, but not all."

"We have to get out of here," Cameron commanded.

The little girl wiggled out of Amber's arms. She skipped to Sean and whispered in his ear.

"She knows a way out without the Chasers following us," Sean said.

The girl took off in a sprint. They made their way through a maze of rooms and offices.

"Through here." Sean's mental link to the child was seamless. He turned an office doorknob, but the door didn't budge. He turned to Eyelee. "How do we get inside?"

She shrugged, but after a few seconds, she reached out to the doorknob. A ball of greenish-white light encased the handle in a sphere. The colors swirled around each other until a click echoed.

They entered a darkened office space, or what had been an office space. The silence inside was palpable. Raz immediately knew the girl wasn't leading them out of the building. He saw all he'd been running from. Shame coursed through him at the row upon row of metal cells in the room. The pain and anguish on Sandra's face was more than Raz could bear. She'd know this was what he turned his back on. It didn't matter that he'd healed her, or that he loved her. She'd leave him, anyway. He was a monster. The proof was in front of their eyes. He was no better than her ex-husband, and the other humans responsible for this room.

Sandra fell to her knees.

Raz tugged her arms in an effort to help her back up. He crouched with her and whispered, "This is my fault. I'll fix it."

"I never thought Thom could be responsible for such cruelty. How could I have not known they were here?"

Cages lined both sides of the room. Each one held a person. Raz couldn't determine if they were human or Sixxer. A handful had a healthy flush, and others had a gray cast etched over their skin. The most heartbreaking was the number of children alone in the cages. None of them cried. Just as Sean's friend hadn't cried. She pointed, leading Amber to the first cell.

A woman with curly blond hair slept inside. She lifted her head and opened her eyes to display the same light brown irises in the same heart-shaped face as the little girl. Her wary gaze followed their movements. She saw the girl, paled, and sat up quickly.

"Zach, how do we unlock the doors?" Amber scratched out, her arms trembling.

Raz had never heard her speak with such raw emotion.

Cameron raced over to the door and examined the lock. He searched the room with his gaze. "Damn it, Zach. What do you have? I'm glad Leon is dead. He's responsible for this. A facility right over our operations. Did any of you have a clue they were here?"

The remaining members of Omega shook their heads.

Zach searched his pockets. "I don't know what will break it. Leon was the one who could break shit. I hadn't expected this to be here. How did this get passed up?"

"Leon used us to hide them." Amber's face had a green tinge.

Raz never thought he'd see Amber lose her tough facade.

When the tears fell, she blinked rapidly and rubbed the heel of her hand over her eyes. "Cam, can't you break it like the medicine cabinet?"

He shook his head.

Amber picked up the little girl and held her.

"Does Taft know you're here?" Zach asked the woman in the cell. "What's your name?"

She didn't answer. Her gaze darted back and forth from Zach to the little girl.

Sandra turned to Raz and Cameron. "We have to get them out. We can't leave them here."

Cameron gritted his teeth as he used a tool he wedged between the door and side of the cell. Leverage wouldn't bust the lock. He heaved against the tool. "A Taft unit is in the next fucking room. What are our choices?"

"I won't leave them here." Sandra added her hands on the tool and pulled with Cameron. Nothing happened.

Cameron stopped. He starred into Sandra's eyes. "Again, what are our choices?"

The woman inside the cage stood and walked toward them. She reached between the bars and touched the little girl's face. She pulled back her hand as though burned. "My name is Veda. We dreamed of you. I wonder if this is another dream, and I'll wake."

"I'm awake. I've been awake," A female voice in the next cell called out.

Zach ran over and clutched the cell bars. "Don't worry, miss. We'll get you out."

"You have the power of the talisman?"

"What? Only Chasers call them that." Zach furrowed his brows. "We have some tech gadgets in a classroom downstairs, but nothing that will pick locks."

"*The* talisman was in my dream."

Raz helped Cameron search for something else that could break the lock. A set of keys would come in handy, but they found nothing. He looked at the woman. "You're not dreaming. I wish to God you were, then we wouldn't have Chasers breathing down our neck."

Veda shook her head. "If I dreamed of you, and you're here ... I dreamed of the talisman, and it's here, too." She turned to the little girl. "Did you see it, my sweet?"

The child giggled and pointed to Raz.

More rustling and movement echoed around the room.

"I just drifted. The connection is weak. My power can't free you. I don't think it would've before a drift. The wrecker is too strong in this building."

Sean tugged on his sleeve. "She said you and Sandra can do it together," he whispered.

Sandra faced Raz. "I have a Nexus connection after your touch. Can I connect to the energy and help you break it open?" She gripped the bars of the cell. Her knuckles turned white and pink with strain.

The woman nodded. "Yes. With him you'll have the right tools. The talisman has to work in collaboration."

Raz watch Zach and Cameron search the room for something of use. "I'm a Transor, but I just used a huge burst of energy to break a false Zenith shield."

Zach bounded over. "I can't find anything. No devices or keys."

Veda reached between the bars and clutched Zach's sleeve. "Talismans aren't always inanimate objects. The Nexus is within all of us. They could use it together."

Drifting had drained Raz. Outside of his circle, the Nexus

wouldn't help anyone in the room. Yet, the little girl had fed his power.

Sandra folded their hands together, and a Nexus hum filled his body. "Is she referring to a T6?"

Raz watched Veda. "They aren't people."

She smiled. "Neither is the Nexus. Try. If it doesn't work, I know you'll come back for us."

Eyelee cried. "No, Mommy. You come with us."

A light surged through them, infusing Raz with awe. The mist swirled around his and Sandra's entwined hands. God, she was beautiful. Looking out at the cells full of people, Raz saw the Nexus light flare in several pairs of eyes.

Raz turned back to Sandra. A stray thought of her ending up in one of these cages sent an ache into his heart. He let go of the past and trusted the Nexus. Sandra was meant to be his. He brought her hand to his lips. "I love you."

A surge of Nexus essence flew from between them and swirled around the room. Amber ducked when the smoky light zinged by her head. Other wisps of energy snaked from some of the cages and from Eyelee and Omega. The floating mist combined into a brilliant stream and went from cell to cell.

The locks unlatched at once.

Veda trembled and pushed open the door to her prison. Eyelee held out her arms, and the woman scooped her into an embrace. Tears ran down her face faster than a flash flood. Over and over, she kissed the girl's hair, neck and face. She opened her still-glowing eyes and whispered to Raz and Sandra, "Thank you. Thank you. Thank you. I haven't held my daughter in almost a year."

Raz's heart lurched. To not hold Sean for a year would be a torture of unimaginable pain. Raz pulled Sandra and Sean into a tight hug.

More people woke and spilled out of their cells. Free.

Whispers of the talisman filled the room. Raz didn't know what they were talking about because it had only been Nexus energy that had freed them. The drift had boosted his power enough to communicate with the rest of the Sixxers surrounding him.

Cameron "How do we get out of here? Chasers are closing."

The woman pointed to the wall behind them. "A stairwell will take us to the ground floor. The service mail room has a hidden exit with vehicles you can use."

"How do you know?" Sandra asked.

Veda turned and her green eyes flashed. "I know because that's how the doctors transported us here."

Raz's gut churned. He'd left M83 to protect his people from infiltrators and keep his child out of Chaser hands. Yet, in his absence his people and their children had been captured and tortured. "We'll follow your lead."

CHAPTER FORTY-THREE

THE LOCKS HAD sprung, but many of the adults weren't strong enough to push open the doors. The kids didn't even try to leave. Sandra hurried to the kids' jail cells. Amber pushed her to walk faster. *What sort of life have these children lived?* Sandra's heart ached at horrors she saw in front of her and the ones her mind imagined. Sean had been so close to being locked inside one of these cages.

Cameron and Raz jogged by and opened the other cells. Sean followed them and helped tug each gate open.

The smallest of the other children stood a head taller than Eyelee. Bigger, with eyes that were too mature to belong to kids, they looked to be between the ages of six and ten. The girl watched them with a calculating gaze. She must've been the oldest, because the two boys looked to her for permission to walk out of the cell.

Not one of the other children had any belongings. They were quiet and alert. Nexus fire lit their eyes, but were they Sixxer, or something else? Sandra glanced at Sean and Eyelee. The swirls of light floating around their eyes were strangely absent.

Amber urged each of the children to line up in the hall between the two rows of cages and touched their shoulders with trembling hands. She examined them for injuries. When she found the bruises and track marks on their arms, murder entered her eyes. They brightened with green light, until one boy sucked in a scared breath.

Nazier had done this to them, and now he was dead. That he wouldn't suffer as they had didn't seem fitting.

"It's okay." Sandra pulled the frightened child near. "We won't hurt you."

Amber stood. "Nazier got off too easy."

Sandra looked Amber in the eyes. "You're the one who ended it for them."

The blonde woman ran over. The little girl with the delicious black curls was in her arms, and the resemblance between the two was striking. "Eyelee knows where to go and what to do. Please, trust her. Take her with you."

Eyelee reached out and fell happily into Amber's arms as only a small child can do. She still clutched Sean's teddy bear in one hand.

Amber's eyelashes fluttered. "I'll keep them all safe."

Sandra touched Veda's arm. "Come with us. Keep Eyelee close to you. You've been apart from each other for too long. Omega will bring the others."

"I'm still needed." Veda looked over her shoulder. Her blonde curls swayed with the movement. "We must hurry. This room is hidden with a wrecker, but once we leave, the Chasers will find us quickly."

Sean ran to Eyelee. Sandra expected he'd take his precious teddy bear back, but he stretched to hand her and each child a package of fruit chews from Cameron's collection of junk food.

Veda stared at Sean for a few moments, a wrinkle on her brow. She crouched to his level. "You have a brave heart, my darling. Thank you for helping Eyelee."

Sean smiled, and his eyes flashed green and purple Nexus light. "You're welcome, Veda."

Veda gasped. Her head tilted up to Sandra. "This is Paris's son. Where is she?"

"You know her?" Amber hustled the kids to the stairwell.

"Yes. She's been helping us plan an escape for months. I initially thought she'd come into the room, but when I saw the soldiers, I knew the prophecy had begun."

Amber harrumphed. "No prophecy comes from Omega. Paris had us fooled. She was working with Nazier."

Veda shook her head. "We hoped for a better life. Once we realized her father's plan, we knew it was too late for us. I was grateful she escaped him, but when we found out she was here ... The danger to her was so great. We didn't think she'd follow through for us, especially with her own child to worry about, but her goal had been to get us out of here."

Sandra stopped. "How long has Paris helped you?"

"Since we were children. She and I grew up together. We lost track of each other several years ago. I thought the worst had happened to her."

Zach and Cameron helped the injured walk out of their cells.

Raz nodded to Sandra. He urged the others to follow her and Amber. As they left their cages, he said, "Don't make a sound. If possible, keep the Nexus handy, but be aware other devices might detect us."

Veda turned away.

Sandra grabbed her arm. "Paris was my friend." She whispered, "She didn't survive the virus."

A sadness shielded Veda's eyes. "As so many of us haven't."

Sandra's heart stopped. Thom's research had indicated his infections were unsuccessful. "How many are sick?"

"Nazier distributed the virus among our group. Four of these captured Sixxers have symptoms."

"He won't infect anyone again." Amber clenched her hands. "He's dead."

Veda pinched her lips together. "Unfortunately, once Dr. Nazier confirmed the infections, Dr. Robins added other facilities to the testing list."

"Do you know where they are?" Sandra asked.

"Yes. First, we have to escape here, or none of it matters." Veda squeezed Eyelee's arm and trotted back to the open cages. She entered a cell where one of the imprisoned hadn't moved since they'd arrived. Veda knelt beside the woman and placed a hand on hers. The Nexus light sparked between their fingers.

Raz gripped Sandra's arms. "You need to lead them out."

Sandra nodded. "Don't linger too far behind me."

"Never." He kissed her.

She hurried down the stairs. The children trembled as they descended three flights of stairs to the first floor. Silent tears streaked their faces. Every innocent sound in the cavernous stairwell made them jump and clutch each other. The few adults able to walk followed them. After the last step, they entered the small shipping center of the building. Sandra turned to Amber and Eyelee. "Which way?"

Eyelee whispered, "Down."

Amber shrugged. She lowered Eyelee to the floor. "I'll secure the area. Wait here."

Eyelee tugged Sandra's sleeve. "Go back to the wall." She pointed to a shadowed corner.

Amber waved at them to follow her. They shuffled farther into the room and wove their way around shipping boxes and packages then waited for the others.

Zach appeared in the stairwell first. He checked the entrance and walked over to them. "The door exits out into the main hallway on the first floor." He kept his tone at a low whisper. "We're opposite the elevators and Sandra's office. A Chaser unit is searching each room. We have to get them to the VW, like now."

"We won't all fit in the VW." Sandra's whisper came out as a hiss. "The team barely fit. We have about fifteen extra bodies here."

Two of the kids gasped and huddled against the wall. Their escape could be short lived.

No! We'll get them out of here.

Raz hobbled down the stairs with an injured Sixxer. Her limp was pronounced, and her arm was around Raz's neck.

The woman reminded Sandra of Paris, in her weaker moments. Her light jacket wasn't enough to stop the shivers running through her body. Sandra ran to the other side of her and wrapped her arm around her waist.

"We won't be able to get the injured out without detection," Raz whispered. "There has to be another way. A back entrance in this room?"

Sandra shook her head. "There isn't one. They use the main hall door for deliveries. Large deliveries are taken to the basement lab dock. The elevators are used as transport to the other floors."

Cameron came up behind them. He helped two injured Sixxers sit on the floor. "We have the advantage of darkness. Lead the children and those who can walk to the VW. Zach and I will take the others out one-by-one."

"It's a stupid plan." Amber pulled her hair and stomped back and forth in front of Sandra. "We have nowhere to hide them. You'll need cover fire to get out. Too many are weak to rely on the Nexus."

Veda pushed to the front of the group. She smiled at Eyelee, caressed her cheek, and planted a sweet kiss on her cherub face. Yet, she didn't reach out for her child. She turned to face Raz and Cameron. "We must leave two Sixxers here."

Zach spun. "I'll get them."

Veda placed her hand on his arm. "They won't make the night. They want to help us and have enough energy left to distract our enemy."

Raz stepped forward. "They gave you their essence?"

Veda swallowed. "Most." Her eyes held the Nexus glow, but they also contained a sheen of tears. She nodded and sucked in a deep breath. "You and your colleagues are strong enough to carry the sick. We'll go out the way they brought us here." She walked over to a wall of cubbies used to sort mail. Neon green light swirled around her hand and searched each mail slot. Every spark and snap of Veda's energy Sandra felt in her bones.

The wall rumbled. Veda rushed forward. Another Sixxer helped her pull the entire unit back to reveal a hidden door.

Veda turned to Sandra. "The tunnel doesn't have any lights inside. Eyelee can be your guide until you reach the end."

What? HUP doesn't have a tunnel on campus. Trepidation rose inside her at entering the black enclosed space. She hadn't been affected since the hospital, but her irrational fear told her all of her previous strength had been a fluke.

Raz hugged her tight. "You'll have all of us with you."

Eyelee and Amber lead the way. The children followed. The Sixxers able to walk on their own entered next. Veda followed them.

Sandra fell back on old habits. *One.* She inhaled through her nose. *Two.* She exhaled out through her mouth.

Raz stepped over the threshold. He offered his hand.

She shook her head. "Take one of the sick. I can go by myself."

He tenderly kissed her then whispered, "Hurry. I can't stand being apart from you much longer. If I have to come back for your ass, then you won't like it."

She smiled. "You can't get rid of me that easily."

He helped two of the injured through the entrance, and they disappeared into the dark tunnel.

Zach was next. "You've got this, Sandra." He chucked her under her chin.

Cameron raised an eyebrow. "You know better than to think I'd leave you behind."

She helped one of the remaining two Sixxers stand and guided her to the door.

The woman held Sandra back as Paris had done days ago when she'd beseeched Sandra to take care of Sean. She was slightly older than Sandra but had a weariness in her expression that aged her. "Remember, the light of love is always inside us. Let it take you." The Nexus glow tingled along the woman's fingers and created a soft haze around them.

Sandra squeezed her hand. The power didn't erase her fear but made her stronger. They smiled at each other. *Three.* Her panic attacks were now a part of history.

"Move it, soldier," Cameron groused. "We don't got all damned day." They entered the tunnel. He pulled the mailboxes closed behind them.

Sandra's Nexus light guided them down a sloping path. Fortunately, the tunnel was short. After a few minutes, they reached the end. Sandra and her charge tumbled out into a massive concrete subway-like tube. Its width had to have been as wide as the entire building. Two white repurposed school buses were parked off to the right. This was how Thom and Dr. Nazier transported captured Sixxers without detection, right under their noses.

Cameron whistled behind her. "How was it possible we had two hidden operations right on top of each other at this tiny university?"

Zach chuckled. "Obviously, Nazier was compensating for something in terms of size."

No shit.

Veda trotted over. "Either of you have talent on how to jumpstart a bus?"

They both pointed to Zach.

"I'll need you, too." Zach cuffed Cameron on the shoulder and walked over to Raz to inspect the large vehicle. "Let's see if my mind-altering Sixxer power can jump this bitch."

Cameron pouted like a child. "I've already been a grease monkey for Amber today." Yet, he was already at the engine.

Veda turned to Sandra. "Most Sixxers treat the Nexus as a thing they can manipulate. It can't be controlled in such a way."

Sandra smiled and shook her head. "They're like me. This is their first taste of the Nexus. There's no harm."

Veda stared at the kids. "The Nexus isn't a thing. It's not some entity. It's … about love. The more you give, the more you'll get back."

Amber laughed. "Your fruity beliefs won't give us any favors. We need to learn how to use renders to boost our power and fight General Taft. The strength the Nexus gives us will help our side win. You were a part of Dr. Nazier and Thom's evil. Don't you want to fight?"

Veda cleared her throat.

Eyelee waved from where she chased her new friends.

Her smile at her daughter was automatic. "The children's energy always returns quickly, doesn't it? They haven't interacted or played for a long time." She turned to Amber. "When you take something from a child, does that action allow the child to love you or hate you? Those are the extremes. Think of all the nuances in between, and what Chasers could do with a power they don't understand. General Taft and the people he's creating are like children, and they'll lash out when their toys are taken away."

"Then help us." Sandra grabbed Veda's hand and squeezed.

Veda stared at Eyelee playing with Sean and the teddy bear. "Our children." She gazed at Sandra's belly.

Sandra shook her head. "How can you tell?"

"It's in your light. They deserve more. I don't know if the prophecy is true. The signs are there, and now we wait for the next one."

Amber rolled her eyes. "Prophesy smrophesy. We got here through lucky timing. We need people like you, Veda, who can help us find others. I have a bullet with General Taft's name on it, but fighting is, also, more than killing. You can nurture and educate the children we find so their hate doesn't blind them. My time for spreading love is long gone."

"It's never too late. I'm coming with you. I don't have any other choice."

They walked over to the group.

Raz scooped Sandra into a hug. He faced Cameron. "Can we get a message to M83 on the total compromise of Hamilton University as an experimental Sixxer facility? Veda informed me she was captured before her daughter was born and has been to other locations."

Cameron nodded. "Her knowledge is invaluable."

"She's going with us. She, also, described where this tunnel ends, which isn't far from the Cutlass."

"We can send communications to M83 when we get there."

Sandra grabbed Raz's shirt. "Did she tell you what Paris was doing?"

Raz's eyes flashed. "Yes. What I did with Paris was wrong. I ran. I hid. General Taft will stop at nothing to use every one of us to further his agenda. Hiding isn't an option."

"Thom will fight, too," Cameron said. "He'll take his time to find us, but we can't let down our guard. He'll want to reclaim his missing prisoners."

Zach shut the hood. "The bus is ready. When I start the motor, it will be loud. I'm not saying it will alert anyone, since it looks like this has been a railway for a long time, but you never know."

"Let's load everyone onboard," Amber said.

Cameron and Zach walked over to Amber and the collection of refugees. They helped everyone climb the steps and find a seat.

Sandra sat beside Raz in the first row. "What happens next?"

"We're a closed and powered circle now. We'll protect our own and search for others who are captured. You and Cameron will find a way to eradicate Thom's virus. The hell with no renders allowed. We'll figure a way to do them without being detected. We'll need all the strength we can find."

The hot shower at the tiny motel invigorated Sandra. The comforts of modern conveniences couldn't be minimized. Two days of travel in the dead of night had left her tired, sweaty and achy. Needy. They were safe and knowing that allowed her to focus on other desires. Her skin flushed and tingled in anticipation of Raz's hands caressing her tonight. She whipped back the shower curtain and jumped.

Raz waited, leaning against the doorframe. Steam floated around his head in a lazy pattern. His gaze raked up and down her body.

She'd wrapped the hotel towel around her in a crazy rush of shyness.

He pushed away from the door. "You're beautiful. And mine. All mine." He smiled and stripped.

Desire pooled low in her body at the sight of his hard abs and semi-erect cock. She stood there in awe at his muscular form. He was back down to a reasonable muscle mass. Not that Sandra had complained about his changes during a blitz.

He stepped in front of her and cupped her face to give her a molten kiss. She moaned. His tongue swooped inside for a taste.

"Soon, love."

She thought he'd take her right then, but he pulled aside the shower curtain and stepped into the tub.

Sandra smiled in satisfaction. He wouldn't deny her after he cleansed his body. She padded on bare feet into the hotel room. She felt like they were a normal couple on a weekend vacation. They had left the cold back in Pennsylvania, and driven to the warm south. The room's temperature reflected the mild fall day outside. No more cold shivers for her.

Veda traveled with them as promised.

Once they'd gotten back to the Cutlass, Cameron had contacted M83.

Zach volunteered to take the refugees to an M83 safe house. They'd hot-wired another car, and the rest of the team headed south to rendezvous with another unit. Then they would break into one of the establishments where Veda had resided.

Sandra pulled aside the frilly window curtain. Three familiar figures stood across the street.

Sean and Eyelee laughed on the playground. Sean showed Eyelee how to have fun on the slide, the swing and the climbing tubes. The child had never had an opportunity to do something so ordinary in her three years of living in captivity. Sean's teddy had officially become Eyelee's. She didn't let the raggedy-doll bear out of her sight.

Nexus power healed them. Sandra had learned to trust the Nexus.

Veda was ever vigilant, and Sandra had every trust and faith in her. Veda would protect the children with her life. The light hovered around the three of them, giving them an ethereal glow in the fading afternoon sunlight.

Raz had assured her they were safer here than anywhere in the country. The farther south they traveled, the deeper they entered M83 territory. Chasers would need a large army to attack them at this location.

Veda wouldn't keep the children outside long, but her desire to provide her daughter with the basic pleasures of a child couldn't be denied.

Sandra understood the fierce protection Veda exuded. She wore the same momma bear coat around Sean and at every thought of Jamie. She watched the kids play, and Veda laughing, with an ache in her heart, but also with a contentment.

Veda and Eyelee were finally a family after years of misery. No one would get the fantasy of the suburban home and trips to the mall, but they had each other. They had love. They didn't crave it or desire it. They had it. Together. Even when they'd been apart.

Raz. Sandra was his. He was hers. After he'd invoked his power in the drift and the Nexus entered her body, he'd marked her as forever his. Wet strands of her hair dripped along her neck and down her chest.

Steam rolled from the bathroom door. She clenched the towel tight against her breasts. They beaded at her thoughts of Raz's mouth on her. A network pattern flashed on her arms, even after her shower. If not muted, her elevation provided her with a constant network of light upon her skin. Raz had been teaching her how to soften it so as not to draw attention.

The water stopped, and Sandra tensed. *Am I nervous?* She turned and spotted Raz.

He'd wrapped a towel around his waist and hadn't bothered using it to dry himself. Droplets of water ran down his brawny chest and trickled along the trail of dark hair beneath the low band of the cloth.

She ate him alive with her gaze. She flushed. Her gaze bounced up to his crystalline irises.

He pushed the wet hair off his forehead. The five o'clock shadow he'd been sporting for the last several days was now a full beard.

What would it feel like when they kissed? On her breasts? Between her thighs? Moisture coated her feminine folds. She shifted her feet, and the evidence of her arousal rubbed slickly between her thighs. Her heart pounded, and her breath came out in short pants. A sexy smile spread over Raz's face and sent hot tendrils of lust and light to the center of her body. Sandra's attraction for Raz and the intense heat of Nexus energy that flared at his come-hither stare.

He leaned against the doorjamb. "Are our charges tucked in for the night?" he asked in a low, husky tone.

"Veda is watching over the children. They're by the play set." Sandra looked out at the three again.

"You don't have to keep watching them. My link to Sean is ever present now. I know when he's hurt or scared. Right now he's happy."

Sandra smiled. *I'm happy when I'm in your arms.*

A mental link from Raz followed her thoughts. *I want to make love to you all night without interruption, my love. That would make me happy, too.*

She rationalized that the hot steam from the shower stole her breath away. More likely, Raz stole it with his lustful gaze.

His eyes darkened at the realization she'd heard his mental musings.

Sandra was still coming to grips with the random communication links between them. She walked closer. "I want that, too," she whispered. So many months of hiding their passion made the revelations carnal and so incredibly seductive.

He cupped her chin, and his tongue and lips sipped and branded her with his love. "I won't ask you to join me in this life."

"You can't stop me. I'll just follow you."

He smiled against her lips. "There's the bulldog I know, forever stubborn."

"Woof!"

They laughed and the sound was pure joy.

Sandra's hands moved to his waist and ran along the beautiful planes of his body. "I always had to rush, to make sure you wouldn't stop. Not ever again."

He leaned down and inhaled along her neck. "Nothing will prevent me from wanting you." He groaned. "I smell your need on your flesh. I'll always know when you need me to take you. When you need me to love you."

An arc of Nexus light leapt between them. Sandra unwrapped the towel from his hips, which did little to hide his erection. This man, this powerful alien man, needed her, wanted her and loved *her*.

He tugged the matching towel from her hand, and it fell to the floor. He cupped her breasts and thumbed her nipples in lazy circles. His power's fire licked her sensitive peaks, and he followed with a cool suckle of his mouth.

She arched her back and cried out. A streak of need ran from her nipple to the apex of her thighs. Her inner muscles swelled and flooded in anticipation of his body's caress. She grasped his penis in a firm hold.

His moan vibrated against her. "You drive me wild, woman. Your smell, your heat, I want it all over me." His tongue flickered out and teased the underside of her breast. Raz wrapped his arms around her and carried her to the bed. He tossed her on her back.

She squealed.

He followed her down. The clean white sheets enfolded them.

His shaft nuzzled her slippery heat. He swept his tongue inside her mouth. The pleasure of his touch was so lovingly accepted.

Raz pulled his head back and brushed her hair out of her eyes. His smile brightened his face. "I never imagined I'd get to have a life with you."

"I wasn't going to live one without you."

The light of love cocooned them in warmth and pleasure. His hands caressed and loved her. She wrapped her legs around him, and he entered her in a slow, erotic thrust. Her hands fell to his hips. They rocked together in a dance of heat and friction.

She gave him all she had, and her love and orgasm burst from her in a wave of vibration and joy. The deep, sexy moan at her ear let her know he'd followed her on the tide to release.

Raz rolled to the side but kept his arm tight around her. He kissed her damp forehead. "I love you so much. We were made for each other."

Sandra smiled. "I love your new sappy romantic side."

He chuckled. "Oh, really? You better get used to it."

"Definitely."

Epilogue

Epilogue

Months Later. Somewhere in the Peruvian Amazon

SANDRA KNEW NO one could design an instrument to measure the amount of love flowing through her body right at this moment. Jamie's eyes were crystal blue, rare for a newborn, and reminded her of Raz. They followed Sandra's every move, and his rosebud mouth cooed and twitched in … amusement?

Sandra laughed. She hadn't decided if his features looked more like her or Raz. Time to figure that out later. His head of dark hair was soft. Tiny fingers clutched one of hers. His strength made her proud.

Sandra's midwife tucked the blanket around them both, despite the humid air. "Dark-blue eyes change as a child grows older, but I can tell this little one won't follow the rules." Her movements in the room created a hint of a breeze. The long skirt and billowy shirt flowed around her in a swirl of colorful material.

Sandra's labor had been difficult, but thankfully short. The awesome sight in her arms outdid Sandra's exhaustion. The wonderment before her had no words to describe it. Her very own child was in her arms. One she'd never thought she'd have.

The midwife wiped Sandra's brow and gave her water to sip. "I'm so proud of you, *mija*." She walked across the military-style tent and placed the water back on a table.

Yet, Jamie was a temptation the older woman probably couldn't resist.

The midwife returned to Sandra's side to place a ring-covered hand on the baby's head. "You're both so strong. The light lives within."

Sandra was getting used to some of the odd references to the Nexus. The people and Sixxers in this village appeared to worship the energy. Some Sixxers sensed her power when a sign wasn't visible. Such detection of her energy seemed more like voodoo than science.

She didn't think she would've given birth inside a hut in the middle of the Amazonian jungle, but months ago, she'd stopped predicting the future. They lived day by day now. It was a lesson she'd learned from the captured Sixxers. Raz and Cameron had liberated about fifty Sixxers at the last hidden Chaser facility, including children. Veda and Eyelee had become the resident mother hens in the camp until those rescued could be relocated.

Zach had been in charge of transportation for M83 rescues, leaving plenty of time to get Sandra to the city for the birth.

Jamie had other plans. He couldn't wait to come into this world.

The flap of the tent ruffled, and Amber entered. "Hi, *bruja*." She smiled.

Sandra knew Amber's joy would burst like confetti around Jamie. She couldn't hold back her delight around any of the other kids they had liberated. The team had been waiting so patiently for Jamie. He was everyone's light now. Amber turned into a blubbering ... girl with ... coochie-coochie-coos coming from her mouth. Sandra wasn't sure how to handle this woman.

Amber pulled over a wooden chair and sat next to the bed. "I see our little *papito* is doing good."

Sandra stifled a yawn. "He's doing wonderfully. Where are the boys?"

"They're coming." Amber leaned over the bed and looked into Jamie's eyes. "They're so bright. Almost as if they're glowing with Nexus light, but they're just his eyes."

The midwife laughed. "Such a distinct feature is a sign of great strength. The prophecy has begun." The bangles on her arm tinkled.

Amber shook her head and rolled her eyes. "What's she muttering about?"

"I'm not sure. She sounds like Veda." Sandra counted fingers and toes. "Do you think he's healthy?"

"He looks perfect. So alert. He's amazing, Sandra." Amber blinked, and her lashes became wet. "You're a mother," she whispered.

Sandra grinned. *Yes, I have been for a long time now.*

The flap of the tent opened again, and Raz and Sean bounced into the room.

Sean raced to the bed and kissed Sandra on the cheek.

"Meet your brother." Sandra pulled the blanket aside giving Sean a better view of Jamie. His arms and legs wiggled in a burst of freedom from the blanket.

Sean's brow wrinkled. "He's a lot smaller than I thought he'd be, Mommy."

They all laughed.

Jamie reached out his tiny hand. Sean blinked at Sandra and then Raz.

Sandra winked. "It's okay. He's saying hello."

Sean held out his finger, and Jamie grabbed it. Sean's smile stretched wide.

A vibration purred low in Sandra's gut. The hum was pleasant and loving. A glow hovered from under Jamie's finger. Sean was saying hello, too. The midwife had said the baby wouldn't have any Sixxer power as a newborn. Sandra sighed and accepted the light from her first son, Sean. His Sixxer abilities had increased in the past seven months, but his power was still shocking to see. Other Sixxers kept their power hidden. Sandra had been taught how to conceal her own energy tones. She looked at the adorable baby in her arms and a sound gently formed within her body. A sigh of music like a wind chime filled the room.

Raz touched her face.

Sighing, she nuzzled into his hand. Her smile stretched her lips so far her cheeks hurt.

"What're you doing?" he asked.

"I'm sleeping with my eyes open. I don't want to miss any of this." Sandra still didn't believe her dreams had come true. After years of believing she'd never have a child, here was a baby from her flesh in her arms. New and sweet. His baby smell intoxicated her.

"You are aglow," Raz whispered. "The most beautiful woman on Earth."

Sandra smiled and tilted her head toward him for a kiss.

Waves of energy surrounded Jamie. Sandra tightened her arms around him and examined him for Nexus light.

Sean's eyes rounded. "He can talk to me, Daddy."

Sandra's gaze popped back to Raz. "Jamie can't contact the Nexus, can he?"

Raz shook his head. "Sean is using his power to light him."

"No, Daddy." Sean pulled his hand away from the baby. "Jamie can talk to me."

"The fortune-tellers have spoken the truth." The midwife laid her hands on Sean's shoulders. "A child with light eyes and the light within is the sign of the coming revolution. His power will be unlike anything a Sixxer has seen."

"Really, *bruja*?" Amber threw her hand in the air. "He's the son of a Transor, of course he'll have power. And, FYI, we're already in a revolution. Haven't you noticed the other soldiers outside?"

The midwife cupped Amber's cheek. "The revolution of your hearts. The Nexus will heal us all. So the prophecy says."

With a wry twist to his mouth, Raz leaned toward Sandra. "You're right. She does sound like Veda. I thought we only had one crazy at this camp." He raised his head toward the midwife. "What're you talking about?"

"The prophecy suggests our alien revolution starts with the birth of a child with crystal eyes, followed by the discovery of the Talismans. Veda already told me they found the first Talisman months ago, during her rescue. Our Sixxer story is very old and full of errors in retelling. The prophecy signs being out of order isn't important. What matters is that the evidence of the predictions are manifesting. I've waited seventy years to see such a child. I thought Sixxers would be destroyed by man, but now I have hope."

"Hope?" Sandra asked.

"Our people will return."

Amber's gasp startled Sandra. Amber didn't react like that. Nothing fazed her except puppies and babies.

Amber jumped from her chair. "That's only a story."

The old woman cackled. "Then this is the beginning."

"What's going on?" Sandra asked. "Fill me in, because I'm missing something here." She feared for her children, and her newfound life.

The love she shared un-ashamedly, un-regretfully and uninhibitedly with Raz was also at risk.

Raz eased up on the bed and wrapped his arms around Sandra and the baby. "My parents told me a story when I was a little boy about our people returning to Earth. My father would act out the fable for me and my mother in a fun, joyful manner. Although, Dad's interpretation might have been a dark comedy, his acting wasn't meant to be interpreted as a true event."

Sandra clasped Raz's hand in hers. "Sixxers are already here."

"No," the midwife said. "The Sixxers here were the ones left behind. Now I have hope the future will bring our people home, and we won't have to hide anymore. We can be ourselves."

To not have to hide. To live and love freely. Sandra's heart swelled with hope. She'd be among her own, and no longer feel alien inside. She'd be normal. No white picket fence for her. No dog, either. Just her and her boys.

Glossary

Anti-NEU (pronounced anti new): a M83 tech device that can sense a Chaser NEU device and reflect the NEU's signal back inadvertently hiding Nexus energy signatures.

Augmenter: a sensor that picks up on a Sixxer's power in the form of harmonics. The device amplifies the sounds and vibrations of the Sixxer's power in order to track a missing circle member. It becomes a sort of GPS to find the missing.

Blitz: a super powerful energy state Transors enter when their circle is threatened. The Transor's muscles will increase in size to give him the physical advantage in dangerous situations. The energy can kill humans who are near.

Blocker (M83 network): a M83 computer network device tablet that acts like an encryption mechanism except it will hide the fact there is a network at a particular location. M83 units using the device can still send outgoing messages, but the receiver will not know from where it came.

Blocker (Chaser): a Chaser device that will block Nexus energy from getting close to them. It's almost like a Transor shield, but relies on technology instead of Nexus energy.

Bond: (also know as a connection) the natural formation of a link between Sixxers' power and Nexus energy. It can also refer to the link between Sixxers within a circle.

Chaser: a human or group of humans who capture and/or experiment on Sixxers.

Circle: an energy bond based on the subatomic electrical pulses of Sixxers' power which is derived from Nexus energy. Provides Sixxers with additional protection and enhancement.

Circle (closed): allows the Sixxers within it to heal others and use the Nexus to enhance their Sixxer power.

Circle (open): allows the excess energy to escape and leaves the Sixxers within it vulnerable to disease and attack.

Cleanse: a process using water and soap to attempt to muffle any excess Nexus energy or Sixxer power. Used more often with Sixxers who are not in a circle.

Dim: when the light of a Sixxer fades and never returns. Could mean death. Could mean a lost of power or Nexus bond.

Drift: when a Sixxer allows the Nexus to control their power. A Sixxer can ultra-focus the Nexus's energy onto one particular subject using this process, but they cannot focus on anything else.

Elevation: the transformation a Sixxer goes through in their mid-to-late twenties when they develop their Sixxer power.

Empath: a Sixxer power. The ability to sense emotions.

Energy transfer: a way of feeding a Sixxer some of another's Nexus energy without a render.

Hybrid: a child born to a human and a Sixxer.

Infiltrator: a human who has volunteered for Chaser experimentation so they can be included in a render without harm. The most typical infiltrators are Zeniths.

M83 (pronounced M 83): an underground militia mostly composed of Sixxers fighting against Chasers.

Mark: a physical tattoo on the skin.

Mark (Sixxer): an ancient practice where Sixxers would tattoo others with a Nexus brand.

Mark (Chaser): an ink tattoo that would designate the individual as a Sixxer. Newer marks could be a small electronic chip placed under the skin to track Sixxers.

NEU (pronounce new) (Nexus Emissions Unit): a Chaser device that can detect electrical signals that are generated via the Nexus.

Nexus (Sometimes referred to as a Sixxer's light.): An external energy force that is the basis of a Sixxer's power and energy signature. The Nexus can be seen as wisps of smoke and light when a Sixxer is using their power. Is the force that allows Sixxers to bond in a circle, telelink, enhance power and render. Can be used for healing other Sixxers. Can act as a warning mechanism when used by a Sixxer Transor.

Observers: M83 soldiers deployed to follow a Chaser or human to gather intel.

Omega: a M83 field unit.

Radiant technology (heat): an outdated M83 science used in anti-NEUs that blocks Sixxers' outgoing Nexus energy and reflects it back to a circle, therefore amplifying their power without needing a render. The science will also create a wave-like barrier near a device. It's used to disable a NEU.

Render: a process where Sixxers use Nexus energy to form a circle. Acts as a protection mechanism by providing the members of a circle a way to use the Nexus to enhance their natural power.

SAFE (Secure Anti-NEU Frequency Emitter): a modified anti-NEU that has two functions. First function is hide Sixxer power and Nexus energy with a barrier. Second function is to detect NEU locations in a surrounding area so M83 units can chart them.

Shield: a physical barrier or forcefield generated by a Transor when his circle is threatened. Usually follows his blitz state.

Sixxer: an alien race that thrives on planet Earth. Each individual has a natural biological power that can appear as magical power to humans. A sixth sense. The power is based off an energy source called the Nexus and uses electrical energy to function.

T6 (talisman): a generic M83 code for technological devices used by M83 military units.

Telelink: after a render, Sixxers within a circle have the ability to communicate with each other mentally using Nexus energy.

The Six: a group of biology students formed at Hamilton University of PA (HUP) campus.

Trank (dart): a tranquilizer created by Chasers and used to slow Sixxers enough for capture.

Transitional: individuals who are naturally changing from human to Sixxer, or Sixxer to human.

Transor: a male Sixxer who has increased ability to control and manipulate Nexus energy with a direct connection.

Wrecker: similar to an anti-NEU, but used by Chasers. The device is a mechanism for containing Sixxer power and Nexus energy to a confined space so captured Sixxers won't give away locations to M83 extraction units.

Xnix-624: a plant virus that was modified to infect Sixxers.

Z-211: a drug variant developed by human scientists that weakens Zeniths' Nexus energy.

Zenith: a human who has been exposed to drugs, usually voluntarily, that makes the individual gain false Nexus energy.

Author Bio: Fiona Riplee

I have always been an avid reader of romance and science fiction. I decided to merge my two reading passions together to create my own version of paranormal/science fiction romance. I love creating new worlds where there are endless possibilities for finding love. I grew up in a small town in rural Pennsylvania and am currently living in Indiana with my hopelessly romantic husband (who would never admit it under torture), the cutest and craziest toddler I've ever seen, and two mischievous dogs. While I haven't sailed around the world I have been to Jamaica where I was married beside the ocean and in a previous career traveled to Germany and Switzerland.

Find me online:

Author Website: http://fionariplee.com
Facebook: https://www.facebook.com/fionariplee
Pinterest: http://www.pinterest.com/fionariplee/
Twitter: @FionaRiplee
Google+: https://plus.google.com/+FionaRiplee
Tumblr: https://www.tumblr.com/blog/fionariplee
Goodreads: https://www.goodreads.com/user/show/43183443-fiona-riplee

65648752R00253

Made in the USA
Lexington, KY
19 July 2017